LIVING NOWHERE

John Burnside has published three previous novels – most recently *The Locust Room* – one collection of stories and eight books of poetry. He has received many prizes for his work, including the Encore Award and the Whitbread Poetry Award. He lives in Fife with his wife and son.

Living Nowhere

John Burnside

Jonathan Cape
London

Published by Jonathan Cape 2003

2 4 6 8 10 9 7 5 3 1

First published in Great Britain in 2003 by
Jonathan Cape
Random House, 20 Vauxhall Bridge Road,
London SW1V 2SA

Random House Australia (Pty) Limited
20 Alfred Street, Milsons Point, Sydney,
New South Wales 2061, Australia

Random House New Zealand Limited
18 Poland Road, Glenfield,
Auckland 10, New Zealand

Random House South Africa (Pty) Limited
Endulini, 5A Jubilee Road, Parktown 2193, South Africa

The Random House Group Limited Reg. No. 954009
www.randomhouse.co.uk

A CIP catalogue record for this book
is available from the British Library

ISBN 0–224–05293–4

Papers used by Random House are natural,
recyclable products made from wood grown in sustainable forests;
the manufacturing processes conform to the environmental
regulations of the country of origin

Typeset in Bembo by Palimpsest Book Production Ltd,
Polmont, Stirlingshire
Printed and bound in Great Britain by
Mackays of Chatham PLC, Chatham, Kent

I will go back to my homeland,
I will cease my wandering.
My heart is still; it stays for its chosen hour.
In spring, the earth flowers
And is green once more
Everywhere and forever; everywhere and forever
The horizon is lit with blue.
Forever . . . Forever.

Das Lied von der Erde

The Perfection of Water

Alina

BY THE TIME they reached the cemetery, Alina could see nothing but snow. It was as if it had been falling far longer here than in the town; falling for days, perhaps, till it had gathered in thick, soft drifts against the headstones and tree-trunks, erasing the paths, blanking out the names of the dead, covering the stale poppy wreaths left over from Remembrance Day and the muddy bouquets of plastic flowers that had lain for months around the stilled graves. Alina couldn't remember whose idea it had been to go there, and the going itself had been complicated and slow. The acid in her blood had really taken hold now, and everything – from a smear of frozen dog shit on the pavement outside the Open Hearth to the magic apple tree that she had found in somebody's front garden, a vision of ripeness standing intact in the middle of a loamy flower-bed, naked of leaves but still bedecked with tiny golden apples that seemed lit from within, lit and warm, still alive, the seeds still liquid in the sleeping core – everything had been a distraction, a moment's pause, a descent into wonder. This was how it worked, she thought, this elixir she had mistaken for a drug. She could feel her mind figuring it out as she went along, finding the pattern then losing it again, but coming to some makeshift understanding, nevertheless. Acid didn't change the world the way she had expected; it didn't fill the streets with apparitions or painted monsters from *The Garden of Earthly Delights*; it didn't make her feel crazy or lost, though she'd known, as soon as the tiny pinkish crumb of the microdot had begun dissolving on her tongue, that this – craziness, loss of control –

was what she'd most feared. Before she took it, watching Francis to see how it was done, she hadn't really known why she had wanted it. Now, with its warmth inhabiting her blood – and this was how it was, a habitation, a blessed possession – a spirit entirely her own had come into being and found itself at home in her body, in the marrow of her bones, in the warm contours of her mind, had found itself at home as if it had always belonged there – because it *did*, it *really did* belong. It had come into being and it was herself as she had been intended from the first, only she'd never seen it. She had never seen it: *why was that?* She wanted to laugh at the sheer absurdity of having missed it for so long, but every time a laugh began, somewhere deep in her stomach, rippling up through her chest and trying to break free, it was as if she were balancing a long, slender, incredibly fragile vessel, a glass column filled with some precious essence. There it was, a long column of glass filled with liquid gold, and she was balancing it in her chest, in her warm body, feeling it tremble the way a fish would feel movement in water, through the whole length of its tender, magnetic body. The one thing she knew was that she needed to hold it intact, to keep it whole. Francis was walking beside her, in his army-surplus greatcoat and black crew cap, still talking, asking if she was all right, seemingly immune to the wave of warmth and brilliance that kept shimmering through her and through everything she saw or touched.

She had no idea how long it had been. She knew it had taken them some time to walk from Francis's house to the cemetery but, other than noticing that it was grey now, verging on dark-ness, and that the snow had begun again, falling in thick slow flakes along Studfall Avenue as they passed the shops, time didn't mean anything to her at all. Or maybe there *was* time – out there, in the world that other people occupied, ordinary people untouched by magic, going about their business, scouting for last-minute Christmas presents or making their way home from the pub: factory girls with tinsel in their hair, coming from a works party to the Open Hearth in gaggles of ten or more, throwing up into the gutter or bawling obscene carols at passing shoppers; the occasional drunk hobbling out from the off-licence or betting shop and teetering along, hands in his pockets, neck craning, his feet stubbing the pavement, his eyes fixed straight ahead, trying not to believe in the possibility of falling over, like a child on stilts for the first time. To Alina, it had all been far away, like something she was watching on a screen, or through the window to a different world. She felt untouchable, utterly intact, and she was surprised at how paranoid Francis became, whenever they encountered other people.

'Come on, Alina,' he'd said, his voice tailing away in exasperation, as she stopped for the twentieth time to peer at something in a shop window, or to stand fascinated over some spill of fruit or broken glass on the pavement.

She'd laughed him off. 'Don't worry,' she said. 'They'll just think we're drunk.'

Francis shook his head. 'Come *on*,' he cried. He kept saying it, like a man with a child to look after – and she kept turning back to him and walking on, aware of the dividing line that protected her from everything else, the dividing line, the membrane, like the cell wall in those biology drawings at school, mysteriously holding everything together, keeping like with like and unlike out, though everything was so fluid and mutable. She had always wondered about that; now, here it was, in action: a living, warm membrane, a bubble of light and energy that could open to take in other things for a time, but would never permit them habitation. It was strange that Francis didn't see it too; strange, and disappointing, that he could step into her bubble, and not recognise that warmth, that he could step in and then, without noticing, step back out, and there would be no evidence of *his* bubble, no current from him of warmth and light. No energy. It was evidence, all of a sudden, of how different they really were, and it made her sad.

Not that she was oblivious to the danger of meeting other people head-on and unprepared; but for as long as she saw nobody she knew, she felt fine. The bubble was protecting her: invisible, paper-thin, it moved when she moved, breathed when she breathed. When she turned to look at something, it shaped itself around her, colours and forms shifting and sliding into new patterns, like the works of a kaleidoscope. When something caught her eye, the whole world streamed into focus: a face, a tree, a light in a shop window – everything she looked at was immediately singled out and made whole. It was true: *everything* was alive; or if not alive, exactly, then filled with energy, filled with some bright, receptive power that came to meet her gaze, responded to her touch, accommodated her thoughts. She noticed an orange on the pavement and glided over to look at it, and she saw immediately that its skin was broken, that it was oozing light, the warm, sweet juice of it seeping out on to the cold stone flags. She bent to see, almost hunkered down, drawing the broken thing into her bubble, breathing the scent of it through the cold smoky air. This was its spirit, this scent. The matter – the pulp and skin and juice of it – was only a vessel; but that sweet, rich orange scent was where its soul dwelled, and she was breathing it, taking it into herself, becoming orange.

'Alina!'

She looked up. It was Francis, turning back for her yet again. 'What are you doing?' He sounded ridiculously unhappy.

Alina shook her head, but she didn't speak. She didn't know what was happening. Couldn't he *see* it? Didn't he know?

'Come on,' he said, quieter now. 'Let's get away from here.'

Alina looked around. Outside the greengrocer's, about six yards away, Michael Mackenzie – the boy from her school that everybody called MicMac – and his twin sister, Lesley, had stopped to watch. Lesley had that look on her face that she always had, as if she was just about to laugh, but was still thinking about it, still wondering if what she had seen or heard was really funny, or just sad. That was how Lesley made her way in the world, that look: a defence, a strategy which, in most people's eyes, only made her seem more stupid. Alina smiled and shook her head again. Then she caught sight of MicMac.

'Come on, Alina.' Francis took hold of her arm and started pulling her away. He must have thought she was going to start a conversation. But Alina was looking at MicMac. He had his hands in his pockets, and he was stooped a little from the cold, but he was staring at her with an expression of pure hatred. Even at this distance, she could see it in his eyes – a hard, set gaze that, in all this warmth and light, in all this glister of the living, energised world, seemed impossibly cold and dead. She shuddered and looked away. Francis was still there, his hand gripping her arm, waiting.

'What is it?' he said, his voice unbearably gentle.

Suddenly the world seemed hideously cruel, unimaginably pitiful. She glanced back at MicMac one more time, as Francis began drawing her away, and she saw that he was still watching. Lesley was laughing now – she had worked it out, whatever it was this time, and she was saying something to her brother, probably telling him, as if he needed telling, *those two are on something, swear to God*. But MicMac was ignoring her. Alina broke away and followed Francis out of the glow of the shop windows and across the road, into the snow that was still falling, thick and slow and continuous, like a shelter from which they had temporarily strayed.

'Are you OK?' Francis stopped them both on the far pavement and lit a cigarette.

Alina nodded.

'Sure?'

She looked up at him and smiled.

'All right.' He seemed relieved. Maybe he had been scared she was going to freak out back there. He handed her the cigarette and lit another for himself. 'Come on,' he said.

The snow had started to settle now, whiting out the pavement, clinging to Francis's hair and coat. Alina felt happy again, all of a sudden. It was like a duty, she realised. Because there was so much that was cold and hard and dead in the world, so much that had been poisoned, you had to hold on to the warmth. You had to swallow that poison and transform it, in your own blood, into something good and true, the way an alchemist would transform base metal into gold. 'All right,' she repeated, softly. She could feel the bubble mending around her, the seal reforming, transforming the snow as it fell into bright, dancing flakes of energy. 'Let's go.'

The graveyard was empty, just as they had expected. It had seemed a good place to hide out after Francis's dad had come home unannounced, when he should have been at work on a double shift. The two of them had been up in Francis's room, listening to *Volunteers* and waiting for the acid to take effect, but just as the record finished they'd heard a sequence of noises below, strangely clear, as if happening inches away, rather than at the foot of a staircase on the other side of a dividing wall: a key in the lock, the front door opening, a series of objects being deposited in the hallway, a box, or a large parcel, followed by the rustling of plastic bags – and two voices, the man's low and deep, the woman's, or maybe it was a girl's, higher, more musical. They sounded deliberately hushed, Alina thought, like partners in a conspiracy. She recognised the man's voice as Mr Cameron's, but she didn't know who the girl was.

'Shit!' Francis jumped to his feet and started gathering his stuff together: a bag of grass, a carton of Marlboros with most of the lid torn away, a box of Swans, three packets of skins and the little pen-knife he'd used to slice the near-microscopic tab of pink microdot into two even tinier pieces for Alina's first trip. Usually, he would drop one or two microdots at once, he'd said, but it was better if you started with just a half, in case there were problems. Alina hadn't known what he meant by that; she'd heard about bad trips, but they sounded too vague and fanciful to be very convincing: monsters crawling out from under the bed, visions of fire and brimstone, or that boy they all talked about – a boy whose name was always different, depending on who was telling the story: Gus Duggan, Bob Russell, Paul somebody – who'd been found wandering naked across the Kingswood sports field, talking in tongues and clutching a Yale key firmly, desperately, in his left fist, as if it were the only thing that would save him from the hell into which he had descended. The story varied in most of its particulars, but one detail was always the same: no matter who it was, no matter where they found him, the ambulance men, or the police, or the doctors at the hospital had had to prise that key from his fingers, so reluctant was he to give it up. Yet later, when he came to, and they asked him what the key was for, he had no idea. That kind of stuff – what Francis called 'a candlelit dinner with Hieronymus Bosch' – hadn't really bothered her, but she'd never considered the more banal emergencies either, like somebody's father coming home unexpectedly when you had just begun to realise you were floating a few inches off the ground, wrapped in your own personal force-field of warmth and light, tuned into the deeper reality of things, but not altogether capable of tying your own shoelaces, or even, come to think of it, of being anything but amused by the concept: *shoelace*. Francis had been sitting cross-legged on the bed, leaving the only other item of furniture in the room, a large, moth-eaten armchair, to Alina. Now he turned off the stereo and began clearing away the visible evidence of their planned afternoon.

'It's Tommy,' he said. He always called his parents by their first names. 'We'll have to get out of here.' He crammed everything into the pocket of his Levi's jacket and headed for the door.

'What?' Alina couldn't quite believe it. He didn't really expect her to go out *now*, did he?

'We have to go,' Francis repeated haplessly, listening all the while to the voices down below. He shot her an understanding look. 'Don't worry,' he said. 'It'll be OK.'

It was easy for him to say. Alina didn't even know how she'd get past his father, never mind negotiate the street, or the world beyond. A minute ago, she had been sitting in the chair, her head tipped back, listening to the aftersound of the music – waves and waves of it seeming to fade away endlessly, to die back into the corners of the room which weren't corners at all, but bottomless tunnels into another space, the guitars drifting far into a distance that was all desert and sagebrush and low wind singing across dry rock. Besides, she didn't know how far along in the trip she was, or how much further she had to go before she came out the other side. She had the idea that it was an hour since Francis had given her the half-tab of microdot, but it could have been longer. Suddenly, the idea of *time* seemed altogether unconvincing.

'Put it on your tongue and let it dissolve,' he'd said; adding with an ironic half-smile, 'like Holy Communion.'

Alina had taken the tiny spot of LSD and held it a moment between her finger and her thumb. It looked like a piece of pinkish dirt. Though she'd told Francis she was sure she wanted to try it – told him several times, because he'd seemed to doubt her as a matter of policy – she still wasn't sure if she was really going to swallow this thing.

'Don't hold it in your hand,' Francis said. 'It'll melt.'

He put his own piece straight into his mouth and, with nothing else to do with hers, Alina followed suit. Then, as they sat quiet a while, she had become painfully attentive to her body and to her surroundings, waiting for some decisive moment of change, fearful and excited at once, but still half-certain that nothing would happen. It was a thought she had entertained several times: she would drop acid, and it would have no effect on her, the way dope never made her as stoned as the others – or as stoned as they said they were, at least. It was OK, she had always thought, but nothing special, just a peculiar cosiness and a feeling that you'd like to laugh out loud for no reason. Music sounded better, and once or twice she'd eaten a chocolate bar and been amazed at how good it tasted, but that was about all. She hadn't quite believed it when people like Francis had described their visions, their new insights, the amazing sounds they'd heard in a simple pop song, every time they had some good blow. This was going to be much the same thing. Francis had tried to tell her what to expect, but he'd quickly given up.

'Nobody can describe acid,' he'd said. 'You have to try it and see for yourself.'

Now, she waited; though she had already convinced herself it was no use. Even though Francis had told her that it took a while for the acid to work its way through the system, she decided that it was having no effect on her at all. She glanced over at Francis: he looked just as normal as she felt. 'Where did you get this stuff?' she asked, impatiently.

Francis laughed and started flicking through his record collection. 'None of your business,' he said.

'It's not working.'

'Give it a chance.'

It was almost nothing, to begin with. She felt warmer, that was all. A slow warmth, building in her body, somewhere deep, under, or maybe inside, her ribcage. Her mind was clear, she wasn't hallucinating – nothing like that. She was aware of something glittering in the dark, something wet, or metallic, glittering close by, but she couldn't quite fix on it. It was there, and it was real; she was sure of this. She was sure she wasn't imagining it – but it was just off to the left somewhere, out on the perimeter of her vision, whenever she tried to focus. An idea was beginning to form, not in her head, not in her thoughts, so much as at the surface of her skin, that this object, this glimmer, was something important, not just a piece of litter, say, or a fragment of scrap metal, but something more, a knife, maybe, or some kind of blade at least. Yes; that was it: a flat, wide-bladed knife with a wooden handle, a ceremonial thing, like the knife a magician would use. She could see it now in her mind's eye: it wasn't dangerous; it wasn't a knife for doing harm. It had a different purpose. The idea of it made her feel – not happy, that was wrong. Not happy, but right. *Just.* As in true, as in authentic. Her whole body felt warm now, and there was something she needed to say, some question she needed to ask. She looked up and saw Francis.

As soon as she looked at him, everything changed. It was as if they had been sitting there for the longest time, and she had forgotten Francis even existed, till she turned, and saw him. He smiled. 'Well?'

She wanted to answer, but she couldn't speak. There were no words. She had been in full possession of herself only a moment before; now everything was gone, as if someone had hit her and she had spun sideways into a long, delicious freefall.

A freefall that had continued, through the waves of music, through the seemingly interminable silences between the songs, through the glimmers and shimmers at the edge of her vision, through Francis swimming into her awareness then away again, his voice coming from a wide, echoey, far-off space that was not distance, or not exactly: he was here, present, it was just that there was something far-off about him, far-off, but not distant. Or not distant the way the music could be, fading into the faraway, still resonant, becoming clearer and clearer as it moved out, starlike, shaved down to the finest quiver of sound. Francis was far, far-off, faraway, in his own space, alone and slightly muffled.

'I love this song,' he had said, at some point. Then – much later, it seemed – he'd said it again: 'I love this.' He'd sat up and pointed at the stereo. 'Listen!'

Alina listened. She could never remember the songs – not the words, not even the titles, and by now she had begun to see that the words didn't really count anyway, it was the sound of it, it was the way the music clarified everything that mattered.

'*We are leaving . . .*' Francis's voice sounded strange, like something he had found at the bottom of a well. He wasn't singing exactly, but saying it to music, joining in. '*You don't need us . . .*'

Alina much preferred the other one, the one about the White Rabbit. Or the one about wanting somebody to love. Or that Quicksilver track that went for a whole side of an LP: 'Who Do

You Love?' But it didn't matter, really, when the lyrics stopped, and she could hear the guitar: a clean sound, like water; then cleaner still, like desert ice.

Finally, the music had ended. She had been trying to calculate, trying to work out the time: how long it had been, how long there was to go, when they heard the door open, and the sound of voices, and Francis had told her they would have to leave. Which was confusing, of course, because Francis had said Tommy would be out till at least ten, and with Mrs Cameron in the hospital again, they would have the house to themselves, mostly.

'What do you mean, mostly?' she had asked

'Well, Derek might come in. But he's no trouble.'

Derek was Francis's older brother. Alina remembered him from school. He'd been quiet, remote, probably a bit shy. He'd left school at sixteen and gone to work at Snakpak. Now he was doing twelve-hour shifts at The Works, trying to get money together, so Francis said, to get into the music business.

'Are you sure your dad won't be home?'

'I told you,' Francis had said. 'He's on a double. He won't be back till well after ten.'

So now, hearing Francis's father come in, she'd thought it was ten o'clock, but when she looked up, it was still light, the sky threatening snow, a thick, bruised cloud filling the window, framed in the glossy white casement like a picture of the sky in an art gallery, or some illustration of storm-clouds from a book on meteorology.

'Come on.' Francis was standing by the door, listening. From the sounds Alina had heard, his father had gone through the house and into the kitchen at the back. She knew as well as Francis did how to listen to people moving about in a closed space, working out where and how many they were, guessing what the mood was, or whether there was any chance of slipping past unnoticed. She had already been doing this – listening, calculating – without even knowing it; from habit, she realised. She stood up.

'Quick.'

They hurried downstairs together and, with an ease and a sense of timing that surprised her, Francis opened the front door so she could slip out unseen, while he – not quite but almost simultaneously – poked his head into the living-room.

'Hello?'

She didn't hear the rest. For a moment, while they negotiated their exit, her head had cleared: she was all focus, all direction. Now, in the shock of outside, that ordinary clarity fell apart. She waited; then, almost immediately, she forgot she was waiting. The first flakes of snow were just beginning to fall. For long moments at a time, she didn't really know where she was. What was she doing here? Why was she *outside*? She looked around. The street was empty. The wind gusted through the hedge at the far end of the neighbouring garden. When it darkened the hedge, the odd snowflake bleeding through as if from some other world, she could imagine another life, a different, cleaner way of being, an elsewhere of light and empty roads she often dreamed about but could never quite remember when she woke: deer coming down from the hills, owls in the woods, somewhere a lit room where someone – herself, not herself – sat reading by lamplight, waiting for something, or not waiting, it didn't matter. She didn't know what this place was – somewhere she had read about in a book, or seen in a film, maybe – it didn't matter. All that mattered was that she could imagine somewhere outside this smoky, poisoned town: light; empty woods; deer crossing a country road in the dusk. This imagined place, this country which did not exist, was *home* for her. Anywhere could have been home for her, as long as it wasn't Corby.

Not that she was alone in that. People here were always talking about *home*, and they always meant some other place, somewhere in the past or the future, a place they had come from, a place they were going to. People who had lived here all their lives, men who had been at The Works for twenty years and more, women whose children had been born and grown up in the glare of the furnaces, would talk about going home for the holidays, or going home when they retired, or, failing that, arranging for their bodies to be taken back to Dunfermline, or Cracow, or Paisley, so they could at least be buried in some other place. All their lives they had lived and breathed The Works; their bodies were steeped in a miasma of steel and carbon and ore; all their stories had to do with the Corporation, or the unions, or what happened in the blast furnaces. That was the irony of it all: after a few months, there was no doubting that they belonged to this place; their bodies were drenched in the stink of coke and ammonia and that lingering undertow, part-carbon, part-iron, that was everywhere – in the soil and the water, on the air, in the fabric of clothes and curtains and bedsheets, in the flesh of the living and the bones of the dead. They belonged to The Works, it had claimed them, and no matter how much they talked about those other places, *this* was their home.

'All right?'

Francis. She had forgotten about him. She tried to say something, but nothing came.

'Come on,' he said, not noticing how far away she had drifted.

'Where to?' It was a pleasure to speak, to know that she could if she chose, that she didn't have to make an effort. She could talk and think about something else at the same time.

'To the cemetery,' Francis said. 'I go all the time. Nobody will be there, not in this weather.' He stood watching her a moment, as if he was afraid she wasn't going to make it. 'Are you OK?'

Alina nodded, but she didn't say anything. It was a pleasure not to speak, too; it was a pleasure to remain silent.

Francis sighed. 'If you're sure you're all right,' he ventured again.

'Absolutely.'

'OK.' He took out his cigarettes and offered her one. 'Let's go see the dead people.'

They found a place to be, a shelter for the graveyard workers next to the perimeter fence, and settled in. Francis forced the lock, and they sat just inside the door, gazing out at the falling snow as it grew darker. In one direction, a few squat trees stood lonely among the gravestones, silhouetted against the empty fields beyond; in the other, they could see the junction opposite the gates, and the windy road that ran off into the dark towards Rockingham. From time to time, a car passed, the headlights scanning their faces then sweeping away on the turn, and it pleased her to think they were visible for a moment to those drivers, not as the people they were, but as others, creatures drawn from the land, or something to be dismissed as a trick of the light, apparitions, figments of a stranger's imagination. Alina glanced at Francis. She couldn't see his face now, in the darkness. Then she turned and looked out towards the fields. On the edge of the cemetery, standing alone at the far end of a gravel path, a low, gnarled hawthorn tree kept filling with light from the passing traffic, then darkening again, as if it were breathing. Beyond that, the land was still: a cold silent emptiness. Alina had been trying not to notice how black it was, a deep black in the green of the yew trees along the graveyard walks, a blackness, even, in the falling snow. She had imagined it would be something terrible, thinking about that blackness here among the dead; but then, all of a sudden, she was struck with a dark, vivid sense of it, of the black in the green of the sap, the black in the white of the snow, like something from a treatise in alchemy, black: *nigredo*, the true energy of the world that wasn't dark at all, or at least, wasn't malevolent, no matter how dangerous it seemed.

She looked at Francis. He was gazing into the distance, off to one side, his eyes fixed on something, or maybe he was just lost in it – she couldn't tell, and she couldn't say anything to make him come back. If she spoke, if she said anything at all, the whole thing would go back to how it had been before, to how it had always been. Instead, she stared at the side of his face, willing him to turn, to see what she was seeing. She wanted him to look out at the fields and see what was happening. She wanted him to know how it was: to know that, no matter what, you had to act as if it was the last evening ever; as if, when the sun went down, it was setting for all eternity. If you did that, if you lived as if every breath, every beam of light, every moment might be the last, you would begin to know what really mattered. You would know passion, you would know the difference between love and desire.

But Francis didn't look round. He seemed far away, far-off, distant. It occurred to her that, sitting out there, looking out at that empty road that seemed to go nowhere, he was beginning to slump, beginning to sink into something that had been there all along, brooding on some hurt that he had kept hidden from her. 'What is it?' she asked.

He started, roused from his waking dream. 'What?'

'What's wrong?' she said, keeping her voice low and gentle. 'Something's bothering you.'

He shook his head. 'Oh, no,' he said, 'not really. I was just thinking about Lizzie.'

'Oh.' Lizzie was his mother. She had been sick, off and on, for the last few years. About two weeks back, she had fallen ill again and had gone into Kettering General. Alina didn't know what the trouble was.

'She's not coming home for Christmas,' Francis said. 'Thing is, Tommy should have been up to see her today. Instead he said he was doing a double shift, to get more money for Christmas, and he'd go up tomorrow.'

'So?'

'So why did he come home this afternoon, if he was doing a double? And who was that with him?'

Alina shook her head. She didn't want to think about this. 'I didn't see anybody,' she said.

'It was some girl,' Francis continued. He hadn't been ignoring her, she knew that, he was just following his own thoughts. Still, Alina felt uncomfortable. She didn't like where this might be leading. 'I've seen her some place.' Francis fell silent, thinking it through.

Alina waited a moment, then stood up. 'I'm getting cold, sitting here,' she said. Francis looked at her then. She reckoned the acid had stopped affecting him ages ago. As for herself, she wasn't sure. Something was there, but it was sitting just out of reach, at arm's length, close enough to touch, but growing colder by the minute. She didn't want it to end so quickly.

Francis pulled himself to his feet. He looked tired. 'Where do you want to go?' he asked.

Alina shook her head. 'I don't know,' she said. 'I just want to be moving.' She didn't say it, but part of her wanted him gone, too, so she could be on her own. She had thought Francis could handle this, that she would be the one who had to take it carefully. Instead, he'd seemed paranoid and unhappy ever since they'd left the house. It was amazing, she thought, how the microdot had made everything so subtle and interchangeable; one thing touched another and immediately it was transformed: filled with light, or hopelessly contaminated, it all depended on which was the stronger, the light or the dark, the clean or the tainted, his mood or hers, the lights from the town or the cool, empty darkness beyond them.

'Come on,' she said. She hoped she sounded reasonably sympathetic. 'Let's walk.'

They walked. And walked. There was nothing else to do. Francis didn't say much; he was probably still thinking about his mother, but he didn't talk about it. They walked right out as far as the top of Rockingham Hill, then they stood at the side of the road, gazing down into the valley beyond. It was beautiful: everything was beautiful at night, when all you could see were the lights and the vast darkness of the world; no steelworks, no houses, no people. The headlamps climbing the hill weren't cars, they were just lights; the spots and pools of gold or silver in the valley weren't pub lounges and front rooms and car parks, they were just spots and pools of light. Mostly, they clustered together, like insects swarming; here and there a single, white porch or dairy lamp stood off by itself, still, silent, faraway and almost within reach at the same time. 'Look.' Alina pointed down at the furthest lamp that twinkled alone in the vast darkness. 'What do you think that is?'

Francis followed her pointing finger. She couldn't see his face now, but she could tell from his voice, when he spoke, that he was sad.

'It's just a house,' he said.

'Who lives there?'

Francis laughed softly and, though she couldn't really see him, she felt him shake his head in the darkness. Suddenly, she was alert again, filled with the same warmth as before, and just as sensitive – only it was subtler now, more controlled. 'How would I know?' he said.

'Pretend.'

'Pretend what?'

'Pretend it's someone you know,' Alina said. She was drawing him in, pulling him out of his dark mood. 'Pretend it's you.' She laughed quietly. 'That's it. Pretend it's you. Ten, twenty, fifty years from now. You live in that house. What are you doing? What are you like?'

She sensed that Francis was thinking. She was drawing him out of himself; she could feel it. What a beautiful expression, she thought. Drawing him out of himself. Bringing him back to the world again. She thought she could feel a smile.

'OK,' he said, conceding something. 'I'm an old man. I live alone. I have always lived alone. I have travelled all over the world, and now I have come here to live out the end of my life in peace.'

'What do you do?'

Francis considered a moment. 'I'm an astronomer,' he said. He was warmer now. 'That's what I'm doing now. I'm looking at the stars. This house where I live is an observatory. In fact, my only valuable possession is a powerful, hand-crafted telescope. It stands alone on the upper floor of this house, trained on the furthest edge of the night sky.'

'How old are you?'

'I'm very old. Maybe seventy or more. But I'm fit. I'm – limber. The rooms are sparsely furnished: a table, some chairs, a few rugs, a battered sofa on the ground floor where I eat and sleep. But above, on the upper floor, the house is empty and wide, a cool, starlit space, all windows, and this beautiful telescope pointing at the sky.'

'What are you looking at?' Alina tilted her head back and looked up. Here and there, a star glittered, but it was mostly clouds.

'I'm searching for an unknown planet,' Francis said.

'What, like Pluto?'

'Yes.' Francis was involved now, looking up, imagining what he could see in the wide black sky. 'Like Pluto. But further away.' He shook his head and turned to her. 'It's the lost planet,' he said. 'No one will ever find it. Not in a million years.' The thought seemed to satisfy him. Alina smiled. She had finally brought him out of himself, and – typical Francis – he had taken it all the way to the edge of the universe.

They stood out in the dark till it was late, staring at the lights in the valley, watching the snow fall. Alina had no idea what time it was, but she knew it was very late.

'I have to go,' she said at last. She felt completely in control of herself now, and Francis seemed better, more cheerful.

'I'll walk you home,' he offered.

'It's OK,' she said. 'Just walk with me till I find a taxi. What are you going to do?'

'I don't know,' Francis answered. 'Go home, I suppose.'

They walked back towards the lights. Above the town, the dull orange glow from The Works filled the whole sky. It was like living in a suburb of hell, Alina thought. At night, the light from the blast furnaces cast a dull glow over everything for miles; by day, tiny flakes of ash and dust drifted on the wind, a taint on the air you could taste, a corruption you couldn't help breathing. Odd to think that, just a mile away, at the foot of the hill, the country lay still and clean, untouched by the poisons their bodies were absorbing, even now, as they walked homeward. Alina thought of the green hedges, the soft new foliage of hawthorn and whitebeam, the daffodils that grew in the public gardens, just a few miles from The Works. They were so clean, so soft. Nothing within the bounds of the town was as clean and soft as that new foliage. And now, looking back from here, she saw that the town was nothing, really. It was The Works, and not much else: Corby Steel Works, like a huge animal drowsing in the dark, breathing men and fire, crouched in its own miasma of smoke and dust, surrounded on all sides by the estates where its attendants lived, like the peasants in some medieval barony, their huts pitched in rings around the great castle. Someone had said once that Corby was nothing more than an industrial estate with a roundabout in the middle; but it was worse than that, because the architects who had built that estate had decided to leave patches of green between the houses, narrow strips of dusty woods, mysterious angles and recesses of greenery and brackish water, wide headlands of trees and shrubs where birds sang in the early morning, odd squares of grass where children played football, or where one tree stood, like the crabbed oak tree near Francis's house, the one they had climbed once, stoned on dope, convinced that an angel, or a demon, lived in its gnarled, grey branches. These patches of greenery were supposed to make the town more attractive to the workers, but they mostly had the opposite effect, reminding everyone of what had been there before The Works arrived. If you walked out of town a short distance, past Kingswood school, say, you found remnants of ancient forest, the dusty ghosts of what had once been clear ponds and rivers full of carp or pike, occasional clumps of wildflowers in woodland clearings, their blossoms impossibly blue, or gold, or blood-red.

They hailed a taxi and shared the ride home. Francis insisted on dropping Alina off first. 'I'll see you tomorrow,' he said.

'OK.'

'Are you all right to go in?'

Alina nodded. It was sweet, really. He looked much worse than she felt. 'How about you?' she asked.

'Oh, I'm fine,' he said. He was being very serious. 'I'll see you tomorrow.'

'OK.'

She waited on the kerb till the taxi pulled away. Francis craned his neck to look back at her, then the cab disappeared and she turned to look up at her parents' window. It was dark. The whole house was dark, in fact, except for the window of Jan's room, which was very faintly illuminated by a warm, yellowish glow. Her brother would be reading in bed, she thought, with just the bedside lamp on. It was a nightly ritual.

Francis and Jan were best friends. They had been best friends since middle school. Alina remembered Francis from that time: a solitary figure, singular, somehow remote amid the gaggle of other boys in the crowded playground. She had noticed right away how stubbornly he set himself apart, how obviously he presented his indifference to all that was happening around him. And it *was* indifference, not contempt, not even disdain. There was no display in it, not the least whiff of defensiveness, on the one hand, or superiority complex on the other. Francis just didn't want to be there, with these others, and, though he wasn't wearing it on his sleeve, he didn't care if it showed.

Alina was a year older than the boys, so even though the boys were close friends, she didn't have that much to do with them. It was a matter of honour, a code: she was a girl, she wasn't in their year group. It would have been beneath her to take an interest when they embarked on their endless cycle journeys, packing strange picnics of pickles and tinned fruit, banana and sugar sandwiches, chocolate bars and those sweet yellow toma-toes you could only find at the height of the summer. The bikes, she knew, were an escape route: sitting at the centre of the Northamptonshire countryside, Corby was surrounded by old country houses, ancestral woods and gardens, tiny sand-coloured villages set around church steeples and manors, ruins of old towers, echoey wells, tidy, quiet farms. The boys explored the country-side every weekend, and they would come back with accounts of the places they had found: Kirby Hall, the Triangular Lodge, Rockingham Castle. It was strange. It didn't surprise Alina that her brother would make picnics and go cycling around the country-side, looking for historic sites. It didn't even surprise her that Jan got a paper round and saved enough to buy a good bike and a camera, or that he started developing and printing the black-and-white film he'd shot in a makeshift studio he'd created in his bedroom. It didn't surprise her because nothing about Jan surprised her. But Francis was different. At first sight, he was so remote, so detached from the world around him, it was hard to imagine him being interested in what was, to Alina's mind, nothing more than a hobby.

Yet it was Francis, more than Jan, who planned these expe-ditions, and it was Francis who made all the best photographs. He probably didn't think so; without ever betraying the least doubt, or the smallest inkling of resentment, he seemed to think Jan was best at everything, to Alina's huge annoyance. Francis probably thought he was just messing about with that camera of his, but there was something about the photographs he took, a closeness to the subject, a fondness, even, that shone, while Jan's pictures were flat, simple records of fact, with no pretence at being anything other than visual documents of a moment, a place, a season. Of course, their first efforts were equally amateurish, and they laughed at themselves when the films came back from the photographic shop, developed and printed on contact sheets so they could see if there was anything worth blowing up. Alina had thought they were foolish to waste all that time and money, especially when Jan had somehow found enough cash to set up his darkroom, but she still hadn't paid that much attention. It was a boys' thing. From time to time, Jan would show her a black-and-white print – they always shot in black-and-white, not only because they couldn't afford colour developing, but also because black-and-white was what the professionals used – and she would try to show some interest. Jan seemed to like taking pictures of hedges, or the sky, or empty stretches of field. There was an unrelenting greyness about it all that probably seemed right to him – just and austere and honest

– but it left her cold. Looking at Jan's pictures, she longed for colour: the real world, the real green of it, the vivid red of a poppy, the deep blue of a summer sky.

Then, one day, the boys were sitting together in the front room. It was odd, but she always noticed it: there was something unsettling about them, something *spooky* that came out whenever they were alone together, a quality she'd only ever noticed with a pair of twins in her class at school, two identical Irish boys with copper-coloured eyes and cropped black hair who seemed, in their selfsameness, almost an offence against nature. Jan and Francis were discussing the pictures, studying contact sheets, deciding what to print. At first, they had ignored her when she butted in, craning over Jan's shoulder to see the blown-up photograph he was holding, and, to begin with, she couldn't quite make it out. Then, when he gave in and held it quivering in front of her eyes, she saw that it was beautiful: a very simple shot of a dead bird lying in a gutter, with a street and a long row of houses reaching away, not quite in focus, behind it.

'I like that,' she said. 'That's the best snap you've taken, by a long shot.' She always called the photographs snaps, to irritate Jan. It never did. Now he stared at her, amused, self-satisfied, as if he had tricked her into something. 'What?' she said.

'I didn't take this,' Jan told her. 'Francis did.'

'Oh.' She glanced at Francis. 'Well. It's very good.'

Jan laughed. 'That's just what I was saying,' he said. 'The trouble with him is, he can't tell the difference between a good picture and a bad one, even when he takes it himself.' He studied Francis, still amused. 'I was just saying, he should send this to one of those competitions in the photographic magazines.'

Francis shook his head and looked away. 'Waste of time,' he murmured.

'He's got more,' Jan continued. 'Would you like to see?' He pulled a sheaf of prints out of a manila folder that was lying on the table. 'Here,' he said. 'Look at this.'

It was a photograph of an old man working in his garden. No – it was an allotment, and the man was working by lantern light, his face lit up like one of those faces in old paintings, a face from an El Greco, or some crazed amateur scientist from Joseph Wright of Derby. It was night, and the man was working with a dibber and a trowel; he needed the lantern to see. But why was he working in the dark? Why didn't he do this in the daytime, like other people? Alina looked at Francis.

'I don't know,' he said, as if she had asked him out loud the question that was in her mind. 'We just saw him like this, on our way home one evening.' He studied the picture; you could see, Alina thought, that he wasn't quite sure, but he thought he probably had something. 'This is how the miners used to grow vegetables, back in the old days,' he said. 'They would work on Saturday afternoons, but that wasn't enough. So they'd bring their lamps out and garden in the evenings, when they got off work.' He picked another photograph from the pile: the same scene, but from a slightly different angle. Alina could see a hedge, a thick scribble of bare thorns at the man's back, echoed somehow, in the face, with its heavy, seamed wrinkles. 'I remember hearing about the mill-workers, back in the old days,' Francis continued. He had forgotten himself, forgotten Jan. He was looking at her. 'Men who used to work in the textile mills, dyeing wool in the West Country somewhere. They made a special cloth, a very bright blue. Uley Blue they called it. An old guy I met told me about them. The cloth was really expensive, but they were paid next to nothing. They had to work every day, all day, including Saturdays. They got Sundays off so they could go to church. There was no time, but they all had gardens, allotments, scraps of waste ground they worked in between the mills, the streams running blue with the dye, their hands and faces and clothes stained a faint but indelible blue.' He looked at the old man in his photograph as if he were one of the dyers from the story. There was, Alina saw, real affection in that look. 'This was how they worked. All the time. With lanterns, at night. Apparently, they grew amazing things: prize onions, marrows, chrysanths.'

'Francis is a gardener at heart,' Jan chipped in, unhelpfully.

The mood was broken. Francis turned to him and smiled. 'Well,' he said.

Alina waited, but that was all he said: '*Well.*'

He didn't ask her out. If he had, she would have said no. She didn't want to go out with anybody. Plenty had asked, and they had all been refused. She knew the boys in her class went about saying there was something up with her, that she was frigid, or a lesbian, and she didn't care. She didn't want to go out with anyone, or not until she noticed Francis. She couldn't help thinking that he wasn't like those others. He made it easy for them to be together, without ever letting it seem they were a couple. He didn't try to take her anywhere, not to the pictures, or to the school dance. He didn't try to feel her up, or get her into bed. He didn't even try to kiss her. Not that she wanted him to. She liked him, but she didn't see why they couldn't be friends. He was friends with Jan, wasn't he? She didn't see why there should be a difference.

Once, he'd asked her if she wanted to go swimming out at the Twenty-Two Foot. It was a place people went because their parents told them not to; it was better than the public baths, with its stink of chlorine and crowds of squealing kids: set apart, out on the edge of the town, it was not much more than a pond, a little muddy in some seasons, but good to swim in, especially in the high summer, when the water was cool and still. Alina had been surprised by the invitation, and charmed, too, for reasons that Francis would never have understood. Though he must have known the story – a story that had been going the rounds for years, ever since Alina was a little girl, and probably for decades before that: a story told to all girls, to keep them from danger, girls who were women now, like the women she saw on their way to Snakpak and Aquascutum every day, women in blue overalls and plimsolls, walking in twos and threes, talking and laughing, enjoying that last moment before they went in, or stopping at the factory doors to finish a cigarette in the dusty summer mornings. The story said that once, a long time ago, a girl had been found dead at the bottom of the Twenty-Two Foot, some time between Christmas and Hogmanay. The girl – whose name was never mentioned, either from respect, or because the teller had forgotten – this anonymous girl, whom Alina had always considered beautiful, had left home on Christmas Eve, on her way to a party. She was dressed in a black satin dress and she was wearing patent leather shoes – and that was what she was still wearing when they found her, suspended in the ice. Her engagement ring was still on her hand and her fake pearls were still around her neck, even though she had been dead for several days when they fished her frozen body from the water. How she had come to be out there – far from home, far from the party – was anybody's guess, but the deepest mystery of all was how she had come to be in the water, under the ice. Everybody who remembered that winter said the Twenty-Two Foot had been frozen solid for days before Christmas, and there was no hole in the ice, no sign of a place where the girl could have fallen through. Alina had wondered if Francis knew that story, and if he did, why he had asked her to go to a place that was haunted by a drowned girl.

Nevertheless, it had occurred to her that going to the Twenty-Two Foot was about as far from a normal date as anything she could imagine. No other boy in the whole town would have asked a girl to go swimming with him out there. Alina didn't know if it was the thought of the ghost, or the fact of Francis's sheer unworldliness that had charmed her, but when Francis had asked, that summer afternoon – casual, nonchalant – if she wanted to go, she had only thought for a moment or two before she'd said yes. It was the confirmation she needed that he didn't think of her as a girlfriend. For his own reasons – and these were quite mysterious to her – he had wanted them to be Just Good Friends. She couldn't help thinking that this was important to him, just as she couldn't help being annoyed at Jan's obvious, and utterly childish, delight in this new development. From the first time she and Francis had gone anywhere together, her brother had started ragging them, calling them names, quoting snippets from *Romeo and Juliet* or sentimental pop songs. Yet, strangely enough, this didn't bother Francis. He seemed to find Jan's behaviour amusing and, all of a sudden, a shift was starting to happen. When Francis started smoking dope, it wasn't Jan he invited round to try it. And today, while Jan was off at the library, or wandering around town with his camera, it was with Alina, and not his best friend, that Francis had shared what he called, only half-ironically, the holy Eucharist of acid – and she was glad of it, glad of having been touched by this warmth, glad he had shared with her what he loved, and not what he wanted, or needed, or imagined he was supposed to have. He had given her a gift; she knew that. She wasn't sure she would ever want it again, but she was glad of the glimpse she had been afforded of a world outside her own.

★

Now, however, coming home in the dark and creeping upstairs, the acid still vivid in her bloodstream, she was terrified of meeting her mother on the landing, or finding her father waiting in her room, as he had done once, when she'd come home late from a school dance, waiting in his pyjamas and the ratty old dressing-gown he'd been wearing for years, his feet naked and white on the bare floorboards. He had been sitting on the bed for God knows how long, bolt upright, waiting, his face eerily blank in that moment when she came through the door and switched on the light.

'What is it?' To begin with, she'd thought something had happened to Jan, or her mother. 'What's wrong?'

Her father stood up.

'Do you know what time it is?' he asked, his voice steady and empty, the voice of a man who has misplaced his trust yet again.

As it happened, she'd had no idea what time it was. She had lost track, dancing, then talking to a pair of wild, funny German girls who had just arrived on a school exchange with the fifth year. She glanced at the little travel clock on the bedside table, a gift from her mother the last time there had been a fight about time. It was not quite eleven thirty. 'I'm sorry,' she said. 'I missed the bus. I had to walk home.'

Her father had looked her straight in the face then, for the first time since she had come into the room. His eyes were filled with an unseemly grief. 'I don't know what to do with you,' he said. 'I ask one simple thing, which is that you come home by ten thirty at the latest. This is not difficult, at your age. You are supposed to be a responsible girl –'

And so it went. In those days, he never shouted; he would just talk at her, without a pause, his voice quiet and resentful. He would say how he counted on her to help him, or how she was killing her mother with all this worry. His accent was more obvious, at times like these, perhaps because this was the most she ever heard him say for days or even weeks at a time. Sometimes he used words he'd found in the thesaurus, or curious little phrases he picked up from the radio and, though she always knew what they meant, she was never quite certain that he did. He said he had allowed her more liberty than most girls her age, because he had thought he could trust her, which was ridiculous, of course, considering how little freedom she had; yet she always felt there was something else, something unspoken behind his accusations, a secret disappointment that he could not bring himself to voice. Another time, he had let her go to a party with some girls from school, making her promise to be home by eleven. She had agreed, of course, because it was the only way she could get out, but when she had tried to stay on, just for a little while, he had suddenly appeared, wearing a raincoat, but still in his grey corduroy slippers, at fifteen minutes past the hour, clutching the anorak she only ever wore to school and embarrassing her in front of everyone.

More recently, things had got worse. Now she would do just about anything to avoid, not just her father, but her mum too. The path from the downstairs hallway to the door of her own room was like a minefield, hostile territory that she had to cross with ever greater care, especially since she'd started smoking with Francis on their supposed dates. She would come home late and paranoid, convinced her parents could tell what she'd been doing just by looking at her eyes, picking up the real or imagined clues identified in those drug information leaflets the schools had distributed to worried parents: *look for dilated pupils, dry mouth, uncontrollable laughter, rambling speech.* Strangely, it had been harder when she'd only been smoking; tonight, still tripping, and amazed at everything that had happened, at how that tiny little microdot had changed the whole world, she was afraid of being caught out by one or the other of her parents, but she wasn't ashamed, and she had no intention of defending herself. If her father had jumped out at her on the stairs and demanded to know what she'd taken, she would probably have told him – as long as he went away after that, and left her to see the trip to its natural end in the safety of her own room. But then, he wouldn't have let her go, even if he'd understood how different acid was from drink, or pills or hash. She wished she could slip him a little tab of pink microdot in his afternoon tea, and let him see what it was like. Maybe then he would realise how desperate his life was.

Reaching the sanctuary of her room was one thing, but stretching out in her bed in the dark, her legs straight and long under the smooth, clean sheets, was something else entirely. Her body felt immense, but it wasn't the size that mattered, so much as the detail. She was aware of herself as something finer and more complex than she had ever imagined. It was like studying the map of a vast city and seeing parks, streets, theatres, fountains, bridges, like following the alley of one sensation – some homeopathic detail of warmth or scent – into a wide boulevard of memorised daylight and music, or tracing a path across her body and finding hints to another creature altogether, something marine, or animal, suspended just a millimetre below the shimmering, tight surface of her skin. She hadn't imagined it would be so physical. What Francis had told her about it suggested that everything would happen inside her head, a swirl of hallucinations and strange notions, a sudden sense of the world as funny, or poignant, or richly populated, a glimpse of the truth under some cliché like 'cosmic laughter' or '*déjà vu*' – but always at the level of thinking, always more or less abstract. She hadn't known it would permeate her whole body.

She was probably starting to come down now. The intense warmth had started to fade, and that sense of being inhabited by something alive, some force that trilled in her veins, was passing slowly. She kept thinking that it would suddenly be over: that, from one moment to the next, the world would slot back into its usual dull, but comfortingly familiar, order. It had been amazing; but she wouldn't have wanted it to last for ever. She wanted to stop for a while, just to lie still and remember it all, to capture the sensation in some image or word or notion, before it slipped away. After all – as she realised with a sudden rush of what could only be described as joy – this experience was repeatable. It was as if someone had just given her the most beautiful gift that could ever be given to anyone, something entirely private and, at the same time, sacramental. It was herself, as she really was. It was a key, a password, a secret mirror.

She was beginning to decide it was all over – and it felt, really, that this was in her power, that she could decide when it ended, just as she could decide, at any time, when to go back – she was beginning to sink, to settle comfortably into the ordinary feel of the bed, the sheets, the coolness of the night air, when she realised something was wrong. It wasn't something she could put her finger on: it had to do with the coolness, with the way the light played in the bedroom curtains, with the fact that the window was wide open, when she was certain, thinking about it, that she had checked it was shut before she'd gone out. Her father was always talking about the crime rate and how an open window was just an invitation to the kind of people who lived around here; he went on about it so much that closing windows, locking doors, making sure everything was secure before you went out had become a matter of routine, something you just did, without thinking. Yet now the window was wide open; the curtains were billowing into the room and there was something missing – or was it that something had been added? Yes, that was it, some-thing new had been added, though she couldn't have said what till the shadow, a dense, vibrant shadow she hadn't altogether registered till now, took form and dropped softly to the floor. At first she thought it was an animal of some kind, a cat or maybe a dog; it was only a moment later, when the figure straightened up and turned to look at her, its back to the half-light outside, that she knew it was human.

'Don't be scared.'

For a long moment, it was hard to connect the voice she heard with this black figure standing at the window, for the voice, soft and more fearful itself than it probably intended to be, was familiar, whereas the shadow in her room was something else, something older.

'I just want to talk to you.'

Alina was surprised to find that she hadn't moved, or cried out. She had not been afraid when the shadow was there: it was part of what was happening, and what was happening meant her no harm. The shadow was real, like a character from a dream, no more or less than that. The voice, however, was something else. The voice had come from the outside, and for that reason she knew it was dangerous. It was a boy's voice, the voice of someone she knew, someone she had met somewhere in the wide, ugly world.

'All right?' The boy sounded more confident now, perhaps because she hadn't screamed, or cried out. 'I'm not going to do anything.'

It was MicMac. She remembered seeing him earlier, outside Studfall shops, with Lesley. But that had been hours ago. How, she wondered, had he gone from five in the afternoon to just after midnight? Had he been there all that time? Had he existed at all, between then and now? As her eyes became accustomed to the room with his presence in it, rather than the original, edgy shadow, she began to pick him out, to notice his check shirt, the streaks of coppery red in his hair. He was leaning slightly against the sill, his back to the window. She wondered if his sister was there too, waiting for him on the street below, and for a moment she thought of calling out, of telling Lesley to come and take her brother away. Then she thought of her father, and she froze.

'Aren't you going to say anything?' The voice sounded closer now, though she could still see his shadow at the window.

Alina shook her head, then realised he probably couldn't see her face. 'Go away,' she said, trying not to sound angry or frightened. Her voice sounded odd to her, as if she had spoken underwater.

'It's all right,' he whispered. He moved, just a little, raising his hand to his face, half-smiling, she thought, though she still couldn't see him. There was a lightness, a kind of shake, in his voice and, for a moment, she thought he was about to laugh, as if the whole thing might be a joke after all. Then, quickly, in one smooth movement, he crossed the room towards her.

'Stop it!' She sounded absurdly like her mother, like any mother talking to a naughty child. 'I'm warning you.' But she hadn't intended what she said to sound angry, or frightened; she only wanted him to understand it as a warning, as a piece of useful advice almost, stranger to stranger. Because he was a stranger, and she couldn't see why he was here, in her house. Did he know about the acid? Maybe he wanted some too.

Now he was there, beside the bed, and she almost screamed, in spite of herself. She'd thought he was going to do something, to hurt her, even, but her voice had died in her throat. All she had heard was a hoarse, rasping noise, and a dull thud as he kneeled down, beside her bed. 'Go away,' she said again, her voice sounding smaller and more distant than before.

MicMac shook his head. 'I'm not going to hurt you,' he said. 'I'm not going to touch you, see?' He held his hands out in front of her face, as if he were about to perform some conjuring trick, and wanted her to know there was nothing concealed in his fists, or up his sleeves.

Alina wanted to close her eyes. If she closed her eyes and waited, he would disappear. She wondered how he had got into the room. 'If you go now,' she said, her voice rising scarily, 'you won't be in any trouble.'

'It's all right,' MicMac whispered. In spite of his promise a few seconds before, he reached out and touched her gently, just above the wrist. His fingers were cold. 'I told you. I just want to talk to you.'

As he leaned closer, Alina could smell the alcohol on his breath. It was sickly-sweet, a combination of whisky and something else, maybe ginger ale. She could hear the way his mouth worked, the stickiness, the motion of his jaw as he spoke. The worst of it was, he didn't seem to think there was anything out of the ordinary in what he was doing. He looked oddly soft to her, as if he was on the point of laughing. 'Get out of my room,' she said, trying to sound calm and firm. She was still scared, but the momentary contact had made her angry, too. 'Go away. Get out.' She reared up in the bed and struck him, hard, on the arm.

MicMac didn't move. She struck out desperately, aiming at where she thought his face was, but hitting his arms, his shoulders, his chest. She could hear him breathing, and he was close, so close she could almost taste the whisky on his breath, his heat and scent mingling with the after-warmth of the acid. Then, all of a sudden, she was striking out into thin air, into empty darkness. For a moment she thought he had vanished, that he had been nothing more than an hallucination. Then she heard a sound at the window, and she saw the shadow again, rising as if it was about to float away.

'I love you, Alina,' it said. 'That's what I wanted to tell you. I'm sorry.'

Then they were both gone: the shadow, and MicMac, disappearing into the darkness. At exactly the same moment, a knock came at the door, and she realised the light was on out in the hallway.

'Alina?' It was her mother. Alina could feel her, standing in her nightie and slippers, on the other side of the door. 'Are you all right?'

Alina jumped out of bed and ran to the window, pushed it shut, and slipped the catch to. The garden was empty; nobody was there.

'Alina?' Her mother sounded anxious. Alina was lucky: her father wouldn't have waited after the first knock; he'd have come straight in.

'I'm fine,' she called. 'I just got up to close the window.' She moved back to the middle of the room. 'I must have left it open.' She could hear her mother breathing; she could feel the tension in her body as she waited, unsure of what to do. 'It's all right, Mum. Go back to bed.'

The tension at the door hovered a moment, then broke. Her mother was gone. Alina slipped back under the covers and lay shivering. She was cold now. Everything she'd had before – the warmth, the softness, the sense of her body as a fine, golden network of sensations – everything she had wanted to keep intact, everything she had wanted to carry over into the light of the next day had disappeared. She felt uprooted. She had made all those shining, vivid connections to a life of her own, to a life that simmered under the surface of the everyday world, and now they were gone.

Sometime during the night, it had snowed again. When she woke, early in the morning, after only an hour of half-sleep, she could feel the change in the air, the bright, true cold of it filling the room, lining the walls, chilling the bedclothes. For a moment as she surfaced, she thought the window was open again, and that she would find MicMac kneeling by the bed, still shrouded in that whisky-and-sugar sweetness. Then she woke and saw that everything was as it had been the day before, and the day before that: bedside table, curtains, wardrobe, books, posters, carpet. The same colours, the same patina of wear and age on the surface of things, the same drabness. She felt like one of those children who get taken to fairyland in an old folk-story, then have to return to their own world, years later, after living for so long with magic. She had heard those stories in school, and she had always been intrigued by them, as if they contained a message of some kind, a message meant only for her. Sometimes the details were different, but the essential story was always the same: the children would go out walking in the woods, or by a lake, and they would meet the King of the Fairies. He would know who they were, he would call to them by name as he invited them into a world that was buried under the ground, or in the depths of a great lake – and out of curiosity more than anything else, they would go. They wouldn't believe they were leaving home, or abandoning their parents; they would just go, because they were the ones who had been chosen, and because there would be no story if they turned away and refused the adventure. Maybe they thought they could live in two places at once: that they could go with the fairy king under the water or into the earth, to a place where time never moved, and there was always sweet music in the air, and at the same time, they would still be at home, where they were needed. When they got to the underground world, they were happier than they had ever been in their lives: they were never hungry, nobody was cruel to them, there was a slow, easy *justness* to things. Everything was alive, even the stones, and nothing ever died.

Yet, finally, after they had been there long enough to know that this was heaven, they were obliged to go back, to return to their parents' world, where nothing had changed, where it was only an hour, or an hour and a day, since they had walked away all those years ago. Depending on which story you heard, the reasons for their departure varied: their parents were calling to them from above, they had committed some offence against the laws of the underworld, sometimes they were even homesick, in spite of everything. In this version, they go to the fairy king and tell him that, even though they are happy with him, even though his domain is the most beautiful place they have ever seen, they cannot help themselves: they miss their own house, they miss their parents and friends. They want to stay, but they must go back.

The king is surprised. He explains that, while he cannot prevent them from leaving, he wants them to understand what they are doing. 'You are leaving paradise', he says, 'to return to a world of hunger and pain. Here no one grows old; nobody dies. Anything you wish for, you only have to think of it, and it is there. Here you have peace, music, beauty.' He turns to gaze around him at a world that is so perfect he cannot imagine anyone wishing to leave it – and perhaps, for this brief moment in the eternity that is his life, his kingdom seems diminished in some way, a smaller, narrower heaven than he had ever believed, less beautiful, and less his own, than he had imagined. For the first time, he is sad. 'Where you are going', he says, 'you will grow old. You will sicken and you will see those you love pass away like spring snow. In that country there is ugliness, despair, pain, injustice. It is a poisoned world.' He has begun to plead with them. 'Do not go back there. Stay here with me and live for ever.' But it is too late. The children have no choice, they are not deciding to leave him, but they cannot help themselves. They belong to the human realm. They are not fairies.

Alina had never forgotten this story. As a child, she had felt sorry for the children, because they had to leave the perfect world they had found; later, though, her sympathies lay with the fairy king, because he had given the children such a beautiful home, and they had refused it. It did not matter to him that they were not rejecting that paradise, that it was their very humanity that obliged them to return to the ordinary world. It did not matter to him because he was not human. He would never understand why the children had to go. Yet his magical world would have become a little less magical as soon as they were gone – and this was what troubled Alina most about the story. In the end, what mattered wasn't how the king felt, or whether the children missed their parents. What mattered was the perfect world. The children had been too young, or too curious, to know it, but as they followed the king, on that first day, they were entering into a contract with the earth. They were taking on a responsibility. Had they but known it, the most fleeting glimpse of perfection would have been eternally binding, but they had been allowed to dwell for years in the underground chambers of a perfect realm, beyond taint, beyond corruption. Until that moment, nothing could have contaminated this world. Had they been older, or more thoughtful, they might have seen that the fairy king loved them more than their parents or friends ever could, that the world they were leaving behind was more real than the home they remembered. All it would have taken was a little imagination.

Alina pulled on her dressing-gown and went to the window. Outside, it was still dark, the snow falling thick and fast through the pools of lamplight along the street, settling on the hedges and fences, on the narrow gardens, on the pavements and paths all the way to the end of the road and out past The Works, past the sludge beds, along motorways and rivers to silent woodlands, empty fields, farmyards packed with wintered cattle, low hills covered with bracken and sweet gorse. Carefully, quietly, she opened the window and held out her hand. She wanted to be cleansed, to wash away something that was bound to her skin, a staleness that was bound as tight and as close as her own warmth, a sticky, tainted staleness that had been with her for a long time, with her but not of her, a taint from outside, a trace of poison she had breathed or swallowed long ago, that had grown and spread inside her till it was almost impossible to decide what was *her*, and what was this other, alien thing. She let the snowflakes settle and melt on the palm of her hand, on her fingers, on her wrists, wanting this coldness, this purity, to fill her, to spread through her nerves and bloodstream till it replaced everything, till she was made empty and new. Finally, when her hand was wet with it, when drops of meltwater clung to her skin like tiny dark pearls, she brought her hand to her mouth and licked the palm, tasting the cold, sooty water, black and metallic in her mouth, like iron filings mixed with morning frost, eternally inter-wined. Yet somewhere – she could imagine it, even in this place – somewhere snow was falling on the side of a mountain, or on an estuary in the far north, and it was made up of nothing but water and atmosphere, in a place governed only by gravity and light, falling on rocks, falling on sand, falling on heather and low trees, blown through the wind or drifting slowly through the grass, like a benediction.

She woke again sometime in the middle of the morning. It was light outside, though it was a grey, improbable light, heavy with snow that had obviously been falling for hours. Alina was lying on the bed, outside the covers, in her dressing-gown. She had to think hard for a minute or more to remember what had happened: she had been awake, or half-dozing, for a long time, but she didn't remember falling asleep, she didn't recall going under completely, hours ago, when it was still dark. She had been standing at the window, looking out, and the window had been open – was this real, or had she imagined it? The window had been open and snow had drifted into the strangely lit gap between the curtains, into the space she had always thought of as magical, a gap between home and the outside world, between confinement and escape. She got up. Why had nobody come to wake her? What day was this? Her father would be gone by now, she thought, off on the day shift; but her mother would be up, getting the house ready for Christmas, scrubbing the kitchen floor, going about with a duster, cleaning the sink, making herself busy as she always did, setting work and movement between herself and the loneliness, or despair, or whatever oblique pain it was that Alina sensed in her, whenever she was still.

She stood a moment and listened. Everything was muffled by the snow, the house enclosed in a cold, hollowed stillness, isolated, stalled, and it would stay like that, suspended in its own light, as long as the snow outside kept falling. She stood, the cold rising around her feet, her body tensed inside the heavy dressing-gown – and then she remembered everything that had happened. With a sense of having failed, of having betrayed herself by allowing the recollection to form, she saw MicMac in her mind's eye, sitting on the floor by the bed, gazing at her with that odd, half-amused expression. She remembered the light in the hall, and her mother coming to the door, and wondered what she had heard. If her mother had been aware that someone was there, surely she would have come in, surely she would have wanted to know what was going on. Or would she? Maybe she had guessed someone was in the room – but if she had, she would probably have thought it was Francis, and she wouldn't have worried too much about that. She liked Francis. Besides, she would have wanted to believe that, whatever it was she had heard, there was nothing to be concerned about. She had probably gone to the bathroom, become aware of someone moving about in the room and, because she hadn't heard Alina come in, she had just checked to see everything was all right. Now, because her husband was away at work, she was letting her daughter sleep.

Alina crossed the landing and locked herself in the bathroom. The acid was a distant memory now, a memory from which all the life had been crushed till it was nothing more than a fact, like a passage from a school history book, or one of those cold frogs they had been told to dissect in the biology class. When she looked at her face in the bathroom mirror, she could scarcely believe that the trip had happened: she looked tired, certainly, but there was nothing to show that she had been away, that she had travelled so far and for so long in fairy country. Francis had told her there would be no hangover, no after-effects of any kind, other than a vague, almost pleasant fatigue, but she hadn't believed him. Now, even though she had barely slept – she had no memory of sleeping, only of being awake – she wasn't even tired and she knew that, had it not been for MicMac's appearance in her room, she would have been fine. As she washed quickly, splashing her face with cold water, brushing her teeth twice to rinse away the stale, sticky-sweet aftertaste of the night, she felt nothing but a quiet, slightly distant apprehension, a troubled state that was not quite fear, and could just as easily have been happening to someone else.

Downstairs, she could hear her mother in the kitchen. Alina resisted the temptation to slip past her, to creep to the front door and let herself out quietly before she was noticed. Instead, she walked to the end of the hall and stood in the kitchen doorway, watching. Her mother was making up a tea tray, putting out biscuits, pouring milk into the little rose-petalled milk jug she'd had for years.

'What is it?' Alina asked. 'Is somebody here?'

Her mother looked round, startled. She had been so absorbed in what she was doing, she hadn't noticed that anyone else was there. She gave Alina an odd, exasperated look. 'It's a friend of your father's,' she said. 'Or so he says. He's brought him a present.'

'What do you mean – so he says?'

'Well. I don't know him. He's very *young*.'

Alina felt the breath catch in her throat. Her father didn't have any friends. It was one of his principles: he kept himself to himself. He certainly didn't have any *young* friends.

'How young?' she asked. 'Who is it? What's his name?'

'Well, he's just a boy,' her mother said, looking more unhappy than ever. She had to know something was wrong, Alina thought – so what was she doing making this boy tea? 'I think he said his name was Michael –'

'What does he look like?'

'Just a boy. He's got reddish hair —'

Alina saw the face from the night before moving towards her in the darkness. It was MicMac. She was certain of it. He had come with a present for her father, or maybe for her, but however you looked at it, he was in her house on false pretences. 'He's not a friend of Dad's,' she said. 'He's a boy I used to know from school. He's playing some kind of practical joke. Tell him you're busy and that he has to go home.' She watched her mother's face darken with apprehension. 'Where is Dad anyway? Isn't he at work?'

'I don't know,' her mother answered. 'He wasn't well last night. He went out for a walk, but that was hours ago.'

'For a walk?' Alina shot a glance out the kitchen window at the thick snow outside. 'In this?'

Her mother's eyes followed hers to the window, as if she thought there would be some answer there, some escape from the unwanted guest in the front room. 'I don't know,' she said. 'He just said he was going out.'

Alina walked back along to the coatrack in the hall and fetched the quilted Chinese jacket she'd bought on the market at Kettering. 'Get rid of that boy,' she said. 'Just tell him to go.'

'Well. Maybe you could —'

Alina shook her head firmly. 'No,' she said. 'I can't talk to him. Just tell him to go home. Say Dad's gone to work.'

Her mother looked doubtful. Then, head bowed, eyes dark with worry, she hurried back along the hall and disappeared into the front room. Alina heard voices, then movement, and she ducked behind the kitchen door, where she could watch the front door without being seen. MicMac emerged from the front room, still clutching the present he had brought. It was a small, rectangular object wrapped in cheap red and green Christmas wrapper, the kind you bought on the market.

'Well,' he was saying. 'Thanks for letting me wait. I'll maybe come by another time.'

Alina's mother nodded. 'I'll say you called,' she said, unlatching the door quickly, and holding it open to let MicMac out. Huge flakes of snow gusted into the hallway, while MicMac stood on the doorstep, repeating his goodbyes.

As soon as her mother closed the front door, Alina slipped on her jacket, and let herself out the back. Now that the snow was finally falling, she realised that she had been waiting for the weather to change and, with the whole town a white shimmer, the snow thick and still on the streets, she borrowed Jan's bike and began cycling out to the Twenty-Two Foot. It was colder than it had been the day before, and the air was utterly white, a vivid, icy whiteness sealing everything, every tree and stone and grass blade, in its cold grip. She had to cycle slowly, the big soft flakes blowing into her face, and the road crusted with drifted snow, but she was determined to continue, to put the town, and its people, behind her.

As she had expected, the Twenty-Two Foot was completely frozen. The ice was thick and clouded, too thick to see through, too clouded to tell whether the eyes of that nameless drowned girl from long ago were staring up at her through the cold water below. Alina moved slowly to the edge of the pond. At its centre, there was a white, vivid space, a magical zone like the fairy king's domain in the old folk-tales, and she wanted to be there, to stand alone in that otherworld, in the middle of the ice. She hesitated a moment, not because she was unsure of herself, or because she cared, one way or the other, whether the ice could take her weight, but because she wanted to register the moment, to make it real, to render it unforgettable. Then, with grace and gentleness and a new respect for the fabric of the given world, she ventured a step out on to the frozen surface. It felt solid under her feet, with just a slight give, like a dance floor, but no cracks appeared and, after a moment, she took another step, her arms outstretched, like a tightrope walker, like one of those tiny silver ballerinas on the high wire at the circus. It was delicious, this momentary sensation, her caught breath, the cool of the air she held in her throat then exhaled, a mist of tiny ice particles suspended on the white air, her breath going in and out like this: the world, herself, the world, warmth and cold and warmth again, a constant measured exchange till it was impossible to say where one thing ended and the other began. A body in the world, breathing. A centre of balance, a breath of air. So much of what she was, was outside her, not her, her, indistinguishable. She took another step, her arms up, her fingers spread, warmth flowing out to the quick of the nails then bleeding away, seeping into the air to become something else, somewhere else in the wide acres of space. Alina could see through the white zone above the centre of the pond to the other side: fifteen, maybe twenty yards away, and the ice the same clouded white all the way across, thick and tense, like a sprung floor for dancing on, dusted with snow and light. She took one step, then another: if the ice broke now, she would go down, sudden and final, falling into blackness. She thought of herself going under, then trying to surface through the hole she had made in falling, but coming up yards away, her fingers scraping against the thick, cold ice. Desperation, icy cold – it was a pleasure, all of a sudden, to play along with this fear, turning it over in her mind like some living thing she had found out in the fields, some tiny animal, hard and clenched and alive. She took another step – it was deep all the way down here, and she wondered again what it would be like to fall through the cold water, her body lost in the pull of gravity, an enchantment she had always felt there, a weightedness and pull, the body's eternal kinship with falling – which was also, she realised, at the root of its ability to dance, its ability to balance, this gift and burden of weightedness, this gravity. She took another step and there was a soft creaking sound, not much more than a whisper under her feet, but it was too late now to go back, or to hurry, it was too late for anything but the course she had set herself upon. Besides, she was content now, more content than she remembered being in a long time: one step, then another, out on to the ice, heading for the vivid white space in the middle of the pond with no more to go on than her centre of gravity, her outstretched arms, her suddenly miraculous body. There was nothing to lose. She knew she wasn't going to fail, she knew the ice would stay whole till she reached the other side, because today the world was hers – the pond, the fields, the sky – if you came out here alone, when nobody else could see you, then it was yours, and only yours, for one perfect and improbable moment when nobody else existed, and the whole world was still, a world that came into being moment by moment because she saw and thought about it, a world that was continuous with her body, her flesh and blood, her skin, her fingernails, her hair. She took three more steps, then stopped – and she was in the cold centre of the pond, her hair charged with electricity, her body singing with the tension of being so far out on the ice. She closed her eyes. Any moment now, the fairy king would appear by her side, and ask her if she wanted to go with him, to live for ever in his inhuman paradise. Alina already knew what her answer would be.

Alma

W HAT SHE WANTED, more than anything, was to remember
the past, *her* past, as a story. To remember being, first in
one place and then in another, and knowing all the stages in
between: the train journeys, the ships at sea, the transit camps,
connected, unified, by a single, watchful mind. What she wanted
was a story she could tell, not to someone else, but for herself,
convincing herself with each telling that this was *her* history.
Nothing was missing, everything was accounted for. But she had
been so young when they left home, and her father would never
speak about the past; just as Marc would never tell her what had
happened during the twenty-three years he had lived on this
earth before he knew her, refusing to return, refusing, even in
his imagination, to relive the pain he had suffered, a pain that
she, Alma, the blessed soul, could never share, and so could never
understand. They had told her in school that this was what her
name meant: *a blessed soul* – and she felt that this ought to have
been her calling: to bless and to be blessed; to forgive, and to be
forgiven. All that was needed was a story: a story to tell and a
story to be told, an exchange in words and memories and gestures.

She had been very young, maybe four or five when they left
home, she and her father, walking, then travelling on a train, then
walking again. All she remembered of the time before was the darkness at Christmas, a deep still blackness that lay upon the land,
so thick and perfect and wide you could reach out of the upstairs
window and touch it, like the dark, live fur of a sleeping animal.
This was what came to mind when people asked her where she

was from: in those occasional, unguarded moments when she allowed herself to think about the home she would never know, a place she couldn't even point to on a map, she always pictured the same thing: a night sky peppered with stars, the snow reaching for miles around her father's house, and the light off the snow like the beginning of a magic trick. She never remembered summer, or if she did, she could make no pictures in her mind's eye, could only hear the words – the words she knew now, in the only language she had – words she would have used to describe the trees, or the birds singing around the lake, or the light on the fields when she walked home from church. She knew it smelled of hay and camomile, but she couldn't recall the scent, she couldn't smell it. Not like the smell of new snow, or the traces of wood smoke on the path to her father's house, more a taste than smell, a taste that came unbidden from somewhere inside her own body, a secret power, always waiting to rise, to take her by surprise and betray her.

It wasn't like that here. They had Christmas, with a tree perched in the front window, all shop tinsel and coloured lights; they had oranges and chocolate bars for the children; they had clear nights when the sky filled with stars and the moon sailed high and miraculously clean over the steel mill. They even had snow from time to time, timid and wet and slow, lingering just long enough to whiten the streets for a matter of days, blanking out the gardens till one plot ran into another, the houses and lives blurred into a continuum of radio and voices and steam, but it was never the snow she remembered from home, it was always provisional, a tentative, fleeting whiteness tainted with smuts and the mixed scent of clay and ore. And that was what you could never get away from: that smell. There were nights when it looked like another place, the streets quiet, the gardens still and mysterious in the middle of the afternoon; there were days when they walked out into what resembled real countryside, with trees and fields of cattle, or they would take a bus to Kettering and walk around the market – but that smell was always present, sooty and metallic and touched with the sweetness of loam, like the houses of the dead in her childhood's lost story books. One Sunday afternoon, out walking on the road past Cottingham, they had been stopped in their tracks by an astonishing cloud, rising as if from nowhere, a vast, dark storm-cloud gathering behind a row of trees like a huge ink stain on the near horizon. The sun was at their backs, still bright, still warm; it lit the trees opposite with a soft gold light, making a mystery of every detail, more real and, at the same time, more of an illusion, bright and transient, like theatre props. Marc could see that it was about to rain and he was casting around for shelter, oblivious to the sheer beauty of the thing, thinking only of how to get the children under cover, to keep them dry, but Alma had scarcely noticed his fuss. Standing at the edge of the road while her husband hurried Jan and Alina on towards the village, she had watched the cloud thicken and stall above the fields, and she had found herself waiting for something, willing it on, praying, even, for a storm that would batter the land for miles, a season of stark rain and day-long winds to wash that dark stench from the air and make it clean again.

Now, on this bleak winter morning, she remembered that moment like a scene from a dream, just as she remembered, or failed to remember, everything that had ever happened. It was as if the present kept slipping away into an improbable past, transformed as it did into something uncertain, something provisional and discontinuous, a series of moments that might have been hers, but could just as easily belong to another. She felt cheated. This was a problem she would have imagined for someone else, someone older, but every day it got worse: she would go about her business, cleaning the house, walking around the shops, tending the garden, and she would be trying to halt the flow, to seize hold of a moment as it flashed past, to seize it and live it to the full, making it hers for ever. At the same time, she wanted to stop people on the street and ask them if they felt the same way, if they had the same sense of having been betrayed, just as she had asked people, from time to time, whether the smell from The Works bothered them. She was sure it did, and she was always surprised when they said they hardly noticed the smuts on the windows, or that dull, steely smell on the laundry.

The front room was cold. She struck a match, held it cradled in her hands till the flame was bright, then she turned on the heater and lit the gas. When the fire was burning, she drew the curtains and switched off the light. Earlier, she had heard Marc getting up, and had lain half-asleep while he dressed quickly and hurried downstairs. When she'd called out to ask where he was going, he had barely stopped to answer.

'I'm going out,' was all he'd said as he opened the front door and hurried away in the morning darkness. Alma knew he wasn't going to work. At one time, she would have worried, she might even have followed him out into the snow, to make sure he came to no harm. Now she didn't care. He went off, and she didn't know what he was doing, but he always came back, and when he did, he was always the same. The night before, he had complained of a headache; then, as he was getting ready for bed, he'd had one of his spells, where he sat on the edge of the bed and stared at the floor, muttering to himself in his own language, a language she had never been allowed to understand. She didn't even know if it was real, what he was saying, or just gibberish. He had sat there for almost an hour, and she had sat on the chair by the dressing-table, watching him, listening, waiting for it to end. He had been like this for months now, and she had gradually come to understand that she could do nothing to help, that he did not want her to help and that – even though he was her husband – she was glad of that fact.

Now it was seven o'clock and she had an hour to herself before the children came downstairs. Alina would come first, trailing down in her nightdress half-awake, her hair a thick, wild tangle like the undergrowth in a fairy wood; then Jan, who always sat up late into the night, reading library books, or looking through his pictures. On school days, they would all have been up and about by now, but Marc let them sleep late on the holidays. Privately, she knew he would rather have them in the house than out on the streets with the other teenagers. He had even joked about it once, about how they couldn't get into trouble if they were in bed, but it had been an uneasy attempt at humour, and she knew he worried about them all the time. He would hear some story at work and come home anxious and angry at the whole world, or he would read something in the paper and sit brooding about it for days, imagining the worst, dwelling on the evil he saw everywhere. At night, he would sit muttering on the edge of their bed, or he would lie awake, staring up at the dark ceiling, and she would lie awake beside him, pretending to be asleep. Meanwhile, she saved and did without and promised herself that it wouldn't be long before they had enough money to get away from here.

The snow was thick now, thick and dark and fast, blotting out the street, erasing everything. For once, this street in Corby could have been anywhere: a street in a real town, where real people lived. The dirt that coated everything, every leaf of every hedge, every pane of glass and window ledge, had vanished for a while, subsumed by whiteness. Alma opened the door and leaned out into the chill air to fetch the milk. It was only as she picked up the first bottle, feeling it cold and solid against her palm, that she noticed something was wrong. At first she imagined that a dog had come and done its business on the doorstep, and it was only by accident that it had somehow found the milk bottles, but it was obvious, on closer inspection, that someone had carried this dirt here and deliberately smeared it on to the caps and around the necks of the bottles. It wasn't the first time something of this nature had happened: there had been days when Alma found vomit, used tampons, dried-up trails of urine, even, once, some kind of animal remains, either here, on the doorstep, or on the path, or scattered across the narrow front lawn. She had no idea who was responsible for this persecution. She had tried talking to Marc about it, but it was useless. He didn't want to know what was going on. He had his own troubles.

Alma wondered if all this was happening because people thought they were German. She remembered the lane in Weldon where she and her father had lived, going on hand to mouth in a tiny cottage, in the years when she had to remember to say, if she was asked, that she and her father were Latvian DPs. She didn't really know what this meant: DP. Her father explained that it stood for Displaced Persons, but that didn't help much and, since it was all he'd said, Alma was none the wiser. She thought it had something to do with her only real memory before they had come to England: a memory she wasn't even sure was real, where she was walking across fields, with nothing behind her that she could recall, and nothing ahead that she could make out. She hadn't even known where she was, walking in that flat country, all she knew was that she was part of a large group of people, men and women and children, walking with no sense of where they were going, though they could see for miles in every direction. For days they had walked, and she had watched her father's eyes harden, his face set, but not once in all that time had she ever felt sad, or lonely. She liked this empty plain. For some reason, she knew it was better than the last place they had been. Here, she could be herself, not displaced, but connected, rooted to the earth, head filled with light under a vast pale blue sky. She knew she had never felt this before, wherever it was she had been before she came there.

She was to remember to say that her father was Latvian. She knew he had sometimes spoken German at home, and his friends also spoke German, but this was to be a secret, because British people didn't understand. Once, at the clinic, when Jan was still a baby, she'd been sent to a different doctor, a Dr Wilkinson. He was a young man, good-looking, friendly, much nicer, she thought, than the others. He'd greeted her when she came in, and she'd noticed he was an Englishman, not a Scot. She liked that; it made him seem more professional. Then, when he looked at her card, he read her name aloud, looked up and said something in German. As far as she could tell, it was nothing in particular, just some pleasantry, and she knew he was only trying to be kind. Perhaps he knew how isolated she was; maybe one of the receptionists, or a nurse, had said something; maybe he'd seen her in the waiting-room, sitting on her own, in the midst of all those other women and babies, by herself in a crowded place, separated from the other mothers as if by a blizzard. Certainly, there was no reason to be suspicious, or unfriendly – but after only a moment's hesitation, she shook her head.

'I'm not German,' she said, in English. 'My father was Latvian. My husband is also Latvian.'

That was what her father had told her to say, if she was ever asked. The English didn't understand, they didn't know anything about Latvia or what had happened there. She didn't feel Latvian, of course; but then, she didn't feel German either. She didn't know how she felt. She had studied books and she had asked some of the older people what they remembered, thinking to steal a past from somewhere and make it her own. One afternoon, she had sat in the library for hours, poring over thick reference volumes about the War and twentieth-century Europe, but she couldn't make any sense of it. It didn't sound like anything she knew; it was just history. She would have liked to sit down with someone who had known her from before, when she was still a child who spoke another language. She would have liked to hear what had happened. Yet, if she could have been anything – and she knew she couldn't, she knew she had no choice – she would have been a little English girl from Weldon, baptised in the little church there, with no need to pretend or to wonder about who she was and where she came from.

She had married Marc when she was just eighteen years old. She'd been lonely after her father died, because she had no one to look after. At the time, Marc had struck her as the kind of man her father would have liked, a quiet man, who kept his own counsel, and he seemed familiar to her, because his name was also German, like her father's. Like hers. She hadn't imagined that anything might go wrong when she made her vow and promised to love, honour and obey a husband whose only distinguishing feature was that his accent sounded vaguely familiar. When she had made those vows, she hadn't expected to have to *do* anything. She thought she was entering into a proven contract, something the Church and the generations who had gone before had tested and found good, thousands of years of wedlock reaching back to the beginning of human time, settling now between herself and this quiet husband, an almost magical weight resting gently between their hands as they exchanged rings. She knew there would be difficult times, that money would be short, that there would be sickness, problems at work, strange people, new places. That was part of any life. All she had expected with Marc was the everyday contract to try as well as they could to live their lives together. It was this simple thing, this living as one, that made marriage a sacrament. But the ordinary miracle she had hoped for had not come to pass. Nothing special had passed between them. Nothing beautiful had happened. She had expected that, at least: some beautiful moment, some happy recognition.

Later, when they moved to Corby, things got worse. Marc had wanted to come; he had the chance of a good job, and he saw it as a means to an end, a way to save enough money to move on. But Alma felt crushed by the place. She was afraid of the furnaces, afraid of the work Marc did at The Works, even though he wouldn't talk about it, just as he would never talk about anything else. She was afraid to know what was in the air, afraid of what her children might be breathing. Most of all, she was afraid of the strange beauty that appeared, from time to time – a beauty that was strange and terrible, like some supernatural phenomenon – in the lights that flickered across the sky, or the folds and ripples of smoke that ghosted through the garden in the small hours. One August night she had seen a cascade of ash, soft bright flakes that she would have mistaken for snow, falling all along the street in the dense summer heat. That had been long ago: in those days she couldn't sleep when Marc was away on night shift, and she would get up and stand at the bedroom window, looking out at the sad clutter of machinery and broken toys in the neighbours' yards, or she would go out into the garden and stare up at the night sky looking for stars, though usually all she saw were smoke-clouds or the glow from the furnaces reflected on the low blue-black ceiling of sky, so it felt like she was closed up inside something solid, some glass ball or Christmas tree ornament. That night, though, it really had seemed beautiful, all those thick slow flakes drifting down on the still air, still half-lit with a whitish glow as if they were somehow alive, a new form of being that had arisen suddenly out of nothing and would go on changing as the cinders floated to the ground and burned out, a last trace of poison decaying slowly on every leaf and pane of glass and the forgotten jerseys on the washing-lines out back, traces that could have been read, had she known how, like the fiery letters of Arabic or Sanskrit. Such moments were rare, but there was something in that livid beauty that frightened her even more than the ordinary smoke and grime that drifted into the garden, into the house even, to contaminate everything – clothes, skin, food, dishes – with their subtle poisons. It unnerved her, that such things could be beautiful. If she hadn't had her garden, and the children, she was sure she would have died. Some nights, she dreamed she really was dead, but still walking around. People could see her in the dream, and they would talk to her; even though they knew she was dead, they would try to include her in what was happening, and she was grateful, but she couldn't say anything, or show that she understood what they were doing. She had that dream for months, then it stopped.

Of course, there were decent people in Corby. As her father

had always said, there were decent people everywhere, even in the camps. That was the only reference he ever made to the past, that rare mention of the camps. But Alma couldn't remember the camps. She couldn't remember anything except the snow of another country and a wide, empty plain. And for as long as she could remember, everything in Corby was dirt. Everything was marked, even the people. When she went outside she could see it; when she went into the garden to hang the washing, or to fetch something from the shed, she could taste it on the air: dirt, carbon, steel, flakes of ore; the smell, not of burning, but of the burned, not of the soil, but of the clay. She could only hang the washing out on certain days, when the wind was right, but even then it never felt clean, it was always touched with grime, and that stink of ore. When she took the bus into town she would sit downstairs so as not to see too much, but it was impossible, really, to avoid it: the bus skirted the entire west side of The Works before it swung away past the little church in the village, through the light industrial estates and up into the bus station by Market Square. At night she could feel it raging at the window, a city of fire crying in the dark. Why be surprised, then, if the people were hard and stupid and dirty? Or not stupid so much as mean, with the brute intuition that comes with meanness, the eye for a weakness, the nose for a secret hurt or fear. From the moment they had moved into this house, they had been set apart; no matter what they said, or did, or pretended, their neighbours had decided, in a matter of minutes, that they were *wrong*. It had nothing to do with where they came from; it was simply a kind of shorthand, a process of reduction that made it clear who was to be included in the circle, and who was to be despised.

A few days after they moved in, she had her first glimpse of what her neighbours were like. She had called after the milkman, to ask about making an order, and she was standing there, a few feet from her own door, listening to what the man had to say, when one of the neighbours walked right up, without even looking at her, as if she didn't exist, and cut into the conversation, in mid-sentence.

'I'll want two pints on Saturday, son, not one,' the woman said. 'All right?'

The milkman nodded, but he didn't take his eyes off Alma. He looked embarrassed.

'Did you get that?' The woman was tall and fat, with long, oily black hair and a mole on her right cheek. She was wearing tartan slippers and a blue housecoat. She seemed angry; looking for trouble; ready for a fight.

'All right,' the milkman said. 'Two pints.'

The woman grunted triumphantly and, with a passing, contemptuous glance at Alma, lumbered away.

'I'm sorry,' the man said, after a moment's pause. He was young and rather handsome, with curly black hair and a thick moustache. 'What were you saying?'

It was always like this. But as Marc would point out whenever Alma mentioned some incident in the neighbourhood, or at the shops, it was much worse for him. He had to deal with it all the time at The Works, and if the women were bad, he said, she ought to see the men. Sometimes he would come home and sit down at the table, looking through his books, his dictionary and his *Roget's Thesaurus*, scanning the pages, flicking from one entry to another, before finally raising his head and fixing her with a look of grim satisfaction.

'Debased,' he would say. 'This is the word.'

'What is?' She knew what he was talking about, but she always asked anyway.

'Debased,' he repeated; then he read out the definition from his book.

In the end, Alma stopped talking about it. She knew that there was nothing to do but get on with their lives; they were stuck here for the time being, and the only way out was to work hard and save, and try to get a house of their own on one of the new developments, or maybe even in an outlying village. She didn't want to think about her neighbours any more than she had to. Besides, they weren't all bad, there were good people too, intelligent and considerate, even kind, in their way – as kind, that is, as a place like Corby would allow. Marc couldn't let it go, however. It nagged at him all the time, how awful these people were, how stupid and mean-spirited they could be, for no good reason. He would learn a new word from his dictionary and use it for weeks afterwards – debased, degraded, gross, vulgar, ill-bred – he couldn't stop himself, he was obsessed. If she complained, he would say it was all right for her, she didn't have to go there, among those men. And it was true, she didn't. She stayed at home and looked after her garden, or she walked to the town centre and spent hours trudging from shop to shop, checking the prices and storing them all in her head, comparing, memorising, studying the special offers, before retracing her steps, buying carrots here, tinned peas there, fish in one place, a cheap cut of meat in another, saving a few pennies by wandering about all afternoon, with the children in tow, but more alone than she had ever felt in her life. Nothing she had ever known was worse than this place, but she was determined not to let it beat her: every penny saved, every bargain negotiated, was a step further in her overall plan to get out, to be free, to be clean again.

Alma went to the kitchen and filled a saucepan with warm water from the kettle, then she carried the pan carefully through the house and poured the water slowly over the contaminated bottles. Some of the dirt washed away, but there was still enough clinging to the caps and neck that she felt compelled to make this trip three more times, boiling another kettle to get water warm enough to wash her milk bottles clean. Not for the first time, she was surprised by her own patience. It was something she had learned over the years, though she had been ashamed of it at first, as if the gaining of such patience had cost her the little pride she had left. The milk bottles were almost clean, and she was almost ready to carry them into the house, when she looked up and saw a tall, reddish-haired boy some six feet away, clutching a Christmas parcel and watching her with an odd, absorbed interest.

'Hello?' The boy seemed nervous. He tucked his package under his arm and took a step closer. 'Mrs Ruckert?'

Alma straightened up and nodded, but she didn't say anything.

'I'm Michael,' the boy said. 'I'm a friend of your husband's. From work.'

'Oh.'

'I just brought round a Christmas present. It's nothing special, just a little token.'

Alma nodded. She was still holding the saucepan. She wanted to say that Marc was out, but before she could, the boy stepped forward and picked up the milk bottles.

'I'll get these for you,' he said. 'You look like you've got your hands full already.'

She was making tea when Alina came down. As usual, she was absorbed in what she was doing, and her daughter made her jump when she suddenly appeared.

'What is it?' she asked. 'Is somebody here?'

Alma looked round. Alina seemed tired and upset, and she wondered again what had happened the night before. Alma knew her daughter had been out with Francis, and she wondered if they had had a row. 'It's a friend of your father's,' she said. 'Or so he says. He's brought him a present.'

'What do you mean — so he says?' Alina seemed suspicious, and it made Alma wonder what she had done, letting some complete stranger into the house, just because he had come with a cheap Christmas gift.

'Well. I don't know him,' she said. 'He's very *young*.' Alma had been surprised by the boy's claim that he was a friend of Marc's, but with what had been happening recently, nothing would have surprised her.

Alina was really upset now. 'How young?' she asked. 'Who is it? What's his name?'

'Well, he's just a boy,' Alma said. 'I think he said his name was Michael —'

'What does he look like?'

'Just a boy. He's got reddish hair —'

Alina was getting more and more upset. She seemed angry. 'He's not a friend of Dad's,' she said. 'He's something else entirely. Where is Dad anyway? Isn't he at work?'

'I don't know,' Alma answered. She was feeling guilty now for letting Marc go off into the cold that morning. Or not for letting him go — there was nothing she could have done to stop him — so much as for the relief she had felt to see him out of the house. 'He wasn't well last night. He went out for a walk, but that was hours ago.'

'For a walk?' Alina waved an angry hand at the kitchen window. 'He's gone for a walk in this?'

Alma didn't know why she was to blame for everything, all of a sudden. Alina was always angry these days. Of course, it was hard for her, with her father being ill. She and her father had always been close, in an odd way.

'Look, you have to send him away,' Alina said, pointing towards the front room. 'He's some idiot from school, playing a practical joke.'

'Well.' Alma knew she was clutching at straws. 'Maybe you could –'

'No,' Alina interrupted her. She wasn't just angry, Alma realised. There was something else bothering her. 'I can't talk to him. Just tell him to go home. Say Dad's gone to work.'

Now Alma saw it. Alina wasn't angry at all; she was afraid. This boy in the front room had something to do with her. Maybe he was someone from school who had a crush on her and was trying to make a good impression on her father with his cheap little Christmas gift. Alma realised she had to get the boy out of the house before her husband got home. 'All right,' she said. 'I'll tell him to go. You wait here.'

She went back to the front room, leaving the tea tray in the kitchen, and told the boy, Michael, that her husband was out, and wouldn't be back till much later. He seemed reluctant to accept this news, as if he thought Alma might be lying, but after a while, she managed to get him out the door, still clutching his Christmas gift. For a moment, she felt sorry for him: Alina was a pretty girl, and it wasn't surprising that a lonely boy like this had developed a crush on her. Still, it was obvious that Alina's affections lay elsewhere.

The boy took a long time to go, the snow blowing up around him and into the hallway as Alma waited to shut the door. She didn't want to be rude. Afterwards, when she went back to the kitchen, Alina was gone. She had slipped out the back way and was cycling off down the road on Jan's bike, unseen by her lovestruck admirer, who was trudging off in the other direction, his hands in his pockets, his gift tucked under his arm. Alma watched him go. It was cruel, she thought, and pointless, this thing about love. She wished the children could know what she knew, that no matter how hard you tried, such love was a passing illusion. Better, she thought, to start a garden, to make things grow, even in a place like this, where it was so difficult.

★

There was a lot to do, to get ready for Christmas. Alma didn't know if it was worth the effort; she couldn't predict how Marc would behave, and she knew Jan didn't like any occasion that involved sitting down together as a family. He didn't like it for the same reason she didn't, because it was false, another hard-won illusion based on half-truths and lies of omission. Yet she had come this far in her life, she had brought up two decent children and managed a difficult husband by going through the motions, and she understood them all enough to know that, sometimes, just going through the motions would carry them through. Most of the occasions of their life were endurance tests, but there was a satisfaction to be had when things were over, when you could look back and say that you had come through. It was even an achievement of sorts, to have something be in the past, so memory could go to work, adding touches of warmth and movement, making it all fonder and less awkward, a semblance of real life, a matter of snapshots and anecdotes. It was in that spirit, then, the spirit of going through the motions and hoping for the best, that Alma continued for the remainder of the day, Marc's continued absence nagging at her, and being pushed to the back of her mind with an ever-greater determination, the more she worked. She was halfway through making a cake when Jan appeared at the back door, in his thick winter coat. His hair was crusted with snow, and he was kicking off his boots.

'My bike's disappeared,' he said, by way of greeting.

'Your sister took it,' Alma answered. 'Where have you been?'

'Out taking pictures.'

'Ah. With Francis?'

Jan shrugged off his coat, and sat down at the table. 'No,' he said. 'I haven't seen Francis for days.' He stole a handful of currants from the jar on the table and scooped them into his mouth. 'I'm hungry,' he muttered, looking around the kitchen abstractedly.

'Well don't eat the currants,' Alma said. 'I need them for the Christmas cake. Make yourself a sandwich.'

'I don't want a sandwich,' Jan grumbled. 'I want *sweeties*.' He stole another handful of currants, then stood up and went to the fridge. He seemed restless, wanting for something, but not sure what it was; or maybe he had something on his mind, something to do with school, or some book he was reading. When he was younger, he would get a book out from the library, and after he had read it, he would come to Alma and ask what she thought about gravity, or some theory she'd never even heard of, some ancient philosopher's notions about the soul, or life on other planets, or whether animals could think the way human beings think. She had never really known what to say at times like that, and she had felt awkward and unhappy that she hadn't read more, afraid that she might seem stupid to him. She had wished, from time to time, that Jan would have these conversations with his father, because it would have done Marc good to be taken out of himself, but she knew, and probably Jan had already learned, that her husband would have made it into something else, some lesson, some homily on life.

Now, when Jan was home, he stayed in his room and read books, or worked on his photography, and she never knew what he was reading, or thinking about. It was as if he had become a total stranger, someone who inhabited a different world, seeing and hearing and thinking things that she could never have imagined – and Alma couldn't help thinking that he had been like this all along, that he had always been different from other children, had always kept himself apart, even when he seemed to be with her, like any normal child, playing, or laughing, or asking questions about books and school. He had always kept something in reserve; there had always been a detachment, a depth in his eyes that she could not fathom. He had an odd, unsettling curiosity about the world, a curiosity that had a cold side to it, a distance from her and from everyone that was neither rebellious, nor defiant, but was, nevertheless, a matter of some importance to him, something he enjoyed, something he *relished*. He was obviously intelligent, and she felt sure he would do something with his life when he grew up and got away from Corby. Still, she couldn't help wondering about him. As a child, he would fiddle endlessly with the dials on the wireless, finding programmes from Finland or Romania and listening avidly to words he didn't understand, as if trying to work out what was being said. Even when he was little more than an infant, she would catch him watching her, watching and thinking about what she was doing, and maybe – this suspicion had bothered her more than she could have explained – thinking about what she was thinking. Alina had been such a different kind of baby, volatile, angry, but also funny at times, happy even, always trying to work out the right response to a situation, trying to decide when she was supposed to laugh or cry, or look suitably penitent. Alma knew this wasn't a trick, it wasn't manipulative. Alina wasn't trying to please anyone, or get away with something. She just had a sense of what was just, an instinctive sense of propriety, of natural laws that she didn't want to betray. There were times, watching her at play, alone, or with her little friends from school, when Alma was struck by a kind of dignity, hard-won and mostly imagined, the dignity of a child who is puzzled by the fact that she has almost nothing, and is determined not to let anyone else see that puzzlement.

Jan was never like that. He just sat and watched, or he followed Alma around the house, to study what she did. His face never showed emotion, just a steady interest that, if Alma was honest, she sometimes found a little frightening. Meanwhile, with each passing year, he became more of a stranger. The older he grew, the more he withdrew from them all. He lived in an invented world, Alma knew this, but it wasn't the usual fantasy world that children create for adventure or escape. It was more of a constructed alternative to everything he had decided he didn't want, and he never bothered to hide the fact that, mostly, what he didn't want was other people. In Jan's world there were trees and birds and running water, but there were almost no human beings. At school, he was praised for his intelligence, but he was obviously something of a mystery to his teachers – and probably to his classmates as well. He was always slipping away from them, travelling on his own path, stepping out of their line of vision. She remembered the class photograph she had bought when Jan was in third year, only to find that he wasn't visible in it: he had disappeared, dipping behind a boy with peat-coloured hair and steel glasses to his left, leaving a blurred space where his face should have been. He was always the one who added the alchemy of studied absence to snapshots of first communions and confirmations, a blur at the edge of the picture like snowfall, or like the wisp of nothingness that storytellers mistake for a summertime ghost: concealed, or in motion, arriving too late or departing too soon, he was the boy who never existed, the boy who spent his free time with phantoms. By the time he was twelve or thirteen, Alma even suspected that she herself was little more than a phantom in his invented world, a wisp of a presence that he acknowledged with the measured affection appropriate to a mother, but with no real recognition, no real kinship. She felt sure he was fond of her, just as she saw that he was fond of Alina in a remote, almost formal way, but she knew she had no real function in that constructed world he inhabited, and it wasn't hard to see that Marc was well-nigh invisible there. At some point – Alma wasn't sure how far back this process had begun – Jan had started to erase his father from his life, a process that reflected not the usual childish anger or the rebelliousness you had to expect from a teenager, but something more akin to a loss of interest, a detachment that left room for a vague sympathy, or perhaps even pity, but not true regard, and certainly not love. The worst thing was, Alma understood this; there were days when she even envied her son's detachment. The only times she was ever happy, the only times she felt real, were the hours she spent in her garden, digging and weeding and sowing seeds, making things grow, waiting for the odd gleam of colour and freshness to appear before the dirt and the smoke from The Works blotted it out. If she could have done, she would have stayed out there all the time, tending her little plot of ground, with no real intentions other than continuing, knowing her task was hopeless, knowing that, no matter what she did, she would never make the garden she wanted.

Two more hours passed before Marc returned. Jan had drifted off to his room with a handful of fruit – an apple, a banana, some dried apricots – and Alina was still out. It was late afternoon when Alma heard the front door and Marc appeared in the hallway, a ghost from the cold, his bare head clotted with snowflakes, his coat ridged white. He didn't see her. She went back to the cooker and stood over the huge pot of soup she was making, stirring it unnecessarily to give herself something to do. It seemed, from the look on Marc's face, that he had walked off whatever it was that had been bothering him – walked it off for now, at least, though it might return in an hour, or a day, or a week – it didn't matter, it was the only thing she could be sure of, the only thing about him that was inevitable. She felt guilty. She knew her husband was ill: he wasn't choosing to be like this, there was something wrong, some imbalance in his memory, some taint in his brain, or maybe a rogue chemical had entered in his blood, some agent the body kept dormant and contained, reactivated by something he had seen or done long ago, in the twenty-three years he had lived before she had known him, or by the fear and anger he felt at The Works, or maybe just by something that floated in the air up there, some tiny particle of dust or metal that he breathed every day, or absorbed through his fingertips. Her guilt was worse at times like these, when she saw that something had given way in his face, that the tension had broken and he would be capable of the slow, banal conversations and silences of normal life – worse, because these were the very times when she most wanted to avoid him. She could hardly bear the illusion they would create, sitting in the front room together, with the children out or upstairs in their bedrooms, an illusion of ordinary life, of two people who could have spoken, or touched, or gone out walking together, if that had been their choice. At least when he was ill – she had to make an effort to think of it as illness, and not as something else – it was the truth, there was no pretence. Marc would sit on the edge of the bed muttering to himself, or he would lie silent and heavy beside her, like someone drowned, and it would be terrible, but it would also be real.

He took a long time to remove his coat and boots. Alma listened as the door opened again, and her husband shook out the wet coat, then banged the boots against the wall outside to knock off the snow. When the door closed, it was quiet for a while, and she was tempted to leave her work, to go and see what was happening. Finally, he came through. He stood on the threshold between the kitchen and the hall, half-in, half-out, and he watched her till she put her spoon down and looked at him. He was smiling, his eyes glistening, his face soft and damp from the snow. Alma made an attempt to smile back.

'You've been out a long time,' she said, trying not to listen to herself and hear how awkward she sounded. 'Are you hungry?'

He shook his head. 'I'm fine,' he said. 'I've been to the shops.' He went back into the hall and reappeared a moment later with two large plastic bags which he set down on the kitchen table.

'Look.' He pulled a large stuffed toy from the first bag, a big furry black-and-white creature that was presumably meant to be a panda. It had round, glassy eyes and stitches for a mouth, and there was something painfully old-fashioned about it, as if he had gone back in time and found a toy from his own childhood, a toy that should have been chewed and raggedy, so that its perfect newness was unsettling, an offence against the natural order of things, like some freak accident. Alma tried not to show her dismay. 'This is for Alina,' he said. He set the panda down on the table facing her, its big glassy eyes staring, and opened the other bag. 'And this is for Jan.'

Jan's gift was a telescope. It was bigger and more expensive-looking than she would have expected, a well-made thing, but obviously meant for a child, in its brightly coloured box deco-rated with stars and half-moons and planets. It was the kind of thing she might have given her son when he was nine or ten, or perhaps even younger.

Alma nodded. 'They're very nice,' she said. 'Now sit down and I'll make you some soup. You must be cold from all that walking.'

Marc smiled and sat down at the table. Alma cleared the toys away, putting them carefully back into their bags and setting them down on the sideboard with as much tact and gentleness and care as she could manage. She wanted to weep. She wanted to run out of the house into the snow and be taken in somewhere, to go back to some other place, some origin where all the deci-sions were still to be made, and start afresh, in another country, with a new life, a new husband, a new self, a clean, cool, untar-nished soul, like the soul she had guessed at, years ago, when snow fell in that place she thought of as home but couldn't remember, or that wide plain where she had walked for days under a vast blue sky. Instead, she took a bowl from the side-board, filled it with soup from the pot, cut some bread and laid it out neatly on a plate; then she set it before her husband, who was smiling softly, drifting from his private thoughts to her and back again, giving her odd, shy glances, boyish and happy and damp from the snow, a man she had never really known, sitting in her kitchen, thinking about Christmas.

Tommy

IN THE BEGINNING was the land. You had to forget all that
Christian stuff about the word, and remember the earth beneath
your feet, the stones and the clay, the bulbs and tubers and tree
roots, the buried dead decaying to become something else, the
ocean of seeds and spores waiting to germinate. Tommy remembered his Uncle Arthur telling him that, thirty years ago, when
they were out in the snow one winter, the snow lying thick on
the ground and in high drifts against dry-stane walls, forming
long waves and ridges across the fields, breaking only for the
conifer plantations that skirted the hills and the broad valleys of
ploughed fields and pasture, dense and still and black, places that
beguiled and frightened him back then, ready as he was to believe
that time would stop, or that he himself would vanish if he were
to venture more than a few steps into those dark interiors. Arthur
worked in those plantations from time to time, just as he worked
on the stane walling, or on the potato picking; he was a man
who could do anything – skilled work, labouring, husbandry, it
was all the same to him, as long as it was out of doors. When
Tommy was growing up his only holidays had been to go and
visit Arthur, wherever his uncle was staying at the time. He would
travel by bus or train to an agreed place and Arthur would meet
him; then they would walk for miles, wandering the narrow tracks
like father and son, stopping every now and then to examine
some detail, some insect or bird or plant. In the summer, he was
allowed to stay for a week or more at a time: Arthur lived alone,
and he liked the company, and Tommy's father thought it was

good for the boy to be out in the fresh air, learning about the countryside. When he was back home in Cowdenbeath, Tommy couldn't wait to escape into Arthur's world, couldn't wait to be swallowed up into the green of it, into the sky and the taste space had when he leaned out of the window of a train and gulped in the cool air off the sea or the grain fields. For weeks after he went back to school, where he did rather badly and daydreamed his way through everything, he survived on the smaller details of memory: the taste of salt or sap on his hands; the dark-gold of the grain in summer; the faint, blue-brown vapour of autumn afternoons that was darker and much sweeter than anything he could have named.

Now, thirty years on, Tommy had travelled so far from the land that Arthur had inhabited it felt like a deliberate betrayal, as if the whole world had plotted to bring him to Corby and bury him in by-products, with the constant stink of chemicals on his skin, the steady, glowering heat of the furnaces sinking into his bones. Back in Cowdenbeath, his father had worked in the pits and it had been taken for granted that Tommy would do the same, but he couldn't stand the idea of going underground. He hated to think of himself stooping into a metal cage and descending into the dark with all those other men for eight hours at a time, squatting, crouching, crawling around in the narrow blackness, hunkering in under stark coalfaces, never able to stand, or stretch, or look up at the sky. People said the pits were dangerous, but it wasn't the danger that bothered him. He remembered days in school when someone from the Coal Board would come to the headmaster's office, and then the headmaster would go from class to class, calling the names of those who had to go home right away. If your name was called it meant your father was either injured or killed or buried alive, and Tommy waited, every time, to hear his own name called, to go home and find his mother in the kitchen with the neighbours, or standing at the pithead with the other women, waiting for news. There was a girl he had liked in school, a pretty red-haired girl called Catherine, who was called out one summer's afternoon, on a day that had seemed far too warm and bright for anything bad to happen, and he had watched her face crumple when she heard her name, a darkness forming suddenly in her eyes, as if she had known all along that something bad was about to happen. He had felt worse for that one moment than he had ever imagined feeling if his own name was called, but he had been glad, that night, when his father came home late after working with the rescue party for hours, and Tommy had crept out of bed to see him standing in the kitchen, talking quietly and looking too old all of a sudden, while Tommy's mother worked at the stove, fixing a late supper.

It was dangerous down the pit, but Tommy hadn't been afraid of the danger. In certain areas, The Works were just as risky as coal-mining, more so even, and Tommy hadn't cared about that. He would have worked wherever they put him, as long as there was a door or a window nearby and enough space to stand up straight and be a man. He hadn't wanted to admit it, when he refused to follow his father down the pit, but he had always felt there was something unmanly about working on your knees, crawling around in the seams of the earth like an ant. It would have been an insult to his father that he had never intended, to say that he would rather do anything than work in the mines, would rather work casual on the building, or travel miles on the bus to Grangemouth, leaving home in the still of the morning and coming back in the late-evening dark. It was only when he married Lizzie, and saw that he needed something more steady, that he decided to travel south and try his luck with Stewarts and Lloyds. It was good money, and Corby was growing all the time, a better place to live and bring up children, with all the overtime you wanted and a good house, not the prefab they were living in on Blackburn Drive, or the condemned house on King Street they had shared with the rats when the boys were still babies.

It was a better life, Tommy was sure of that. Still, it hadn't been what he'd intended, growing up. When he was ten, and fifteen, and even when he was working as a hod-carrier on building sites, he had dreamed of living on the land like Arthur, maybe even having his own little plot, somewhere up north, away from the smoke and the taste of coal that was always present in the air, even on the coldest days. It was the same dream Arthur had harboured all his life, that patch of ground to work and sweat and bleed over, a dream that hardened in the older man's soul like a tumour and eventually killed him. Tommy knew, by the time he was eighteen, and Arthur was dying in the hospital at Bridge of Earn, that he would never live on the land, that people like him never got themselves that little patch of ground they dreamed about. Up north, where Arthur had gleaned an existence for years, the land was dying. The people who owned it didn't care; they knew what it was worth for fishing and shooting, or forestry, but they had never loved anything alive, they had only ever loved money, and the things they possessed elsewhere, farms and town houses and rare porcelain, gun-dogs and horses and the well-spoken wives they had picked up casually on their way through the comfortable, easy life that had been planned and managed on their behalf for generations.

Or so Arthur said, when he took Tommy out into the woods and fields, stealing a pheasant or a salmon from land and water that was owned by somebody else. Arthur was full of stories about a Scotland that had once existed, but Tommy could never tell if those histories had happened ten years or ten centuries before he was born, and no matter how persistent the boy was, Arthur always managed to avoid answering questions about when and where and who, specifically, all this had happened to. As a child, listening to Arthur's stories, Tommy had never understood how the people tolerated the inhuman behaviour of the rich land-lords. When Arthur told him how the people starved, even though there were deer in the hills and fish in the rivers, or how, if a man was caught stealing a pigeon from the landlord's doocot, he would have his hand cut off in front of the whole village, Tommy couldn't help wondering why they didn't rise up and fight back. Better to die, he thought, than live so dishonoured. One day they had gone on a long walk, and Arthur had shown him a hidden road, or rather, the ruin of a road, buried under grass and weeds – not tarmac, but old stones and gravel laid down who knew how long ago by the mythical inhabitants of Arthur's Scotland. This was one of the ghostie roads, Arthur said; there were hundreds of them all over the country, roads that had been used for years and had suddenly disappeared, lost in the snow, or buried under drifting sand, or just grown over, like this one, when the people had been driven out by the landowners. Arthur told him about a secret village he had come across in the north somewhere; or rather, what remained of the village, a ruined place, its walls tumbled into the surrounding undergrowth, the doorways and lintels colonised by ferns and ivy, the one street almost imperceptible amid grass and weeds. There was a story about the place, how the men who lived there had gone out to work one day and had been caught in a snowstorm. It was a small community – maybe four or five families, maybe even fewer than that – and there would only have been a handful of them: whatever they were doing that day, they got hopelessly lost in this storm and they all died, lost in the snow, freezing to death as they wandered, unable to find their way home. Then, when the men didn't come back, the women and children had decided to abandon the place and go to the nearby town, or to another village: they were probably dispersed all over the place, Arthur said, their names lost, their history broken.

'You have to remember that, in those days, women depended on men for their livelihood,' he said. 'Just like they do in the pit-towns today.'

'What happened to the village?' Tommy asked.

'It vanished,' Arthur said. 'For a long time nobody knew it was there. When I found it, everything was overgrown. Trees had come up through the foundations of the houses. Weeds were growing on the streets.'

'Is it still there?'

'I suppose so.' Arthur looked thoughtful. 'I've not been back. It gave me a bad feeling. Places like that, you just have to stand there and look around to know why people believe in ghosts.'

'Do you believe in ghosts, then, Uncle Arthur?'

Arthur had laughed. 'Of course,' he said. 'Take a look around you sometime. Take a look around when you're back in Cowdenbeath, walking down the High Street. Look carefully and see how many ghosts you can see.'

Tommy hadn't understood this at the time, but he'd thought about Arthur's words later, when his uncle was in hospital, and Tommy could see the ghost taking shape in his eyes. He had wanted them to stop what they were doing, all those nurses and doctors, keeping that ghost alive against his will, but there was nothing he could do, and eventually he had watched as Arthur faded into the blue-white hospital sheets, already elsewhere, walking home to wherever he belonged on a ghostie road that had been the main thoroughfare at one time, but was just a track now, a phantom line running between wheat fields or pasture, something barely discernible at the edge of a wood, or a shimmer appearing faintly in a snowfall, where before there had been almost nothing. After his uncle died, Tommy had started finding ghosts everywhere: mysterious places still remembered in the words that lingered on in street names, another land hidden under the conifers and light industrial estates, old highways gleaming through the salted roads in winter, and those salted roads themselves, already suggesting the ghosts they would one day become, foreshadowing their own vanishing into whiteness and dust, the ghostie roads of an undecided future.

He worked the continental shift system, like most of the men, and he had a set routine for each shift. On days, he rose at four thirty and carried his clothes to the bathroom, where he could wash and dress without disturbing Lizzie. For a long time, he had thought there was no point taking much trouble over it; by the time he was half an hour into the shift, he'd be dirty again anyhow, face and hands grimy and bleared with that chemical taint that never quite left his skin. That was before he'd met Katrina, though. Now, he took a little more care over his appearance than he had done, even if he knew he would only see the girl for five or ten minutes at the most. He didn't eat before work, but on day shift he would go downstairs and fix himself a brandy and egg, drink it in one, then walk to the newsagent's to pick up the paper. He had always liked the paper shop, even before Katrina started working there; he liked the way it was lit up in the dark, and at Guy Fawkes, or Hallowe'en, or Christmas, there would be fireworks, or scary masks, or tree-lights glittering in the shadows. The first time he'd met Katrina, she had been unpacking papers on the floor of the shop. He'd reached down to get the *Mirror* from the pile she was unwrapping and, though she hadn't said anything, he'd been aware of her smile, an open, friendly smile that made her seem happy with who she was. Or so it seemed to Tommy. From that day on, he would stop to talk and it had gradually built into such a ritual that he would walk down early for the paper even when he wasn't on days, so he could ask her how she was, or what she'd done at the weekend, or how her studies were going, and he would catch himself being awkward and happy at the idea that they were flirting.

Once he'd got his paper, he would walk to the bus stop and wait for the bus, the paper folded up neatly and tucked under his arm. He wouldn't read it till later, at breakfast, when he could take a proper look. His journey took him up through the town and then out, past little playparks and stretches of waste ground, and he would sit upstairs, on his own among the crowd of men smoking and reading their papers, his face turned to the window. He wanted to store the cool of the air in his body, carry it with him into The Works, make it last till his eight hours was over. He also found himself thinking about Katrina more and more, not just on the journey, but well into the shift, picturing her fresh, open face, her honey-coloured hair swept back and bound in a pony-tail, her pale blue eyes, bright and alive and watchful, taking everything in, taking his measure, figuring him out. It was her eyes that told him he was acceptable to her, that she knew, in spite of the difference in their ages, that he was a real person, someone she could have talked to, or even spent time with, had things been different. Not that things could ever have been different. Tommy was forty-four years old; he guessed Katrina was no more than nineteen or twenty.

He didn't have breakfast until he got to work. The canteen was subsidised, so he thought he might as well take advantage, and besides, it was a pleasure to get the first hour and a half in, then cross the yard in the breaking light, or the winter dark, and sit down at his usual table with a mug of steaming tea and a plate of eggs and bacon, and eat it slowly, lingering over the warmth and comfort of it all, the paper spread out on the table beside him at the racing page. In the old days, before he got married and before betting was legal, he'd been a bit of a gambler; now, he just studied the form, and maybe had the odd flutter on the Derby or the Lincoln. Never the National, of course: that was for women and amateurs, and there was no predicting what might happen, any horse could win as long as it stayed on its feet, some disaster could occur, some mass pile-up, and a hundred-to-one shot could come romping home from out of nowhere, like Foinavon. It had disgusted Tommy, when Foinavon won. To him, the only thing worse than losing was to win dishonourably.

In the mornings, he only looked at the sports pages; later on, when things were quiet, he would read the paper from cover to cover, absorbing everything in equal measure, the Middle East, the sex scandals, the celebrity news, the adverts for girdles and thermal vests that came between the news and the sport. Sometimes he would go to the door of the shed and stand with his face to the cool outdoors, smoking a Kensitas and, though he tried not to dwell on things, he would think about Canada. It had been touch and go, back in '65, whether they had come to Corby or emigrated for good. He and Lizzie had talked about it, and Tommy had fancied the idea of Canada. He didn't know what it was like, but he'd read there weren't many people, and that the land was huge, whole territories still almost uninhabited, still fresh and wild and undamaged. He imagined it as a quiet place, a wide country where you could ride for days through open prairie, and if you lived outside the two or three cities, you would be in that half-wilderness he had seen in nature films, with deer woods and clear lakes fringed with pines. That had appealed to him – but Lizzie hadn't wanted to go so far away from her home and family. Her mother had been ill at the time, he remembered, though it hadn't been just that. Lizzie was afraid of change, she wanted everything to stay the same. She hadn't even wanted to move from Scotland, though she knew there was nothing for them there. So he had travelled south, and got a job as a labourer in the blast furnaces. It had taken a while to get used to that, but he'd worked hard, and he'd gradually got himself into a better situation, in by-products. Still, he thought about Canada from time to time, and he wondered what it would have been like. He didn't have anything against Corby; people said bad things about it, and it was true, the town had its problems, but it was better than it was made out to be – better, for sure, than those clannish pit-towns back home.

He had come down in '65, on the rail ticket and subsistence, stayed in the Church Army hostel, joined the union and put his name down on the housing list. Within eight weeks he got a house on the Beanfield, which was a good part of town, not too close to The Works. His first impression of The Works itself had been of something impossible to navigate: a vast labyrinth of rail lines and machinery glimpsed through wide shed doors; smoke from the coke ovens drifting into the open yards between the mills, shrouding the men in a soft, dusty monochrome, like the light in an old Cagney film; heat billowing out and wrapping him close in a blanket of what felt like actual fire as he wandered through the huge machinery of the place, blinking and gasping for breath, but trying to look as if he was accustomed to it all. Until that moment, he had always worked out of doors; maybe that was the reason he hated it so much, and why he was so surprised by how casually the other men accepted the place on its own terms. For Tommy, during those first few weeks, every day he was there was like walking into hell. He hated the noise and the heat, he hated not knowing where he was supposed to be, or what he was supposed to be doing, and he knew how dangerous that was. He resented the idea that he might get hurt, or even killed, before his family could travel south and begin their new life. What he hated most, though, was walking across the furnace yard when a train was passing, slag spilling out from the ladles, white-hot and unpredictable. For the first time in his life, he found himself thinking about all the ways a man could die, and he couldn't think of a worse fate than to die by fire.

After a while, he started searching for gaps between the sheds, stretches of open ground that he came to know as cool, empty places, quiet enough for a stolen cigarette break and a chance to hear himself think. But nothing was certain. The place kept shifting: what he remembered as a sanctuary would vanish overnight, displaced in his memory till he began to think he had imagined it. A corner he had convinced himself was safe would suddenly fill with noise, the air tense and straining in the heat like a sail filling with wind. For the first two weeks or so, he thought he would never find his way back out once he passed through the gate and started walking to where he thought he was supposed to be. Then, when he was out again, he thought he would never find his way back in – nothing was the same from one day to the next, he had to remember the men coming on shift with him, making their faces and work-clothes his land-marks, patches of human detail and colour in all the smoke and noise and metalwork.

Then, after a month or so, he was one of those men. Slowly, without really noticing, he'd got used to it. There were still days when he was afraid, especially around the blast furnace, but after a while, he knew what he needed to know. He knew his spot, and how to get there from the gate, or the canteen. He knew where the toilets were – on his first day, nobody had told him, and he'd waited ages for a break, so he could go outside and relieve himself. This was how he lived, one man among thousands who had learned his own strip of territory, then kept with it. The rest of the labyrinth was irrelevant to him. Stray into the wrong area and something would go wrong – like the man he'd seen one night coming off back-shift, a man his own age lying crushed under a load of steel, his leg torn out at the roots, his face a pool of grey and black. Or had he seen it? He knew what had happened, and he remembered the details he had been told, but hadn't he held back, hadn't the man been screened from him by the cluster of bodies, some men on their knees or crouching, wanting to help, others standing, telling them to wait for the emergency team, all the textbook knowledge useless in the face of real injury. They had blackboards at various key posts; you could read them as you walked to your place, or watch some first-hand wiping the board clean at the end of his shift: times and types of injury, broken thumbs or lost fingers, local burns, spills, falls, temporary and permanent blindings. These things happened for one of two reasons: either you took a wrong steer, and ended up where you shouldn't have been, or fate simply chose your particular post, the place where you had to stand fast for eight or twelve hours at a time, to make its inexplicable yet – after it was all over – wholly predictable visitation. That was why you stuck to your own spot. That was why you had routines. That was why you were careful around a stranger, in case he broke the rhythm of the place and made something happen that your whole life – on shift and off – was calculated to avoid.

In the summer, when he was on double shifts, he would think of the first three months, when he'd come down alone and stayed in the Church Army, waiting for his name to come through on the housing list. Back then, he'd spent his days off swimming or drinking beer and he wished he could go back to that, it had been so simple, so clear what he was doing. Everything had seemed to be in the future then, and he had been fitter and more inclined to be happy. He felt a vague, warm expectancy, as if he'd been given a promise; it was how he felt at the bookie's sometimes: he could do no wrong, he was his own man, everything was set to the exact level, the perfect pitch for success. Then Lizzie had arrived, and life had changed. He had been so proud of the house he'd got for them, and the money he was bringing in, but she had barely noticed, or if she did, she didn't care. All she talked about was Scotland, wondering how her mother was, going across to the phone box to wait for the call from her brother John, who had a telephone of his own, just to get the latest from home, news about people she barely knew – Mrs So-and-so from the end of the road had just had an operation; young Kenny McGhee had got a place at Edinburgh University to study law.

It wasn't just Lizzie who caused him problems, though. Tommy knew he had changed while he was away and it shouldn't have surprised him that the whole family noticed it. After his first month or two at The Works, he had learned to look for the signs in a man's face and body and clothes that showed which department he was in, how long he had been there, and how much damage had been done to his flesh or his soul or his self-respect. It didn't take much to read these men: everything about them was defined by their occupation. A furnaceman would have a cherry-coloured burn on the end of his nose, or on his forehead, from lifting the furnace doors; another man might have fingers missing from working on the machines, or his clothes would be peppered with tiny holes from being showered with hot metal sparks. Every part of The Works had its own smell, its own colours. Traces of dust would soak into a man's skin, sometimes oxblood red, sometimes green or pale blue, but mostly a grey-black, the underground tones of ore and sinter and slag. Tommy knew his own body was similarly tainted; within weeks, his skin was already a map where every spill, every gust of heat, every shift was signalled by some after-stain of carbon or metal. But it wasn't just the physical changes that were visible. There was something in the eyes of every man who worked on Steelside, a look that acknowledged a kinship with this dark machinery of fire and metal. Tommy couldn't see it in himself, but it was there in others, and he knew if it was there in them, then it was there in him. By the time Lizzie and the boys arrived, coming off the bus in the middle of the day, The Works had already claimed him, though he only understood how much when Francis turned aside for just a moment, his face creased, as Tommy picked his son up and held him aloft.

'How's my boy, then?' Tommy had said.

Francis had sniffed. 'You smell,' he'd said, not just stating a fact, but meaning to be cruel, and Tommy had glanced at his wife, who stood watching, the empty birdcage she had insisted on carrying all the way from Scotland set down beside her on the damp pavement. Tommy wanted to explain to them that things were going to be better now, that he had a good job, and they would be living in a nice house; he wanted them to understand what he'd had to go through to get them here, all those doubles and nights, crossing the furnace yard, standing for hours in the heat, avoiding slag spills and splashes, learning what he had to do as he went along, with no help from anybody. He remembered the special regard accorded to the pit-workers back home, how Lizzie thought so highly of her brother John, because he worked underground, and he wanted to tell them how it was at the furnace yard, working eight or sixteen hours at a time in the indescribable heat – but he didn't say a word, he just pretended to laugh it off, all the while watching Lizzie, who smiled her weary, reluctant smile then picked up the empty birdcage and looked at him, her face empty of everything but fatigue.

The distance between them had deepened that day, which had bothered him much less than he had expected. There had been a coldness, a more or less functional element in their marriage for some time and, though he had thought coming to Corby was a good move, a way of giving her some of the things she wanted, he wasn't really surprised when she disliked it. Lizzie disliked so much, nowadays. After Francis, she hadn't wanted sex – which had been fine by him, since he'd discovered, not long after they were first married, that he derived no pleasure from their awkward lovemaking – and she had been easily upset, retreating into her own little corner whenever things didn't go the way she wanted. Back home, he had been mystified by this: he'd said she should get down to the doctor's, to see if there was something wrong with her, but she'd taken no notice.

'It isn't me that needs the doctor,' she'd said, laughing bitterly. 'You should maybe think about yourself on that score.'

'What's that supposed to mean?'

'It means you're the one who needs to see a doctor,' she said. 'You're the one with the problem, not me.'

'What problem's that then?'

'You know fine well,' she'd said, but she hadn't elaborated and, when he pursued it, she had just clammed up and gone back to her knitting. Later, when he'd told her about the job in Corby, and how he would be going down first to get things set up, she had just looked at him, her eyes empty, that half-smile playing about her lips, as if she knew something he didn't. He tried telling her about the opportunities at The Works, and how she would have all the things she had dreamed about – a new cooker, a proper washing-machine, nice furniture from one of the big stores – and she had listened quietly, nodding away, half-smiling, the empty look in her eyes like a reprimand, never to be spoken, but always present. He had told her it would be good for the boys, too. 'What future have they got here?' he had asked. 'The pits are all going. There's no work.'

Lizzie hadn't said anything, but he knew that she knew he was right. There was nothing for any of them in Cowdenbeath. So he had come south, and he had hoped for a change – a new life, a new start. Instead, the distance between them had grown, till they hardly spoke to one another – only began speaking, in fact, when Lizzie first fell ill, and it began to dawn on them both that it was serious.

The worst thing, though, was that she had turned the boys against him. Or Francis, anyway. Derek was a good kid, he could always see both sides of an argument, and he didn't judge. But Francis was a different matter. When Tommy had left Scotland, Francis had clung on to his jacket, saying he didn't want him to go. Now, just eight weeks later, he was ice-cold, distant, touched with that same aloofness Lizzie had, smiling the same knowing half-smile. He was only nine years old: he hadn't come to be like that by himself. Lizzie had done something: she had allowed herself just one luxury, just one act of resistance, but this had been the slow, subtle poisoning of his son's mind against him. Why else would he have done what he did, and said what he said, the moment he got off the bus?

When Tommy turned to him, it was obvious Derek hadn't known what to do. Maybe Lizzie had had a go at him, too, but Tommy knew the boy was made of stronger stuff. Now, as Francis turned aside, that mocking look on his face, as if Tommy weren't good enough for him, and Lizzie stood by coldly watching, Derek stepped forward and took hold of his father's arm. 'Hello, Dad,' he'd said. 'We missed you.'

Tommy nodded. 'That's all right, son,' he replied. 'I missed you too.'

Lizzie had insisted on getting a job. She said she wanted some money of her own and, though Tommy didn't like the idea, he couldn't bring himself to stand in her way. She had only been at Snakpak a couple of months, though, when she had the first attack of her mysterious illness – an illness nobody understood, which made everyone assume it was cancer – and she couldn't go on. Meanwhile, the boys were settling in, in their different ways. Derek made friends with the other boys round about, and Francis fought with them. Tommy couldn't believe how angry the boy was: he would fight with anyone, for any reason; it didn't bother him how old they were, or how many. If someone said something he didn't like, he just lashed out, which frequently got him into trouble at school. Once, he had been going out to the shops with Lizzie, and a boy from across the street had passed by, a wiry, mean-natured little fourteen-year-old called Liam, whose father Tommy knew as a wiry, mean-natured forty-year-old on the coke ovens. The boy had spat, just outside the door, and said something – Tommy never found out what – that Francis had taken as an insult to his mother. Later, when they were trying to sort it all out, Tommy was surprised by this: Lizzie might think Francis was fond of her, just because he had turned against his father, but he wasn't, not really. He wasn't fond of anybody. He was too angry. The insult, real or imagined, had prompted Francis – who was only eleven at the time – to a swift and vicious response: without a moment's hesitation, he'd run over to the bigger boy, who'd probably been too surprised to react, and punched him hard in the face, just once, but it was enough to bust the kid's nose. Liam went down with a stunned look on his face, blood everywhere.

Tommy had witnessed this scene with dismay. It wasn't that he had any problem with fighting, it was just that Francis was too willing to fight and Tommy had learned early on in life that you have to choose your battles, otherwise life just wears you down. He'd been a bit of a hard man, years ago, and he knew how to handle himself, but he knew the worst thing you could do was let yourself become a target. As he'd soon learned, there was always somebody bigger, or meaner, or more ready to fight dirty than you were. He'd built up a bit of a reputation, after Arthur died – more of a reputation, probably, than he deserved. Then, one night, he'd been on his way home from the pub and he'd seen three men getting on to a boy he knew from Grangemouth. He didn't know why he'd got involved: it wasn't his fight – but he'd been angry, all of a sudden, seeing three on to one, and the boy he knew, Ray, wasn't much of a fighter, wasn't much good at anything, really, when it came down to it. Tommy knew he should have kept right on walking, but he hadn't: he had happened along just as things were about to get ugly, and he had gone over, wanting to know what was wrong. He'd had a few drinks, and he was always more inclined to lose the head when he was drinking, but he'd surprised himself that night. When he stopped to see what was happening, one of the three boys had turned on him. He was a big man, with curly black hair and a black moustache.

'Mind your own business,' he'd said. 'It's nothing to do with you.'

Tommy glanced over at Ray. The boy had blood on his face, a fat lip, nothing too bad – yet. In the half-light under the street-lights, it looked like he was crying. Tommy hoped he was wrong about that. 'He's all right,' Tommy said. 'I know him. Anyway, I don't think much of three on one.' His head was clear, in spite of the drink, and he was pretty sure the big man was all he had to bother about. The other two looked like they were hangers-on, along for the ride. 'So why don't you leave him alone and fuck off back to where you crawled out from,' he added quietly.

As Tommy had expected, the big man didn't hesitate. He came

charging straight in, his face flushed with drink, his eyes empty and black. Tommy stepped aside, let him stagger on, then, when the boy turned, he stepped up and put the head on him. As the big man reeled back, blood bursting out of his nose, Tommy hit him again, same place, the meat and bones of his face soft and yielding, a wet, smashed mass. The other two had been standing back, holding on to Ray, but when they saw their mate go down, they let their prisoner go and started backing away. Tommy had guessed right: they didn't have the heart for a fight, not once they'd seen blood. He took a couple of steps in their direction and they turned and ran; in that same moment, the one with the moustache started pulling himself up off the floor and Tommy smashed his boot against the side of his head, then followed on till the big man went down once and for all. He looked round to see where Ray was. He thought, at first, that the boy had done a runner, but he hadn't; standing off to the side, under a street-lamp, he was watching, his face white, but the expression was one of sickly fascination.

Tommy called out to him, 'You all right?'

As soon as Tommy broke the silence, the boy came to himself. He looked at Tommy. He seemed scared, as if he thought his rescuer would start on him next.

'Go on home,' Tommy said. 'Before somebody comes.'

Ray nodded, but he didn't move.

'Go on. It's all right.'

Ray seemed to think about it a moment, then he turned and started away, half-walking, half-running, looking back over his shoulder, as if he thought Tommy was going to come after him – and it was insane because, just for a moment, with his blood up and feeling a sudden contempt for the boy, Tommy had to resist the impulse to do exactly that, to go after Ray and cut him down, to do to him whatever those drunken bastards had intended doing. The impulse passed almost as soon as it came, but for that moment, standing on a half-lit street between two rows of privet hedges, the night air suddenly cool on his face, Tommy felt something rise in his throat, a thick tide of exhilarating anger he'd not been aware of till now, something cold and steady, a new readiness to judge and find lacking and strike down, like some Old Testament God disappointed by the human race he had wanted so much to love, erasing whole cities with a single, arbitrary word. All of a sudden, he understood that disappointment. He hadn't got into the fight for Ray's sake, he'd just seen what was happening, weighed up the opposition and taken action for its own sake, because he could, because he had an excuse. It didn't matter to him that he could have been wrong, that one day he would make the wrong call, and he would be the one on the floor with his face caved in, or worse. What mattered – what he felt most surely as he walked away from the scene – was that one day he would go too far. Events like this were just an excuse: what he wanted to do – he knew this now, for the first time – what he was ready to do was kill someone. Next time, or the time after, that would be exactly what happened, because that was what he wanted. At some point, without knowing it, he had been contaminated with an anger he didn't understand, tainted against his will with an extraordinary capacity to hate other men. It was only one part of him, he knew, but it was strong: now, all of a sudden, he saw where it could lead – and he was afraid, the fear a cold flame in the marrow of his spine, absolute fear mingled with an unexpected recognition, a kind of black joy.

So this is how it is, he thought, as he walked home in the darkness. This is how I am. The idea kept repeating itself in his mind, and he couldn't shake it off, even after he had climbed the stairs to the bathroom and stood at the sink, splashing cold water on his face and listening for the normal sounds of the house. For the first time, he saw how far he had come from Arthur's world – and, for the first time, he understood that he could never go back there, not even on a visit.

Now, in Corby, he was even further from that world – and on that first day, when Francis had turned away from him, he knew how far he had come. All he could hope for was that his sons would have a better life than the existence he had been unable to avoid. He was grateful, at least, that he didn't have a daughter. Boys had a chance to get out, if they used their heads – which was why he didn't want them to be fighters. He wanted them to know what they were about, and not be drawn into anything by other people, or by the ugly logic of the world they had been born into. They had to know how to look after themselves, but he didn't want them to fight, not because he believed there were any peaceful, reasonable solutions in life, but because he didn't want them to get trapped in situations that made no sense, with people who weren't worth the bother. He didn't want them to be victims either, though – and from the time they were just wee boys scrambling around after a football, he had taught them how to look after themselves. When they were old enough, he had shown them how to do enough damage to another man that he wouldn't be able to strike back, but he had also told them that the best thing to do was to avoid a fight altogether when-ever they could.

'If you can walk away,' he would say, 'then walk away. But don't run. Never run.'

He had taught them to be cautious, to see what was coming and be ready for it. He'd told them about all the tricks: how a boy would come up to you on the street, looking all friendly, ask if you had the time, or a light, then when you were distracted, or had your hand in your pocket, someone else would come at you from behind. Or maybe you would be walking home late and you'd see somebody on the ground looking like he was sick or hurt, but when you went over to help, you'd discover, too late, that it was all a set-up, that the boy on the floor was just a decoy and you had walked into a trap. He'd told them to forget all that stuff about fair fights: it wasn't about putting your fists up Marquess-of-Queensberry-style, he said, anyone who thought that wouldn't last long. He wanted them to understand that there was no such thing as honour; that the men they had to deal with every day of their lives could not be trusted. He knew that wasn't always true – he would have trusted Arthur with anything, for example, and there had been others over the years, maybe two, three at most, that he knew were all right – and he knew he was robbing them of something, talking like this, but he would rather they lost whatever it was he was stealing than see them lose their self-respect, or their lives, on some street corner at closing-time.

Lizzie hated all this, of course. She didn't know what it was like – she hadn't seen what Tommy had seen, she didn't know what men were capable of. She thought Derek and Francis would just sail through life because they were her sons and she wanted them to do well. She didn't think about them alone, out in the world, among other boys, among other men. Maybe that was what spoiled it all, maybe that was why Francis had never listened, because his mother had always been there with her other version of life, spoiling him, making him think it would be easy. Derek listened, of course, and he took it all in; that was the kind of boy he was. He didn't say much, but you knew he was listening.

As soon as they arrived in Corby, though, Tommy knew it was Francis he had to worry about. Derek was his mother's son, when it came down to it: a bit of a dreamer, no danger to anybody, more of a thinker than a doer. He could sit in his room for hours, picking away at his guitar, or reading the music magazines, and most of the time you wouldn't even know he was there. But Francis was a chip off the old block, everybody said it, not knowing what they *were* saying, recognising in the son the same darkness, the same homicidal anger that the father had taken so long to recognise in himself. It made Tommy afraid. The boy was too quick to judge, too quick to take offence; most of all, he was too quick with his hands. There had been incidents ever since they arrived when Tommy was called to the school, or when he had to go out into the square in front of the house where the boys played football and intervene, just like that time with Liam, when Francis had broken the boy's nose. It had been bad enough, doing it in front of Lizzie, but what Francis didn't know was that Liam's older brother, a twenty-year-old on leave from the army, had seen the whole thing from the window across the street, and had come running out, looking for blood. If Tommy hadn't been there – alerted by the fuss Lizzie was making, he'd hurried downstairs, just in time to see what was going on – he didn't know what would have happened. The one thing he was sure of was that Francis wouldn't have backed down, no matter what. In the end, he had managed to smooth things over, more or less, by sending Francis back into the house to see to his mother, while he faced down the brother. The boy was wiry, like his father, he was probably quick and fairly strong too, but he wasn't too bright. Tommy didn't fancy getting into something with a soldier, especially not in a place like this, where it was all Protestants and Catholics, but in the end he hadn't needed to. He took pride in that – took pride in how calm he could be, in how well he could keep himself in check. It was something he had won, against his own nature, and he knew it was something Francis would have to win, against that same nature, handed down from father to son, a taint, a form of sin. Tommy had never been one for church, but he read the Bible sometimes, and he remembered that phrase: *the sins of the fathers*. He had always thought of that sin as something active, a chosen path, a sin committed by a man in full possession of himself; now he knew that sin could be present in the blood, lying in wait, unsuspected. You couldn't avoid it by saying your prayers and living by somebody else's commandments or rules; you had to seek it out in the corners of your own being, seek it out and expunge it, sucking out the poison before it grew strong enough to kill you, cutting into your mind and your spirit and draining the venom, the way a doctor might cut into a wound, or a snake bite. Tommy knew he could do that for himself, but he couldn't do it for Francis – nobody could – and he was afraid that, because of him, because of the sin he had passed on, the boy would have to endure some hard knocks before he did it for himself.

In the beginning was the land. That was what Arthur had told him, and Tommy knew it was so, knew it best when the weather changed, when summer came, or when it snowed, as it was snowing at that moment, falling in a slow, dark wave all along the street as he stepped down off the bus and walked the hundred yards to Katrina's house. For a long time, changes in the weather had been all that really happened in his life, other than worrying about the boys and the odd argument with Lizzie. The longer he had been in Corby, the more Tommy had come to believe that a happy life was one in which nothing happened: each day following the next in a predictable routine, day shift, back-shift, nights; the odd day out to Kettering or Northampton on the bus; Sundays at Mass, when he had the weekend off, to keep Lizzie happy. Every day, he looked into his face when he was shaving, and he saw the slow changes that were happening around his mouth and eyes. People always said you couldn't see the changes you lived with, you didn't notice yourself growing older, because the process was too long, the changes were too insignificant to notice day-to-day, but they were wrong. As he grew older, Tommy saw how his face changed, how his eyes paled. Once, he'd had the bluest eyes – everyone had remarked on how blue his eyes were when he was a boy; now, the irises were paler, as if the smoke from The Works had clouded them, and his mouth was darker than before, a little tighter, a symptom of the disappointment he had had to manage, day-to-day, and of the work he'd had to do, holding himself back, smothering the fire he carried in his blood. There were even times when he saw changes from one morning to the next, a slow fade, the spirit he remembered from his days with Arthur settling deeper in his body, like sediment. It hadn't bothered him – or not until Katrina had turned up. He had thought it inevitable, and there had been a satisfaction, of sorts, knowing he was doing what he needed to do for Lizzie and the boys. It hadn't even bothered him that this slow subsidence of the spirit had happened unseen, unrecognised and unappreciated. Lizzie was too wrapped up in her own problems now even to know he was there half the time and the boys were remote and self-absorbed, especially Francis. Tommy had watched them grow and he'd been glad when Francis had made friends with the foreign boy, Jan. Jan's father worked in the welding shop, a dour, quiet-spoken man with a dark hurt in his eyes, a DP, somebody had said, from Latvia, or Estonia, they thought, though he never talked about himself, never talked about anything much, in fact, other than work. Jan was a good kid, and a good influence. He'd brought Francis out of himself, made him think about a wider world, Tommy could see that. Meanwhile, Derek was happy enough, playing music, listening to records. Though he'd hoped for better, Tommy hadn't minded when the boy left school and got a job in Snakpak, hadn't even minded when Derek had come to him, a few days before his eighteenth birthday, and asked if Tommy could get him a job at The Works. He wanted the money for a reason, Tommy knew that, and he was fairly sure that it wouldn't be for ever, that Derek would do more with his life than he had done.

Things had been fine, then, till Katrina had turned up. That first day, in the paper shop, Tommy hadn't given it much thought: he'd felt something shift at the back of his mind when she looked up at him and smiled that smile, a smile he recognised from long ago, though he didn't know where from. He'd laughed at himself back then, thinking about this girl on the bus to work, remembering her face, her honey-coloured hair, her pale blue eyes. He'd seen her the next day, going in for his paper, and he had caught himself thinking about her in the quiet times at work, walking to the canteen with her smile in his head, or her voice, coming unbidden, sneaking in on him when he wasn't paying attention – and from that first week till now, four months later, it had all been drift: chance meetings on his days off that were not quite as accidental as he pretended; long conversations outside the shop or at the bus stop; finally, after about a month or so, a walk by the boating lake, in the middle of the afternoon, something more or less arranged and so, for the first time, a source of guilt, a matter for Tommy's conscience. Though he had nothing to feel guilty about – or so he thought when he reasoned with himself, after each of their occasional meetings in the library, or their slow walks in the woods. Nothing untoward had ever happened: he had never touched her; he had never even begun to tell her how he felt, even if there were times, alone at work, or lying awake in bed with Lizzie laid out beside him, heavy and still as a bale of wool, when he had allowed himself to recognise how he did feel, if only for a moment, before he shook it off, incredulous and ashamed.

Nothing untoward had ever happened, and he had nothing to feel guilty about – or so he told himself as he stepped down off the bus and walked into the snow that was falling, thick and slow, on Gainsborough Road. The worst thing he had ever done was to bring Katrina home, and even that had been an accident. He had been out buying things for Christmas and she had met him by chance at the bus station, on her way home from the library – she was studying part-time at the Tech, and it was easier to work in the library, she said, than at home, when her dad was off work. It had been an accidental meeting, and she had only come to the house because she'd offered to help carry his bags. When he'd heard the music coming from Francis's room, he'd thought about sending her home, but he hadn't, he'd forgotten his caution for a moment and invited her in for a coffee. Ninety-nine times out of a hundred, he'd reasoned, Francis would have stayed exactly where he was. This time, though, he'd come down right away, just as Tommy and Katrina were putting the bags in the kitchen.

'Hello?'

Francis had stood at the door of the front room, as if he was afraid of intruding, or of getting caught up in something, but as soon as he saw Katrina, he had frozen, his face a mask of suspicion.

'I'm just going out,' he'd said, looking at Tommy with a fixed, oddly determined air, as if he had decided to pretend Katrina wasn't there.

'All right,' Tommy said. 'This is Katrina. She's helping me with the shopping.' He wasn't prepared to play Francis's game.

Katrina looked embarrassed. 'Hello,' she said.

Francis nodded, but he didn't look at her. He seemed ill at ease, his eyes too dark, his face haunted by something – and Tommy saw that something was wrong with him, something that had nothing to do with Katrina. 'Are you all right?' he asked.

Francis shook his head. 'I'm fine,' he said. 'I just – I thought you were on a double today?'

Tommy looked at him. Now he saw it; there could be no mistake: the boy was on something. He was drugged up – on cannabis, probably. Tommy had suspected something was going on, he'd caught the odd whiff of something on the landing, late at night, or in the middle of the afternoon, when he'd come in from day shift and, even though nobody was there, he'd guessed the house had just been vacated an hour before. Francis thought he was stupid, of course, he didn't know how obvious it was – and it was true that, until now, Tommy hadn't wanted to believe the evidence of his senses. 'Where are you going?' he asked, quietly. He wondered if Katrina had guessed what was going on.

'Just out.'

'All right. Will you be home for your tea?'

Francis shook his head. 'I'll have my tea at Jan's,' he said. 'Are you going to the hospital?'

Tommy nodded. 'Later,' he said.

Francis pursed his lips. 'All right,' he said. 'Tell Lizzie I was asking for her.' He glanced at Katrina, then looked away quickly. 'See you,' he said.

As soon as the front door closed, Tommy went to the window and looked out. As he had suspected, Francis wasn't alone; he had Alina, Jan's older sister, with him. He wondered if she was the one who had given him the drugs, or whether it was Francis who had started her off. That seemed more likely. Katrina came and stood next to him. 'Is he all right?' she asked.

Tommy nodded. 'He's fine,' he said. 'He's a bit unsettled at the moment.'

'He was probably surprised to see me here.'

Tommy looked at her. She was standing close to him, almost touching his arm and for a moment it would have been the easiest thing in the world to have bent down and kissed her, just once, just lightly, on the lips. It even seemed, just for a moment, that this was exactly what she was waiting for him to do, and Tommy felt suddenly weightless, the light off the snow blue-white all around them, transforming the room to some magical place where anything could happen. Tommy had forgotten how it felt to want a woman – and maybe he had never felt it like this. His desire for Lizzie, even when they had first met, had been something abstract and, at the same time, expected of him, a choice to be made among limited possibilities, like choosing a job or a house. No one had ever seemed to him so beautiful or as improbable as Katrina was at that moment – and it was this that saved him, this inability to imagine that she could want him as he wanted her that saved and damned him at once, damned him for ever to inaction, a hesitation born out of disbelief, rather than duty to his wife or the sense of honour that could be salvaged from self-denial. The light was on Katrina's face, their bodies were almost touching, and he could see, or thought he could see, that she was waiting for him to do something – and he let it go, in the space between one breath and the next, let it go without even knowing that that was what he was doing. It was nothing more than a movement, a step back, or not even that, but it was also a covenant between them, an admission of possible guilt, and Tommy knew that she had seen and understood, that she had read his face like a book. From now on, for as long as it lasted, that guilt would be present in everything they said and did, contaminating time itself, sweet and dark and indelible. Katrina smiled and shook her head.

'I'd better go,' she said. 'You've got things to do.'

That had been yesterday, and now, against his better judgment, Tommy was on his way to meet her again, a brief, stolen meeting between work and the hospital, a kind of lie, to the world and to themselves, but better, Tommy thought, than never seeing her again. Because that had seemed the only choice, in that moment after Francis had walked out the door, leaving the taint of his judgment behind, a choice between touch, or giving up, and Tommy had been too afraid of giving up not to construct something, even if it was a lie, that would allow him to see her again – and the day before, knowing what he was supposed to say and do, he had followed her to the door and they had stood a moment, watching one another, waiting for a sign.

'I'm at home tomorrow,' she had said, finally. 'Dad's at work.'

Tommy nodded.

'You could come round. We could go for a walk.'

Tommy nodded. He felt weak with longing.

'He's on back-shift,' Katrina said. 'Can you come at three o'clock?'

'Yes.' It was all he could manage. Something was fluttering in his throat, like a bird trying to escape and he wanted her to be gone, wanted time to collect himself. Katrina reached out and laid her hand on his forearm. It was the first time they had ever touched.

'I'll see you tomorrow,' she said. Then she turned and walked away in the thick snow, and Tommy watched her go, alive for the first time in years to the soul he had buried inside himself, the man who had swum in the Twenty-Two Foot that first summer here, the boy who had walked for miles in the summer light with his uncle, naming birds, listening to the land as it spoke to him in a voice he had forgotten now, feeling the pull of gravity and the wide arch of the sky over his head, and knowing that life was good.

Derek

WHEN HE WAS alone in the house, he could hear music in the distance, a far-off glimmer of sound that reminded him of the introduction to the Etta James song 'I'd Rather Go Blind'. It was that same discreet bass, that slow walking rhythm in his bones that made him realise he wasn't hearing so much as feeling it: the exact, just measure of song in his flesh filling him out, making him true. That was what music was for, but when he tried to play it himself, it sounded thin and empty. He had started with a lead guitar, but he'd quickly switched to bass; what he really wanted was an upright, something in a warm, dark wood, a physical thing, a shaped gravity matching his body like a twin. He could see himself – not now, not yet, but one day – he could see himself finding that just measure, and everything would fall into place, the pictures would all make sense, the sounds would come right, and he would be playing behind King Curtis, or John Coltrane, like the great Paul Chambers. Or he would be standing off to one side, almost invisible, laying down that discreet bass line while Etta James or Bessie Banks sang a slow-burning soul ballad. That sound – a sound that was there for him, and no one else – was all he had to go on, but it was real, it belonged to him, it was a clue to what he needed to be. Sometimes it seemed far away and almost too soft to hear; but he had nights, alone in the house, when it sounded close, almost distinct, almost playable. Once, a teacher in school, Mr Conway, had said that every life had its purpose, but that most purposes were hidden, secrets buried deep in the soul, or in the heart. It was a remark that came out of nowhere: Mr Conway taught history, and most of what he said had to do with battles and kings and laws about corn or enclosures, but that one day, hovering over Derek on one of his slow perambulations about the classroom, Mr Conway had interrupted himself and said it, quiet, reflective, maybe working something out for himself, something to do with home, or his family. Every life has a purpose, and our only task is to know what it is. We are secrets to ourselves, he said, and this is what makes history so interesting – and he went back to what he had been talking about before, probably thinking nobody had taken in what he had said. But Derek had taken it in. He understood. His life had one purpose, and it was the finding of this rhythm, the learning of this half-heard music that came to him at night out of nowhere.

That was why he had taken this job at The Works, to get money for his music. He didn't like to be at home when everyone else was there, he couldn't stand seeing his mother ill all the time, couldn't stand Tommy's hurt silence, so he'd got himself on permanent day shift, working twelve hours most days, saving what he could, and using the rest of the time to sleep and practise. He hardly ever got a chance these days to plug in and actually play, but he was always learning new stuff by just listening to records. You had to listen all the time, soaking it all up, taking it in. You could learn from anybody: Miles Davis or James Brown, Stravinsky or John Coltrane, King Curtis or Elvis. He wished he could listen to music at work, but it was too noisy. Tommy had got him a job at the plug mill, and all he heard, twelve hours a day, was the rumble of tubes as they spilled on to the cooling racks, and all the background noise of The Works, day in, day out, the sound of steel ramming into steel, the creak and strain of old machinery and men's voices calling out across the yards or the mills, harsh, grating, shot through with muffled anger. Every man Derek knew was angry, they just had different ways of carrying it. Some wore their rage on the outside like a badge or a tattoo, others smothered it deep in their bodies, so it only shone through at odd moments, a terrifying gleam in the eyes or around the mouth. Some transformed it into other things – hobbies, drinking, fantasies, even music – but it was never completely buried, and it came out whenever a man had to raise his voice to be heard, the hard note of anger glinting like steel through a shout or a warning. Derek had known about that anger all his life: as Tommy's son, he had grown up with it, treating it as another presence in his life, like a wild dog that had taken shelter in the house. What had surprised him, starting at the plug mill, was how universal it was, how every man carried that same anger with him, as if rage was not just a part, but the essence of manhood. Here, he had learned that, even if they laughed, men never really smiled. Here he had learned that a man's guard was never down, that he never let himself be seen by others. Most of all, here he had learned – finally, as confirmation of something he had suspected all along – that he himself was not altogether a man, because he smiled all the time, and he talked, and when he looked at himself, or listened to his own voice calling out across the floor, he did not see, or hear, or feel the smallest trace of rage. It made him afraid, a little; it felt dangerous, like working close with white-hot metal or heavy machinery and having no shield, no protection. Here, from the first day till now, six months on, he felt naked.

On that first day, he had found his station by the cooling rack and stood waiting for the first batch of tubes to roll out. Derek's job was to keep the batches separate, to count them out and mark every tenth tube with chalk, to check the numbers in each batch against the expected numbers on the production sheet. You had to be sure to keep tubes of different width apart: two from separate batches could look very much alike, with only a few centimetres' difference in the bore, but those few centimetres were crucial. On that first day, Andy, the shift supervisor, had explained how important it was not to get the batches mixed up. That could lead to accidents, or loss of business. He had taken ten minutes to impress this detail on Derek's mind, then he had shown him how to use an air-jet to blow out the tiny pieces of steel that would adhere to the inner surface of each tube like soot in a chimney. Derek wanted to know where his protective clothing was.

'How do you mean?' Andy seemed genuinely puzzled. 'What protective clothing?'

'They said in the office that I'd be provided with protective clothing.'

'What, like overalls?' Andy said.

'I don't know.'

The supervisor gave a short hard laugh. 'I expect they meant the glove,' he said. 'There's an asbestos glove kicking around somewhere. I wouldn't wear it, though. It's too hot. Your hand'll turn to putty in that thing.' He was already turning to go. 'You OK, then?' he said. 'Know what you've got to do?'

Derek nodded, but Andy was walking away now, his attention caught by something at the far end of the rack. Suddenly, Derek was alone, wrapped in the heat and the noise of the mill, alone and not at all sure what he had to do, with eleven hours and thirty minutes to go before he could walk back to the gate and catch the bus home.

He wasn't alone for long. The pattern of work at the plug mill was a short period of activity, while a batch of white-hot tubes rolled through, followed by a wait of anywhere between a few minutes and two or three hours before the next batch turned up. The busy times kept each man occupied at his post, two at one end of the rack, about ten or so yards apart, Derek on his own at the other, with his chalk and his air-jet, spraying out the tubes and marking them off in tens, all the while trying not to burn his hand on the hot metal. Occasionally, he would push the nozzle of the air-jet too far into the tube and tiny particles of hot steel would blow back on to his arms and body, burning needlepoint holes in his T-shirt and spotting his skin with tiny blisters of steel. Once, while he was chalking off a tube, his hand slipped, and he got a thin sliver of a burn along the edge of his wrist, but it hurt less than he had imagined it would, and he kept working, intent on going unnoticed. After the third batch of tubes had run through, he remembered that he hadn't asked Andy about breaks.

'You the new boy?' A fat, red-faced man with wispy blondish hair had crept up behind him and stood a couple of feet away, holding a ragged glove that was covered in smudged burns and grime. 'You're supposed to wear this.'

Derek shook his head. 'Andy said I wouldn't need it,' he said.

The fat man shrugged. 'Suit yourself,' he muttered, and retreated back to the other end of the rack.

Alone again, Derek made an effort to take in his surroundings. To begin with, the place had seemed empty and lifeless, a space for machinery and nothing else. Now he saw that there were birds high up in the roof of the shed, starlings he thought, ten or more of them, twittering and flitting to and fro among the metal supports. And that wasn't all. Here and there, in between the big, dark machines, he could see there were cats, at least four or five, and probably more: a large, weary-looking tabby with a sad, hurt mouth; a pair of tortoise-shell kittens with long flickering tails; a lean, mean-eyed black-and-white, with a soft-looking scar above one eye. In between batches of tubes, Derek tried to get the kittens to come to him – not because he particularly liked cats, but because it was something to do. The kittens kept their distance, however, as did the other animals. They weren't pets. They were wild. They probably lived on mice and the occasional bird, he thought. Or maybe the men left food out for them – but then, how had they come here in the first place? Why would anything that could go elsewhere choose to live in this heat and noise?

About two hours into the shift, a thickset, grey-haired man of around fifty appeared. He was wearing overalls that had once been white, and a grey cap. 'You Tommy Cameron's son?' he asked. His voice was like wet gravel rolling around in a tin can.

Derek nodded, and the man held out his hand. 'I'm a friend of Tommy's,' he said. 'You'll probably not remember me. Sammy Cahill.'

Derek didn't remember at first, and then he did. This was a man who had come to the house a few times, years ago, when they first moved to Corby; then, after about a year, the visits had stopped. Derek guessed that this had something to do with his mother. Lizzie would take a dislike to someone, for no particular reason, and Tommy would have to tell them they couldn't come to the house any more. It had happened more often when she got really sick, and because she was so weak, Tommy had never argued, never put his foot down.

'I remember,' Derek said. 'Mr Cahill.'

'*Sammy*,' the man said. 'Anyway, how's it going?'

'Fine.' Derek was trying not to smile. He always liked people that Lizzie had taken against. It was a matter of principle, almost.

'I'm just going on a break,' Sammy said. 'You want to come?'

Derek looked around for Andy. He knew he was supposed to

wait till he was relieved before he left the floor, but he had no idea when this would be. 'I'm not on a break yet,' he said.

Sammy shook his head. 'Don't bother about that,' he said. He turned and looked back across the floor to where the fat man stood, swinging a long crowbar. 'Hey, Peter,' he called out, his voice just loud enough to carry over the noise of the machines, 'come and look after the rack, while the boy here takes a break.'

Peter looked unhappy, but he came over to Derek's work station, still swinging the crowbar.

'This is Peter,' Sammy said. 'He's not supposed to be working here. When he does work, that is.'

Peter frowned. 'I can't do without the money,' he said.

Sammy shook his head. 'Peter's got a heart problem,' he said. 'He's supposed to stay out of the heat. They offered him a job somewhere else, but he wouldn't go. Not enough money. Only, if he stays in the plug mill, he's going to die. Aren't you, Peter?'

The fat man shrugged. 'We're all going to die,' he said. He was looking at something out of the corner of his eye. Derek turned slightly and saw – and as soon as he saw, he guessed something bad was going to happen. One of the cats, the black-and-white, had strayed close to where the three men stood. It was watching Peter with a curious expression, as if it expected something from him, maybe food, or a petting. Derek could see that Peter was watching the cat too, that he was waiting for something, waiting for the right moment – and he wanted to intervene, to make him stop. He looked at Sammy. His father's friend seemed not to know what was about to happen; or if he did, he didn't care. Meanwhile, Peter flashed Derek a malevolent look, a look that showed he had guessed how soft Derek was, a look that let him know that it was this, more than anything, that had sealed the cat's fate. At the same time, with a sudden loud bang that made Derek jump, Peter's crowbar crashed down on the cat's tail, severing it cleanly. The animal screamed and darted away, but it left the black-and-white tip of its tail behind. Derek felt sick.

Peter laughed. 'Stupid fucking things,' he said. 'They never learn.'

From that day on, Sammy had been his friend. He had taken time to show Derek the ropes, to make sure nobody took advantage.

He had probably seen something in the younger man's face, something he recognised from long ago perhaps: some sadness, some notion of loss. Derek was always checking himself, hoping his face wasn't giving him away when men like Peter did or said something cruel, or someone in the canteen told a story about an accident that had happened down at the coke ovens or by-products and he felt that shimmer of fear running through his body, a bright shiver of horror, touched with a sympathy for the wounded man that he knew he had to keep hidden. Still, he was surprised at how quickly he got used to the plug mill. It was the same routine every day: a few batches of tubes, the odd minor burn, Sammy coming by at break-times. Derek could never see the logic in this routine; the office had told him that he would get three breaks each shift, two of fifteen minutes, for a cup of tea, and one half-hour for lunch, but Sammy came round whenever he felt like it, and they walked out into the cool air, crossed the yards and sat down in the canteen for as long as Sammy saw fit to do, ten minutes on some breaks, half an hour or more on others. No matter how long it was, Sammy ate something every time, then smoked a cigarette, either at the table, or on the walk back to the plug mill. He would order bacon rolls, or a large bowl of chips, then smother everything in salt and brown sauce. He told Derek they had to eat a lot of salt, to replace what they lost in the heat. It wasn't that bad where they were, he said. The boys in the blast furnaces had it a lot worse. Some of them even ate the salt tablets that management handed out.

Derek had quickly fallen into a routine. He would get up just before five, have a cup of tea, then catch the bus from the stop opposite Beanfield shops. It was familiar to him, this morning ritual, like getting up for paper delivery all over again, getting dressed in the dark and moving about quietly, while the wind gusted around the house and everyone else lay sleeping. Sometimes Tommy would be on day shift and they would pass one another in the kitchen, or on the stairs, but they never stopped to talk. Tommy was like a ghost in the mornings, hardly present, almost insubstantial. Most days, though, Derek was alone. His father would still be out on night shift, or if he was on the two to ten later that day, he would still be asleep, snoring quietly behind the door that was always closed now. Derek knew his mother was in there, too, but Lizzie lay so still in her bed it was as if she wasn't quite there. In the other room, the room across the landing that stood separate from the others, Francis would be sleeping too, and Derek would always be aware of him, in his narrow bed, a taut, detectable presence, like a clock, or an idling machine. He felt an odd power, then, being up and about while his brother slept. He felt older and more mature, the one who had to go out into the dark while Francis lay dreaming, his face at rest, his body in repose, still and quiet. When he stepped outside Derek would stop a moment to feel the wind in his face, fresh and cold from a wider world, a clean wind from somewhere far away, from a country of ozone and rain and great trees beyond the vast blur of The Works.

At a few minutes to six, Derek would get off the bus and walk up to the gate in the early morning dark. He would pass through the damp yards under the murmuring white lights of the gantries, pass the welding sheds where men stood smoking and gazing out at the perimeter fencing, pass the showers, pass the accident boards where, every shift change, one of the supervisors came and read through the list of injuries – burns, lacerations, chemical spills, broken bones – before he copied them into an old-fashioned ledger and wiped the blackboard clean, ready for the next shift. The plug mill was one of the easiest jobs on Tubeside. After a couple of months, Derek was moved to the far end of the rack, where he had a hut for shelter, newspapers to read, and a comfortable chair to sit in. All he had to do was control the racks: keep the speed steady, stop them if anything went wrong, make sure every tube was straight in the teeth of the rack before it dropped off at the far end and on to the conveyor line. If a tube lay at an angle, he had to climb up on to the rack and set it right; one time he didn't notice that a long, narrow-bore tube was going through uneven until it hit the conveyor at the far end, one end dropping head first on to the wheels and bouncing fifteen or twenty feet into the air, in a shower of sparks and noise, almost hitting the roof of the shed before it came clattering down, just missing the hut where Derek sat reading the paper. Most of the time, though, he kept on top of things, dreaming his way through twelve-hour shifts, sitting alone in his dark hut, hunched over a music magazine or a crossword puzzle, only coming alive when he got a break and walked out into the big, empty yards, the second skin of heat that had formed on his chest and face dissolving in the cool air. First thing in the morning was his best time, especially as autumn drew in. It was almost worth being there in all the heat and noise, just to step out into the night, to walk the hundred yards to the canteen in the dark, small rain falling, or a light wind blowing in his face, the fire-glow up ahead seeming close at times, then receding, a chill fiery light on the sky and along the tracks that ran everywhere. One morning in late October, Sammy came by early, on his way to a break. As always, Derek joined him, leaving the hut to Peter, who just nodded, now, whenever he left his post. Sammy looked too bright, as if he were trying to hide some upset or hurt that he couldn't let anybody else know about.

Outside, the air was fresh and quiet, after the heat and noise of the plug mill. It had just rained, and everything was clothed in a silvery wet film under the overhead lamps. Sammy took a deep breath. The sky overhead was a milky blur, a few last stars glittering through wisps of cloud and smoke. Sammy looked up. 'Stars,' he said. 'Look.'

Derek craned his head back. He nodded. They had stopped walking, halfway across the yard. Suddenly, Sammy laid a hand on his arm. 'Close your eyes,' he said. 'Take a deep breath.'

Derek felt awkward, but he closed his eyes anyway. He didn't want to offend Sammy. Besides, there was a seriousness about his father's old friend, a sudden, strangely innocent seriousness that demanded respect.

'That's right,' Sammy continued. 'Take a deep breath. Now you can smell it. Taste it. You know, your sense of smell isn't independent of taste. It's all the same. Which means that what you are detecting now, by smell, by taste, is something you are taking in, the way you take in food, tasting it, absorbing it into your body. It's in your body now, becoming a part of you for all time, for your lifetime and beyond that. Even when you're in the ground, it's still there. If somebody digs you up, centuries from now, some archaeologist, say, he'll find it in whatever's left of the clothes you were buried in. He'll find it in your bones.' He laughed softly. Derek wondered what was going on. Sammy could talk, he knew that, but he was never serious like this. 'Everything you touch, every breath you take, the food you eat in the canteen, it's all tainted – and it's all becoming part of you. It's part of your blood, part of your nervous system. It's in the marrow of your bones. It's part of your thinking, part of your dreams. It's there – in all your senses – smell, taste, touch, hearing –'

Derek opened his eyes. Sammy was staring up at the sky, like Jesus in those catechism pictures of the Ascension, as if he was trying to figure out how to rise into the air, to rise above it all, to ascend through the haze of milky, roseate smoke into the stars. After a moment, he turned to Derek and shook his head. 'This is something I do every chance I get,' he said. 'I stop and remind myself of what it is I'm breathing. What it is I'm becoming. That clay smell, for example: that's iron ore.'

Derek nodded, but Sammy wasn't really talking to him now. Maybe this was something he had said before, to other men; maybe he was just giving voice to years of quiet, contained thought. He turned his head and scented the air like a dog. 'Smoke: yes. But you have to think about it. Because there are so many different kinds of smoke that, to live in a place like this, you need a whole new language for it, like all those words the Eskimos have for snow.' He smiled sadly. 'I'm getting old,' he said. 'I'm going a bit soft in the head. But I've been here since very nearly the beginning, and I say you have to keep reminding yourself of all this. You can't let yourself get used to it. Because that's what they want. They want you to get used to it. They want you to take it for granted. They want you to *be* that smell.' He turned back to the sky. Derek hadn't known what to say then, but it didn't matter, for Sammy had broken out of his trance and started walking again, towards the canteen. Now he was the same as before, remote, detached. 'Don't trust anybody here, son,' he said. 'Not management, that goes without saying. But not union, either. Don't trust anybody but yourself. You'll not go far wrong, if you remember that.'

Derek had no idea where this came from, but it was an ordinary pronouncement, something he'd heard from Tommy, and from some of the other men in the canteen. He nodded. He didn't know if he agreed with what Sammy was saying, any more than he could agree when the other men said that what the country needed was another war, or National Service, or the birch. It was talk, something done to pass the time. As they stood at the counter, Sammy engaging the canteen assistants in the routine banter that Derek always found so embarrassing, he studied the man that he'd come to think of as something like a friend. He had felt privileged at first, to be singled out by the older man, but he was worried too. He didn't really want friends. Not here. He had his music, he had his plans. All he wanted from work was enough money to get away, to buy a new bass and make a clean start somewhere. He wasn't going to be contaminated by all this, not like Sammy, or Peter. He wouldn't stay at the plug mill for ever. It was only a means to an end. Still, he would never have said such a thing to those men. They might hate The Works, they might feel soiled by the smoke and dirt, but they were proud of what they were. Mostly what they hated was being told what to do by the foremen, and the way management was always cutting corners to save money. They didn't really dislike the work, though. It was what they did. They were steelmakers and that was an honourable trade. Derek knew that if he let them see, even for a moment, how much he dreaded being caught up in their life, they would have hated him for it.

Most of all, that life was a story these men enjoyed telling. They talked about terrible accidents that had happened in the past, repeating the details with grim relish and unmistakable pride. Sammy's favourite was the one about the father and son, working together in the blast furnace. It was something that was supposed to have happened years ago: the man had got his son a job, and it was the boy's first day; they were working together, when the son had got caught up in a bogey, or maybe he had tripped, but somehow he had ended up falling into the furnace. In a last effort to save himself, he'd grabbed hold of a safety bar, but his lower body was already being consumed by the intense heat, and his hands were holding on in a mere reflex. His father, who had turned away for a moment, had looked back then, and seen what was happening; without a word, and without a moment's hesitation, he had pushed what remained of his son's body into the fire. The reason, as Sammy explained, grimly, was that he didn't want his wife to see her son's body all burned up like that. Better to see nothing; better to think only of ashes.

When the men weren't telling stories – most of which seemed

highly unlikely to Derek, though real horrors happened every month or so, somewhere in The Works – when they weren't repeating the myths they had grown up with, they would sit in the canteen and argue about the worst place to work. Every man had his own idea of where it was: some said the coke ovens, others the blast furnace; Sammy thought it was by-products, because that was where all the poisons were gathered into one place. For Derek, it was an image he had formed of the soaking pits, a place he dreaded, even though he'd never seen it, and didn't even know what was done there. It was the soaking pits he dreamed about, on those rare nights when he did dream. He would be standing by a fiery trench, the length and width of a new grave, and someone would come up behind to push him in. He didn't know who that person was, he never saw a face, never heard a thing. There had been one night, though, when he'd caught a glimpse – or not even a glimpse, just a hint, a suspicion of who it was behind him. He couldn't believe it. If it had been Sammy, or Peter, or one of the other men, he wouldn't have been surprised. He wouldn't even have been upset if it had been Tommy. But the face he saw, or rather didn't see, the cold half-smile he conjured from the last wisp of a nightmare, had nothing to do with The Works, and was the one person in the world he wanted to trust. It was his brother, Francis.

As children, he and Francis had been close, two brothers against the world, known to one another, one flesh, one blood. Derek felt sure that this was so, but he couldn't remember when that time had been, or exactly when it had ended. As children, they had been so similar. Francis was big for his age, so that, even though he was two years younger, he always matched Derek for height and weight, and because Lizzie dressed them in near-identical clothes, strangers would sometimes take them for twins. Derek had imagined he was proud of that. At the same time, though, he had always felt less important than Francis, less noticed. Because they were always together, and seemed so close, people back home in Scotland had treated them as a single unit. When their parents' friends, or the teachers in school, spoke about them, they never referred to them by name; for the whole town, they were 'the Cameron boys'. Yet, on the street, when people said hello, or asked how their mother was, it was Francis they spoke to directly, even though Derek was the oldest. They were talking to them both, of course, but it was Francis they looked at, and it was Francis who replied, polite and seemingly interested, saving that little look of his, that superior, mocking smile, till the people were gone.

Not only did they dress the same, they also had their hair cut in exactly the same style. When they were children, Lizzie would give them some money and send them off to the barber's together. The barber was an old man with a grizzled face and thin grey hair. His name was Frank Peebles, and he was a friend of Tommy's from the pub; sometimes he would do their hair on the cheap and they got to keep whatever money was left over from what Lizzie had given them. They had exactly the same haircut, every time: short at the sides, square at the back, a little longer on top. For Derek, this monthly ritual was one of life's best pleasures: he liked watching Francis in the barber's chair, liked the way old Mr Peebles draped the bright blue nylon sheet around him, tucking it in neatly, with a little towel at the neck to keep his collar clean. When his brother sat down in the chair, Derek would glance at him through the mirror and imagine there were not just two, but four of them, and Francis would look back at him through the mirror and flash him that little smile he had, that half-mocking smile that made everything seem like a game, something from which they both stood apart, like strangers from some far-off, superior civilisation. That was what drew people to him, Derek thought, that smile. He made everything look easy and pleasurable and faintly ridiculous, even school, even going for a haircut.

Francis always went first at Mr Peebles's. While he was being shorn, Derek would sit off to one side, and watch as his brother was transformed. Any variation in their matched lives, even a difference so slight as an inch or so of hair, was new and curious to them both. When it was his turn, Derek loved sitting in the chair his brother had just vacated. He loved the feel of the nylon sheet billowing out, then settling around him. It was like crossing to another world: under that sheet he was mysterious and inde-terminate, suddenly capable of transformation, or gifted with the power to vanish at will. Quietly, systematically, Mr Peebles would go to work, first with the clippers, then with scissors, shaving and snipping, paring him down to the bone. It didn't matter that a thin layer of skin covered his skull: he was beyond flesh, and his face became lean and pure as the old man worked, like the faces of the saints in church. It always surprised him when he saw pictures of Jesus, with his long, floating hair and soft features. To Derek, Jesus was hard and clean, his hair neat and stubbly, as if someone had just run a Number 4 clipper over his head.

Then, one day, he had changed his mind. Suddenly, he didn't want that neat hairstyle any more, and he didn't want to look like Francis. He wanted to be different. It had started with something they'd seen on television. To begin with, Lizzie had been suspicious of television, but after a while she had relented, and Tommy had got one on the cheap from a friend of his who worked in an electrical goods shop. For the first year or so, Lizzie been strict about their viewing habits. They weren't allowed to watch it on weekdays, but on Sunday afternoons the whole family would sit through the film matinees – Hollywood classics, like *Meet Me in St Louis*, with Judy Garland, or Spencer Tracy in *Fury*. They watched every week for several months, not so much interested in the stories as in the sense it gave them of America; over the weeks, the stories shifted and melted together, running from film to film, sending Joan Fontaine out into a world feathered with new, cinematic snow, haunted by Rebecca, pursued by Orson Welles, or dying of some clean, subliminal disease under the patient gaze of nuns.

One afternoon, they watched *Samson and Delilah*, and Derek remembered how much he wanted to experience the soft tug of the blade in his hair when Hedy Lamarr stole in upon the sleeping Samson. He wasn't really sure why she was cutting Samson's hair, and he had a vague sense of the absurd theatricality of it all, yet he was immersed, utterly, in the naked beauty of the moment: the ghost of something soft, something Babylonian, rising to the surface of his skin, his body suddenly smudged with a dark sweetness, a blur of warmth and myrrh on his lips, like the bloom on a plum. He glanced over at Francis and saw that his brother was watching him. Neither of them said anything, Francis just flashed that faintly mocking smile of his and turned back to the screen, but Derek knew he had *noticed* something. He had seen through him, and, for the first time, Derek understood that his brother saw everything, even what he was thinking, even his dreams.

The next time they had gone to the barber's, as soon as Francis stepped down from the chair, Derek had asked Mr Peebles to cut his hair really short, to set the clippers to Number 2. At first, the old man had refused, and Francis had stood to one side, watching the two of them with a curious, kindly expression, as if he knew what was going on, and wanted his brother to understand that none of this was necessary. Finally, Mr Peebles had agreed to give Derek a crew cut, running the clippers quickly over his head, as if he wanted to have the work over with, to send Derek away as soon as possible. Francis watched the entire operation without comment but when Derek stepped down from the chair, he reached out and ran his palm across his brother's newly shaven head. 'It feels surprisingly soft,' he said, in a mock television advert voice, as Mr Peebles handed Derek a towel and turned away, busying himself with his instruments.

Derek nodded. He felt like Samson in reverse, as if the crew cut had revealed something unsuspected, some hidden potential that he hadn't known was there. It wasn't till they were about to leave, as he was paying Mr Peebles the money Lizzie had given him, that Derek caught sight of them both in the mirror and, suddenly, for the first time that he could remember, he saw that they looked altogether different, like two ordinary boys who happened to be in the barber's at the same time, going about their business; unique, dissimilar, free.

Now, though, he felt that that moment had been the beginning of something – something he himself had started unintentionally. Not long after that haircut – which had horrified his mother – Tommy had got the job in Corby and had gone south on his own, to stay in the Church Army for a few weeks till he could get them a house. Neither Derek nor Francis knew where Corby was, all they knew for sure was that they didn't want to go, they wanted to stay home, to continue with the life they knew. Derek was pretty sure his mother didn't want to move either, but when he asked her about it, she had said it was a good chance at a fresh start, and they'd have a nice house, with new things. Corby was a new town, she said, and there were plenty of opportunities. Derek didn't understand what that meant – and he was even more mystified when Tommy sent them word that he had a house, and they all travelled south on the train, going with nothing but a couple of suitcases and an empty birdcage. The bird had died a few weeks before, but Tommy had said to bring the cage anyway, they would get another bird as soon as they settled in. On the train, it was Derek's job to carry the cage, and he sat for hours, all the way south, in the lingering smell of lime and millet, as if he were carrying the ghost of the dead budgerigar.

Corby had been a shock. It wasn't like anything he had expected, and the first thing he was aware of was the smell and the dirt from The Works, even though the house they'd been given was on the far side of town, not far from Kingswood, with its open woods and its avenue of sequoia trees left over from some estate that had been there years ago. By the time they were ready to go, Francis had convinced himself he was excited about the idea of moving to England; as soon as he saw Corby, however, he hated it — and he made it clear that he blamed his parents for bringing him there. He started to refer to Tommy and Lizzie by their first names, but there was no affection in it: it was as if he was referring to people he had read about in a book, or seen on a television programme, people he found it mildly interesting to observe, but for whom he had no particular emotions. When Lizzie first got ill, he was helpful around the house, but he never brought her flowers or little presents the way Derek did, not even on Mother's Day, or her birthday. Meanwhile, Tommy seemed lost, bewildered by the realisation that nobody else was happy, after he'd gone to such lengths to start a new life. Tommy liked Corby: to him, Derek thought, it was good money and a new start, but it was also something else, something to do with a myth of comradeship. The men at The Works were hard and sure of themselves, partly because they lived with danger, but there was also the history of the place, a history you walked into on your first day, a group memory of the furnaces and the cauterised dead, memories sweetened by drink and the long hours of night shift. Or so Derek thought. As far as Francis was concerned, the whole move was a mistake, and it was a mistake Tommy had made, because he was stupid. Derek remembered their first day, walking around the empty house in Handcross Court, Lizzie stopping in each room to glance out at the garden, or the grassy square outside the front door, as if she was waiting for something else to happen, something that would make this building home. Their life in Scotland had been the prefab; it had been filling the heater with paraffin and sitting close to get warm; it had been the woods, the football pitch, the walk to school, the stone angels in the graveyard on the Old Perth Road, quizzical and bright, with silver on their skins, like the people in early photographs. Corby was just smoke and grime, even if they did have a garden with a high wall all around it and a proper bathroom with an immersion heater. Tommy must have thought they would all be happy here: the boys could have a bedroom of their own, and he had saved money, working doubles and Sundays, to buy all new furniture and a good cooker for Lizzie. He couldn't understand why they hated it so much.

Derek disliked Corby, but he tried not to let it show. He helped Tommy in the garden on his days off: Tommy had a job in by-products now, and he would bring home bags of urea, which was supposed to be a great fertiliser. That first year, they dug the whole garden over, two long beds of rich-looking, brown soil, then they spread it all carefully with the urea, making sure it was applied evenly throughout and digging it in, a spitful at a time. Tommy explained to Derek how you had to let it sit a while, so it would be absorbed into the soil before you planted – but that while turned into a year, and Tommy didn't plant anything, he just let the earth soften and crumble in the rain, two long beds of fallow ground, empty and brown for a while, then etched over with weeds and grass till they went out and dug it again, and applied another few bags of urea. So it went, year after year, and Tommy would always talk about what he would plant when he got enough time to do it properly. For Derek, that garden summed up everything about their lives: the plans, the promises, the waste. Francis thought it was funny.

'Why do you bother?' he would say, when Derek came in from the garden, his hands caked with loam. 'He's never going to plant anything.'

'He's doing his best,' Derek would reply. 'It's not as if he's got much time.'

'I know he is,' Francis said. 'That's the point, isn't it?'

'What does that mean?'

But Francis didn't answer. He just turned back and stared at the garden, where Tommy was finishing up, scraping mud off a spade, looking lonely and old all of a sudden, the way men do sometimes when they are working alone, out in the open. Derek had always thought of this work – digging, turning the soil – as honest, even dignified; seeing that look on Francis's face, though, he suddenly felt sorry for Tommy, and for himself, as if the two of them – father and son – had allowed themselves to be deceived in some way that only Francis could understand.

He had lived in Scotland for nigh on twelve years and now he remembered almost nothing. He had fragments of streets and a dark pithead in his mind, pictures from the outlying fields and the old water-house where he had been told not to go and to which he went all the time. There had never been much to do there, but it had a vague atmosphere of danger that drew him in. There were names in his head, memories of school Communion breakfasts, snatches of conversation overheard outside Mass on Sunday mornings. There had been a cinema, a Woolworth's, a bakery with sweaty-looking cakes in the window. There had been a butcher's shop with sides of meat on hooks all along one wall, the last blood dripping slowly on to the coarse, pine-scented sawdust. That was his clearest memory of home, that butcher's shop. It had been his favourite stop when he went shopping with Lizzie: as soon as they walked into the shop, he would see four or five carcasses, sometimes more, hanging on a rail by the far wall, the meat a dark crimson, bruised here and there to oxblood red, the fat smooth and sculpted around it, like a sheath of wax. For as long as he could remember, he had been fascinated by the slow fall of the blood dripping into the sawdust from the severed necks and thighs, just as he had always loved standing outside the fishmonger's shop, gazing at the brindled skins of herring and mackerel through the constant stream of water that flowed down the window to keep the produce cool. He wanted to see through those blank, button-shaped eyes, to know what the fish knew in the sea; in the butcher's shop, he wanted to hold his hand out, palm upwards, under the slow drip of old blood, to know what it felt like, if it was cold, or still warm, if it was thicker than water, the way people always said it was. Most of all, he liked the smell of the meat. It was a comfort to know that death smelled like flesh, an antidote to the priest at Mass talking about ashes, and how everyone who lived would return to dust. On Ash Wednesday, the priest would anoint Derek's head with the oil and ashes, and he would walk back to his place among the others with what he thought was a solemn look on his face. As soon as he was away from the church he would wipe away the mark, even though the teachers said he had to leave it untouched until it came off of its own accord. It was a sin, they said, to wipe it off, and they always questioned him when the ashes disappeared mysteriously an hour after Mass. Derek couldn't tell them that he didn't want essences; he couldn't say that what he wanted was substance, not ashes and scented oils and the promise of the soul. He preferred the magnetic quality of the meat hanging on those hooks to incense and holy oils and the body of Christ reduced to a thin wafer stuck to the roof of his mouth and melting away, leaving that sickly, unleavened taste that lasted for hours.

He liked the butcher's. He wanted his mother to buy the beautiful, marbled steaks, the pink cuts of pork loin, the dainty medallions of lamb – but she never did. Usually she bought bacon, or sausages; sometimes she bought scrag-end, but she seemed not to notice the better meat that Derek found so inviting, so rich and sweet and red, laid out on the marble slabs. It seemed perverse to him, this insistence on offal and offcuts, he didn't understand her choices as having anything to do with money. He remembered her standing at the counter one time, asking if they had any scraps for the dog, and he had been surprised, because there was no dog, just a goldfish he had won at the fair. He could see her, in the dark blue coat and headscarf she always wore, not looking at the cutlets and sides of sirloin – but it was more a picture than recollection. But then, that was how it was with everything he remembered. Even when there were details he was sure of – the smell of daffodils in the church at Easter, the smell of blood or fish in shop doorways – it was never real enough, never quite finished. It was as if he were picturing a life that had been described to him by someone who had been there, but no matter how detailed these pictures were, they were never quite real, never quite in focus. And he himself was never quite there.

He could see his mother, he could see Francis. He could see his Gran and Uncle Tam. But he could never see himself.

Lizzie was always talking about Scotland, about going back some day when they had made a bit of money and were ready to retire. Every summer, she would ask Tommy if he wanted to go home for the holidays, but he always managed to avoid it. Or almost always – there had been one trip north when his Gran was sick, about five years ago. It was in the middle of the summer, so they had gone as a family, travelling overnight on the coach and arriving in Edinburgh sleepless, grimy and stale from the crowded bus. Derek was fifteen. He had been away for almost four years, and already he couldn't remember his Gran, or anything about Cowdenbeath. He couldn't remember what the High Street looked like, or his old school, or any of his friends. He had a vague memory of the prefab, and the garden where he'd played with Francis in what seemed like another time, another world – but when they went to visit his grandmother he thought they had got the wrong house, because he was sure he had never seen the place before. They had knocked at the door, all of them standing there in their Sunday clothes, Tommy uncomfortable and vague, Lizzie pale from the illness she was already trying to conceal, Derek fidgety and nervous in his uncomfortable shoes. Only Francis seemed relaxed. When the door opened and their Aunt Eleanor had shown them in, with the dark courtesy that descends upon the houses of the dying, Francis had stood in the hall while the adults spoke in whispers, looking around, taking it all in. After a moment, it was decided that Tommy and Lizzie would go up to the bedroom for a short visit, while the boys waited downstairs. Eleanor didn't think their gran could take too many visitors at one time.

As soon as the others had gone, and the brothers were alone in the front room, Francis turned to Derek with that cold, mocking look on his face. 'Smell that,' he said. 'Isn't that amazing?'

'What?' Derek couldn't smell anything.

'Can't you smell it?'

'What am I supposed to be –'

'Wool. Soap. Aniseed. Damp newspapers.' Francis paused for a moment, testing the air, considering. 'Firelighters. Dog. Some kind of sweet cake. Dundee cake, maybe.'

'It's a bit musty,' Derek said.

'It's not just musty.' Francis smiled grimly. 'It's somebody dying. It's the whole history of someone's life, frittering away on the air.'

It was true. Derek hadn't guessed before, but as soon as Francis said it, he knew their grandmother was dying in the upstairs room where Tommy and Lizzie were no doubt standing at that very instant, awkward and upset, trying to think of something to say. Derek was appalled at how calmly Francis had described the thing, how utterly remote he was from their pain. The way he talked was the way people talked in books or television documentaries, his curiosity abstract and sociological, without a hint of feeling.

'It's funny', Francis continued, 'how your own house doesn't smell of anything much. Or not to you, anyway. Other people's houses smell so different. So − rich.' He looked around appreciatively.

'Our house has its own smell,' Derek said.

'Does it?' Francis looked at him. He seemed amused. 'What's that, then?'

'It's lots of things,' Derek said, defensively. He didn't know why they were having this conversation, or why he felt he was somehow defending his grandmother from some unspecified criticism. 'Baking. Food. That kind of thing −'

'Well, yes,' Francis said. 'But that could be anything. And it's temporary. This is permanent. Even when she's gone, this smell will be there long after.'

Derek lifted his hands to his face. He couldn't listen to any more of this rubbish. Their grandmother was dying, and Francis was talking about smells.

'What?' Francis looked innocent. 'What's wrong?'

Derek shook his head. He wanted to cry. 'I don't understand you,' he said. 'I mean − don't you even care? If you're so sure she's dying −'

Francis's expression didn't change. He just sat there, watching, taking it all in − and it struck Derek that everything was interesting to him, so nothing really mattered. He didn't care about anything. He never had. 'I know she's dying,' he said finally. 'I can't change that.'

'I didn't say you could,' Derek said. 'But you could at least pretend.'

'I'm not going to pretend anything,' Francis said. 'I'm just different from you, that's all.' He stood up and walked to the foot of the stairs. Nobody had lived up there for years, not since their grandfather had died. Until she had fallen ill, Gran had spent her whole life in the kitchen, sitting in her big chair by the stove, day and night, drifting from sleep to waking, from waking to sleep. Derek couldn't understand why his aunts and uncles had let it go on. 'You've never really understood, have you?' Francis continued. 'You think everybody's the same.'

'No I don't.' Derek was hurt.

'Ah, but you do. You even think we're the same. And we couldn't be more different.' Francis gave Derek a sweet, understanding smile. 'I don't really belong to this family,' he said. 'I'm not like you. I'm not saying I'm better, or special, or anything. I just accept the truth. We're different, we always have been. Lizzie used to dress us up in the same clothes, give us the same toys for Christmas, all that, to try and make us look like brothers. But it didn't work. I'm nobody's brother. And I'm nobody's son.' He was still standing at the foot of the stairs, looking up, listening. 'You want me to pretend,' he said. 'But I can't.' He looked at Derek. 'I don't feel anything. I don't even know what it is I'm supposed to be feeling.' Somebody moved upstairs and he walked back into the front room quickly and sat down.

'I don't believe you,' Derek said. He couldn't think of anything else to say.

Francis smiled and shook his head. 'Too bad,' he said.

A moment afterwards, Lizzie came into the room and said their gran was too tired to see them and they would have to come back later. Derek couldn't help feeling relieved, but at least he managed not to let it show. When he glanced across at Francis, however, the look on his brother's face was unmistakable, and he knew Lizzie would have seen it too. It was a look of indifference, not relief, not satisfaction. He had probably been quite prepared to go upstairs, but it didn't matter much one way or the other. He didn't care. His whole manner was calculated to make that clear. He didn't care. He had never cared. He never would care. He was a stranger to them, mildly interested, but with other, more important things to consider.

A few days later, their gran had died. Tommy had been keen to get home to Corby, but they had stayed for the funeral. After that, they hadn't gone back. Not that it mattered. Now that he had been there, Derek didn't miss Scotland any more. He'd thought he did, when they first moved, because that was what you were supposed to do: you had left something behind, and you were supposed to miss it, because that was where you came from, that was where you belonged. Derek didn't miss Scotland, because he didn't know what Scotland was. The mythology said it was the *Sunday Post*. The White Heather Club. The Highlands. Shortbread. But they never had shortbread at home, not in Scotland, and not here, except at Hogmanay when everybody turned into cartoon Highlanders, wandering the glassy streets with coal and bread in their coat pockets, leaving their doors open so anybody could walk in, as tradition demanded. Men they barely knew would come to the door with whisky and salt; fussy, unhappy women would gather in the kitchen with his mother, sniffing at their glasses of advocaat and munching Dundee cake. There would be shortbread then – and there would be Jimmie Shand, The Alexander Brothers, Moira Anderson, Andy Stewart singing 'Donald Whaur's Yer Troosers?' and all the men joining in, cheery for a while in the first flush, before the drink really set in.

Scotland was a myth. Burns suppers, tartan, Bonnie Prince Charlie, knowing what clan you were supposed to be in, it was all a bad myth. But then, that was all they wanted. Bill McInnes, their usual first foot, wandering in to sing 'Wooden Heart' to Lizzie in the kitchen while Tommy stood by, embarrassed, almost smiling; Jim and Annie Lavin, with their however many children tagging along behind clutching grubby shortbread fingers and trying to steal sips of whisky from the abandoned glasses that littered the sideboard and mantelpiece; sullen, good-natured Mull, always on his own, never quite as drunk as he pretended, nipping round in his cardigan and slippers, his eyes dark and still, like two chips of granite. None of these people came from Scotland – or not from the Scotland you saw on television or read about in the *Sunday Post* – but they were all going back there to retire and die: back to the hills and the summer rain, back to haggis and shortbread and finnan-haddie, back to Robert the Bruce and Bonnie Prince Charlie and Harry Lauder.

Derek wondered why they talked about going home all the time when it was no different from where they were now. And then it struck him. They didn't want to go back to what they had left, because what they had left wasn't much different from what they had here. They wanted to go back to an invented place: they wanted to go home, but there was no such place as home. The only home they could have had was where they were now. They were no different from him, Derek realised. They didn't remember Scotland any more than he did, but then they didn't want to remember. Whenever anybody went back for the summer holiday, they would be based in Lochgelly, or Paisley, or Dundee, staying with family, probably, because it was cheaper, but they spent their days out in Crieff and Crianlarich, or on the roads between. They visited Edinburgh Castle and thought about Rob Roy; they took walks by the shores of windy lochs, or trudged up the Birks of Aberfeldy in damp raincoats and plastic head-scarves, breathing the clean country air and working out how long it would be before the pubs were open.

They didn't want home, they wanted the same Scotland the tourists got. Scotland might have been home once, but it had never been the home they talked about now, it had just been estates and steelworks and poky wee shops and pubs that looked like outsized Anderson shelters with grilles on the windows and grey, shamefaced men gathering around the doors at six o'clock, waiting for opening time. They pretended there was something back home – wherever home might be – that was better than what they had here, but Derek knew, just as they did, that home was coal and shipyards and steel, and the mythical communities they dreamed about were just estates and tenements, no better or worse than the Beanfield, as bad mostly, as the Exeter, where dogs roamed wild and the one pub was nicknamed the Bucket of Blood. There was nothing here that they hadn't brought with them, these misty-eyed Scots and Irish and Poles: the home they talked about so fondly was a lie, and they knew it.

Francis was different. He hated Corby, he had hated it from the first day, but that didn't mean he had any nostalgia for some mythical home ground. He was smarter than that – and there were times when Derek suspected that it was the strength of his hatred, of his anger at having come here, that made him so. His cruelty took different forms, but Derek felt it most in the distance Francis put between himself and his family, the seeming indifference he displayed towards what his mother called kith and kin. When he'd said they were different, Derek had known it was true, of course. But he also knew that they were brothers, they had grown up together, and neither of them knew any other life than the life they had shared. That was what bothered Derek most, that Francis seemed to believe that this life, the only life they had, had never happened, that he had somehow been living a parallel existence all along. He didn't want to be close, nothing like that; he just wanted Francis to recognise that they had stuff in common, that they had grown up thinking the same things, talking to one another, watching the same films and reading the same comics. He wanted Francis not to pretend that they had never sat together after Mass in the little classroom at St Bride's, eating the packed breakfasts their mother had made early that morning, in the prefab's icy kitchen. He wanted Francis to remember the time they had persuaded Alice Dow to take off her knickers and show herself, to remember that miraculous nakedness, the same, smooth, unfledged nakedness of baby mice, and how, even then, they had both guessed, without saying anything, that there should be something else, something softer, not hair exactly, not even fur, like the fur of an animal, but something warmer and more vivid. It was something they shared, this knowledge, the way they shared the same vocabulary, taking to school the words they had learned each week when Tommy brought home the Sunday papers, and they had read them together, the boys leaning over Tommy's chair on a Sunday morning, and saying the words aloud, with occasional corrections or explanations when they came across a new word, or a difficult sentence. Tommy would buy the *Sunday Post* and the old *Record*, with their quirky snippets of local news, or those mystery stories they ran in series like *Stranger than Fiction*. Reading those accounts of mysterious events – like the trail of devil's footprints through the snow in a Cornish town, or the boy who was snatched by a giant bird and carried away, somewhere up north – Derek realised the world was a dangerous place, but there was a beauty in the danger. The world was threatening, dark, even murderous, but it was only the kind of danger you saw at the pictures. That was the world they inhabited. He wanted Francis to come back to that world because, without his brother, Derek wasn't sure he could believe in it – or not altogether. He needed Francis to remember it all: Saturday matinees and first puffs on cigarettes and the way they had surprised themselves the first time they swore; girls they had liked and boys they had fought with; the smell of the prefab; the smell of the hallways at St Bride's. But Francis denied it all. He seemed genuinely to remember nothing, when Derek reminded him of things that had happened years ago, in Cowdenbeath, or when they first came to Corby. It was as if Francis had no past, as if he was frozen in the present.

Derek knew Francis was taking drugs, dope for sure, acid probably, he wasn't sure what else. The trouble with his brother was that he was one of those clever people who thinks everybody else is stupid; he was too full of himself to be careful. There had been times when he'd sat down to dinner stoned – though never when Tommy was there – or he would sit watching *Top of the Pops*, while Lizzie sat knitting in her chair by the fire, and he would be out of his head, giggling and muttering to himself, while Lizzie kept her head down, or sat tutting quietly whenever a singer she particularly disliked appeared. She hated The Rolling Stones most of all, especially Mick Jagger, but she was pretty indiscriminate in her condemnation of anyone who struck her as funny-looking. Years before, she had taken an instant dislike to Donovan, so Francis would pretend 'Universal Soldier' was his favourite song of all time; whenever he wanted to get a rise out of her, he would break into a chorus of 'Hurdy Gurdy Man', or 'Catch the Wind'. Lizzie fell for it every time. Derek didn't have the heart to tell her that Francis couldn't stand Donovan: if she had known what her sons really listened to when they were shut away in their rooms she would have been round to the presbytery like a shot, begging Cash Cromwell to come and perform an exorcism, or some such thing.

Derek had been alone for an hour or more, and was beginning to wonder where Tommy and Francis were, when he heard the door. He decided to ignore it; then he wondered if he'd missed something. Maybe he was supposed to be at the hospital. Maybe Tommy had said something, and Derek had forgotten the day, or the time, and, even though he had no memory of anyone saying anything, he went to the window and pulled back the curtain an inch, to see who it was. If his father and Francis had gone for a pre-Christmas visit, expecting him to turn up in the waiting-room with a present or one of those poisonous-looking poinsettia plants that everybody was buying, Tommy would have sent Francis to phone old man MacColl next door – Tommy wouldn't have a phone in the house; he wouldn't even use one, if he could possibly avoid it, nobody knew why. Since Lizzie had gone into the General this time, Tommy had travelled over every second day or so, but Derek thought they were supposed to go as a family, for a kind of substitute family celebration, on Christmas Day. He wasn't looking forward to that: Tommy and Lizzie were so awkward together now, and the fact that they always did as much as they thought was needed to seem like the usual happily married couple only made it more obvious that whatever there once was between them – love, affection, some kind of basic respect – had died long ago.

It wasn't Mr MacColl, though; it was Alina Ruckert. She was standing on the doorstep, in her padded Chinese-style jacket, looking up at Francis's window and knocking the snow off her boots. Derek went out into the hall and opened the door.

'Hi.' Alina smiled. They had been in the same class at school till they were sixteen, and Derek had always liked her – though that sounded so banal, like 'fancying' somebody, or thinking they were nice-looking. Derek didn't think Alina was nice-looking and, if he thought about it, he didn't really fancy her. If he could have described what he felt, he would have said that he thought she was beautiful – but nobody ever said, about a girl, that she was beautiful, because it sounded stupid. You could talk about a beautiful day, or a beautiful goal, but never a beautiful girl. Maybe that was why he had never dared to ask her out: it wasn't fear or shyness that held him back, it was a kind of reverence. Besides, Alina was one of those girls who made it clear they were not available. Even though she always made a point of being polite, even though she could be kind, she was surrounded by an aura of remoteness, set apart from other girls in his class who were so obviously concerned with how they looked, or what people thought of them. Alina always looked good, but she didn't seem to care if anybody noticed. She was also the only girl he knew who went around on her own. It was something Derek had noticed, perhaps because he was so shy: you hardly ever saw a girl sitting off on her own, reading a book, or whatever, they always went about in twos or threes, and there was usually one who was prettier than the others. Being pretty was what mattered; it defined a girl. Even if the girl was clever, it was always how pretty she was that got her noticed. How pretty, and how popular – but Alina didn't seem to care how popular she was. In fact, she didn't seem to care about anything that girls were supposed to care about. She lived at a distance that had always seemed to Derek impossible to cross, but that wasn't the only reason he felt so diffident on the handful of occasions he'd been obliged to be in her company – and because he had harboured this reverence for her for so long, it had upset him terribly when he'd learned, a couple of months back, that Francis and Alina were going out. It was bad enough that he'd liked Alina so much all these years, but it was humiliating to discover that his ideal girl was going out with his younger brother.

'Is Francis in?'

Derek shook his head. Alina smiled again, and he realised he was being rude. 'Come in,' he said. 'You must be freezing.'

'It's all right,' she said. She looked cold, but there was something else too – an unease, the too-ready smile a cover for whatever it was that was bothering her. She looked pale and tired, and Derek wondered if Francis had given her something when they had been out the day before – dope, maybe, or acid.

'He should be back soon,' he said. 'You can wait where it's warm.'

'OK.' She stamped her boots one last time and stepped across the threshold. Derek caught a thin trace of perfume through the cold ozone smell of the snow on her hair, and stepped back while she shrugged off her coat.

'I was just about to put the kettle on,' he said, aware of how like Lizzie he sounded. 'Would you like some coffee? Or tea?' He watched as Alina hung the jacket up on the hall coatrack, more at home in his house than he would have expected.

'I don't want to put you to any trouble,' Alina said.

'It's no trouble.'

'All right.' She nodded. 'Tea would be nice.'

Derek had decided, when he heard Francis was going out with Alina, that it had something to do with his being friends with her younger brother. Where Alina was remote, but mostly well-enough liked, Jan was strange. Nobody in school could make him out and he was generally, if not disliked, then treated with suspicion, even by the teachers. It was as if some strange creature had wandered into their midst and stood there, observing them all with a kindly yet somewhat bemused curiosity – and it was this curiosity, this fact of his watching them, that made them uncomfortable, as if they saw themselves in this watching and realised, even though Jan never commented or made judgments about what he saw, how absurd they were. Without ever doing anything deliberately to offend anyone, Jan was marked out as someone to avoid, a stranger in their midst, remote, unnatural, one of the weirdos. Not that Jan gave a damn. He kept himself to himself, you had to say that much for him. Still, Alina must have been grateful to Francis when he took her baby brother under his wing. It was odd to everyone else, seeing the two of them together, but nobody said anything. If you were friends with someone that nobody else liked, it usually made you unpopular by association – but Francis was exempted from this rule. It was accepted that his friendship with Jan was just another facet of Francis's unpredictable, but essentially likeable, personality. Everyone believed he had made friends with Jan from kindness. Maybe it was this suspicion that made him so fiercely loyal – whatever it was, no one could say a word against Jan in his presence.

Which was how the feud with the Niven brothers had started. The Nivens were a pair of hard nuts from the G-stream with half a dozen brain cells between them, but they saw themselves as something, with their StaPrest and Doc Martens, their Crombie coats and skinhead haircuts, stomping around the school like a couple of storm troopers, trying to act big. They were pretty generally despised, but when they attracted a couple of the other brain-dead to be in their little gang, most people started giving them a wide berth – something the Nivens mistook for respect. Derek figured the illusion of power had gone to their heads, but he didn't think much about people like the Nivens unless he had to – and he didn't have to until the wet December day in his last year of school when Mickey Davidson found him in the corridor and said he'd better go outside, because his brother was killing Stewart Niven in the playground. By the time Derek got there, the action was over: one of the Nivens was on the ground – Derek could never tell them apart, though one was a year older: they just looked like skinheads the way all skinheads just looked like skinheads – and Francis was standing off to one side, listening, or pretending to listen, to Mr Harris, the metalwork teacher, who had obviously just intervened to stop the fight. The Niven boy's face was bloody, and he wasn't moving, just lying there, as if stunned. Derek found out later that Francis had smashed Niven's head against a brick wall several times after he was down; kids were saying if Harris hadn't turned up, Francis would probably have killed the boy. Now Harris was talking to Francis very calmly and quietly, but with that edge to his voice that made it clear where he stood. Harris was a big man who had been in the Royal Navy for years; these days, he was the one other teachers called on if a particularly vigorous caning was to be administered. At the very mention of his name, some of the younger boys would fall silent with awe and the fear that most teachers would have mistaken for respect, but Harris didn't seem to like his reputation much, and Derek had an impression that he was really quite a decent bloke, underneath.

It was probably Harris who kept Francis from being expelled. He was the one who listened to Francis's story and, though he made it clear he didn't condone fighting in the playground, he put the case for leniency to the headmaster, the demonic Mr Collings. It turned out that the Nivens, along with their little gang, had cornered Jan Ruckert in the playground and tried to cut his hair with a pair of kitchen scissors. The attack had been witnessed by around ten or fifteen boys: Jan hadn't tried to fight back, in fact, he'd put up no resistance at all, but somehow, as they were hacking off handfuls of Jan's thick, soot-coloured hair, one of the Nivens had cut his face slightly, and the sight of the wound had frightened the gang off, leaving Jan bloody but not particularly rattled. He'd stopped a moment to look at the boys who had been standing by, watching but doing nothing to help; then he'd headed for the boys' toilets, where he'd used a handful of paper towels to stop the bleeding. Later, thinking about it, Derek respected the boy for not wanting to make a fuss; at the time, though, he'd thought of the whole thing as a humiliation he would never have been able to bear, and he understood Francis's reaction, even if it was excessive.

In the end, Francis had been let off with a warning. Or at least, he'd been let off by the school; for the Niven gang it was a different matter. As time passed, they had become nastier and so more dangerous: Derek knew, because Tommy was always telling him, that the universal law when it came to men was that the people you had to fear were the stupid, the mean, the cowardly, the ones who had no self-respect, and so nothing to lose. The Nivens were the kind who would stab you in the back, or jump you when you were walking home late on your own; only a couple of months back, if you believed the rumours, the whole gang of them had got a greaser in a telephone box and tried to cut his fingers off with a pair of garden shears. According to the story Derek had heard, the only thing that had saved the boy was the fact that the shears were blunt, so all they did was saw away at the flesh, cutting as far as the white of the bone, but no further. Still, they had done quite a bit of damage. Why the whole gang of them hadn't come after Francis yet was a complete mystery to Derek. Maybe they were afraid of Tommy. Everybody Derek knew was afraid of his father.

Derek set about making tea while Alina waited in the front room. He wasn't sure if he was doing it right: he thought you were supposed to put one spoonful in for the pot, then another for each person, but that didn't seem a very reliable method and, after he'd waited for it to brew a while, then poured a cup to test it, what came out looked thin and watery. He didn't know, either, whether he was supposed to put the tea in a cup, with milk and sugar on the side, or if he should leave it in the pot, for her to pour. If he did that, he'd need a tray, and there wasn't one. He couldn't help thinking how much easier coffee was: you put a spoonful of it into nearly boiling water, then you drank it. No milk, no sugar. He'd learned to drink coffee from his big cousin Jackie back home; whenever he was asked how he liked it, Jackie, who was in the Merchant Navy, would call out, 'Strong and black, like my women.' He'd said it to Lizzie once and the whole house had fallen silent. Lizzie hadn't known where to look.

Finally, thoroughly confused, he'd popped his head into the

other room. 'How do you like it?' he'd asked, sure he was doing something wrong.

Alina was sitting on the sofa, staring at the fireplace. She looked really tired, but it was more than just fatigue. Something was bothering her. She glanced up at him. 'Milk,' she said. 'No sugar.' Derek couldn't help noting that this was how Francis always took his tea.

'OK,' he said. 'Coming up.' He winced. Every word just seemed to make things worse – but Alina hadn't even noticed. He doubted if she'd even heard him.

He went back into the kitchen and poured some tea into one of Lizzie's special bone-china floral cups. It was the service her mother had given her for a wedding present, and it only ever came out for proper visitors, like the priest, or family. The tea looked stronger this time, so he dashed in a little milk and carried it through, cup and saucer, thinking he ought to have had a plate of biscuits, the way Lizzie always did when she had people in.

'Here we are,' he said. He stood useless in the middle of the room a moment; then, when she didn't reach for the cup and saucer he was so obviously holding out for her, set them down on the low coffee table in front of the dead fireplace. It was too far away: that was obvious, but he didn't know what else to do. He looked at her. 'I'm sorry, we've got no biscuits,' he said. 'Mum's in hospital.'

Alina nodded. 'I know,' she said.

At exactly the same moment, when Derek – who had just said 'Mum' in front of her – was just about ready to flee into the kitchen and hide in the press, he heard a key in the front door and, a moment later, looking angry and wet from the melted snow on his hair, Francis appeared. He seemed surprised to see Alina.

'Hiya,' he said. He looked at Derek. 'Did you make tea?'
Derek nodded.

'Christ.' Francis turned to Alina. 'I wouldn't drink that if I were you. Not if you want to see Christmas.' Then, seeing the state she was in, his face softened. 'What is it?' he asked, his voice suddenly gentle, solicitous.

Alina took a deliberate sip of the tea and smiled weakly.

'Nothing,' she said. 'I'm tired. Didn't get much sleep.' She glanced up at Derek.

'Ah.' Francis nodded. 'Well,' he said. 'Don't worry.' He gave Derek a meaningful look, then went through to the kitchen. Derek followed, embarrassed.

'I just saw Tommy with that girl from the paper shop,' Francis said, rounding on him, his face angry again. 'He's walking around in the snow with her, for anybody to see. And he had her round here yesterday.'

Derek didn't know what to say. He'd seen Tommy with a girl too, just once, briefly, at the bus stop, but he hadn't known who she was. 'So?' he said.

Francis shook his head. 'Something's going on,' he said. 'That's obvious.' He poured himself a mug of tea, looked into it incredulously, then added some milk. 'Anyway,' he said. 'Me and Alina are going upstairs, OK? If Tommy comes in, don't tell him we're here.'

Derek shook his head. 'I'm just going out,' he said, without knowing why. He'd been planning to stay home, not go out wandering in the snow, but he couldn't bear the idea, suddenly, of being in the same house with Alina and Francis – especially if Tommy came back and he had to lie.

'OK.' Francis nodded. He carried his mug through to the other room and said something to Alina. Derek couldn't hear what it was, but he didn't care. He stood in the kitchen, listening, till he heard them go upstairs, then he put on his coat and boots, and went out into the snowy world.

It was already beginning to get dark. This was his favourite time to be out in wintertime: the end of the afternoon before the beginning of the evening, the streetlamps newly lit, the snow coming thick and dark through the hoops of light, women coming home from the shops with their kids trailing behind, the lights from the shop windows suddenly golden in the almost dark, the odd solitary girl stepping off a bus or coming out of a shop, touched with the beauty of the snow and the light, miraculous and impossible, like the girls in his mother's catalogues. Lizzie was one of those people who got new catalogues all the time; she liked to sit by the fire in the evenings and look at the goods – the leather furniture, the kitchen appliances, the garden ornaments and speciality

Christmas gifts – not, Derek thought, because she actually wanted any of it, she just found it reassuring to know such things existed. She was always clipping coupons in magazines and sending off for catalogues and brochures, though she hardly ever bought anything and the few things she did order were disappointing, somehow, when she unpacked them in her own front room.

The catalogues held another appeal for Derek, however. Occasionally, when he was on his own, he would get them out and flick through the women's fashions, looking at the models in their brand-new summer dresses and swimwear: beautiful girls not much older than him in printed cotton pyjamas; women in their late twenties, exotic and clear-skinned and beautiful, in tailored jackets or heavy winter coats. He carefully avoided the temptation of the underwear section; he'd skimmed those pages once or twice, but it wasn't sex, it was something more elusive that he was after. There were no words for it that he knew, but if he'd been forced to explain himself, he would have said it had something to do with the mystery of women, not women naked and pouting with their legs wide open, like in the porn mags he'd seen at school from time to time, but women in their ordinary lives, women going to the beach, or walking in the woods in autumn, their hair pulled back, their faces calm, with nobody looking at them as they went about their business. He'd always been embarrassed by the porn mags – yet, and though he was ashamed of this fact, he also knew it was true, he would rather have admitted to Francis, or any one of his friends, that he had a stack of *Fiesta*s a foot high in the bottom of his wardrobe, than have them discover him leafing through Lizzie's catalogue and dreaming about those fully dressed, self-sufficient women in their banal narratives of shopping and days out with the children. He would never have admitted to these fantasies, just as he would never have admitted to being shocked, when they'd first come to Corby, and he'd heard boys in his class talking about jam-rags and some not quite defined scene involving a Mars bar and a naked woman. He would never have admitted to having fallen in love, at fourteen, with one of Aretha Franklin's backing singers, or to carrying a torch for his brother's girlfriend ever since he'd first had to talk to her, in French one day, when the teacher had split them up into boy-girl pairs and made them practise the conversation exercise for *Un bonhomme de neige*, the only French conversation he could still remember, either because it had been so simple – *C'est l'hiver. Paul et Nathalie Thibaut jouent dans le jardin* – or because it reminded him of Alina, the way he had imagined them together, in a French suburban garden, making a snowman, in their dark French-looking coats and coloured gloves.

He knew Francis would say he was being sentimental: Francis, who would hover over Lizzie sometimes, as she sat watching some bad film on television, making fun of the love scenes, or laughing at the absurd twists in the plot that drew people apart then brought them together again, as if the whole world were just a backdrop to their miserable romance – 'Oh look, she's found the letter, I wonder why her father didn't destroy it, instead of leaving it on the table for anyone to see, I suppose now she'll make it to their rendezvous under the clock after all' – and Lizzie would be annoyed, telling him to be quiet, wanting to see what would happen, even though the conclusion was already long-decided and Francis knew she was only pretending, that she enjoyed the attention, just as he knew she was secretly disappointed when he went out, ten minutes before the end, announcing that he couldn't take any more of this rubbish. Francis made a big deal about seeing through them all: Lizzie with her sweets and Sunday matinees, Tommy with his fallow garden, the neighbours, the teachers at school, Cash Cromwell with his Bingo games in the Social and his regular Sunday tirade on money, robbing the people of what little they had with threats and promises. Francis saw through everybody, and he seemed genuinely disappointed, as if he knew how things could be different, even if he couldn't be bothered to explain it. He was disappointed in Derek too, that was obvious. It was a kindly disappointment: Derek felt how well-meaning his brother was, behind the mockery and the seeming irritation.

'You like her,' he'd said, just a fortnight back, when Alina had been round for the afternoon. The two of them – Francis and Alina – had been upstairs for hours, listening to Francis's music, while Derek skulked around downstairs, wanting to practise, but beyond concentrating.

'She's all right,' Derek answered, reluctant to talk like this about the person he thought of as his brother's girlfriend.

'You should ask her out,' Francis said, as casual, as matter of fact as he would have been if he'd been suggesting Derek buy the new Bonzo Dog Doo-Dah Band album.

'Don't be stupid.'

'Why not? She's not my girlfriend, you know. I don't own her.'

Derek shook his head. 'That's not the point,' he said. He hated Francis when he talked like this. 'It's got nothing to do —'

'If you like her, ask her out. What's she going to say?'

'I'm not listening.'

'Yes.'

'Shut up.'

'Or no.' Francis looked at him curiously. 'So what have you got to lose?'

That was what Derek didn't understand. Francis didn't seem to care about anything he cared about, yet he was his brother, his kith and kin. They had grown up together, and they had been so alike, or so it had seemed to Derek, back in Cowdenbeath when they were boys with the same address, the same history, the same dark future that they tried to ward off with charms and spells, reinventing the world, making it larger and more accommodating. Derek remembered the day he had found something in a school textbook, one of those endless addresses that gave every detail, winding its way out into the stars, to the very edge of the known, and he had hurried home after school and written his own version into the inside of his satchel:

> Derek Alan Cameron
> 17 Blackburn Drive
> Cowdenbeath
> Fife
> Scotland
> Great Britain
> Europe
> The World
> The Solar System
> The Milky Way
> The Universe

And he kept thinking there had to be more, details he had forgotten or didn't know, some way of teasing out the borders of his tiny world, some way of easing the burden of being who and what and where he was and finding an entirely new space to inhabit, a space that was at once eerie and beautiful, like the space in a film. It was like the space he imagined for all the legends and folk-tales he had read at school: a space for the blue men who emerged from the waves and pulled you overboard when your boat stalled halfway across the Minch; a space for the sea-trows and sirens, bright voices singing across the water, unbearably sweet and compelling; a space for those creatures who emerged from the snow and stole a man's mind, leaving him dumbstruck and staring on a lonely path across the moor; most of all, it was a space for the svelte aboriginals of that mysterious country, quiet men setting their nets on the shore for curlews and godwits, always with an eye on the sea or the woods, on the infinite possibilities that dwell in water, or the wind, or snow. Those stories were about more than superstition, or the casual fatalism of people whose lives were governed by the random – Derek knew that, just as he knew the Devil could walk across a village in the dark, leaving his footprints in the snow, across rooftops and lawns, and up and down the sides of buildings, odd claw-like prints filled with wet, black shadows like ink stains, and a faint smell on the air like coal-tar or paraffin. Those stories weren't about something invented, they were about something that had been lost: if he knew anything, it was that. Something important had been lost, and all he had ever wanted was to find it again.

That next morning it had been bitterly cold; there had been a hard snow in the night, and he and Francis had walked to school slowly, almost losing their way in it, the world they knew altogether different, all of a sudden, with new spaces to cross, as if the houses and gardens he knew by heart had hunkered down into the earth, or even disappeared altogether, whiteness and buried cars here and there, then all of a sudden, a mirage, like the milkman's horse standing at the corner with a rug over its back, in thick wreaths of warmth and steam. Over it all, there was a faint bluish light, as if the town had been transformed into a theatre, or a nativity play. When they finally reached the school, they learned that the pipes had frozen in the night. Strange men were walking up and down the corridors in wellingtons and waterproof coats, slushing around in the puddles of black water with engrossed looks, as if the whole thing were some elaborate, even enjoyable game, and Miss Gould was standing at the door, meeting the children as they arrived, and telling them there was to be no school that day. Derek was overjoyed. It was as if his charm had worked, as if he had made the world new, just by writing those words inside his satchel.

It was Francis who suggested going to the old kilns. They had been forbidden to go out there, not by Lizzie, but by Tommy, no less, so they knew it was dangerous. Lizzie told them not to slide down the sides of the pit bings on scraps of linoleum; Lizzie told them not to go climbing in the old quarry; Lizzie told them not to go into Mr Henderson's garden after their ball – and because Lizzie told them, they knew there was only a slight danger, the kind of danger boys were destined for. George Anderson had gone climbing in the quarry on his own: he had fallen from somewhere high and broken his leg and some ribs and had to wait hours before anybody came looking for him, and though everybody agreed he could have died out there, it only made the quarry more of a magnet to every self-respecting boy for miles around. But the old kilns were something else. There was no obvious threat, or nothing that the grown-ups could explain – and maybe that made all the difference, because the fear they inspired wasn't based on any rational explanation. The kilns were a mystery, a place apart, protected by nothing but damp air and ancient taboo.

But they hadn't made it to the kilns. Just as the town had seemed altered by the snow on their walk to school, so the woods had become an altogether new and almost unnavigable space, the usual landmarks hidden under drifts of white, the paths they knew petering out, or branching away unexpectedly to clearings they had never imagined were there. Everything was larger and wider than Derek remembered and they had been walking for less than an hour when he stopped and looked at Francis.

'We're lost,' he said.

Francis snorted. 'No we're not.'

'Well, where are we then?'

Francis looked around. The woods lay still and white and featureless around them and for a moment he seemed puzzled. Then he laughed. 'We can't be lost,' he said.

Derek shook his head. He was the oldest; it was his responsibility. 'I think we should go back,' he said.

'No.'

'It's freezing. And we're lost —'

'We're *not* lost.'

'We ought to go back. Mum will be worried —'

'Why will she be worried? She thinks we're at school.'

Francis had carried on walking then, but they had continued arguing, Derek becoming more and more certain they were lost, Francis insisting he knew where they were, and where the kilns were, saying there was nothing to worry about, they would get home in no time. That was when they saw the man. He was tall and gaunt, with dark, unkempt hair and a damp, straggly beard, a man about their father's age, standing off among the trees away from the path, watching them. He had to have been watching for some time, but he hadn't said anything. Even when they noticed him, he didn't speak, but just stood watching, as if he had never seen two boys before. Derek was afraid. He grabbed Francis's arm. 'Come on,' he said. 'Let's get out of here.' He had heard somebody say that at the pictures, and it sounded odd, hearing himself say it.

Francis didn't move. His eyes were fixed, not on the man, but on something else, something Derek hadn't noticed. 'What's that?' he asked.

Derek looked. The man was carrying a large brown sack, like the sacks they used for coal, only longer and wider and though it was hard to see, he could tell there was something inside, something alive, struggling to get out at the bottom of the sack, which the man was holding slightly up and away from his body. It was something about the size of a cat, but it could have been anything, a small dog, a fox, even a large bird, Derek couldn't tell, and he didn't care. All he wanted now was to get away from there.

Francis had other ideas. Taking a step towards the man — just a step, though it seemed an impassable distance, a step off the path and into the new snow — he looked curiously at the man. 'What have you got in the bag, Mister?' he said.

The man didn't answer. For a moment, Derek thought he was about to come at them, and he flinched. It was the smallest movement, a half-step, but it was enough for him to know that his body had intended to run, to leave Francis there and make good his escape, even if his mind had no such intention.

'What you got in the bag?' Francis asked the man again, his voice louder, singing across the space between them on the white air.

The man shook his head. 'None of your business,' he said, a half-smile playing around his mouth now.

'It's scared,' Francis said. 'It wants to get out.'

The man glanced down at the bag and nodded. 'So what?' he said. He lifted the bag slightly and Derek could hear noises – muffled, but distinctly plaintive sounds that anything could have made.

'You should let it go,' Francis replied. 'It's scared.'

Suddenly, without warning, the man lifted his head and gave a loud cry, almost a roar. It wasn't an angry cry so much as a cry of frustration, as if he had suddenly grown tired of people coming into his woods – there was no doubt, in Derek's mind, that these were his woods, that he belonged here in some way that they did not – and meddling in his business. It was too much for Derek: he grabbed Francis by the arm and started dragging him away along the path, watching the man all the time, to see if he would follow. Francis didn't resist, or not altogether, but he came reluctantly, his eyes fixed on the bag where whatever was inside was struggling more than ever now, making those small, plaintive cries that Derek still couldn't identify. 'Let it go,' he called back, one last time, but Derek could see he was losing his nerve now, and when the man took a few steps towards them, Francis turned and broke into a run, which allowed Derek to give in to the fear he'd been holding back all this time, allowed him to let Francis go and run for dear life, even though he had seen, with that last backward look, that the man had only intended to scare them off, that he wasn't really following. They had run and run, not knowing where they were going, only finding the familiar path that led out of the woods and back to the street by chance. Even then, they hadn't stopped; they'd kept on running, slipping and skidding on the icy pavements all the way home.

Derek had been sick with flu for a week after that. Lizzie had kept him out of school, and the snow kept falling all the time he was in bed, feeling like a fake, even though he did have a temperature and, at night, lay sweating and feverish in the suddenly wide bed, alone for the first time since he was a baby, because Francis wasn't allowed to be in the same room, in case he caught whatever it was his brother had. Derek couldn't remember ever being alone at night, and he had been afraid, sometimes, when he woke in the dark and it was silent, nobody there, no magnetic presence of another body, nobody breathing quietly in the gap between himself and the wall. He had been dreaming, and though he couldn't remember the exact details, he knew something had frightened him while he'd been asleep, some demon, not of the dark, like the demons in films, but of the daytime, a dark figure coming towards the house across the neighbours' gardens, half-concealed by the snow, hurrying towards them all through fields of rotting cabbage stumps and frozen laundry. It was the dream he had always had, in the long hours of catechism or arithmetic, a half-waking dream that startled him awake sometimes, when the teacher was talking about God or the times tables, and though it was always different in its smaller details, it was really the same dream every time – a dream of someone coming, someone who meant him harm. He would notice something on the way to school – a trail of footprints crossing the lawn, a scatter of coal, a cigarette end burning in the snow – and he would know that that person was coming, a man with flinty nails and nicotine-stained fingers, tall and soft-spoken and cruel. In the dream, that man would come to the house and slip in when nobody was looking – and when Derek and Francis came home from school, he would be waiting for them.

Now, walking into town in this year's snow, Derek realised that he hadn't quite understood what he had been afraid of, so long ago. He had thought he was afraid for himself, afraid that someone would come for him in the still of the afternoon, or the dead of night. He had thought of himself as haunted by those demons from his story book, and he had imagined himself as one of the chosen – but he had been wrong. He had always been wrong and he had always known it. He wasn't one of the chosen, he wasn't one of those singled out by fate. But Francis was. All his life, Derek had been afraid, not for himself, but for Francis. Francis, who was so clever; Francis, who was always so sure of himself; Francis, who knew no fear. There had been times when he

resented his brother – resented his luck, his cleverness, his arrogance – but even then, in the midst of resentment, he had been
afraid for him. It didn't make any sense. He wasn't his brother's
keeper, and even if he was, his brother could take care of himself.
Francis, who had always been smarter, and better-liked, and harder;
Francis, who didn't have a sentimental bone in his body. Why
would anybody be afraid for *him*? Derek had no answer, yet he
was afraid, just as he had always been afraid that Francis was the
chosen one, the one who had been marked out, that day in the
woods, or on some other day long ago, when nobody was there
to stop it happening. That was what made him special: that mark.
That was why – and Derek realised it with a shock, as if he had
been caught out in some unspecified crime – that was why Derek
loved his brother more than he loved anyone else, even himself.

Keeping Fire

Alma

S HE WAS TRYING to find space in her house for another dead child.

She remembered the day, all those years ago, when her first baby died. The child had only been four days old, but she had been real, a real daughter with eyes and fingers and a tiny, desperate mouth that kept trying to cry, then giving up. Renate: that would have been her name. Alma imagined her growing tall and wise and going home to the place where her grandfather had lived, learning to speak her own language, finding her lost grandmother, solving all the riddles. She had never wanted to give up, not for one moment, but someone had taken her baby away, not long after the birth, and she had never seen Renate again. There had been complications with the delivery, the doctor said, and she knew from the first visit he made to her bed, a tall, thin man in an immaculate white coat, that he was trying to prepare her for the worst.

They had kept it a secret from the children that there had been another child before they were born, a sister who was already dead before they even spoke about her, a ghost on all their lives. Sometimes she felt that was wrong – she thought Jan and Alina had the right to know they'd had a sister – but Marc insisted. He didn't want them thinking about that, he said. What good did it do? What point was there in dwelling on things when there was nothing you could do about it? That had been his constant refrain in those days: you have to move on, he would say, you can't afford to dwell on things. He liked that word; *dwell*. It meant to live, to have a house, to be sheltered, but it also meant this other thing, this dwelling on, this being caught up in something and unable to move on. He'd heard someone use it, and he'd looked it up in the dictionary, noted it down in his little book, started saying it whenever he could. He thought of the house as their dwelling place. He refused to dwell on the past. 'I'll rather dwell', he said, 'in my necessity.' It was a quote he had found in the dictionary, and he loved to repeat it, though Alma wasn't convinced he actually knew what it meant. As the years passed, she came to hate that dictionary.

Meanwhile, she had stayed at home and devised a life of her own, a secret life hidden in every corner of the house, to honour the child she had lost. She had created a little altar in the corner of the kitchen, on the shelf above the fridge. She hadn't thought of it as such, it had just emerged, of its own accord. It had started with a vase she had found in Woolworth's, a cheap thing that Marc wouldn't notice; she had filled it with flowers and set it out where she could see it if she was working at the sink, or sitting at the table making pastry or cutting vegetables for stew. Later, she had added other things: a bowl from a jumble sale; a scrap of bright blue fabric from a draper's shop in Kettering; a child's wax-crayon drawing she had found in the street. The drawing had been wet with rain, clouded with those ashy smuts from The Works that blew around for days and settled everywhere, on the bedroom windows, on the laundry, on the leaves of the trees. It wasn't very much, just half a page torn from an exercise book: a picture, in pink and green and yellow crayon, of a tall, narrow house, with a tree to one side, and a thick, waxy sun overhead. The child must have made the drawing in school, then lost it on the way home. When Alma found it washing along in the gutter on her way back from the shops, she had fished it out and carried it home, a small trophy that was at once more precious and fragile than anything she had ever possessed. She had washed it carefully, rinsing away the dust and grime, sponging off the mud with a tea towel and setting it on the windowsill to dry. The colours had faded a little, but that only made it more beautiful in her eyes.

She had been trying half-heartedly to make something of the

garden ever since they had moved in, but it had been hard, dispiriting labour. The dirt from The Works got everywhere; the soil was thin, a wash of silty mud over thick, dead clay; the garden seemed to sit in permanent shadow, The Works brooding above it like a vast beached ship, oozing smoke and carbon and the microscopic flakes of iron that you couldn't help breathing every time you opened the back door. When Renate died, she had begun again, in the long, patient earnest of grief, working every spare moment, turning the soil, making compost from kitchen waste, digging out stones and fist-sized lumps of clay and carrying them to the dump one or two at a time in an old shopping bag. It had been slow work, and she had been grateful for it. Marc had his job: in those days, he hadn't hated it as much, and it was somewhere to go, something to do. He signed up for all the overtime he could get: extra hours, double shifts, standbys. He didn't notice the changes she was making around the place, or the work she was doing in the garden and Alma didn't care. For once, she was doing something for herself, for herself and for the child that Marc refused to mourn.

Meanwhile, her work in the garden created an interesting by-product. Every now and then, as she rooted around in the cold earth, breaking up lumps of soil and sifting out the larger stones, she would find fragments of another world, another time: tiny pieces of blue and white china, shards of terracotta, pebbles of smoothed glass, even the stem of an old-fashioned clay pipe. They seemed oddly beautiful, like evidence of a lost civilisation, beguiling clues to an elegance long forgotten. One fragment of china, about the size of her thumbnail, was fretted with tiny blue veins that might have been roots, or pine needles from a Willow Pattern bowl; another, even smaller shard was hatched with a herringbone pattern, a feather, or the leaf of some tropical plant. Elsewhere, in one dark corner, in soil that was one-tenth loam and nine-tenths clinker, she found a massy cache of broken glass, just three or four inches from the surface. She dug it out, rinsed it, and picked out the best pieces, tiny jewels of Bristol blue and leaf green; then, together with the best of the china pieces, she set them out on the shelf above the fridge with her other finds. Slowly, a design was beginning to emerge, a separate zone of greens and blues and golds, complete in itself, different in quality from the rest of the house. It was less like a shrine now than a threshold, a portal into some other world. Sitting at the table making dough, or standing at the sink peeling potatoes, she could look up and imagine herself passing through to another space, like the separate reality of folk-tales or the stories she had heard from the farm workers, growing up in Weldon.

Everywhere she looked, there were clues. A flicker of shadow, a shaft of light, the sound of rain at the windows in the small hours when Marc was on night shift: it all added up to something and Alma knew that she was close to that something, that it would take no more than a slight shift of attention to find what she was looking for. It was so close, just a matter of inches, just a heartbeat away. After months of work, she planted out the garden; bulbs first, then seeds, a couple of hybrid tea-roses, some tiny, slightly ragged violets. She hadn't spoken to Marc, she had just saved money from the housekeeping, a penny here, sixpence there, till she had enough to set it all out. What she was making, she had decided, was a memorial garden. At the same time, it was more than that. It wasn't just a garden, it was a place to be; even with The Works looming overhead, even with the dirt and smoke drifting in, blackening the leaves, tainting the daffodils as soon as they emerged, even though some of the plants died, and the grass never really knitted into the lawn she had hoped for, it was a refuge, a separate world, where the souls of the dead – not just her daughter, but all the dead, the known and the unknown, her father, her friends from the farm, the mother she had never known, all the people who had died in the war, or in The Works, burned or scalded or crushed to death while they worked – all the souls of the dead who were dead, all the souls of the dead who were still living, could rest a moment, could take up residence, and find a dwelling place in a flower bud or a leaf, or in the snowdrifts that formed against the back fence, sparkling white for an hour or more in the first fall before the tainted air made them grey and dull. Whenever she found something – a new fragment of porcelain, a length of ribbon – she would add it to the shrine above the fridge. One day, in the library, she found an old Christmas card inside a book: it was tiny, no bigger than the palm of her hand, the front wreathed in holly and forget-me-nots, the inside inscribed, in clear, strong copperplate: TO DEAR NELLIE, FROM LILLIAN, CHRISTMAS 1893. Alma wondered about these women. Where had they lived? How had they spent their days? What were they to one another? Sisters? Friends? Allies? She placed the card on the special shelf, and it seemed as if her dead child had found new friends in that other place where she waited, silent and untroubled, to be reborn.

All this time, Marc was creating his own world, closed up in his silence, poring over the dictionary, scribbling in his notebook, increasing his vocabulary. Alma was afraid he would stop long enough to think about the shrine above the fridge some day, and ask her what she thought she was doing with all that clutter, but he never did. Slowly, with no obvious decision on his part, he had withdrawn from the kitchen, and he hardly ever went out into the garden at the back, even after she had made it quite presentable, with its patch of lawn, its narrow beds of roses and poppies and a single red peony that had somehow survived, in spite of the smoke and grime. It was as if they had come to an unspoken agreement that this would be her part of the house, her private space, her dwelling. He had his words, she had her flowers. He had work, she had the kitchen. It must have seemed a fair trade to him, if he even thought about it at all. Alma wanted to tell him that he was cheating, not her, but himself, but she never did. Three years after they lost Renate, Alina had come along, and she had been perfect, a live, noisy baby with a shock of sable hair and big, china-blue eyes. She had laughed all the time as a child, and she had run everywhere – *full of joy*, Alma had thought, *full of joy*.

Now Jan had gone through that gap in the light, to sit with Renate and his grandparents and all the others. She had not expected to see this again, not like before. When her baby had died, they had taken her away, they had made her invisible; now, when they had come to the house and told her Jan was gone, they had already begun the same quiet, steady conjuring trick they played with the dead. From the first, they had done all they could to make her a stranger to her son. Before she could let him go, he was disposed of; before she could understand what the questions were that she needed to ask, they were turning away, making themselves busy, taking each moment of the present as it happened and burying it in a far, improbable past. In the days before they carried the box to church and set him down in the ground, Jan was being transformed so thoroughly into an absence that she sometimes forgot him. Because of how he had died, the police couldn't release the body right away, and they had to wait, till those strangers were finished with him. Then he was sealed up in a closed coffin, so she couldn't say goodbye, couldn't kiss his face or touch his hair. Before he was gone, he was gone. That was what they did with their dead in a town like this.

At one time, in the country, in the village where she had lived for a while as a stranger – and here, too, probably, why not here, in the days when children were still their mothers' children – at one time the women would come to the place where a body lay to prepare it for burial. They would wash the skin with warm water and spices; they would comb the hair; lay a man out in his Sunday best; dress a woman in her wedding clothes. They would come together and they would work silently, in the common knowledge of what had to be done, the younger ones watching their elders and learning the ritual, the old ones closing the dead soul's eyes and repeating the words – quietly, almost inaudibly – repeating the spells or prayers that had been handed down from time immemorial. Alma remembered this, but she had never seen it: she had read about it in books, and her father had told her a story, long ago, before he died and was taken away, of how the peasant women at home would sit all night with the dead, talking in their low, dark voices, giving a little part of themselves over to the dead one, to make his journey easier.

'What journey?' she had asked.

Her father had shaken his head, and Alma understood, too late, that this was a story that did not allow for questions. 'A journey,' he had said, simply. 'When people die, they go on a journey.'

'To heaven?' She hadn't been able to stop herself. It seemed to her that he was remembering something, something that made him sad, and she had wanted to understand.

'Perhaps,' he had said – and he had smiled then. It was a sad, faraway smile, and Alma had realised there was something else he wasn't telling her, something he had thought about telling, before deciding against it. To begin with, she had minded, but after a while she understood. It was in the nature of adults to have secrets; she had always known that. Her mother was a secret, the past was a secret, the children she had known before they had come to live in this new place, the clock she remembered, the little narrow street where she had seen blood in the snow – they were all secrets, guarded by adults for her sake. It wasn't till much later, when she had begun to think of herself as separate, that she had seen this secretiveness as a betrayal, a refusal to grant her a history that she could tell herself when she needed to remember who she was, and where she had come from.

As a child, she had thought heaven was real, because she knew her mother was there. Now, she didn't believe in such things. She didn't believe in the God she had been told about; she didn't believe in Jesus on his cross, or the Holy Virgin ascending into the sky with that odd look on her face, as if she was surprised by what was happening, or unsure of where she was going. Most of all, she didn't believe in the Church. When the priest came to the house, she sat in the kitchen, waiting for him to go; when the others came – men from the funeral director's, come to talk about the arrangements, the policemen whose job it was to ask questions about her son, that woman from the Corporation, who sat a while and didn't say anything, so that Alma hadn't known, afterwards, why she was there – when all these people, who were strangers to her, came and sat in her front room, talking quietly, never looking her in the eye, suspicious-looking, secretive, embarrassed, she had sat in her chair by the fireplace and waited for them to be gone. This is how it is now, she thought. There are always people, but they are always strangers. She did not know their names, or the names of their children. She had never been to *their* houses, or sat in *their* front rooms. They were people she did not know, yet they were in her house, talking, moving about, trying to help. Couldn't they see that she didn't want them there?

The worst of it, though, was how they talked. They talked so easily, they found words that seemed to satisfy them, words that had been selected for such occasions, sanctified by habit and a more or less casual acceptance of their inevitable inadequacy. These strangers offered their condolences, or they spoke about faith, and they waited for her to respond with some accepted formula, but Alma had nothing to say. She knew they thought it would do her good to enact the appropriate ritual, to make the correct gestures and say the approved words; but now, in her only language – a language she had grown up with, always troubled by the thought that it wasn't really hers – the words she needed did not come, and she wondered if there was something else, something she could have said in that other language, not German but the one her father had given up, that would have satisfied these others and made them leave her alone. One word in her true language might have been enough. Her father had always said how important it was to speak well, to know what it was you wanted to say, and Alma had often thought he must have spoken his own language beautifully – but she had never heard it. His true voice was a secret from her.

She remembered watching over him as he died, the cancer in his throat spreading into his chest, his face emptying, the faintness in his eyes dying out altogether, till there was nothing left but bone and hair and skin. The doctor hadn't known what to do, other than prescribing painkillers, and her father refused to go to the hospital; so, at seventeen, she had tended him – and she remembered thinking, as he lay mute in the tiny upstairs room of the cottage, that her history would be lost for ever now; that, even if she could have framed her questions in a way that would have induced him to answer, even if he had been willing, finally, to tell her who she really was, where she had come from, how they had travelled from there to where they were now, at that very moment, even if she could have found a way to make him see how important it was that she know her own history, he was no longer in a position to speak. One day, surprised at herself that she had taken so long to think of it, she brought him a pen and a notebook and asked him one last time to write down what he remembered, since he could not say it aloud. She had pleaded with him, aware of the fact that she was taking advantage of his condition, but unable to help herself.

Her father had looked at her for a long time, his face still, each hard-won breath sounding as if it might be his last. She could see the dismay in his eyes, she could see that he knew what she was asking, and why, and she knew, in that moment, that he had always known what he was denying her. Finally, he picked up the pen and, with no small effort, began to write. His hand was feeble; he could hardly control the pen; but it did seem that words were forming, a scratchy, wild script unfolding across the page, first one line, then another, then a third. Alma watched. It was true, she was sure of it, slowly, sentences were being shaped, word by jagged word. As her father worked, the effort showing on his face, she thought about what she knew – what she knew about him, what she knew about herself, what she remembered for certain and what she thought she remembered, all the wisps of recollection and half-formed imagery ghosting across her mind like incense across an altar, and she was stunned by how little there was. How could she have lived for seventeen years, and remembered so little? How would she go forward from this moment, what future would she have, if there was no past to build upon? She felt desperate, as she watched her father's hand, so thin, so insubstantial; and she wanted to see what he had written, wanted to hurry him up so he would finish before he was too weak to continue – and it was at that very moment that the pen wavered, then slipped from his fingers, spilling on to the bedclothes, the notebook sliding to the floor. At the same time, her father's head fell back and his eyes closed.

'What is it?' she said. 'What's wrong?'

Her father didn't answer. He had the drugs the doctor had given him for the pain, but Alma knew his only release – a release that was both provisional and brief – was unconsciousness, and everything told her to let it go, to let him slip into the peaceful darkness for however long he was permitted to rest. At the same time, she looked at the notebook on the floor, where she could see only three lines of writing, and she wanted to wake him, to make him try again. It was only a moment before that temptation passed, but she remembered, long after they had buried him, how she had felt for that single moment, the moment when he had first slipped away from her, almost a week before he died.

She carried the notebook downstairs, leaving her father to

sleep in peace. In the kitchen, while slow rain fuzzed the tiny windows, and the air darkened outside, she tried to read what he had written. She tried for a long time, bewildered by her inability to make anything out, but it was no use. At first, she thought it was something in another language – Latvian, say, or some local dialect from his unknown childhood – and she thought, if that had been the case, no matter how obscure it might be, there would be a chance of something. She could have found someone who knew, someone to decipher and translate these three lines he had scratched across the pages of her notebook. It would be a start, then, she thought, even three lines would hold some key, if they could be understood. Finally, however – and she knew this was the end, that she would never ask him again about their lost life – she saw that what he had written was nothing, three lines of meaningless, almost illegible nonsense words. She didn't know if this had been deliberate, a last attempt to cling to his secret. She suspected not, but there was no way to be sure. She thought not. She hoped not.

In the end, though, it hadn't mattered. All that had mattered was that she was a displaced person, a lost soul, a present without a past – and now, as she prepared to bury her only son, she felt that the future had been taken from her, a future that was no more her own than the past, but to which she had been connected, through Jan. She still had Alina: she knew that, she told herself that, but she also knew, deep down, with shame and with total certainty, that Jan had been her real future, her only way of living beyond all this smoke and grime. It didn't matter that he had detached himself from her, that he lived in his own, private world. Ever since he was a baby, she had dreamed about the life he would have one day – and all that time, as her two surviving children were growing up, that had been the difference between them, a difference that Alina had probably guessed at long ago: the difference between thinking and dreaming, between care and hope. When Alma lay awake at night, she would think about Alina, she would worry about her, the way any mother would worry about a child, living in such a place; but Jan was the one she dreamed about, the one she dreamed *for*. Jan was the one she believed in, the one on whom she fed her hope. Now he was gone and, with him, the future had disappeared. Everything was the present: this moment, then the next, then another; isolated pieces of time, disconnected and seemingly random, with no story to hold them together. That story should have been herself, but she wasn't there any more, she was nothing more than a function, a body that moved and occupied space, because it could not do otherwise. Now, without a story to tell, she wanted nothing but to be left alone; because, when she was alone, it was like no one was there at all.

When she was alone, she went out into the garden. She couldn't bear to be in the house, now that Marc was there all the time. The bosses at work had told him to stay home, to look after his family, but after the first few days, when he had wandered around, naked and mad and talking to himself, all he did was lie on the bed, staring at the ceiling, his face set like a stone mask, as if he was the one who had died. Alma wished it was. Then, all of a sudden, and without being asked, Alina took over. After the first empty days, she was the one who dealt with the visitors; she talked to the funeral men; she called the police station to ask when they could have the body back. She told the right lies and listened to the useless condolences. People came and went, and Alma stayed alone in her garden. Sometimes she did a little weeding, or she cut the grass, but mostly she stood at the back fence and looked out at The Works. It seemed further away now, smaller and less monstrous. At night, she could see the flames, she could taste the smoke and the rusty taint of the ore, but it was gentler now, less corrosive, less real. Perhaps, after all these years, she had become immune to it. Perhaps a balance had been reached, a bargain struck: there was just enough carbon and ore and ammonia in her blood that no more could enter; perhaps the poison she had breathed all this time had made of her its natural dwelling, and she had accepted it, taken it in, made it, if not her friend, then at least her accomplice. Wasn't that how they used to cure people, in the old days, before these useless doctors? The patient had gradually learned how to live with the poison, and not let it kill her – and that, all of a sudden, seemed the most natural thing in the world. How else would we be cured, if not by poison? How else would we know we were alive, if not by grieving? If there was no story, there was at least that. Whatever there was, it was all she had: iron and corms and blood, laid down in the earth, named and anonymous, remembered and forgotten.

Derek

IT WAS WARM, the morning of Jan Ruckert's funeral, warm and a little clammy after a night of rain, a faint smoky vapour rising from the grass at the far end of the cemetery, the people gathered around the gates shuffling and uncomfortable, wanting to be elsewhere, but drawn here by curiosity, or a vague sense of event, a sense that something important had happened. Derek was surprised at the numbers: men he knew from The Works, women his mother had known and, most surprisingly, crowds of younger people dressed in the best funeral clothes they could manage, dark shirts, black jeans, old school shoes, the occasional pair of black plimsolls. They stood in rows, quiet and respectful, their heads bowed; it could have been a school assembly. In the midst of all this, the one group that looked out of place was Jan's family, Alina pale and angry-looking in a black jacket and skirt, her mother dignified, walking slowly along the gravel path, her eyes fixed on the middle-distance. It must have come as a surprise, all those people. Derek couldn't see anyone who looked like he might be Jan's father. He looked around, trying to locate Francis. He knew his brother was there, because he'd seen him leave the house early that morning in the same black clothes he'd worn for Lizzie's funeral. Francis had good reason to attend this funeral, of course, unlike these others; unlike Derek, for that matter, who might not have felt so awkward if there had been fewer people – spectators, really, most of them – but was becoming less sure of his reasons for being there with each passing moment. He hadn't known Jan. He hadn't even talked to him until that last night, when he'd let him go out into the streets and get himself beaten to death. Derek kept wondering what would have happened if Jan hadn't gone off on his own; over the last week, he had veered wildly between guilt and self-exoneration, and he had wanted desperately to find Francis and tell him how it had happened: how he had tried his best, and how Jan had told him he would rather be left alone.

The night Jan died, they had all been at a party. Derek had gone with Gary and Mitch to the Nag's Head, and they had drifted along to a house on Station Road, where half the town was crammed into two rooms, drinking and smoking dope. Derek hadn't known Francis was there, but he'd seen Jan and noticed how out of place the boy looked, sitting in a corner cradling a glass to his chest, watching the room as it heaved and swelled around him. Jan was wearing a bright blue shirt and white jeans; he looked like a spy as he sat observing the crowd with an unhappy, oddly penitent expression on his face. Derek didn't know the boy to speak to, so he didn't feel bad about avoiding him, even though it seemed obvious that Jan was depressed, or fed up. He was also very obviously drunk. Derek was surprised by that – he had never thought of Jan as a drinker, though he had wondered about acid from time to time, knowing he was a friend of Francis's, and knowing Francis's history in that particular field. Derek didn't approve of acid. Dope, yes, that was OK, but it didn't really bother him much, one way or another. He liked alcohol, in moderation; he had listened to Tommy all those years, talking about all the mistakes he had made, and telling both his sons not to do as he had done, and oddly enough, considering what a bad example Tommy had been for much of that time, it had stuck. Derek drank beer for the taste, but he didn't bother much with spirits, and he hated wine. He hated anything sweet. On the few occasions he'd drunk wine, he had woken the next day with this thick, cloying sweetness on his tongue and at the back of his throat, and he'd felt sick and tainted, as if he'd spent the night chewing on marshmallows.

He didn't like parties much, either. Most nights, he would rather have gone home, to listen to music on his headphones, or practise, but when he had been rehearsing with Gary and Mitch, they would drift naturally to the pub and, after a couple of drinks, the other two would be looking for somewhere to go on to, and Derek would tag along, in a spirit of what he knew was an entirely artificial solidarity with the rest of the band. They'd been playing together for over a year now, and Gary was good at getting them work – on the cheap, cash-in-hand, it was true, but it was experience, and Derek liked playing with other people. Sometimes they rounded up a few other musicians and did a party or a wedding: Gary knew a mad old sax-player called Billy who had been hurt in a motorcycle accident so couldn't play for more than half an hour at a time – it was something to do with the supply of air to the brain – but when he did come in, he was amazing. Billy knew jazz, and he could play all the old standards, but he didn't mind what he played as long as people were appreciative. He liked to be in front of an audience. Derek sometimes wondered if the air to the brain thing wasn't a little bit of an exaggeration so Billy could look like more of a star, coming in for half an hour then bowing out on a high note, the audience, such as it usually was, clapping and cheering, partly because Billy was good, but also because he was such a character, full of himself, but touched with sadness, a crazed loneliness in his face that got all the more poignant when he smiled.

When he did go to parties, Derek usually wound up on his own, flicking through record collections or sitting in a stranger's garden looking at the sky. At night, The Works was unavoidable: wherever you were, there would be that dull orange glow overhead, or a hint of smoke on the air. Depending on the wind, tiny black smuts would drift across the gardens, settling on people's faces and clothes. For a long time, Derek hadn't thought much about it, he had just taken it for granted, as if this was how things were, how they had to be. Now, though, after three years at the plug mill, he was starting to resent the smoke and the dirt, starting to feel its claim on him, the way it settled into his skin and lungs, marking him out. He hadn't planned to stay so long; now, he wanted to go, to move somewhere and find other musicians to play with, guys who would challenge him, talented people who would force him to grow. He looked across the room at Gary, who was trying to pick up a small, dark-haired girl Derek vaguely remembered from school. Gary had taken on himself the role of player-manager: he fixed up gigs, argued about money, looked after transport. Derek didn't mind that – he knew it was something he wouldn't have wanted to do – but Gary wasn't that much of a guitarist, and Mitch was even less of a drummer. They were comfortable to play with, because they knew their limits, but Derek knew he wasn't progressing. They didn't want to take the music any further: if they could make a few quid and have a good time, they were happy. Mostly, what Gary wanted was to be a guitarist, so he could tell girls like the one he was chatting up now that he was in a band, and they were about to cut their first record. They had been about to cut their first record for a year now.

After a couple of beers, Derek was ready to leave. It was obvious Amy Mackay wouldn't be coming to this particular party and he didn't see any point in staying otherwise. Gary was still working away at the dark-haired girl, with no great luck by the look of things, and Mitch was off smoking dope with a bunch of people from the Nag's. Derek didn't really know many other people at the party, and he was glad of the fact. He was heading for the door, hoping the others wouldn't see him and drag him back, when a voice called out from somewhere on the stairs above him.

'Derek?'

He looked up. It was Francis.

'How's it going?' Francis was wearing the look he always had when he was about to ask for something. These days, ever since he had started going to college, it only made him seem more of a stranger.

'What do you want?'

Francis laughed. 'I don't want anything,' he said. 'I just –' He came to the foot of the stairs and grabbed Derek's arm. 'Listen, I've got to go somewhere. Can you just keep an eye on Jan for me? Make sure he doesn't get into trouble –'

Derek sighed and shook his head. 'Am I my brother's keeper?' he asked, with enough irony so Francis would know that his request was unfair, but not so much that he expected to be refused. Derek had never refused Francis anything, or not directly.

Francis laughed again, an odd, uncharacteristically nervy, excitable laugh. Derek figured he was high on something. 'Very funny,' he said. 'Just keep an eye on him. Please?'

'Why can't you keep an eye on him?'

Francis didn't say anything — but there was no need. Behind him, standing at the foot of the stairs, trying to look like she wasn't waiting for anyone, was a girl Derek thought he knew, a face he half-recognised but couldn't place. 'Oh,' he said. 'Well, I saw him earlier. He seemed fine.'

'I know he's fine,' Francis said quickly. 'It's just that — he was acting a bit funny for a while there —'

'So what's new?'

'Aw, come on.' Francis put on a wounded look. 'Don't be like that.'

Derek nodded wearily. 'All right,' he said. 'But I'm not staying long.'

Francis beamed. 'Thanks,' he said. 'See you later.' He was already starting for the door. The girl turned and gave Francis a shy, slightly unsure smile.

'I'm telling you.' Derek stood up and went after him. 'I have to go —'

'That's fine,' Francis said. 'Just keep an eye on him till then. See he gets home all right.'

He disappeared before Derek could say more. The girl followed. It was only after they had gone that Derek remembered where he had seen her before, and even then, he couldn't quite believe it.

Derek hadn't done what Francis had asked, though he had tried. After another hour, it was obvious Amy wasn't going to show, and he was feeling like a fool, half-cut from too many beers, and ready to leave. He needed air. He hated being among so many people when there was no dividing line between him and them, like the edge of a stage, or even the little marked-out area for the PA and drum-kit when they played at pubs. Still, he felt obliged to check on his brother's friend, even if he didn't much like the guy.

He found Jan sitting in a plastic chair, just outside the back door. He was still cradling a pint glass full of clear liquid to his chest and watching the people, who had spilled out through the kitchen and into the garden, gathered together in clumps, smoking dope and swigging beer from tins. 'Are you OK?' Derek asked.

Jan looked up. His eyes were blurry, his face muddled. He didn't say anything.

'Listen,' Derek said. 'You ought to go. You're a bit drunk –'

'So I am,' Jan muttered, grinning sadly. 'So I am. But in the morning, I'll be sober. Isn't that how it works?' He was slurring his speech, though not that badly.

'In the morning,' Derek said, 'you'll be hung over.' He realised there was an insult buried in there somewhere, but he let it go. 'But if you stay much longer, you'll be very hung over.'

Jan made an effort to pull himself together. For the first time, he seemed to notice someone else really was there; now he was studying Derek, as if trying to work out who he was.

'I'm Francis's brother,' Derek said, as if the question had been asked aloud. 'Derek.'

'I know who you are,' Jan said. He seemed confused. 'So where's Francis?'

'He's gone home.'

'Really?' Jan looked around. The garden was even more crowded now, a mass of bodies spilling out from the house looking for more drink, or somewhere to collapse, or trying to figure out where the dope was. 'When?'

'An hour ago.'

'Oh. Well, I don't blame him.' Jan surveyed the heaving crowd with obvious distaste. 'Who'd want to stick around here?' He laughed. 'What better proof of evolution, eh?'

Derek gave him a tight smile. Right now all he wanted to do was get away.

'Evolution,' Jan continued, talking to himself again. 'A messy business. All this useless surplus just to produce the odd Mozart. I mean, what's it all for?' He turned to a plump girl who had backed into their tiny square of space and gave her a nasty, contemptuous smile. 'What do you want,' he muttered. '*Lebensraum?*'

Derek was pretty sure the girl hadn't heard, or if she had, hadn't understood, but she recognised the tone of voice, and her face twisted into a sneer as she edged away, back to where her friends were. 'Look,' he said. 'I think it's time to go.' He tried not to sound too half-hearted.

'What? Are you kidding?' Jan regarded him with mock-surprise. 'Just when it's starting to get so lively?'

'OK.' He hovered a moment, but Jan didn't say anything. Derek decided he'd done enough. Just as he turned to go, however, the other boy grabbed his arm.

'Who were your favourite characters in Rupert?'

'Rupert? You mean, like in the books?'

'Yes.'

Derek shook his head. 'I don't know them,' he said. He wasn't quite lying: he had seen the books, when he was younger, because Francis had always liked them, and Derek had been curious as to what all the fuss was about. He hadn't really seen the point, though. It was a world he didn't recognise, this piece of England populated by polite bears and public school elephants, and he soon gave up on it. He much preferred *Alice in Wonderland* or *Gulliver's Travels*; mostly, though, he'd read comics and the music papers.

'Really?' Jan seemed surprised. 'Francis always liked Freddy and Ferdy. You know – the fox twins?'

'Is that so?' Derek wondered if this was true. From what he remembered, Freddy and Ferdy hardly ever appeared, they were outsiders to the main group, but whenever they did turn up, they would get into trouble, and they always seemed out of place, a little sinister even, compared to Rupert and Algy and the little Chinese girl whose name he couldn't remember. Like Tweedledum and Tweedledee, Freddy and Ferdy were the products – and the practitioners – of a different logic, which made them at once interesting and peripheral to the action, curiosities, outsiders, not the kind of characters you could identify with. It sounded like Francis. 'I wasn't that keen on books,' he said – and he almost wondered aloud what he was doing here, discussing children's books at a loud party with a near-stranger. 'Listen, I was thinking about getting out of here. Maybe we could share a taxi home.'

'Why?' Jan looked up at Derek as if he'd just told a great joke. 'What's at home?'

'You need to get some sleep,' Derek said. He was careful not to seem too concerned. Concern usually inspired contempt.

Jan raised his glass and took a long swig, but he didn't say anything.

'What's that you're drinking?' Derek asked.

'Water.'

'Really?'

'Vodka.'

'Oh.'

Jan grinned sadly and took another swig. It seemed the conversation was over, in his mind at least. Still, Derek thought he'd give it one last try. 'Look,' he said. 'I can drop you off. It's on the way.'

'Nah.' Jan shook his head and looked out at the room full of bodies. 'You go on. I'm going to stay here for a while and practise my social skills.'

Jan had been right about one thing: it wasn't much of a party. Derek had only gone because he'd thought Amy might be there: even if she was with Alan, it would have been good to see her, just to stand in a room and look across at her, knowing she was aware of him, hoping that she still wanted to reach out and touch him, all the time pretending she had no idea who he was.

He'd met Amy the previous Christmas. He had been on his way to the Corinthian with Gary and Mitch when she passed them on the street, a small, vivid girl walking home alone in the first snow of the year, her shoulder-length dark hair spotted with snowflakes, her eyes catching his as she passed, a momentary look of recognition, of some sudden kinship, passing between them, unnoticed by the others. Derek had wanted to stop and follow her to wherever she was going, but she walked on quickly, barely pausing for a backward glance. Then Gary said something, and they were passing by, the distance lengthening between Derek and this amazing being, the sense that he was making a mistake, that he was letting something go that he couldn't afford to lose, growing more urgent by the minute. For a moment he thought of turning back: he could have followed the girl's tracks along the pavement and found her, he could have stood at her door and waited till she answered, he could have made her laugh when he turned up out of the blue, cold and awkward and totally obvious. Instead, he walked on into town with the others. Gary had set them up with the chance of a gig playing Sunday lunch times at the Corinthian and, though it wasn't much, it was paid work, and Gary had said they could play what they liked, even jazz. Derek didn't want to let the other boys down by not turning up. Besides, he didn't know who the girl was – but he reckoned Gary would. Gary knew everybody.

'Did you see that girl who went by just now,' he said, trying to sound casual. 'Wasn't that Mick Johnson's girlfriend?'

Gary laughed.

'That's Amy Mackay,' he said. 'She's a bit out of Mick Johnson's class, I'd say.'

'Oh.'

'She's married to Alan Mackay,' Gary continued. 'You know who *he* is.'

Derek nodded. He didn't know Alan Mackay personally, but he had a good idea he was one of the rugby club lot, an ugly piece of work. 'Oh,' he muttered – oh, as in no big deal.

But Gary was watching him. 'You don't fancy her, do you?' he asked, with a look of amused incredulity. 'Cause if you do, forget it. I don't want to have to go looking for another bass player.'

Derek shook his head. 'I've never seen her before today,' he said. 'I thought she was Mick Johnson's girlfriend.'

Gary grinned. 'Of course you did,' he said. 'Anyway, she isn't. She's Alan Mackay's wife. So don't go getting ideas.'

It had snowed for days. It was the best and the worst winter for years: cars buried in drifts by the roadside, the whole town shimmering under the snow, the bus to The Works juddering along in the morning at not much more than walking pace. Derek was still working at the plug mill, but he had promised himself that this would be his last year: by the summer, no matter what, he would be gone, ready to start again elsewhere with the money he had saved over the three years or so since he'd first started at The Works. He had made a similar resolution a year before, just after Christmas, but Lizzie had been sick again all through that spring, and he'd decided to stay on to help Tommy. With Francis away at college, he reckoned, he had no choice but to hang on a little longer. Now, he saw that Lizzie wasn't getting any better – that, if anything, she was getting worse, and he knew there would never be a good time to go. Another Christmas, another spring, and now, with the promise of a few gigs, some experience under his belt, and he would be gone. He knew he couldn't play with guys like Gary and Mitch for ever.

He had never met Amy in all the years they had been growing up in the same town; now he saw her all the time – out shopping on Corporation Street with an older woman he guessed was her mother, coming out of the Strathclyde with two other girls just as he was going in, granting him the same fleeting smile that he remembered from their first meeting, waiting at a taxi rank with a girl Derek remembered from school and two men, one of whom he supposed was the famous Alan Mackay. It wasn't till a few days before Christmas, though, that he saw her alone. He'd been to the Strathclyde with Gary and Mitch that lunch-time, but he'd left them around two, to do some last-minute shopping. He didn't know when – or even if – Francis was coming home from college, but he wanted to get him something, and he was crossing the market square on his way to the record shop when he recognised Amy walking towards him through the snow, laden with plastic bags. She had seen him first, and she was watching him, a smile forming that Derek thought was less of a greeting than a challenge.

'Hello,' he said. He considered her load of shopping bags. 'Do you want a hand?'

'Thanks.' She stood smiling at him, not moving. 'I was just going home.'

Derek couldn't tell if this was a yes or a no. 'OK,' he said, feeling stupid and helpless.

Amy laughed. 'What are you up to?' she said, glancing off to one side, as if she was afraid someone might be watching. Her voice was soft and, to Derek's mind, impossibly musical.

Derek shook his head. 'I'm just –' He thought hard. 'I was just going to the Charolais for a coffee.'

'Ah.'

'Would you like?' He looked off to one side, as if *he* was afraid someone might be watching. 'I mean. Would you like to go for a coffee?'

Amy laughed a little louder this time. 'Yes,' she said. 'I'd like to go for a coffee.'

They sat for an hour and a half before Amy said she had to go. The conversation over coffee and tea cakes had been easy and natural, in spite of the fact that Amy was another man's wife. Derek had expected to feel awkward; instead he had told her about music, and what he planned to do, and how he liked to be alone at Christmas, not with the family, sitting around the television eating cold mince pies. He had told her about his mother, and how she had been ill again – Amy seemed to know Lizzie, or to know women who had known her when she worked at Snakpak – and how he was hoping that this Christmas wouldn't be her last. For her part, Amy didn't say much. She sat listening, smiling, occasionally murmuring the odd casual response or comment, a knowing look in her eyes, as if she wanted him to know that she knew he was just going through the motions. Finally, Derek asked her what she was planning to do for the Christmas holidays.

'I'm going to be busy,' she said. 'I've still got so much to do. I should be doing the tree this afternoon. Still, I can do it tomorrow.' She smiled. 'I'm on my own tomorrow.'

Derek nodded thoughtfully. 'Are you?' he said. He couldn't think of anything else to say, and he knew he must sound clumsy and boyish to her – but then part of him knew that she liked that, that a woman like her probably had smooth bastards after her all the time, even if she was married to Alan Mackay.

'I like a nice Christmas tree,' she said, a little laugh in her voice that left him dizzy. 'You can come and see it, if you like.'

Derek nodded, aware that he looked far too serious. 'I'd like that,' he said.

'Well.' Amy stood up and started putting on her coat. 'Come tomorrow at two o'clock.' She told him her address on Station Road. 'I'll open a bottle of something,' she continued, 'and you can tell me how nice my tree looks.'

The next day, he was standing at the lower end of Station Road at a quarter to one. He had been up and down the street a couple of times, to locate the house, now he was waiting to see that Alan Mackay was definitely coming out, before he went in. He could see all he needed from here: he hadn't wanted to be noticed hanging around at the other end of the street, where people he knew might be going by on their way to the Nag's, but he could just see Amy's house from where he was, and he was unlikely to draw attention down here, opposite the factories. It had been snowing all morning; the snow had settled on the hedges and verges, everything white and still, with that empty, week-before-Christmas feel, the buses moving slowly by at the far end of the road, the odd muffled, anonymous figure walking to the pub or the village shops in a heavy winter coat, dark and small against the snow, like the people in old photographs. Derek waited, trying to look inconspicuous. Finally, at one fifteen, a dark, thick-set man emerged from the address Amy had given him and, even from this distance, Derek could see it was Mackay. The man waited a moment at his front gate, looking out, then he hurried off towards the village. Derek watched him vanish into the snow, then looked again at his watch. One twenty. Amy had said two o'clock, and he didn't want to be early. He remembered the old Corby village church – he'd been to a christening there once – and he decided to take a walk in the grounds to pass the time.

By the time he knocked at Amy's door, at three minutes past two, he was freezing. The cold had numbed his fingers to the knuckles; he couldn't feel his feet any more. He had been walking round and round the little churchyard, making lists to occupy himself: favourite albums, favourite tracks or singles, favourite all-time bass lines. Mingus: *Dynasty*. King Curtis: *The New Scene Of King Curtis*. Etta James: 'I'd Rather go Blind'. Bessie Banks: 'Go Now'. Paul Chambers on 'Dr Jekyll' or 'Sid's Ahead' from the *Milestones* album. He had thought about it randomly at first, then he'd started putting things in order. Then he had gone through the personnel on all the Miles Davis records he had ever heard. Cannonball Adderley, John Coltrane, Red Garland, Paul Chambers and 'Philly' Joe Jones on *Milestones*. Herbie Hancock, Chick Corea, Wayne Shorter, Dave Holland, Joe Zawinul, John McLaughlin and Tony Williams on *In a Silent Way*. Then he had gone back to thinking about bass players. That guy Pierre Michelot on the *Lift to the Scaffold* soundtrack. It was amazing how everything built around the bass, how the same people sounded just like themselves and at the same time just that little bit different, depending on who the bass player was.

Amy appeared as soon as he got to the door, almost before he had time to knock, and he wondered if she had been watching, keeping an eye out for him, wondering if he would show up.

Maybe she had even seen him hanging around earlier. She showed no sign of it, though. She didn't speak at first, but swung the door wide to let him pass; then, as Derek stepped in out of the cold, she grinned. 'You must be freezing,' she murmured happily.

Derek nodded. He could feel the warmth off her, could smell the warmth of her body touched with perfume and just a hint of the house, the glow of a coal fire, an intimation of citrus and old wrapping paper.

'I've been doing the tree all morning,' she said, as Derek stood waiting for her to tell him where to go. 'Do you want to take your coat off?'

Derek felt uncomfortable now, standing there in another man's house. He hadn't thought of Mackay before, other than as an obstacle, but he sensed him everywhere now: real and alive, getting ready for work, not wanting to go, thinking twice about it at his front gate, hurrying off to catch his bus. For the most fleeting moment, the thought crossed Derek's mind that he should go now, leaving everything just as it was, but when Amy smiled and reached to take his coat, he couldn't help himself: something had begun, a story with its own logic, its own energy. He shrugged off his damp coat and Amy took it and carried it down to the kitchen, leaving a trail of bright, glistening drops of melt-water all along the linoleum floor. She hung the coat over the kitchen door, then she switched on the hall light and turned, still smiling, but expectant, waiting to see what he would do – and Derek felt suddenly how important it was that he should do nothing, take nothing for granted. He stood motionless, watching her, waiting.

'It's all right,' Amy said. 'There's nobody here.'

He nodded. 'I know.'

'Then relax.' She looked serious all of a sudden. 'It's almost Christmas. Let's make this an afternoon to remember.' She turned back to the kitchen and looked around. 'Go through to the front room,' she said, after a moment. 'I'll bring some drinks. Would you like champagne?'

'Champagne?'

'Yes. Champagne. The real thing.'

Derek had never known anyone drink champagne, other than at weddings, and even then it was usually something else, something fizzy *pretending* to be champagne. He shook his head. 'Don't you want to keep it? For Christmas Day –'

Amy pursed her lips. Derek could see that she was wondering about him, wondering if he was going to spoil it all, with – what? His nervousness? His diffidence? Maybe she was thinking he had misunderstood. She had made it clear enough, what she expected, but he still didn't feel he could do or say anything to make her know that he did understand – and he did, he understood every-thing. He even understood that she didn't normally do this, that it wasn't just some game she was playing to get back at Mackay. 'I'd love champagne,' he said.

They drank a glass of champagne, then another, while Amy put the final touches to her Christmas tree. After the third glass, Derek realised he was feeling a little tight: he hadn't eaten since the night before and he wasn't used to champagne. He wasn't used to anything other than beer, and the effect was quicker than he had expected, quicker and more pleasant than anything beer did, a tight warmth in his face and hands, a softness to everything, a sudden magic in the Christmas tree lights and the baubles that Amy kept holding up against the tree, letting them dangle and spin on their cotton threads among the dark, citrus-scented branches. Finally, she was done.

'There,' she said, stepping back. 'What do you think.'

'It's beautiful,' Derek said. He meant it, too; it was the most beautiful tree he had ever seen.

Amy smiled. 'I told you I made a good Christmas tree,' she said. They were standing close together in the glow from the tree, closer than Derek had realised. He felt warm now: warm, and touched with magic, not just from the champagne, but from the proximity of her body, of her hair, her scent, her mouth. The decision he had made before, that he would do nothing, that he would presume nothing, was still there, at the back of his mind, even when he was kissing her, so he didn't know if he had been the one who had made things change, their bodies touching then folding together, the warmth of her mouth on his, her hand raised to touch his cheek, the astonishing presence of her flesh drawing him in, dissolving his resolve, making him at once more real and less decided. He had been determined that he would do nothing, and he had allowed himself to believe that nothing would happen; now, as he sank into the inevitability of what was happening, he saw that no decisions had been necessary, or even possible – that neither he nor Amy had decided upon this, or not really. It had been there from the first moment when they passed one another in the street, and that look had bound them together; it had been present ever since, in his mind and in his blood, a logic waiting to unfold, just as it was unfolding now: their bodies merging into the light of the tree, into the glimmer of tinsel and the sweet citrus-and-conifer scent that held them both, while the snow fell again outside and the window began to darken.

Most of what Derek knew about sex he had gleaned from magazines and Hollywood movies – and he was smart enough to know that, in this respect, he wasn't much different from the other boys he knew, just as he knew enough about the world to understand that the dirty pictures he'd seen in the playground, or floating around at The Works, were pure invention, a lie about power that, even as he'd stared at the naked women and the odd positions the couples got into in the story books – it was so obvious they had been arranged that way for the camera – he had been dismayed at how banal and calculated it all was. From the more explicit films he'd seen, he knew sexual intercourse was supposed to be a noisy, energetic affair, a not-too-gradual burn building up to a violent blaze, followed by cigarettes and fitful conversation. On a couple of occasions he had met a girl called Aileen at the Nag's Head or the Maple Leaf and she had taken him to her older sister's house, where they had gone to bed in the spare room and done all they could to make the night cine-matic, Aileen giving soft little cries and gasps that Derek wasn't convinced were altogether involuntary while she dug her finger-nails into his back and thrashed around, the bed creaking and shaking, and Derek all the time conscious of the sister, whose husband would be out on nights, sitting in the front room directly below them, filing her nails and sipping vodka and orange while she watched the late-night film. The relationship hadn't lasted long, maybe because the conversations were too fitful, maybe because Derek didn't like to smoke in bed, and Aileen hadn't seemed too disappointed when, at their last meeting, Derek had told her he couldn't go back to her sister's because he had to rehearse with the band. Though he would never have said it aloud, Derek couldn't help thinking that sex was not all it was cracked up to be.

Now, in an instant, everything was different. With Amy it was all touch and lingering contact, her fingers and lips drifting on his face and neck, leaving trails of sensation in his nerves, a surprising warmth that seemed to originate somewhere in the almost imperceptible borderline between his skin and hers, a borderline that kept shifting and melting away, so their bodies seemed to shimmer as he surrendered to a slow process that didn't build to a movie climax so much as lead him gently to the edge of a precipice and then, calmly, in one long swoop of pleasure, tipped him over and let him go, so that he was falling in mid-air, falling slowly, like Alice in the rabbit hole, lost to himself and, at the same time, aware of every nuance of touch and scent and taste, every sound, every movement. It had surprised him, that first time, how beautiful Amy became when they were lying together under the tree, locked in their own separate world, the taste of her mouth mingled with the scent of fir and the glitter of tinsel, her slender, pale body so very precise and lithe and true. When he had seen her on the street, he had noticed how pretty she was, but lying there inside her, in the glimmer from the Christmas tree lights, he realised that she was the first woman he had ever known who was truly beautiful, and he was gladdened for a moment by the half-formed suspicion that she was being beautiful for him in a way that she had never been for anyone else. It was as if some spirit hidden inside her skin had suddenly risen to the surface and come into the light and he couldn't help thinking, or at least wanting to believe, that this emergence, this awakening, had happened because of him.

The affair had lasted for four months; then, without warning or explanation, Amy had decided to end it. That afternoon they met at the boating lake and had gone for a walk in the woods. It was early in the spring, still, but it was warm, and the air smelled fresh, touched with sap and the promise of blossom, so close to nothing but sweetness it was hard to believe The Works were still there, about a mile away, in a fug of smoke and carbon. Derek had been happy that day, as he had been happy for weeks, for no good reason: Amy had never promised anything, they hadn't even discussed the possibilities that he'd imagined when he was alone, sitting up late with his guitar or listening to records, dreaming of a different life somewhere, like some kid in a '50s film noir. She had often talked about how much she hated Alan: it had turned out, she said, that her husband was a pig – which didn't surprise Derek much, though he was surprised at her surprise, surprised that she'd ever even thought of marrying him – and though he didn't hit her as such, he treated her badly, ordering her around, shouting at her when she did anything wrong, more or less forcing her to have sex when he came home drunk from the rugby club, telling her off like a kid when she spent money on something he didn't approve of. One night he'd come in pissed and crashed around the house for a while; she had heard him come in, and she'd tried to turn over and go to sleep, but she couldn't. Or maybe she had, because she was only half-awake when he'd appeared in the room, shaking her by the shoulder.

'Come on.' He was almost shouting. 'Get up. Come on. Wake up.'

She sat up in bed. 'What is it?' she said. She really thought something was wrong. She thought maybe he'd been in a fight. But he hadn't answered. He'd just made her get up and follow him downstairs to the hall, where he stopped and glowered at the floor. Repeating it to Derek, Amy had laughed at the memory, but he could tell she was disgusted. 'He'd been sick,' she said. 'And he wanted me to clean it up. That's why he got me out of bed. To clean up his mess.'

'So what did you do?' Derek asked, though he already knew the answer.

Amy smiled bitterly. 'What do you think?' she said. 'I cleaned it up. At least he didn't wake me up for a fuck.'

Derek was always surprised when she said things like that. Fuck. Cock. Buggery. She liked saying fuck, she liked to shock him a little, telling him what she wanted him to do, in Alan Mackay's bed. Sometimes it seemed that was all she had. Words. But that afternoon at the boating lake, she hardly spoke at all. They had walked for ages in silence, his happiness wearing down to doubt; then, when he was ready, she had said what she wanted to say – what she had obviously rehearsed saying – very quietly, while he listened, with the gradual realisation dawning on him that, behind the carefully maintained screen of his happiness, he had been expecting her to say it, sooner or later.

'I think it's time to call it quits,' she was saying. 'I mean, there's no future in it, not for us. I'm never going to leave Alan, and even if I did, I don't think it would last between me and you.' She considered a moment. 'It's been special. I'll never forget what we've had. But it makes sense, don't you think, to get out now, before we have to get out?'

Derek was confused. He didn't want to get out. He'd decided, long ago, that he loved her, and he wanted to take her away from Alan Mackay and Corby and the whole bit. He wanted to marry her, and live somewhere good and work at his music. He had wanted her to be free, just as he would be free. He had also been smart enough to realise how absurd that would sound, if he ever said it out loud.

'I knew you would understand,' Amy said. 'It's not that I don't –' She broke off and looked at him. 'Well. You know,' she said.

Derek shook his head. 'I *don't* understand,' he said. 'Why can't we just go on as we are?'

Amy looked unhappy. 'We can't,' she said, simply.

'Why not?'

'Because it won't work,' she said. She looked close to tears. 'You know it won't –'

'I don't know anything.'

'God, Derek. Please. Don't make me cry.'

'Why not?' He was angry now. 'Go ahead and cry.'

'Don't.'

'I want to be with you,' he said. 'I was going to ask you to come away with me. I was going to say –'

She raised her hands and half-covered her face. 'Don't,' she repeated. 'Please don't.'

'Why not? Who's going to stop us?'

She lowered her hands. He'd thought she was crying, but she wasn't. 'I am,' she said. 'Now, if you really care about me, you'll let it go. Just say goodbye, and keep what we had. Nothing can touch that.'

That was how it had gone, back and forth for an hour longer, not getting anywhere – and the worst thing was, Derek had let it go. By the time she left him, out in the spring woods, he had agreed not to try to see her, or to communicate with her in any way. If they met on the street, even if there was nobody else around, he was to walk right by and not say a word – and by the time Amy left, even though Derek had made no promises, she knew he had agreed to her demands. It was only then, when she knew she'd won the battle, that she let him see her cry – let him see and then, a moment later, turned on her heels and walked quickly away, knowing he would not follow. And it was only after she was gone that he realised what he had lost. He had let her go, just like that, standing in the woods, watching her walk back towards the town, a bird singing somewhere in the undergrowth, the sun starting to dip behind the trees, and he hadn't really registered that this was *it*: this was for good, the end. Even if he saw her again every day, passing her on the street or seeing her with her idiot of a husband on a Friday night at the White Hart or the Nag's, he would never be alone with her again, he would never touch her, or see her naked, or lie with her quietly in Alan Mackay's bed with that smell of her hair and the warmth of her on his mouth and hands. She was the only woman he had ever really known, even if it had only been four months. He had touched her, he had seen into her. He had been her lover, which was different from being in love, or having sex. All those years he had been half in love with Alina – or imagined he was in love with her – he could never have imagined touching her, never mind going to bed with her. Amy was the woman in all the songs he had ever wanted to play, and he had let her go, just like that. For weeks afterwards, he had gone over it again and again, trying to work out what he had done, what he hadn't done, what he should have done. He could have followed after her and told her whatever it was she needed to hear, said to her whatever it was he hadn't said, or hadn't said right, to make her stay. But he had let her go. He had watched her walk back towards the town on that muddy path they had set into the grass all the way from the back of the swimming pool to the boating lake; then, when she disappeared, he had turned and walked slowly home. It was days before he realised what had happened, days before he understood that her going was final, that the assumption he had made all along that their affair was leading to something had been a mistake. All that time, he'd kept at the back of his mind the simple, unchallenged notion – part wish, part romantic love song – that they would be together some day, and he'd never seen that Amy didn't believe in it, that she had never believed in it. He had wanted more; she had been ready to take whatever she could get, and leave it at that. Something had happened – Mackay had got suspicious, someone had seen them together and threatened to tell – and she had decided to give up everything they had. For a while, she had believed in something – he didn't doubt that – but she had never believed in the possibility of leaving Mackay and starting again. And why should she? Her life had been no different in most respects from his: everything happy was a daydream, a temporary condition, a handful of moments stolen from the run of things, tiny spots of colour in a wide desert of ash, momentarily bright, like the lights on a Christmas tree, beautiful and insignificant in the dark.

He had meant to take a taxi home, but as soon as he left the party, his mind started up with the usual argument: a taxi fare was money he could spend on other things, it was a good night, clear and warm and light, the streets empty, the stillness quiet and welcoming. Occasionally, he would take the risk and walk home late at night after the pubs had closed and the gangs were gone – the worst time was just after closing, when people were out looking for taxis, and gangs of boys were roaming up and down, angry and stupid and dangerous, looking to do damage. One night, outside the Candle, a man had been waiting for a taxi, standing on the kerb eating a poke of chips, and some boy had come up and asked him for one. The man shook his head, and said something like 'Get your own chips', not really meaning it, just as a joke, and the boy had pulled a razor out of his coat pocket and slashed the man's face from his ear to his chin, slitting the cheek open, blood everywhere, some girl screaming, a bunch of other boys standing off to one side watching, doing nothing. You were better off staying away from the taxi ranks and the area around pubs at closing-time, Derek reckoned, better to pick your way home through the quieter streets, or take a short cut through the woods, following those ghostly yellow paths through the dark, out past the boating lake and on up to the Beanfield, keeping your eyes peeled when you got back to the street, ready to melt back into the shadows if you saw anything suspicious. Tommy had told them about all the tricks, told them how some boy might approach you on a quiet street and ask for a light, and when you had your hands in your pockets, his mates would come up behind you and put you on the floor before you knew what was happening.

'What do you do', he would ask, 'if you see somebody lying on the ground, late at night, say, when nobody else is around?'

Derek would always shake his head and wait. He knew better than to answer.

'The boy might be genuinely hurt,' Tommy said. 'He might need help.'

Derek listened, looking serious.

'Then again,' Tommy would continue, 'it might be a trap. You go over, you lean down to see what's wrong, and somebody comes up, hits you from behind. That's it. So how do you know?'

Derek looked serious and waited for an answer – but Tommy just smiled enigmatically and shook his head. 'You don't,' he said. 'You never know.'

Which didn't help much. Derek wasn't sure whether he was supposed to treat everybody with suspicion, or whether there was some trick – some skill, some special awareness – that he had to acquire so he could tell the difference between what was real and what was a lie. Not that it ever mattered. When he was out at night he avoided people as much as he could, not just because he was afraid of what might happen, not just because there was something ugly, something morally unacceptable about the idea of falling victim to people like the Nivens and their ilk, but because it offended him even to admit that such people had any power at all, other than in numbers. Francis had told him, once, that he should ignore Tommy.

'Tommy's worried about us,' he said. 'But he never worries about himself.'

'That's because he can look after himself,' Derek answered. He knew his father's reputation, though it surprised him to think Tommy was so feared. It didn't seem right.

'So can I,' Francis said. 'I'm not afraid of anybody.'

'Well, maybe you should be.'

'What can you do?' Francis was shaking his head, looking serious for once. 'As Lizzie says: *what's for ye will no go by ye*. You have to live your life. It's a calculated risk.'

Derek snorted. He knew there was no such thing as a calculated risk. He'd heard the words used, read them in books, heard them on the radio, or the television, and he'd thought: what a luxury, this calculated risk, this danger over which you had at least some small portion of control. In Corby, there was no such thing. On any Saturday night, on the way home from the club, or the Nag's, a gang of men you had never even seen before could step out of the dark and beat you for so long and so hard you would never walk again, like Paul Cash, who'd been in Derek's year at school, but was in a wheelchair now, and didn't go out much, even in that. Or you would be standing at the bar in the Raven, ordering drinks and thinking about some girl you'd met on the dance floor a few minutes before, and some bastard would glass you for no reason, because he thought you were screwing him, or you'd jogged his elbow, or maybe the girl you'd been talking to was somebody he'd fancied for years, and he was pissed-off that you were having more success than he was. That had been how it happened to Max Phillips that time, Max Factor everybody called him, an old hippie who wouldn't have hurt a fly and always laughed along with people when they laughed at him, a dumb-saint of the mind, according to Francis. You couldn't calculate those risks: you were at the mercy of chance − chance, and the banal, stupid violence of boys like the Niven brothers and their gang. For as long as he could remember, Derek had been scared − not so much of what might actually happen, as of the squalor and humiliation of being one of the victims, of being stabbed or given a kicking in the public thoroughfare, of lying on the steps of a pub like Max, with blood seeping through your hands, while a bunch of half-sobered people stood watching, waiting for the ambulance to come. Whenever he left the house, he was all attention: listening, watching, his body tensed, the very marrow in his bones attuned to the possibility of something, some shift in the darkness a few feet away, a raised voice in the next street, the sound of running feet through one of the anonymous little courts around the Maple Leaf. Whenever he was out, he was always ready for something that, when it came, you couldn't be ready for. Once, when he was just a kid, he had been walking home from Our Lady's in the snowy woods and a bigger boy had appeared from nowhere, a boy of about sixteen, big and ugly and mean-faced, lurching towards him out of the twilight, a glimmer of malice in his eyes. Derek had thought about running, but something in him had rebelled at that – it was like an admission of something, an acceptance that this boy had some kind of natural right, by reason of his size and strength, to inspire fear. Derek had stopped and stood stock-still: he wouldn't accept it, he would not admit the boy's power, no matter what – and he could see that the boy had been surprised, even a little taken aback, in the moment or so before he had walked right up and nutted him. Derek hadn't felt anything, not even pain; he just stood looking at this boy, who had walked away a little startled. It had felt like something, that moment: not quite a victory, more an appropriate refusal.

What he had been refusing, he realised later, wasn't the power of the other boy, or his own weakness – it was the commonplace nature of his malice, the assumption that the attack was somehow natural. A year or so back, he had been playing a free gig at the Corinthian. It was as much a rehearsal as a gig, just trying things out in front of an audience they knew would mostly ignore them anyhow, but it had been experience, and some of the crowd in there – mad Bob, a couple of the other regulars – had been fairly appreciative, even clapping after a couple of numbers. They'd been stretching themselves, finding their limits – which hadn't been that difficult – playing a mix of jazz and blues, with some old R&B thrown in, and it had started to go pretty well after a while, Derek and Gary and Mitch, along with a guy called Oscar the Greek from Kettering on piano. Oscar was pretty good – better than the rest of them – and it had lifted them all. They had started not long after the place opened, and they had played non-stop, trying stuff out, breaking off now and then for a drink or a cigar – Oscar smoked these thin, sweet-scented little cigars that he produced from a tin every time they stopped for a rest. Because the place had been nearly empty when they started, they'd felt free to do anything they wanted, and they hadn't really noticed new people coming in: odd guys straggling in for the first drink of the day; boys with hangovers looking sheepish as they wandered to the bar and ordered hair of the dog; old men who hadn't shaved from the day before huddled over pint glasses or standing around with cigarettes hanging from their mouths, looking mystified; the big cheery-looking Sikh who always seemed to be in there, getting drunk slowly and deliberately, smiling when anybody spoke to him, but not saying much. It was an odd crowd – it always was in the Corinthian – the kind of ragtag band of wasters and solitaries you usually found in a town-centre pub, but that suited Derek fine. At one point, between numbers, a man in a pale blue raincoat came in and stood at the very end of the bar, close to the door. His cheeks and nose were flushed, the redness shot with tiny purple veins; to begin with, he seemed unhappy, worried about something and, at the same time, in a state of preparedness, ready, if necessary, to apologise, to placate. Joy the barmaid went over and he looked at her questioningly, as if he thought she was going to deliver a reprimand or throw him out. Instead, she smiled and he smiled back, relieved. Derek noticed there were stains on the sleeve of the coat, distinct, dark splashes that might have been blood, but could just as easily have been food, or paint. 'A pint and a half,' the man asked, in a breaking voice. He had noticed the musicians, and was turning to look at the band, interested, cheering up already. When the next number ended, he applauded, and a few of the other men at the bar joined in. Derek saw a surprised smile flicker across Joy's face.

That mood – led by the obvious appreciation of the man Oscar had quickly christened Famous Blue Raincoat – had deepened for an hour or so while the bar gradually filled. Derek had barely noticed the change; he was into the music now, into Oscar's playing and the idea that you could do stuff like this in a place like this, into the idea that there were people like Famous Blue Raincoat in the world, weary and unhappy, waiting to hear someone play jazz on a rainy Saturday morning in a smoky pub above a bus station. It wasn't till they were nearly finished that he noticed the atmosphere had begun to alter, the enthusiasm of the older men who had been there from the start subsiding gradually into a careful silence. That was when he saw the Nivens and their cronies, in from the rain and sitting off to one side of the room, around a table covered with freshly drawn lagers, watching the proceedings, waiting for the right moment to break in. Stewart Niven and MicMac kept looking at each other, the same fixed expressions of disbelief on their faces. They didn't have to say anything, that look said it all. Finally, Stewart stood up and walked towards the band.

'What the fuck is this?' he said, talking to Gary. 'You call this music?'

Gary shot Derek an unhappy look. Stewart Niven wasn't the kind of person he wanted to be discussing the finer points of jazz with. 'We're just playing,' he said. 'You know. Anyway, we're almost finished.'

'So what is it you're playing?' Niven placed extra emphasis on *playing*, turning back to his gang and grinning. The whole room was listening now. Derek looked at Joy, standing behind the bar, and shook his head.

'It's jazz,' Gary answered quietly.

'Jazz?' Niven grimaced. 'How is it jazz?'

'You know. Improvising.'

Niven turned back to the table where his brother and the rest of the gang sat watching.

'Hey, Andy,' he said. 'He says they're improvising.'

Andy laughed. 'Nah,' he said. 'They're just making it up as they go along.'

Nobody laughed – though Derek thought this was pretty funny, coming from someone like Niven. A moment later, Joy appeared from behind the bar.

'All right,' she said. 'The entertainment's over. Let's have a big hand for –' She looked at Gary, suddenly puzzled, and Derek remembered they didn't have a name. They were just four guys playing in a bar on a Saturday lunch-time. A few of the older men clapped, and Oscar even stood up at the piano and ventured a bow, but the atmosphere they had built that morning had been destroyed.

Still, when he thought about it later, Derek realised that what mattered wasn't the way their gig had ended, but what had happened before the Niven gang came in. They had touched people. Famous Blue Raincoat, for example. Derek wished he could have spoken to him, and found out who he was, but the man had disappeared as soon as the set had finished, and Derek had never seen him again. The Nivens had hung on, watching, making what they probably thought were smart remarks. They were particularly interested in Oscar, with his long black hair and his thin cigars, and for a while Derek had worried that they would be followed out to the car park, when they came to piling their stuff into Gary's van. It wouldn't have surprised him. Nothing about the Nivens would have surprised him. He'd remembered a Saturday lunch-time a few weeks back, when he'd been here with Gary and Mitch, and the whole gang of them – the Nivens, MicMac, Danny the Frog and a couple of other boys whose names he couldn't remember – had taken up residence at the next table, pulling their chairs up round a ring of lagers like pigs going to swill, mumbling insults at one another and staring around the place, waiting for someone to return the look, so they could get started. Derek knew the routine. He was always surprised, at such times, that the Nivens didn't recognise him as Francis's brother – but then, maybe they did. Maybe they were scared to go after Derek because of Tommy – there was something about the way they never looked at him, or looked right past him, as if he didn't exist at all, that made Derek wonder what strange charm being Tommy Cameron's son had conferred upon him.

It had been quiet, that Saturday lunch-time. A few of the old boys were standing at the bar, managing pints and chasers. The big Sikh was already drunk, smiling vaguely at the room in general, getting down on one knee occasionally and balancing his pint glass on his thigh, the way he did from time to time when he was drunk, all concentration, performing for himself, ignored by the other boys at the bar. Nobody in the Corinthian had ever seen a Sikh before this boy turned up in his big maroon turban and a tight jersey exactly the colour of the grammar school's uniform jumper, but an unspoken agreement had been reached, that first day, that nobody would bother the boy, as long as he wasn't bothering anybody else. Derek had never understood how this worked: even the Nivens left him alone, though they would stop what they were doing every now and then and watch him with an air of satisfied contempt as he swayed to and fro, or did his balancing act on the floor by the bar, setting his pint on his thigh and stretching out his arms like a tightrope walker, pleased with himself, drunk and remote and happy. The Sikh never appeared at night, only at lunch-time, and he never spoke, other than to order his drinks. Derek had never seen anybody get so drunk so quickly.

It had been quiet, and slow, even when the pub began to fill up. Some days were like that, rainy and slow, the nothing-doing kind of days when you had a few pints and drifted home, or off to the bookie's or the Charolais, and waited for the evening. Still, nobody had noticed The Kid when he turned up, a wee boy of around twelve or thirteen in a damp T-shirt and raggedy jeans, sneaking in the back door from the car park side and sloping up to the nearest table clutching a purse, his face carefully set in an expression he probably thought of as winsome. It was just his luck — probably the kind of luck that followed him around — that he chose the Niven gang's table to slope up to. Derek noticed him not long after he appeared, silent and watchful, ready to bolt, in a desperate hover at MicMac's elbow, and he stopped listening to Gary, who was droning on about the band they were planning to put together with him as front man. The Kid was thin, shifty-looking, about as winsome as any weasel, in spite of his best efforts. If Derek had been asked to sum him up in a single phrase, he would have said 'deserving victim'. He was one of those kids who always looked guilty, the boy the teachers picked on at school because — as they always said — even if he hadn't done what he was accused of doing, he had obviously been up to *something*. From the look of it, MicMac was working on the same logic.

'Please, mister,' the boy said, addressing MicMac, but looking around the whole table, cautious, hopeful, ingratiating. 'Can you buy me a drink?' He held up the purse. 'I've got money.'

MicMac smiled. He looked, for a moment, like somebody's older brother. 'What do you want?' he said. 'A coke?'

The Kid looked at the pint glasses all around the table. 'Is that a lager top?' he asked.

MicMac nodded and the boy nodded back. 'I'll have a lager top,' he said.

MicMac laughed. The others were watching now, waiting to see what would happen.

'You're a bit young, aren't you?' MicMac said.

The Kid shook his head. 'I'm old enough,' he said. 'I've got money, see?'

MicMac looked at the purse and nodded. He was playing it slow. 'So I see,' he said. 'Where did you get it?'

The wee boy looked at him and told a barefaced lie – and everybody, himself included, knew it. 'I found it,' he said. 'Out there. In the car park.'

'Ah.' MicMac reached out his hand. 'Can I see?'

The Kid wasn't sure now, but he must have figured he had gone too far not to hand the purse over. MicMac seemed harmless enough. All the faces around the table looked friendly. As soon as MicMac had the purse in his hand, he opened it up and looked inside. Then he turned to the boy. 'This is a lot of money,' he said, still playing the new-found older brother. 'You could buy a lot of drinks with this.' He snapped the purse shut.

The Kid swallowed. Too late, he began to see his mistake. 'I just want a pint of lager top,' he said, adding, desperately, 'and one for yourself, if you like.'

MicMac laughed. 'That's good of you,' he said. He looked at the others. 'What about my pals here?'

The Kid nodded quickly. He was calculating how much he was going to lose. 'One for them too,' he said.

Suddenly MicMac's mood changed. Now, instead of the amused but indulgent big brother, he was all moral indignation. 'You didn't find this purse, did you, son?' he said, looking around at the others. The Nivens sat glowering now, like a bench full of judges. MicMac winked at Danny the Frog and turned back to the boy quickly, his face all accusation. 'Tell me the truth now,' he said, his voice rising just a little. 'You stole this purse, didn't you?'

The Kid looked scared, but he was ready to try bluffing it. 'I didn't,' he said. 'Honest.' He was staring at the purse, which MicMac held in his firm grip. 'I found it.'

'All right. Where did you find it?'

The Kid looked desperate. 'Out on the street,' he said. 'It doesn't belong to nobody.'

'It must belong to someone.'

'I found it,' The Kid said. 'It's mine.'

'Finders keepers, losers weepers,' MicMac said, his voice dripping sarcasm. The boy didn't answer. MicMac looked at him a moment, then he opened the purse again and removed the handful of notes inside. Derek could see it was about thirty pounds in fivers, maybe more. MicMac slipped the notes into his pocket and handed back the purse. 'Take this back to your mother,' he said.

'It's not my mother's,' The Kid said, his voice close to a whine. 'It's mine. I found it.'

'Well take it and fuck off,' MicMac snapped. 'What are you hanging about here for?'

The wee boy started to cry. 'Come on, mister,' he said.

'Fuck off,' MicMac said quietly, his voice even. 'Or I'll call the manager.' The Nivens were laughing now, as MicMac slipped the empty purse into the boy's pocket.

'It's not fair,' The Kid cried. 'That's my money –'

MicMac stood up quickly and walked towards the bar. It was Big Dave's day in, and though he wasn't the manager, he must have looked pretty imposing to The Kid, who didn't wait for MicMac to speak, but bolted out the back door the way he had come. MicMac watched him go, then he fished the stolen money from his pocket and strutted back to the table. 'What'll it be, boys?' he asked.

Stewart Niven let out a low whistle. 'You really are a fucking bastard,' he said, with obvious approval.

'Yeah,' MicMac said, 'but I'm the bastard who's buying.'

Derek was always surprised at the routine malice of people like the Nivens and MicMac. Lizzie would say there was good in everybody, if only you could find it, but Derek knew she only thought that because the Church told her so, told her not to judge, but forgive – even though the Church was always judging, and never forgiving, condemning people to hell left, right and centre. If Cash Cromwell had had his way, everybody who put nothing in the collection on a Sunday, every wife whose husband had spent all they had on drink the night before, waving an empty hand over the scatter of coins and occasional notes on the plate and hoping nobody would notice, everybody who didn't do their utmost for the upkeep of the church would burn in hell for all eternity, no questions asked. The funny thing was, Derek didn't believe in forgiveness – not for people like the Nivens. It was important, he thought, to feel a righteous contempt for such people, to refuse their world and put forward another way of being, a world that theirs would displace if it could. Why would he choose to believe in forgiveness? Why would he choose to forgive? If Jesus really did forgive us, why was there a hell at all? It was absurd. As a boy, Derek had always gone to Mass to keep Lizzie happy, but he'd never thought about God, just Jesus and the Holy Ghost, the one closer to him than any man he could think of, the other beautifully remote, part spirit, part questing bird. Yet even though the canopy above the altar showed a huge white dove hovering over the tabernacle, Derek preferred to imagine the Holy Ghost as a wind moving on the waters, inscrutable and elusive, than as some glorified pigeon. Then, when he was about sixteen, he and Francis had decided, quite independently, that they couldn't bear to hear another of Cash Cromwell's sermons on the upkeep of the church, and they had stopped going. Of course, he'd given up much more quietly than Francis. With his little brother, missing Mass had been a piece of theatre: rebellion, arguments, Lizzie's tears, Tommy's anger, Francis's steadfast refusals. They had probably given up going for the same reasons, but Derek had just slipped off somewhere – to the woods, or the boating lake, where he'd sit by the water, reading a book, thinking about the future, planning his escape. He couldn't understand his parents and their good Catholic friends: even if they didn't agree with Francis's objections to the way Cash Cromwell went on and on about money, milking them for all he could get and always complaining that they weren't giving enough, or with the hypocrisy of a Church that was supposed to care for the poor, but stored up huge treasures here on earth in exactly the way Jesus said you weren't supposed to do – even if they didn't agree with all that, surely they could see there was something impossible about Christianity itself, about living by these particular commandments, about turning the other cheek, about loving everybody. Christ, how could he – how could anybody – love his neighbour as himself? Why would he want to? He didn't want anybody's *love*, he just wanted to be treated with some basic decency. All those people talking about love, they were lying and cheating and robbing one another all the time, and nobody seemed

to care. Maybe that was why they'd made up that impossible religion of love, Derek thought: because it was impossible, and everybody knew it, there was no real pressure to live up to it, no real
need to do anything but go through the motions, carrying on
with business as usual in the meantime. And business was always
about taking advantage. If they'd had another system, another set
of rules based on the ordinary, possible decency of which people
were capable, everything would be different. People wouldn't be
set the impossible task of loving their neighbours, they would
just have to treat them as human beings. There would be no
excuses.

Now Lizzie was dead, he wished they had kept up the pretence
a little longer for her sake. Francis would get angry — a lie was
a lie, was how he saw it, but there were lies and lies. Lizzie's life
had been a struggle to keep the lies by which she lived in one
piece, more or less, a struggle to keep going as well as she could,
with dignity and self-respect, in a world that would do anything,
it seemed, to strip that dignity away. For years she wore the same
coat, with the same navy-blue headscarf he had bought her from
his saved-up pocket money one Mother's Day, when he was about
thirteen. He remembered her going round the shops, checking
the prices, and storing them in her head, then going round again
and buying what was on offer, saving a few pennies here, a few
there, taking hours about it but feeling, at the end of the day,
that she had won something, that she had asserted some value
she felt was important. All the money she saved in a day wouldn't
have paid for a round of drinks down at the Hazel Tree, but that
wasn't what mattered to her. The only thing that mattered was
that she had control of something, besides what Tommy gave her
'for the house'. Whatever she saved she had won for herself, for
the odd box of Black Magic to share round, watching television
on a Saturday night while Tommy was at the pub, or a bar of
good soap that she would hide away in a cupboard under the
sink for months, so it would harden and last longer. She liked
taking baths, and she liked the smell and feel of good soap. It
was the cheapest way of having quality in your life, to spend a
few pence extra on a bar of soap, so you knew that, in one thing
at least, you had something like the best. The first job Derek had,
tending the fruit and nut machines at Snakpak, he'd bought her

a whole pack of Imperial Leather and some nice talc out of his wages, just to see the look on her face when he gave it to her. All his life, he had wanted to make her happy and all his life he had known it was an impossible task. Nothing could make her happy: she was too disappointed. The doctors said she had died of cancer, but Derek knew that she had died of the same thing that killed everybody else here, the same thing that would probably kill him sooner or later – disappointment.

He had meant to take a taxi, but he hadn't, even though he almost always got a taxi on summer nights, in spite of the arguments he had with himself about money. He knew enough to know that summer nights were the worst times to be out on the streets because, even though there were fights in the winter, acts of drunken rage or madness around Christmas and Hogmanay, it always seemed crueller and more pointless in summer, on the long grey-green evenings, leaves on the trees and that scent on the air of sap and honeydew, and some gang stepping out from the shadows, hard-eyed, stupid, attuned only to their own dull rhythm, like hunting dogs. On summer nights, the violence felt more calculated, boys from the Rangers Club ducking into the Catholic disco, singling out some kid near the door and beating him senseless, or waiting outside the Nag's or the Open Hearth for some straggler and cutting his face or throat open with bottles or knives. It never took more than a minute or two, the five or six on one circling quickly and moving in close, moving into the rhythm, raining down blows and kicks, aiming for the head, the neck, the ridge of the spine. None of those boys would have done anything like this on their own. None of them would have known how. Everything depended on rhythm, everything was determined by the group.

Now, as he walked back in the soft half-light, it felt to Derek that the attacks were getting closer and more random all the time. Two streets away from where he was walking was where Paul Cash was attacked on his way home from a date, knocked to the ground and beaten so badly that he'd been left crippled for life. At the Raven, Derek had been standing at the bar, listening to the band, when Max Factor suddenly went down, just a couple of feet away. Derek hadn't seen a thing: one minute the guy was there, trying to get a drink, the next he was on the floor, a hole gaping in his neck, while a girl stood screaming three feet away and two other men worked with bar towels, trying to staunch the flow of blood. Derek had helped carry the guy outside – someone thought the cool night air would slow the bleeding, or at least calm Max down – while they waited for the ambulance. Later, he couldn't get the image out of his mind, not just of the wound, but of the look on Max's face, surprise more than fear, bewilderment as much as surprise – and under it all, that ancient grief of men like Max and Derek, the solitary, the defenceless, the ones who couldn't have belonged to the group rhythm even if they had wanted, and so were constantly singled out, like rogues separated from the protection of the herd. It turned out that Max had jostled some guy's arm as he went to pick up his beer, and the guy had cut him so he wouldn't look bad in front of his mates, who were standing a few feet away, watching, seeing it all. Everybody knew who those guys were, but nobody said or did anything. The Raven was neutral ground: if something like this had happened in the Catholic club, say, there would have been reprisals, gangs working their way back and forth through the summer, laying traps, springing ambushes, rapt with the rhythm of the group, with the beautiful machinery of attack. Meanwhile, the trees flowered in the parks and gardens; the long nights grew sweet and still; the darkness deepened around them like the wings of a theatre.

There were nights when anything seemed possible. A man out walking his dog on Occupation Road was attacked with an axe and left for dead; a fifteen-year-old boy was singled out on his way home from the fish and chip shop opposite the Phoenix: while four of the gang held him down, another pulled out his two front teeth with a pair of pliers. It was ten thirty; people walking by would have heard his screams. That was the worst, Derek thought: to be in the power of others, and to know that nobody would lift a finger to help. Sometimes he could feel it in the air: freedom and violence, the rage of summer, the simmer of the group everywhere he went. Though he couldn't really afford it, he always took taxis on nights like that. He was aware of the fact that people knew he was Tommy Cameron's son, but that could as easily have made him a mark as anything else. It was odd. Francis went wherever he liked, on foot, and nobody ever bothered him. Derek couldn't get away with that.

Still, he was almost home safe when he found Mickey D. The boy was in a bad way, lying on the ground at the edge of the road, his face bloodied, his shirt ripped. Derek remembered what Tommy had told him about finding somebody on the street at night, then he hurried over to Mickey and crouched down beside him. He didn't really know the boy – he remembered him vaguely from school – but he knew there was no harm in him. 'What the hell happened to you?' he said.

'Fucking Nivens,' Mickey spluttered, spitting blood. It looked like they'd broken some of his teeth. 'Five of them. The Nivens, Mackenzie, fucking Danny Boyd –'

'Can you get up?'

'Nah.' Mickey struggled hopelessly then sank back. 'I think my leg's broken. Fucking Danny the Frog jumped on my leg, can you believe it? If that bloke hadn't come along –' he looked off to one side.

Derek looked too, suddenly alarmed. Maybe it was a set-up, only different from the one Tommy had described. 'What bloke?' he said.

Mickey lay back and pointed. 'He's over there,' he said. 'They gave him a real battering.'

Derek stood and took a few steps off into the half-dark where Mickey had been pointing. The sky was beginning to lighten now, a pale greenish gloaming out beyond the houses. When Derek got to the kerb he saw a body splayed on the pavement about fifteen feet away. He was surprised he hadn't seen it right away. He knew he was breaking all of Tommy's rules – don't get involved, keep on moving – but he walked over to where the body lay: a shapeless bundle that only gradually resolved into a human form lying on its side, blood pooling around the head. If it hadn't been for the bright blue shirt, he would never have guessed who it was: the face was raw, the nose and mouth smashed, the eyes blacked out, the hair a welter of blood. He felt sick: it was obvious, even at first glance, that Jan was either dead or dying. He glanced back to where Mickey lay watching. At the same time, he heard the sirens, away in the distance. Too late, as usual.

'Is he all right?' Mickey called. Derek shook his head. He

couldn't say anything. He remembered Francis asking him to keep an eye on Jan at the party hours ago. So how had the boy got here, when his house was on the other side of town? What the fuck was he doing *here*? 'You'd better get going,' Mickey shouted. 'The boys in blue are on their way.'

Derek nodded, but he stayed where he was. He told himself he should do something, get Jan into the recovery position, try giving him the kiss of life, but he couldn't move – and he wasn't really sure what the recovery position was, when he thought about it. All the time, he was wondering how Jan had gone a good mile and a half out of his road. Meanwhile, the sirens were getting closer. 'It's time to go,' Mickey called. 'Go on.'

Derek looked at him. The boy was on something, that was sure, and he remembered people talking about Mickey, saying how he'd take anything he could get – Mandies, speed, H, anything. Now, when he was all bloody and probably had a broken leg, he was more concerned with what happened to Derek than anything else. He was right, of course. It wouldn't do to be found here, especially not now. 'You're sure you're OK?' he asked.

Mickey nodded. 'Why did he do it?' he asked, suddenly. 'I mean – he must have known, right?'

Derek nodded. 'I suppose so,' he said; then, as the sirens approached, he walked away quickly, steady, not running, and turned the corner into the green of the morning twilight.

Francis was gone. He had disappeared some time between the funeral service and now. Derek had guessed as much, but he wasn't sure till Alina caught him up on the way to the gate, sombre and oddly elegant in her funeral clothes, her face much older now than Derek remembered from school, just four years before. 'Thanks for coming,' she said. 'It was a nice thought.'

'I had to come,' Derek said, and it occurred to him that he couldn't ever tell her why. 'He was such a good friend to Francis.'

Alina nodded. 'Have you seen him?' she asked. 'Francis, I mean.'

Derek shook his head. 'He was at the church,' he said. 'I've not seen him since.' Suddenly, he realised. Everybody knew what had happened: Mickey D hadn't said anything to the police, but he'd told his brother at the hospital, and his brother had told somebody else, and soon the word was all over town that the

Niven gang had killed some kid who'd tried to stop them killing Mickey. Mickey hadn't told why they picked on him in the first place, but it didn't matter, Francis would have known by now who was responsible and he would be planning something, some kind of revenge, some kind of *justice*. That was how it worked, everybody knew how it worked, you didn't talk to the police, you waited for your chance and, as soon as you could, you hit back, an eye for an eye, a tooth for a tooth. A life for a life – that was what Francis would be thinking now, one life, or maybe two, maybe five, the Nivens, MicMac, Danny the Frog, whoever else Mickey had said was there. Derek remembered he'd said it was five of them, and he realised, standing in the warm August sunlight with Alina in her simple, terrible black suit, that Francis would know who they all were, and that, sooner rather than later, he would go after them. He was probably out there at that very moment, Derek thought, setting his vengeance in motion, waiting in the deep summer shadows somewhere, nursing the cold hard weight of his anger against the warmth of the summer sun.

Tommy

A S THE FAMILY and their guests walked back to the cars, Tommy realised that Francis was gone. He'd been there at the beginning: standing outside the church he had looked grief-stricken and lost – much more grief-stricken, Tommy thought, than he had at Lizzie's funeral less than a month ago. Which shouldn't have come as a surprise, knowing how much Lizzie had suffered over the last six months, and over the years for that matter, sick with something or other ever since they had come here, so it was almost a release for them all when it was finally over. You could hardly measure something like that against a boy's life, especially a boy like Jan Ruckert, who had shown so much promise. Still, it was odd, after all those years of being Lizzie's favourite, that Francis had seemed so cold, so still in himself at *her* funeral, as if he had been intent, not on holding something back so much as not pretending to feelings he didn't have. Now, his feelings were impossible to conceal. He wasn't in tears, he was just as still as he had been in this same church among the handful of friends who'd come to Lizzie's service – Tommy could hardly believe how many people were here now, maybe a hundred, maybe even more than that, watching, saying nothing, just taking it all in – he was just standing off by himself, beside the hedge in the warm July sunshine, pale, desolate and completely untouchable. Francis had seen him then, when everyone was assembling outside the church, standing out on the pavement having a last cigarette before the service and waiting while some detail was sorted out, but he hadn't spoken, just shown, with a slight shift of expression, that he'd noticed Tommy was there, before looking away. A few minutes later, the crowd had started filing into the church, the men out on the pavement taking last drags on their cigarettes and tossing them into the gutter, the women and children falling out of the quiet, murmuring groups they had formed in the grounds and joining their husbands as they entered into the darkness of the church.

Tommy hadn't been to St Brendan's for years. He had stopped going to regular Mass not long after they'd moved south, much to Lizzie's annoyance. It wasn't so much that he had stopped believing as he'd got tired of the idea of belief. He had been brought up to think that faith was precious, that God concealed Himself to test us, that faith was nothing if it was not irrational. If you had proof, that wasn't faith. If you never doubted, then you never really believed, because to believe was to overcome doubt, to carry on in the absence of proof, just as our Saviour had done in his final hours, when it seemed his own Father had abandoned him. It had seemed a beautiful idea to Tommy when he was fifteen, even when he was twenty-five, but by the time Lizzie fell ill, and his boys grew into strangers, he'd seen through the deception – because it was a deception, this call to irrational faith – and he had stopped going to Mass, stopped praying, stopped even thinking about it. In the beginning was the land, that was what Arthur used to say – and Tommy had never doubted him, but he had never really understood that you couldn't have both, that the God in heaven and the divinity Arthur found in the earth were beyond reconciliation. It had taken years to see what the old man was getting at: the land wasn't just Scotland, or the fields they had explored all those years ago, it was everything. It was life itself: it was the birds of the air and the deer in the hills, it was the trees, the grass, the wind, the earth, the water. To begin with, Tommy had been aware of a loss: he had grown up in the Church, his family and their families had been believers – Arthur excepted. In the end, though, it was a relief, even a kind of happiness, not believing. Or not believing in what he had learned to believe and finding his way into something else – some old, dark, earthly thing – a step at a time, working by touch and guesswork, recovering something from the depths of his body, like a man finding a wreck, or some cargo of precious metal at the bottom of a deep, quick-flowing river.

Yet, now, when he thought about it, with the worst of the struggle over, he saw that he had always doubted the faith of his fathers. For years, he had envied the Presbyterians their bleached, angular spaces, the clear windows and whitewashed walls where God was suggested only by an absence. What he wanted was quiet; all this theatre – the vestments, the incense, the stained-glass windows that muddied the light as it fell in one long ray of light on the boy's coffin – all this grand opera was more than he could bear, twice in one month – and he realised he had always disliked Catholicism, even when he had gone to Mass every Sunday morning, kneeling to atone for the failings of the week, or the frequent excesses of Saturday night. He had hated it all along, with its dark cupboards packed with fabric and spices, its pink-cheeked statues of St Anthony and the Holy Virgin, its damp, slightly too masculine smell under the contrived surface of wax and lace – hated it, and never once dared to admit how much. He had been brought up to believe in opposites: presence or absence; life and death; God and the Devil; something, or nothing.

Now, it felt like an achievement that he had stopped believing. Katrina had been part of that – all those books she had made him read, all those questions she had put into words – but, most of all, he had given up believing around the time Lizzie had first fallen ill, as a kind of preparation for what was to come. For he had known all along – from the first operation to the last miserable, drugged days – that Lizzie was marked. Nobody could have grown up as he had, watching his mother and father, his uncles, his neighbours go down one by one, hearing the whispers in hallways and sick-rooms, catching that faint loamy smell that clung to the linen and curtains, without knowing cancer the moment it entered the house, before the doctors knew, or said for sure that they knew, before the thing took hold, before the smell of death – a smell at once darker and sweeter than cancer's metallic perfume – took up residence, familiar and almost reassuring in its finality, spreading slowly from the sick-bed, filling the curtains, slipping quietly downstairs in the night to colonise the front room, so guests would know, the moment they passed through the front door, what the patient upstairs was working so hard not to understand. In those first days of Lizzie's illness, Tommy had prayed, but his prayers had been offered up in a condition of quiet desperation that convinced him, far more than any of Arthur's arguments could have done, that belief was no longer possible – and that was when he had repented of his life, repented, not of his sins, but of his mistakes, which were different, and far more damaging than any sin the Church could condemn him for. He repented, and it was this repentance that sealed him off for ever from Lizzie, because all that he repented of was exactly the faith she dwelled within, simple and doomed, while the promise their lives had once held decayed into silence and misunderstanding. He repented, and his repentance seemed to him bitter and good and necessary, but it was, of necessity, a private matter, a secret he'd thought he would be obliged to keep for the rest of his life, until he met Katrina.

He hadn't seen Katrina at all during those last weeks when Lizzie was fading away in the bedroom, fading like a stain that had been there for years, dark and at the same time faint, like an ink-mark bleaching out in the sun. He hadn't seen her, not because he was guilty about what they had shared over the years – it wasn't sex and he didn't think anyone had the right to prohibit friendship, not even Lizzie, who had taken so much else from him – but because he didn't want her to be tainted by that darkness, he didn't want her to see it clinging to his skin, or smell the sickly-sweet aroma of it on his breath. He hadn't seen her for weeks, and she had known enough to stay away – she had exams, and then she had been on holiday, travelling around France with a friend, a girl she knew from college, happy to be getting away from home, away from Corby, probably away from him too, though she had never said it. Then, when she came back – it was the day after Lizzie's funeral – they had met on the street by accident, and they had stood talking a while, awkward all of a sudden, though they had never been so before. Katrina had said he should come round some time when her dad was out and see the pictures she'd taken on her trip and Tommy had said he would, knowing in his heart that he wouldn't, knowing that something had changed between them. He had talked to her for about twenty minutes, maybe half an hour, and he hadn't even told her about Lizzie, but it didn't matter, because she didn't need to know. He hadn't noticed Francis till after she was gone, walking away on the sunlit street, suddenly remote and young, and so unlike himself in nature and temperament that he was surprised they had ever been friends, if friends was what they had been. He wasn't sure about that – he had tried every way he could to bury his desire for her, not a sexual thing, just a wish to reach out and touch her, a wish to connect with her, and maybe not even with her, but with anyone, after all those cold years with Lizzie. He hadn't seen Francis, so he didn't know how long the boy had been there, but it was obvious from the expression on his face that *Francis* had seen *them*, and had judged accordingly. It was a judgment that Tommy knew was fair, even if, technically, it wasn't right. He could hide that wish to touch Katrina from them both, and they could both pretend he had been successful, but any outsider could have read him like a book, and Francis was no fool, in spite of the fact that, in everything that mattered, he was.

They hadn't spoken since. Tommy had heard from Derek what happened to Jan Ruckert, and he had decided to attend the funeral on principle, because he had liked the boy, what he had seen of him. It was something he'd needed to do, to go back to the graveyard and pay his respects, just fifteen yards from where they had buried Lizzie: being there, he felt he was in touch, not so much with her, as with all his dead – with Arthur, with his parents, with Lizzie, with the boy he had scarcely known, but liked, for no good reason. He had been brought up to think of the dead going to an afterlife, but that afternoon, standing in the warm sunshine with half the town looking on, he had wondered if this was all there was, this return to the earth, not ashes to ashes, not dust to dust, but water and salt and carbon returning to the wet earth and becoming something else, something new. The thought – the thought of becoming the very thing that replaced what had gone before – appealed to him. It was better than that old Catholic idea, the resurrection of the dead, or the notion of ghosts, waiting till the day of judgment, crowding the earth, looking for what they had lost. Imagine the ghosts we would have, he thought, if all those spirits returned – not just the people, but everything: the animals, the birds, the children dead in childbirth, the trees felled to make way for factories and roads. Think of the slow fade of those ghostly stains on the air, in the grass, in the earth. Better, he thought, that everything decayed to those smallest particles, atoms and molecules, drops of water, grains of salt. He remembered how Katrina had told him about the painters on Lake Baikal, working on their tiny, beautifully detailed miniatures, how they rowed out to the centre of the lake to work, so not a single speck of dust could fall on the wet paint, so everything would be perfect. Those miniatures – tiny boxes, painted eggs, exquisite and absurd beyond beauty – were the only objects in the world untouched by the dust of what had gone before. That was probably what made them so precious.

Derek came level with him on the road home. He looked worried. 'Have you seen Francis?' he asked, almost breathless from catching Tommy up.

'I saw him,' Tommy said. 'Then he disappeared.'

'What do you think he's doing?'

Tommy shook his head. 'I wouldn't know, son,' he said. 'Your brother's not talking to me.'

'Why's that?'

Tommy stopped walking. They were standing outside the shops, not far from the place where Jan had been attacked. 'He thinks I did wrong by your mother,' he said. 'He thinks I let her down.'

Derek was puzzled, but only for a moment. Tommy saw it in his face – the boy knew about Katrina, or he knew something about what had been going on. The understanding that dawned on his face betrayed as much. 'Anyway, it's been a long time since Francis talked to me,' Tommy added, as much to distract himself from that look as anything.

Derek shook his head. 'I don't know,' he said. 'I think he's maybe going to do something stupid.' He looked unhappy, as if he wasn't sure he should be saying any of this. 'I don't know,' he repeated, looking away.

'What are you talking about?'

Derek looked up. 'He's not said anything about all this,' he said. 'Not a word. And now he's just disappeared. He didn't even speak to Alina, or her mum. He just walked away.'

'So?'

'So maybe he's going to do something.'

'Like what?' Tommy already knew what his son was saying, and he felt that old chill in his heart, when he thought of Francis in one of his cold rages, striking out, icy and determined, bent on destruction.

'I think he'll try to get the people that did this,' Derek said. 'The police won't touch them. Nobody will say anything. But Francis knows who they are. Everybody does.'

Tommy didn't know who they were. He'd not even thought about it. Gangs, boys in the night, fools with too much drink in them. That was all he'd thought. 'Who was it?' he asked quietly, trying to seem casual. He already knew what he was going to have to do.

'Stewart and Andrew Niven,' Derek said. 'Michael Mackenzie. That gang.'

'How do you know?' Tommy asked.

'Everybody knows.'

Tommy nodded. He knew about the Nivens and their kind. He'd worked for a while with their father, before the man had been thrown out of The Works for stealing, and he'd seen the boys around. They didn't come into the Hazel Tree – they wouldn't have dared – but Tommy had noticed them in the town-centre pubs, swanning about, acting big. They were miserable little shits; it was no surprise that they'd been the ones to go four or five on one on a boy like Jan Ruckert.

'Well,' he said. 'I wouldn't worry about it. He'll calm down after a while.' Tommy almost believed it himself: Francis was smarter now, he'd been to college, he had a future. Would he really throw it all away on rubbish like the Nivens? He started to walk on slowly, thinking. There was a bunch of flowers on the ground opposite the pub, where the Ruckert boy had been found by the ambulance. It took him less than twenty yards to decide what he was going to do, but he didn't want Derek to guess what he had in his mind. He could see the boy was looking at the flowers, a hurt look on his face, as if it had all been his doing, as if he was the one responsible. 'Don't worry,' he repeated. 'I'll talk to him.' He knew that Derek knew he wouldn't, and that, even if he did, it would make no difference.

People thought Tommy was a hard man, but he wasn't really –

and he felt sorry for the real hard men, the boys who sat lonely in their reputations, cold as stone, afraid to smile or say too much, burdened by the need to do something every now and then to send out the message that they were still big. Tommy knew you had to be afraid of something to spend that much time and energy on an image, and there was nothing that frightened him that much. He could handle himself, that was fair enough; but since he'd been in Corby, he'd not allowed himself to get into a fight just because his pride demanded it. Hard was about being cold, capable of anything, chilled to the bone by the fear of seeming soft; hard was about that undercurrent of fear that ran through the lives of all the men he worked and drank with. What made Tommy dangerous – he knew he was dangerous, and he thought he knew why, even if he couldn't do anything about it – what made him a danger to everyone, when the mood was on him, was a lifelong disappointment. For a while, he had imagined he was angry – and he had good reason to be, born in a coal town, with nothing to look forward to other than the pits, growing up in the dirt while other people, people he could see, people who were no better than him, drove by in their cars and fancy clothes – yet he wasn't angry so much as disappointed. Anger sprang from fear, it flared out, it was uncontrollable; what Tommy felt was cold, steady, a constant flame burning at the back of his mind, blue and clear, like a pilot light. He wasn't disappointed in life. That was what people liked to believe, that it was life that disappointed men like him, life, the world, being alive, whereas, in fact, the opposite was true: Tommy loved the world, he loved trees and water and stones and the sky, he loved the earth, he loved swimming in the river on a hot summer's day, or walking in the snowy woods in the middle of winter. He wasn't even disappointed in people, or not really. What disappointed him was the world people made, the institutions, the rules, the conventions by which they lived, whereby one man's life was richer and easier than another's for no good reason and – worse – those rules by which the poor, the weak, the deceived, the disadvantaged perpetuated their own condition, looking for a boss, believing what they were told, obeying the joyless laws that were made for no other reason than to hold down and contain every spark of life in their hearts and minds and bodies, every last glimmer of energy, or imagination, or everyday joy.

He hadn't realised any of that, though, until he'd met Katrina. She'd made all the difference to him, talking about books, talking about the world beyond, a world he'd never really considered. Or if he had, it had only been to dream – like the time he'd thought about going to Canada and starting a new life. There were boys at The Works now who talked about that, boys who said trouble was coming, another Depression maybe. Just the other day, one of the lads on his shift, Terry, had announced that he was going to move to some place near Toronto, where his sister was. Tommy knew he had no chance of getting in, or getting a job, but he understood what the boy was saying. The boys at The Works were always talking about Canada, or some such place. It was a myth, like the stories they told about The Works, the stories about ghosts in the furnaces and the man who haunted the yards, a phantom from years ago dressed all in black, hovering at the edge of a man's vision when he was crossing the yards on his way to the canteen or the showers. Tommy had seen the phantom himself once, a shadowy figure standing at the far end of a shed in a haze of light, no more solid than the dust-motes dancing around him, like one of those Brocken spectres he used to see, out walking in the hills when he was a boy. It reminded him of something Arthur had told him: how, after it had rained and the sun was beginning to come through, or as the first snow began, a phantom house would appear at the far end of the road that ran through the village where Arthur was living at the time. It was just another of the old man's stories, Tommy knew that, but there was a truth to it, nevertheless. There was a truth to it because the men needed it to be true. They needed something to be a visible mystery in their lives, just as they needed the story of a better place with snow and mountains and space for everybody. Terry wouldn't really go to Canada, he wouldn't go anywhere much, he just knew that the good life he had hoped for was somewhere else, not here, and he wanted to say so, even if he couldn't do anything about it.

Tommy had had the same dream himself, years before. Now, what he had was his stolen conversations with Katrina, and the books he borrowed from the library – books on gardening full of the names of flowers and apples; books on travel; history books. Tommy didn't like novels much: he didn't want stuff that was made up, he wanted the real world, that real world they always talked about in the Sunday papers back home as 'stranger than fiction'. Yet the more he read about that world outside his own, the more he understood just how much he belonged to Corby, how much he had been destined for this place from the beginning, in spite of all those country walks and night-time poaching expeditions with Arthur. He was Corby through and through, just as he would have been Cowdenbeath through and through if he'd stayed at home: men like him didn't escape, they just moved from one prison to another, from the pit to the steelworks, from mother and father to wife and children, from being told what to do at school to being told what to do by politicians and managers and television. Yet his life was a story too, beyond all this surface nonsense of work and duty and contained rage. Katrina had made him see that. Sometimes, when he was getting ready for the day shift, with his family asleep around him, Tommy would think about the lights in Crosshill, or the moon above the fields on his walks with Arthur. He would remember Lizzie's dad going off to his job at the pit, walking off down the road through the falling leaves and he would remember the month or so he'd lived alone before Lizzie and the boys had come south. He remembered night shifts at the blast furnaces when he first started, the heat of the furnace in his bones, and he remembered going on his break, aware of the wide-open door at the back of the shed and the whisper of birds out in the perimeter fences. There was an underlying reality that had nothing to do with work, or people, nothing to do with money or politics or religion. It was about the night and the wind, the rain at a window, the quiet of the early morning. They were taking everything else away from him, but they had always been poised to do that: he had come to learn, over the last few months, that the only defeat was to let it bother him. You can always choose what you care about – that's what Katrina had said one day, for no reason, when they'd been out walking in what was left of the King's Woods, where the big avenue of redwoods grew, the bark soft and rich and dark red, as if there was blood underneath, red blood coursing through the veins of the wood. But that story of himself was buried most of the time, buried deeper, even, than the disappointment he worked so hard to contain. Even finding traces of the story – fleeting memories of Arthur, or those few weeks after Derek was born – was work now, whereas the disappointment – the disgust – came to the surface unbidden, in a long hot surge of fire that blinded him, so by the time he regained control of himself, it was usually too late. The first time he'd been to a pub outside Corby, the barman had given him a disdainful look.

'I'm sorry,' the man had said. 'I didn't get that. Do you speak English at all?'

Tommy didn't say anything. He was aware of the other men in the room, watching to see what would happen. The barman waited a moment, then snorted softly, almost imperceptibly. 'Come to think of it,' he said. 'Do you speak any language?'

Tommy saw the barman's head bouncing off the polished wood of the bar, the pool of slops he had been about to mop up with the cloth muddled with the blood, the other men frozen, watching. He had known, coming in, that no single one of them was dangerous. It was always like that: if his blood was up, he didn't care. It didn't matter who it was, or how many there were.

Now, though, the situation was different. Tommy wasn't one of those men who could make plans and coolly execute them. He had to feel something, he had to be in the thick of it. With the Nivens, he would have to work it all out, he would have to decide what he needed to do to stop Francis doing whatever *he* was planning to do, if he hadn't done it already. He didn't care about people like the Nivens and their gang, they were nobody, it wasn't right to take people like that seriously. You had nothing to do with them, and that was that. They were too cowardly to get in the way of anybody who could handle himself, they were the kind who picked on the weak, the kind who ganged up on one boy, a boy who probably wouldn't have fought back even if he'd known how. Now, Tommy had to deal with them, before Francis did something stupid. Because he knew, as sure as he could know anything, that the police wouldn't get the Nivens for what they had done. It would be up to somebody else to exact a just punishment. Only it wouldn't be Francis. Not if Tommy could help it.

★

The Hazel Tree was deserted when he arrived that evening, just after six.

'Where is everybody?' he asked Billy, the boy behind the bar. Billy had the look of a Hell's Angel, all damp beard and a grin of jagged grey teeth, but he was smart, and he made a good barman, always watching, able to tell when one or another customer was getting out of hand, with the good judgment to know when to leave things to sort themselves out, but imposing enough to step in when he had to. He liked the older regulars, men like Tommy and Sammy, and he showed them a keen, almost exaggerated respect, but he watched the younger guys like a hawk. Now he was his usual self, quiet and contented-looking, drying glasses behind the bar while he waited for another night to begin.

'Dunno, Tommy,' he said. 'The usual?'

'Pint and a wee one,' Tommy said, nodding. 'Listen, Billy. What can you tell me about that Niven gang?'

Billy scowled. 'You've heard about that, then,' he said. He put the pint down in front of Tommy and fetched a shot glass from the back counter.

'About what?'

'The Mackenzie boy,' Billy said, with obvious distaste. 'He's one of that lot. Or he was. They've just fished him out of the Twenty-Two Foot. Seems like the boy forgot how to swim.'

'Mackenzie?'

'Michael Mackenzie. His old man used to come in here, with what's his name Niven. Till they got barred.'

'So do they know what happened?' Tommy's mind was turning around desperately. He couldn't imagine Francis *drowning* somebody.

Billy snorted. 'Accident, they're saying. The boy had been drinking. They think he tried diving in or something. He was probably too stupid to know it's not twenty-two-foot deep all the way out. Not in the summertime, anyhow.' He set the whisky in front of Tommy and went back to drying glasses.

'So it was an accident,' Tommy said, trying not to seem overly interested.

Billy shook his head and breathed out through his teeth. 'Maybe,' he said. 'Or maybe something else.'

'How do you mean?'

'Well.' Billy put on a sceptical face. 'I did hear tell that he'd been involved in some fracas a while ago. Some boy that got killed outside the Pluto.' He gave Tommy a quick confidential look, as if to say he knew about the connection and was more than ready to let this line of conversation go. Tommy nodded for him to go on. 'So there's talk that he was overcome with remorse. You know.' He drew a finger across his throat. 'Though I don't see it myself. I mean, since when did a boy like that develop a conscience, all of a sudden?'

Tommy shook his head. 'I don't know,' he said. He finished his drink and had another, then he stood at the bar, listening to the music on the radio, till Sammy came in.

It was a dark night. It seemed right to Tommy, a few nights after the funeral, that it should be so still and black, as if the whole town was in mourning for the boy who had died for no reason. Time singles people out, he thought, ignores who and what they are and makes them into something else – signs, or emblems, keys to the myth by which they all lived, without really knowing what it was. Once, years ago, in a waiting-room somewhere, Tommy had seen a photograph in a magazine: a man in a suit and tie, old school, though not that old, was sitting at a desk, looking the very spit of a City businessman, except that he was wearing a blindfold, a length of immaculate white material tied around his eyes. The caption under the picture read: NO MAN IS AN ISLAND. That image had stayed in Tommy's mind ever since: it expressed something about the way they all lived that he couldn't put into words, something to do with the way they pretended they knew what they were doing, pretended they believed, pretended they were talking to one another when all that was going on was random noise. But then, every now and again, something happened: a boy set himself on fire in a square some-where, or a bunch of soldiers raped a fifteen-year-old girl in front of her whole village, and you saw that everything your world was built around – politics, trade, the news, the stories people told each other over breakfast or over a game of crib at the Hazel Tree – everything you were meant to take for granted and live by and not question was a lie. It was like Church, all that incense and colour there to screen the emptiness where God should have been, all the hymns and sermons filling the air to distract you from the obvious silence around the altar. It was easier if you went for the whole package – God and heaven, the Free World, the nuclear deterrent; the Royal Family, the House of Lords, the bosses; the Unions, the Party, the working class; family values, better living conditions, world peace – but, Jesus Christ, how many clues did you need to know it was all a lie? Nobody cared about Jan Ruckert, or who killed him, but half the town had turned out to watch a stranger being laid to rest, and they didn't know why, other than that some obscure grief had been brought to light for a moment and had to be appeased. That grief wasn't for this one boy, or even for all the boys who died on the streets, or in the blast furnace, or down the pit, it was for the world that was being laid to waste around them, for the land that had been stolen from under their feet, for the future they didn't believe in, even as they worked for it, scrimping and saving, doing double shifts at The Works and going without so they could go home one day, as if home had ever existed.

Home. That was the word that had haunted them all this time. Tommy heard it every day of his life: it was the one promise he had made to Lizzie that he couldn't keep. She had always talked about going home, if not when they retired, then at least at the end. She had made him promise she would be buried back in Cowdenbeath, laid to rest in a graveyard that had never existed, under old, moss-covered stones and rain on the Old Perth Road. All the time she was sick, she had talked about those places – Cowdenbeath, Hill of Beath, Pittencrieff Park – as if they were something special, something holy. Then, when things got worse, she had stopped. She had probably known she was dying towards the end, but they never talked about it. Tommy thought he'd been protecting her; she had probably been protecting him. Meanwhile, she had been trying to keep something else alive with all that talk of home – something abstract, something that had nothing to do with her any more but might apply, one day, to her sons. She probably knew as well as Tommy that home was outside their price bracket: you needed more than they had to call any place home and not have it wither around you.

It was dark on the Lincoln Estate. Tommy didn't mind: his vision was good in the dark from all those years of night-walking with Albert, out poaching, or just wandering across the fields in the moonlight when it was easier to believe that it was just land, and not somebody else's private property. Tommy had kept the senses he'd developed back then, the sense of touch that could distinguish one thing from another in total blackness, the sense of smell, the keenness of vision – none of it had atrophied over the years at The Works. The child he had been all those years ago was folded inside him, intact and awake, ready to decipher every least sign on the air, aware of every nuance of sound. He'd noticed, from time to time, how he could tell when something was there, even in total darkness. Once, when he was out in the King's Woods, before they took the trees down and built the new estates, before Lizzie and the boys had come south, he'd been walking in almost total darkness, on one of the long paths that cut away from the main avenue, where the trees grew in close, and he had met something – some presence, some force – that made him stop. Even though he'd seen and felt nothing, he'd known something was there – and it *had* been there, where it shouldn't have been, an animal, a heavily pregnant deer, lying on the path, cold and dead. He'd never seen a big animal lying dead like that out in the open, they always crawled away somewhere to die, if they could, but the deer lay still, in the middle of the way, and when he saw what it was, feeling his way in the dark towards the gravitational pull that he'd detected before he saw anything, feeling his way in the dark, then striking a match when he caught sight of the darker blackness in his way, he saw that it was huge, preternatural, its face empty, its eyes dulled. He could have imagined sensing it there without seeing it, if it had been alive – there was an energy to any live thing, a gravity to any body that registered in a hundred ways on the surrounding air. Living things had a resonance, a rhythm to them, that was easy to detect. But this deer was cold and lifeless, it was nothing but bulk.

That was when Tommy had realised that a man had more than five senses, it just wasn't in his interests, most of the time, to use them. Or not if he was a working man, tied to a machine, locked into the rhythm of a wheel or a rack, his whole function reduced to the supply of coals or ore to an oven or a furnace, his only attention paid to a simple pressure gauge or thermostat. He'd read somewhere – in one of Katrina's weirder books, no doubt – that there were tribespeople who believed that everyone had two bodies, one on the outside that could be seen and touched, the other enclosed, a private self. The bodies were identical to begin with; then, depending on how a man lived his life, they diverged: the outer body became harder and less aware, inured to the world's knocks, overused, deadened, but the secret body remained untouched, still aware, still capable of travelling between this world and the next, still a spirit. If a man was careful, he could learn to see and hear and feel with this private body; if he could just stay tuned to its frequency, no matter what went on around him, he would be capable of amazing intuitions, blessed with a sensibility that could never be explained in the outer world. Tommy thought Arthur had stayed in tune with that inward self. He had been in tune with it all his life and that was how he stayed so in tune with the world around him. He'd said as much once, when he'd taken Tommy out poaching one night.

'You have to learn how to think like the animal,' he'd said.

Tommy remembered nodding, thinking he'd understood. He'd read stuff like that in books, seen it in films about Indians. It was *The Last of the Mohicans*. It was Hawkeye.

Arthur was watching him. After a moment, he laughed and shook his head. 'Naw,' he said. 'Not like that. You have to learn to think like the animal. And then you have to think like a man again. Only this time, a man who can think like the animal.' He was still shaking his head good-naturedly. 'That's if you want to catch anything.'

When Tommy remembered that good-natured shake of the head, he would be glad again. Good-natured. That was the word everybody used about Arthur without ever thinking what it meant. Good-natured. Tommy wished he'd done whatever it took in a man's life to be like that, because that was the best he could think of for any man, to be good-natured. Not that it mattered now, or not for him. When a man had sons, all that mattered was how they lived their lives, the chances they had, the future they would live in when he was dead. Tommy thought about the boys all the time, and how he'd wanted them not just to be able to protect themselves from the world – that went without saying – but also to grow up good-natured, able to see the differences between one thing and another, not reading everything as a possible danger – and he worried all the time that bringing them here, to Corby, had been a mistake, for Francis at least. Tommy knew that Derek was probably all right, he had his music and even if it never took him anywhere, it was probably enough; but Francis was another thing altogether. Tommy worried about Francis every day; he thought about him; he planned his life for him, half-convinced in a superstitious way that the sheer force of his own will could make the boy's way straight. Even when he was occupied with something else, the plan was always there at the back of his mind: or not a plan so much as something he imagined, imagined and hoped for, imagined and believed in, the way he had imagined and hoped and believed all those years at church, praying that something would come and touch him and make him different. Tommy didn't know where the image had come from, but he had imagined Francis as the owner of a small orchard, a commercial enterprise, growing apples and pears and maybe cherries, working the property, living on it, standing out at night under a summer sky, doing his rounds on a winter's morning, shaking the snow off the apple boughs or painting the stems with wax to protect against pests, whatever it was orchardmen did in the winter, working late into the evening at harvest time, filling box after box with the sweet, ripe fruits. He had no idea where this picture came from – he knew nothing about apples, nothing at all – but it was as clear as anything he saw in his day-to-day surroundings, and it grew more real and more varied as time passed, the details filled in, the changes of light and season seen and remembered, every leaf of grass warmed by the sun or streaked with frost. He knew that Francis might never even think about an orchard, or anything to do with the land, but then the boy would have his own ideas, his own dream of something, and that was what mattered.

The Nivens lived in a close on the Lincoln Estate. Tommy was always amazed by these new developments that kept springing up – this one had got prizes, had its picture in all the papers, the whole bit – and by how the people that designed them knew nothing about the people who had to live there. This place, for example. If your basic populace was law-abiding, decent folk, no doubt there was good reason to make an estate all lanes and closes and dead-ends like some kind of Cretan labyrinth with little nooks and cul-de-sacs and alleys into the dark. But what if your basic populace was a bunch of drunks, crooks and bastards with knives and hatchets hidden in their jackets? Tommy had had a drink at the Lantern once with a boy who'd showed him proudly the wee loops that his mum had stitched inside his coat, so he could hang his 'tools' off them on a Saturday night; he could still recall the look of it, the boy's shirt pocket with its wee tartan trim and the gleaming steel suspended inside his Crombie-style coat, all neat and tidy, pleasing, in an odd way, though Tommy knew stuff like this would get the boy killed, sooner or later. The Lincoln Estate was perfect for boys like that, but it was also the perfect place to catch them out: step up quick out of the dark and the boy would have no chance, the body would be found later, wrapped in the black coat with its loops and polished metal-work, messed up now, in its own dark pool of blood, another victim. It was the one religion that united everybody here: don't become a victim. You heard it everywhere you went: at The Works, in the pub, on the street. Don't be a victim – and the town was full of them. Big men and trade-union boys and hard-faced women: victims all. The only thing worse than being a victim was being a victim waiting to happen. Being a victim and not even knowing it. Now Tommy was about to make another boy into a victim. He was doing it for a reason, but that wouldn't matter to the boy's maw, or that wee cunt of a faither who'd been chucked out of The Works for stealing money out of other men's coat pockets.

He found the right street and waited. It was a warm night, the sky clear and high, a wide dome of wind and stars. You could see them out here, far enough from The Works that there wasn't just that dull orange light on the sky from the furnaces: here, out beyond what remained of the woods, the night was blue-black, clean-tasting, deep. Tommy could have been anybody, standing just outside a ring of streetlight, smoking a cigarette, hardly visible: a man waiting to keep an assignation, the way he had sometimes waited to meet girls before he was married, waiting for them to slip out a back door and come to him in the dark, still warm under their coats. He could have been some drunk on the way home from the pub, caught in a wave of sentiment and stopping in the dark to look for something lost, something he knew was missing, though he'd no idea what it was. Drink did that to you sometimes: it made childhood, or love, or self-respect seem suddenly real and physical, a lost object like a watch or a ring, something that could have been recovered, if only you could find it.

'Hey!'

Tommy ducked back into the shadows – but it wasn't him they were calling out to, whoever it was who had called. It was somebody else, somebody he hadn't seen till now, standing at the far end of the alley. He couldn't see who it was that had shouted, either, but he knew the voice from somewhere, or he thought he did.

'What the fuck?' The voice was different this time: it came from the figure he'd caught sight of just a moment before, a thickset boy at the far end of the alley, who'd suddenly emerged from the shadows, taking Tommy by surprise. He was about ten yards away; he had passed suddenly through the light, then vanished back into the dark, into almost total darkness, at the very moment Tommy realised there were two of them, two boys there, one after another. There was more noise, it sounded like a scuffle, a pair of bodies moving in the dark, then stopping, as one body moved away, the sound of his footsteps slow at first, then hurried, vanishing into the blackness. Tommy hurried forward, sliding along the wall, trying to remain invisible. The man he had seen was still there, taking short, helpless little breaths, gasping for air. Tommy walked forward into the shadows and the light seemed to follow him, or enough of it, at least, to see the boy Niven, his face white as a sheet, leaning against the wall of the close, his breathing a low mechanical hiss now, blood on his clothes, a small, dark object poking out from his chest. The boy managed to stay standing a moment longer; then, when he saw Tommy, he tried to move, lost the equilibrium that had held him up and fell, heavy and dumb, like the animals Tommy had watched being slaughtered back in '63, when the foot and mouth outbreak came to Fife, and he'd been a volunteer, helping to kill and dispose of cattle all over the country.

Niven had been drinking whisky. Tommy could smell it on him. The dark object he'd seen in the boy's chest was a screwdriver –

and Tommy remembered what he'd said once, about how easy it is to find a weapon that nobody could trace to you, a screw-driver, a hammer, something you borrowed from The Works, say, and put back later, on your next shift, so nobody would be any the wiser. But then, if you left it behind – with fingerprints on it, for all you knew – you'd done exactly the opposite of what Tommy had been suggesting. Whoever had done this – he was trying not to think it was Francis, that it could have been anybody, that the Nivens had plenty of enemies – had started out with a good plan, but had botched it halfway through: they'd left the boy alive, they'd left the screwdriver behind, they'd been a few seconds away from being seen, by Tommy, and by God knows who else.

Now Niven was moving his legs, trying to get up, or maybe turn himself around, like a dying animal wanting not to be seen. Or maybe he wanted to ask for help. His lips were moving, but there was no sound coming out, just a blood-thickened gurgling. And here it was again, that horror of a man dying in the open – a man, yes, but an animal too, when all was said and done – that horror and the strange, sickly beauty of the human body giving up its warmth and movement and tension on a street corner for anyone to see. To share in this moment – and Tommy had shared in it a couple of times, standing by and feeling that kinship with a decaying life – to share in this moment was a privilege and a curse. Tommy knew he would die – he felt as if he had always known this, even when he was a small child – and he had never once been afraid of dying. Death was something most people didn't understand: Tommy thought they would be more accepting if they could see how mineral it was. But the idea of dying in public horrified him. More than anything else, he wanted to die alone in his bed with a radio playing some-where in another room, or birds singing at the window in the early morning. He had sometimes thought about possible endings: bleeding to death on a verge after a road accident, or dying of cancer in a house that would feel suddenly empty, the way Lizzie had done, in a matter of months, during the worst heat wave for years. He had seen men die and it had left him feeling empty and cold, as if their deaths had taken a little of the warmth from his own body, but he knew he wouldn't mind dying at all when his time came, as long as it didn't happen in public – even like this, with one witness to stand and watch, corrupting the moment, leaning in, watching, just as he was leaning in, looking into the boy's face as he reached out and took hold of the screwdriver.

'You did wrong, son,' he said. 'You know you did wrong.'

Niven whined and tried to turn away, his head straining to the side. It probably hurt like hell, even if the boy was partly in shock, when Tommy twisted the screwdriver upwards, and then down, tearing something inside, watching the boy's face widen, then collapse into nothing, his eyes dulling the way hot metal did when you doused it in water. He wondered if the boy had known anything, if he had felt remorse for his sins, in the moment of his punishment. Probably not. For most of these boys, things happened in the night and there was no reason, no connection between one event and another. It would have been fine if Niven had known why what had happened had happened: you didn't have to believe in God to believe in retribution, or the repentance of sins. But then, Tommy couldn't be sure of what had happened, or why. He didn't know for sure who had run away in the dark, leaving this mess for him to clear up. All he knew for sure was the emptiness in this boy's face. He leaned closer and examined Niven's eyes then, satisfied, he pulled the screwdriver loose and slipped it into his pocket. It was evidence. Blood was evidence, too, but he would deal with that. He just hoped that Francis – or whoever it was that had been there a moment before – had the nous to do the same.

Alina

IN THE MORNING, when she was getting ready for the service,
Alina couldn't help thinking that she should have been going
to a wedding, not a funeral. Her friend – it was the wrong word,
maybe; not quite accurate, but as close a term as she could find
– her friend from work, Heather Durie, was getting married at
three o'clock at the registry office on Saturday. She would be
wearing a white dress, carrying a bouquet – Alina could see every
detail in her mind's eye, so often had Heather described them to
her – and she would be thinking of – what? That was the strange
thing: Alina had never met Graham Walker, the man Heather
referred to as her 'intended', but she was sure this Graham was
the wrong choice, and more often than not, whenever she thought
about the wedding, and even on the one occasion she had talked
about it to her mother, she had used the words – silently, in the
recesses of her own mind, or on that one occasion, aloud – the
words that she couldn't help thinking were an omen: 'What in
God's name is she thinking?' At one time – it made her smile
ruefully to think about it now – Alina had imagined that she
would be married some day. Once, idly, she had even thought
she might end up with Francis Cameron. That had been a long
time ago, before they had started 'going out', before she had really
noticed him. There had been a bit of trouble at the school and,
because he was the one who had started it all, Francis had suddenly
seemed different from the other boys, at once foolish and graceful
and defiant enough to be taken seriously. Maybe that had been
what led the way to their brief friendship, a couple of years back.

There had been a special school assembly that day, during which the mad headmaster, Mr Collings, had been going on and on about how sinful they all were, how they did not deserve God's mercy, yet God had sent his only son, Jesus, to die for us. He had become quite emotional finally, talking about how Christ had suffered, how he had been scourged, nailed to a cross, left to die in the blazing noon heat, scoffed at by criminals and unbelievers, and even though he could have stepped down from that cross at any moment, even though he could have stepped down and cast his enemies into Hell for all eternity, he had accepted death for our sakes. 'Jesus died for our sins,' Collings had cried finally, exulting. Alina thought he was about to jump off the stage and start working the third year up front like Elmer Gantry in full flow. He settled, however, for the power of infinite repetition. 'Can you even begin to imagine that?' he asked, daring them to answer. 'It's impossible even to conceive of it, yet this man, this Son of God, man in god and god in man, died for us. This merciful God, in his infinite mercy, died for YOU –'

'Not for me, he didn't.'

The voice had been quiet, almost conversational: an aside, a plain statement of fact. Everyone froze. A few looked round to the middle of the hall, where the speaker stood; most, especially the third and fourth years at the front, fixed their eyes on their shoes. Mr Collings stood dumbstruck, a wounded, grieving look in his eyes. Any moment now, he would have one of his fits and descend upon them, his black gown fluttering around him, like the angel of God's vengeance. Somebody had to stop him, thought Alina. And somebody had.

'Who said that?' Before Mr Collings could say another word, the deputy head – a thin, waspish man named Parrish who tried hard to look like one of those air force pilots on television – strode from the stage and out into the assembled classes. It was his role in life to act as the agent of the head's divine wrath, to intervene before something truly awful, some truly inexcusable blow or insult, had been delivered by the old madman he served. He carried his cane everywhere, twitching it from time to time so it looked like it had a life of its own, an elemental force coming to life in his hand, and capable of anything. 'Who's the comedian?'

he demanded again, as he strode through the hall. 'I'll not ask twice.'

'You already have.' The voice came again from the ranks of the fifth form. Alina stood on tiptoe to see who it was, but she needn't have bothered. It was Francis Cameron and, as he spoke, he raised his hand and waved it softly in the direction of the astonished Parrish.

'Quiet!' the deputy roared. 'What is the meaning of this insolence?' He strode towards Francis, the ranks of fourth- and fifth-formers parting before him like the waves of the Red Sea. Finally he stood, his cane poised, face to face with the offender. 'Well?'

Francis, who had been staring straight ahead, turned to look into Parrish's eyes. His expression was friendly, pleasant, unafraid; Alina half-expected him to smile. 'I didn't ask anybody to die for me,' he said.

Parrish was outraged. More precisely, he was visibly outraged. But his outrage was an act, Alina could see this, an act for the school, and an act for the head, whose erratic moods he probably feared more than anything else. Francis was looking straight ahead now; he had said all he was going to say. Meanwhile, Parrish played out the part allotted to him. Alina could see him thinking – how to handle this without involving Collings, that was the question – and she could see he wasn't sure. All the staff was watching him from the stage – and suddenly Alina knew that they hated him just as much as any kid in that school. She had never thought of it before: she had seen them all as a unit, working together, unified by their general dislike of children, especially clever ones. Now she relished the thought that they didn't like Parrish, and they were embarrassed by Collings. They didn't really like one another; they probably didn't much like themselves. Finally, Parrish decided his only strategy was to make an example. He raised his cane and pointed it at Francis. He looked determined; but he was also afraid of something. Francis was unpredictable; he had the reputation of being just crazy enough to have struck the man down where he stood and not cared about the consequences. Parrish hesitated – and the whole school saw, and relished, that moment's pause. Then, when the moment had passed, his opponent, with something approaching grace, let him off the hook: before the deputy head could say anything, Francis very slowly and deliberately extended his right arm, palm upward, fingers extended.

The whole school was watching now, even the third years. There were boys present who hated Francis Cameron, for one reason or another, but this was different. Everyone was with him now. Any fool could see that. The staff certainly could. They stood on the stage, frozen in – what? Horror? No, loathing. At this moment, everything they loathed about this job sat heavy upon them, a visible weight, for all to see. The cane hissed through the air. For a moment, Francis stood dead still. Then he lowered his right hand and, with the same fixed, staring expression, raised the left, palm upwards as before.

The cane hissed again. The staff watched as the process was repeated, once, twice, three times. There was a murmur from the lower school, like the murmurs among the crowd that always precede a rebellion in history stories. Maybe Parrish realised, then, what he had done. He stepped back. 'What do you have to say for yourself now, boy?' he asked, slightly out of breath.

Francis kept his eyes front.

'Well?' Parrish couldn't quite keep out the note of fear in his voice.

Finally, after a long pause, Francis spoke. 'Thank you,' he said. The whole school, lower and upper alike, allowed itself an audible smirk.

'What was that?'

Francis turned to the man pleasantly and smiled. 'Thank you,' he said again and, almost imperceptibly, just enough so that those around him could see, though everyone else said later that it hadn't really happened, he gave a slight, grave, half-smiling bow. But Alina had seen it, standing off to the side among the lower-sixth prefects, and she had been taken with him, for a day, or a week, she couldn't remember how long. Maybe he was the right boy, if there had to be a boy at all. Maybe he was different. For a day, or a week, she had almost been convinced.

And at the time, she had wanted to be convinced. A boy – a man – was what she had been trained to hope for and expect ever since she was a little girl: a husband, a house, children, happiness. It was all too clear that, if she didn't find these things, her life would be meaningless – and for years, she really had thought in terms of a man and a home and things she would own and clean and insure. As far as her parents were concerned, she still thought in those terms, she just hadn't found the right boy. As far as Heather was concerned, it was the same problem, and Alina had been careful not to disabuse her of the notion, had worked hard, in fact, to ensure Heather thought of her as normal, not because she wasn't normal, or at least, not because she was abnormal in the way some of the boys she had refused had suggested, but because she didn't know what she wanted, other than knowing that she didn't want a husband, or a house, or children. Not now, not ever. She'd even said as much once, sitting in the canteen at work, but Heather had just laughed her bright, delicious laugh and said Alina would change her mind soon enough, when the right person came along. Which had just made Alina wonder if she really wasn't normal, after all, or rather, if she wasn't somehow abnormal in some mysterious way that those boys were incapable of imagining. Maybe it was abnormal to want to be alone, to want not to be touched. Maybe everything was abnormal, other than the basic, ugly, hurtful life that her parents had endured for over twenty years.

Alina had returned from college reluctantly, tempted by the thought of staying in Bristol and finding a job in a bar or a restaurant, but relenting finally and coming back to her old room, a job at Snakpak, and her father's increasingly bizarre moods. Packing nuts at Snakpak, or biscuits at Daddies Cookies, or crisps at Golden Wonder, was the only work available to a female student over the summer, and she needed the money to keep her going in books and extras for the autumn term. She didn't like coming home; in fact, she hated coming home, not just because of her father's condition, but because, whenever she did, she saw MicMac again. After that night, three Christmases ago, she had seen him all the time, a dark presence hovering at the edge of her world like a kestrel hovering over a field of grass, waiting to descend, waiting to strike. He never did, though. All he did was watch her dolefully, like some betrayed lover. Sometimes she thought he was waiting for her to say or do something, as if he thought he'd done what he needed to do, had given her the signal, and it was up to her to let him know how she felt. And she wanted to let him know how she felt, she wanted him to know that she loathed and despised him for what he was doing. She wanted him to know he disgusted her. But even if she could have brought herself to tell him so straight out, she knew she would never give him the satisfaction of having had her attention, if only for a few minutes. That would have made him part of her story, part of her life, and she was determined not to allow that to happen. She knew she had to ignore him, for that was the only power she had. She had to ignore him and she had to be vigilant at all times, so he could never enter her life again. When she saw him on the street, or in a pub, she looked right past him. Sometimes she felt the joy draining out of her, though, just keeping up the act, and it was a blessed relief when she'd been able to go away, to be out of his sight once and for all. All she had to endure then was the vacations.

She could have looked for work elsewhere, but most of the money would have gone on rent and food; by staying at home, she could save more, and for the first two years it had been worth it. Stamping out gaskets at Scandura on piecework rates she quickly became one of the fastest workers on the big presses, much to the annoyance of the permanent employees, some of whom couldn't make as much as she did. That had led to problems by the time she was ready to leave: nothing she couldn't handle, but there had been remarks, and small acts of meaningless sabotage, like the day someone punched her card out ten minutes after she clocked on, or the time she came back from break to find her press was mysteriously down, with an engineer working on it, even though it had been fine when she'd gone to the canteen. After that, she had applied to Snakpak, and got a job for the summer two years running: it was hot, repetitive work, but if she stayed busy the time passed fairly quickly, and she could make reasonable money.

Every woman who worked at Snakpak started on the packing line. It was the most boring job in the world: the women stood in lines of three or four on either side of a conveyor belt; each had a pile of display cards, with slits cut into each card in a grid so the ridged tops of the cellophane packs of salted peanuts, or cashews, or fruit and nuts could be secured to the card, until it was fully covered. Then, when the whole assemblage was hanging in a pub or shop, and people bought the product, the picture on the card would gradually be revealed. The drawback to this approach, of course, was that Alina had to look at the pictures that were to be so slowly uncovered for around eight hours every day, as she covered each card as quickly as she could – this was piecework – then picked up the next, clean card and the next, and then the next. Which would have been bearable, she reckoned, if the pictures had been of anything other than Page 3 Lovely Beverly Pilkington, her come-hither smile slightly too white, her improbable breasts jutting, the skin honey-coloured and bathed in a sheen of light. Alina wondered how they did that: did they photograph the woman wet, or did they cover her in some kind of oil, like the glazing oil in the tanks upstairs, so the light would cling to the skin the way salt would cling to the glazed peanuts after they came off the fryer? Did they carry out any kind of market research to see who actually ate nuts? Was it only mechanics and darts players who liked cashews? Didn't women and Church of England vicars eat fruit and nut mix? Alina wondered what the other women on her line thought about being forced to stare at this half-naked woman all day while they sweated in the heat, their fingers itching from the plastic and the salt, their legs and feet numb from standing. They all had to wear little peaked caps with hairnets at the back, though there was no chance of hair getting into the sealed packets and everyone knew what got into the nuts further up the process, where the men worked. Fran, who worked in quality control, was always finding fag ends and chunks of grease, fingernails, and even, on one occasion, part of a comb, the brown plastic teeth finely coated with hair-oil and dandruff.

It was an undemanding job – a job precisely suited to women, as she'd heard a visiting manager say. In summer the place was incredibly hot; hot enough, at times, to cause stoppages. According to the union rules – the women in Snakpak were unionised, though the men were not – once the temperature rose above, or fell below, a specified level, the rep would advise management that work would cease until reasonable working conditions were resumed. This never happened in winter, no matter how cold it was outside; in summer, however, the heat from the fryers, combined with what the rep called high ambient temperatures, brought them several hours of cheerful respite once or twice a year, time to go out and sit on the cool grass, the women pulling off their net caps, their bodies sticky and glowing, in spite of the fact that most of them wore nothing but a bra and panties, or a modest slip, under their nylon overalls. Alina didn't mind the other women; most were older, hard-bitten, funny, and at the same time strangely self-contained and easy. The men, on the other hand, were awful. That first year she'd worked there, they had been after her as soon as she started, and they didn't let up till nearly the end of the summer:

—Hey, Alina. That's a nice name. What is it? Polish?

—How are you this morning, beautiful?

—Alina. When are you going to let me take you to the pictures?

—Hey, Alina. If I said you had a beautiful body . . .

and – mysteriously – from a scrawny little pipsqueak of a boy called Tony, who looked about fifteen and normally wouldn't say boo to a goose:

—Alina. Meet me outside after work and I'll show you the big estate.

Alina ignored them, or she pretended to ignore them. Some days it was harder than others. It was all surface – on their part, on her part – but it still stung her that she knew better than to turn around and tell them, in no uncertain terms, where to go. That would have been disastrous. It wasn't so much that the men were watching her; it was the other women, too. She knew they would measure her by how she played the game – it was a favourite expression there, as it was wherever men and women worked together. Play The Game. Meaning: be a girl. Smile, walk on, pretend the whole thing is just a joke. Never let it be obvious that you would rather drink a gallon of waste glazing oil than be alone with any one of them for a single second. 'Ignore that lot,' Maggie, the woman who worked next to her on the line, would say, in her quiet, superior voice. 'They haven't got a brain cell between them. Especially that Alvin.' Alvin was the shift supervisor, and used his position to dodge work and pester the girls, making sly, lewd comments when they were stuck on the line, or on the way back from the canteen. The best thing about the shift system was that, every second week, when his shift was on backs, Alina only had to see Alvin for two hours a day. The worst thing about the shift system was that the men didn't work nights here, like they did at The Works, so every second week Alvin would be there for most of the day, dividing his time between strutting around the upper level in his supervisor's coat, telling the men in overalls what they already knew they had to do, and leaning over the gantry railing, right above Alina's head, watching her work. He never said anything; he just stood watching with a satisfied smile on his face: a short, wiry little man, unaccountably blessed with a modicum of power and bottomless self-regard. The word was, Alvin had been made a supervisor because his mother, who worked in quality control and was universally referred to as Goodnight Eileen, was having an affair with the manager, Mr Stanton, her own man having vanished years ago, owing money to everyone who had ever been stupid enough to be taken in by the likes of him. The trouble was, Alvin made Alina's skin crawl, even though she knew there was nothing to him. When he tried chatting up one of the other women – Maggie, say – she'd give as good as she got, if not better, and it would all be a huge joke. Once, Maggie had been passing the gantry on her way to the canteen and Alvin had stepped out in front of her.

'Hiya, Darlin',' he'd said, all innocent smile and shifty eyes.

'I'm only one man's darlin',' Maggie had replied, without a moment's thought. 'And it's not you.'

Alina could never have said that. She wished she could, but she knew she couldn't. Whenever Alvin came anywhere near her, or even if he threw her a casual glance, something froze in her throat and she knew he could see that she loathed him. For a man like Alvin, that was good enough. He could read it, and would read it, as an acknowledgment of his power. And how could she tell him it was otherwise? Someone like Alvin would never understand what she knew, what she knew without a doubt as soon as he was gone, which was that he was nothing more than an emblem, an ugly but, in his own right, negligible reminder of a world that Alina would one day leave behind for ever, a world of sidelong glances and innuendo and self-abasement that she would forget as soon as she stepped off a train, or a bus, in the world towards which she was travelling as surely as Alvin would never go anywhere, or know anything, other than Corby.

It was still quite early in the summer, on an afternoon so hot that a special break was called, when Alina first met Heather Durie. The first thing she noticed about Heather was her hair: long, sable-coloured, it cascaded over her shoulders as she walked into the canteen pulling off her cap and laughing at the back of the queue with the two older women who had come in with her. Alina thought she had never seen anyone as beautiful: vivid, graceful, her body full and rounded and lithe under the nylon overalls, Heather was a walking contradiction to everything around her. She looked glad to be alive, no matter where she was. She seemed to be charged with energy, talking, taking everything in, laughing out loud as the woman behind the counter made some remark Alina didn't hear. At the same time, she appeared restless, impatient, wanting something. One moment she was joking with the others; a moment later, she was scanning the room, looking for an empty table in the crowded canteen. When she saw Alina, she smiled, said something to one of the other women, and crossed to where Alina was sitting.

'On your own?'

Alina nodded.

'You don't mind if me and my friends join you?'

Alina shook her head.

Heather laughed. 'You don't say much, do you?'

Alina smiled and shook her head. Heather sat down opposite her, grinning. 'I've not seen you before,' she said. 'Are you new?'

'I suppose so,' Alina said. 'I'm just working for the summer. I was here last year –'

'So you're a student?' Heather looked interested. 'Well, that explains it. I've only been here a couple of months myself. I'm not staying much longer, either.'

'Really?'

'Really.' Heather was still for a moment as she thought about something precious that, for her, was far off and separate from where she was now; then she grinned and came back to the conversation. 'So. What are you studying?'

'History.'

'Really?' Heather looked surprised. 'What do you do with history?'

'What do you mean?'

'I mean: what kind of job do you get?'

Alina shook her head. 'I don't know,' she said. 'I just like history.'

Heather laughed out loud. 'Well, good for you,' she said. Alina couldn't tell if she was being serious or not, and before Heather could say anything else, her companions had arrived, settling in at the table with tea and biscuits like women who had the rest of the afternoon to talk and eat for once, rather than a hurried fifteen-minute break.

The next day, they met again, first over lunch, then on their afternoon break. It felt easy talking to Heather, easy and relaxed, the way it never felt with the other women. Alina liked them well enough, those other women in their ugly hats and white overalls; more, she respected them – but she couldn't talk to them. They thought that she thought she was special, a cut above: Alina knew this, though she had no idea why. It had something to do with not knowing what they knew, not following the plot of *Coronation Street*, not reading the papers, not having a boyfriend or a fiancé. There was no resentment; if anything, the women showed more concern for Alina than anything else, afraid she might do something to let herself down. Day to day, they were polite enough, but they stayed at arm's length – and Alina had to admit she was glad of it, even though she realised that they, the women, were aware of that too. Yet – at the same time, and wholly conscious of the contradiction in her own thinking – Alina regretted her tacit exclusion from their world, a woman's world of invention and laughter that she sometimes saw in glimpses, a magical shifting world to set against the hard, close-cropped existence of the men. Alina recognised that world, but only from the outside, like an anthropologist, having its customs and rituals translated to her word by word and gesture by gesture. Meanwhile, at the back of her mind, no matter who she was with, no matter who she talked to, she knew these women mostly just felt sorry for her. They weren't angry with her, they didn't blame her, they just felt sorry for her. They knew she despised the work, just as they despised the work; they knew she was smarter and better than the jobs she was allowed to do, just as they were smarter and better. The only difference was, they got on with it, they didn't dwell, they made their own lives. Most of all, they Played The Game. When Alina talked about politics, or history, they would listen politely and nod, but she knew they were sorry for her, that she took such things so seriously.

Her conversations with Heather were different. They were conversations you could drift in and out of, held in instalments, meandering, aimless, self-renewing. After a while, the two women were meeting at every break, Heather badgering Alina about what she planned to do in the future or talking about her fiancé, Graham, who was some kind of works manager with good prospects, Alina answering her questions and listening, mostly listening, enjoying the sound of Heather's voice, closing down just enough whenever Graham was mentioned that, after a while, Heather didn't talk about him as often. Most of the time, they sat alone, often carrying their lunches outside and sitting on the grass verge to take in the sun; when somebody did come and sit with them, they would suspend their private conversation and turn to greet the stranger, courteous, take-it-or-leave-it friendly, as if stepping out from some inner sanctum to meet the world on common ground. They always came off the floor at the same time – smoke-breaks, tea-breaks, lunch. When the shift ended, they would meet up outside, as if by accident, and walk to the bus stop together. Heather would pull off the net cap whenever she left the floor: Alina loved to watch as she shook her long dark hair loose and it tumbled over her shoulders as if it had a life of its own. It was a sign, Alina thought, the emblem of Heather's life, of her soul, and it came as a surprise, later, when she announced she was getting it cut for the wedding.

In the meantime, they were new best friends. Or so Alina thought. There were times when she entertained fantasies of going away, of talking Heather into leaving Corby, leaving her stupid fiancé and her tidy future, and going off to the far north of Canada, or America, say, and walking in the mountains, or the desert, going out into the wilderness and seeing dust storms, sunsets, giant cacti, landslides, the real silence of the solitary places. Alina had never managed to take Graham seriously; most of the time he seemed to her little more than a figure of speech. In truth, she couldn't understand why women like Heather bothered with men at all. It was as if she didn't know what men were like, as if she had never heard or read all the stories you could hear or read anywhere, anytime.

Like Fatty Arbuckle. Alina told Heather the story of Fatty Arbuckle one lunch-time, taking the whole half-hour to describe every detail of how Fatty had taken an aspiring young actress named Virginia Rappe to a hotel suite and killed her with a broken bottle. Other guests at the hotel heard Virginia's screams, but they did nothing till Fatty emerged from the room, giggling softly to himself. When she was discovered, Alina said, Virginia Rappe was covered in blood from the numerous slashes on her body; her last words, whispered to the nurse who took her to the hospital, were, 'Fatty Arbuckle did this to me, don't let him get away with it.' She then went into a coma and died five days later. Fatty's career was ruined, but he was never charged with the murder.

When Alina stopped talking, Heather laughed. All the way through the story, she had been smiling, listening, watching Alina's hands a little too closely, watching her face, bemused and slightly taken aback. 'That's horrible,' she said, at last. 'But why do you think about stuff like this. It's so — morbid.'

Alina shook her head. 'It's not morbid,' she said. 'It's how it is.' She wanted to say more; she wanted Heather to see that men were like gnats on a summer's evening — a nuisance, nothing more: insignificant, alien, utterly meaningless. The way they lived wasn't interesting, it was just an existence: a half-world of cars and money. What mattered was something else, something as different from the mere existence of those men as a live bird, or a frog, or a deer was from tarmac and road signs. She could see from the way her friend was looking at her that Heather thought she was angry — with men, or with the world, or with some particular man, some old lover, or her father maybe, or someone who had rejected her. But she wasn't angry. She couldn't be angry, because you didn't get angry with gnats, you just walked away from the marshy ground where they congregated and out into the open air, into the pale evening light. Men were like a different species: they were strangers to her, a species that was damaging

the world, a species that seemed determined to destroy everything she loved. With a few exceptions, the men she knew treated
everything they touched with contempt, but that was because it
was life itself they hated and feared – feared more than hated.
That was the point of the journey – to get away from that world
where men made the rules and set the terms. There was another
world out there, a world bigger than Corby, and she wanted
Heather to see it.

Heather lingered a moment over Alina's story, then she forgot
it. It didn't belong in her vision of the world. She glanced up at
the clock. 'It's time to go back,' she said.

Alina nodded. She could see that it had been a waste of time.
As they made their way back to the line, Heather brightened.
'You know, I can't wait for you to meet Graham,' she said suddenly.
She looked radiant. 'Come to think of it, I'm surprised you two
haven't met already.'

Alina didn't say anything. She looked out of the last half-open
window, caught a glimpse of green and filed it away in her mind.
It was bright outside, the air sweet and fresh and touched with
the scent of cut grass.

'Still, you'll meet him at the wedding,' Heather continued
happily. 'That's if you're coming.' She stopped walking, as they
reached the double doors to the factory floor. 'It's decided,' she
said. 'Next month. We don't want to wait any more.'

Alina couldn't believe it. She could feel the future she had
planned – the mysterious, unpredictable future – melting away
in her mind, the journey she would never take becoming a phan-
tasm, an impossibility, absurd and immature as any child's
daydream. The journey they would have taken together, finding
who knew what on the way, discovering new depths and angles
in their friendship and in themselves, had been a mirage all along:
an endless expanse of sumac and melting snow, it had gained in
power from being only half-formed, a shimmering, elusive thread
that had run through their conversations, mythical and so much
more real than the everyday world of Snakpak. What had brought
them together, Alina had thought, was a shared solipsism: she had
always wanted to create that world of lakes and autumn woods
where someone – she could never decide whether it was herself,
or someone else, maybe someone she loved, or at least trusted –

would be sitting in a large empty house, in the first days of thaw. Now, she was ashamed to think that she had imagined Heather had thought that way too: Heather, who talked about Graham every day, no matter how hard Alina tried to change the subject, with that real, self-deluding affection that every bride-to-be harbours, against all the odds, till the week, or month, or year after the wedding, when she finds out what the man she married is really like.

Then, all of a sudden, it was over. The dreams she had entertained, and the frustration of those dreams, seemed naïve and self-deceiving set against the world that had destroyed her brother in the space of a single night. Alina had been asleep when the police came; she was ashamed, later, that she had slept through everything, through the police chapping at the door in the small hours, through her mother's first shocked reaction, through the event itself, an event that had taken place on the other side of town, but should still have had such resonance that it would have shocked her awake and driven her out into the dark, to be there before Jan had faded away into the summer heat. As it happened, she hadn't woken till it was nearly morning – she would never understand why her mother had let her sleep – and then, as she came downstairs and saw her mother's face, she had known right away, not just that something bad had happened, but that it was Jan – Jan, not her father – who had died. According to the police, her father had been called out from The Works overnight, but he still hadn't turned up, leaving his wife to deal with everything. Yet it could so easily have been her father they were here about – it even made more sense, somehow: the whole family had worried about him and resented him and waited for him to come back to them for so long – and that was what Alina saw in her mother's eyes, that wish, or that sense of the logic of it, at least, that it should have been the father, and not the son, who had been taken from them.

Alina had come down to the kitchen in her nightdress – she slept late now, whenever she could – her hair a mess, her face smudged with sleep and warmth. She was aware of herself, even as her mother told her the news, aware of a half-made, dishevelled quality, rich with the sweetness and warmth of sleep, turning suddenly to chalk in her mouth and on her skin, something dry and heavy as talc clogging her throat and pores so she could hardly speak, could hardly even move when her mother stopped talking and sat, her eyes turned towards the back window, as if she was thinking about what needed doing in the garden. It was like being sealed inside some solid thing, closed up in a stone or a seam of coal, the stillness unearthly, her body suspended, not in air, not even in water, but in something material, something immovable.

She was ashamed. That was the first thing she understood, when the power to think returned. She was ashamed of having slept, ashamed to be wondering if there had been some mistake, because she hadn't been there to listen and take in what the police had come to say. There had been two, it seemed, a man and a woman; Alina wondered where they were now, and why they had left her mother alone – and perhaps there really was some mistake, perhaps they *had* come to the wrong house. For a moment, she was on the point of going upstairs and checking Jan's room to see if he wasn't there after all, sleeping in his own bed, oblivious to all that was going on, just as she had been – and then she saw, in her mother's face, that the same thought had occurred to her, that she had probably wanted the police to go because she had needed to go up and look, hopeful and desperate, afraid of, needing, wanting, not wanting confirmation of the fact, one way or another. Or maybe she had thought that, if they were gone, she could pretend they had never been there. Maybe if they were gone, they had never existed. The logic that had applied before they came, the logic of her life, the simple arithmetic, could be resumed as soon as they were out of the house.

The thought occurred to Alina then that her father should be there with them. She decided – deliberately, not waiting long enough for doubt to creep in – that he would have been taken to the police station, or the hospital, or wherever they had the body – those very words, that very idea of 'the body' passed through her mind, as if she were thinking of nothing more awful than a very suspenseful or tragic television play – to identify, or claim, or whatever it was they made you do when someone you loved was dead. She had seen that moment a hundred times on television: a body, a curtained window, an anxious relative or spouse being asked if they were ready, or told to take their time, before the curtain was drawn, or the sheet pulled back and the body revealed, horribly still, barbarically composed. Did they really do that? Alina had never seen the point of the exercise, but it was presumably something that happened. Perhaps her father was somewhere at that very moment, in a darkened room with strangers, gazing at Jan's battered corpse. But surely that would have been hours ago. Surely he should have been back by now.

She looked at her mother. Alina could see she was waiting, so she waited with her. They waited a long time, without really knowing for sure what it was they were waiting for. After a time, they didn't speak or look at one another; at one point, her mother got up and walked out into the garden and Alina followed, as if she were expecting to be shown something, some new blossom, or a bird's nest in the rose bush. It was light now, the sun was up. The garden looked clean and well-tended. Alina watched as her mother crossed the patch of lawn and stood by the fence, her back to the house, her body shaking. It seemed she was sobbing, sobbing with as much control as she could manage, but sobbing none the less – or so it seemed, until she turned around, and her face was composed again, empty of emotion, a woman in her ordinary garden, looking for something perhaps, or waiting for someone to come, a welcome visitor, an expected guest.

Later, people came to the house. The police again. Someone else – someone Alina thought should not have been there, a social worker, or a psychiatric nurse, she didn't know – and finally, waiting at the door, unsure of whether he should come in, the parish priest, absurdly round in his black suit and thin, silky shirt with the dog collar. At first Alina hadn't known how to respond to what had happened; now she did the only thing she could do, in her father's absence – she took over. Her mother received the police in the front room, and she seemed to be listening to what they had to say, but Alina knew she wasn't hearing a word. She received the social worker, or whoever she was, with the same apparent courtesy, but paid her no mind at all. She was numb, Alina supposed; she showed no emotion, she seemed patient, detached, courteous, but she wasn't really there. Not until Father Cromwell arrived.

She wouldn't see the priest. She sat in the kitchen while Alina received the man. They were both still in shock – even in shock, Alina knew that – but afterwards, when her mother emerged from the kitchen with a blurred expression on her face, she was aware of how badly she had received the priest. Father Cromwell had delivered what might well have been a prepared speech, his voice low and honeyed, so different from the strident, angry tone he had used in the days when Alina had still felt obliged to attend Mass.

'I know these are early days,' he said. 'But I hope you can find it in your heart to forgive.'

Alina shook her head. She had almost made it through without comment, letting the priest do his job, waiting him out and seeing him out, while her mother sat staring out of the back window at her garden. 'No,' she said. 'I can't forgive this. I don't want to forgive. I think we all forgive much too easily.'

Father Cromwell looked uncomfortable. He'd been doing his duty, trying to fulfil his appointed role. Alina knew that. She knew he'd probably dreaded this visit – but that was exactly why she was angry with him. All those years, when he'd expected her to attend his church, it had been as if a promise was being made, or at least implied. Now that promise was broken. If he had come to the house in ordinary clothes she might have been able to let him go without the show of bitterness, but the black suit and the collar were too much.

'I hope I can find it in my heart to forget,' she added. 'Because the people who did this don't deserve to be remembered. But they don't deserve my forgiveness either. I'll remember my brother; I won't remember these others. I'll forgive my brother for not seeing the danger from these – people. And I will remember him for the person he was.'

Father Cromwell nodded – but Alina wasn't going to let him off the hook. 'My mother's in shock,' she said. 'I don't think she fully understands what has happened. All she knows is, her God has deserted her.' The priest half-raised a hand in dissent at this, but Alina carried on. 'I don't believe in her God. I don't think I ever did. And I always felt bad for that.' She looked into the man's cloudy grey eyes. He was concealing something now – anger, maybe, or maybe disappointment. 'That was your job,' she said.

'To make me feel wrong for not going to church. For being a sinner.' She smiled. 'And this is your job, too,' she said. 'I know that. But now you've done your job.' She stood up. The priest sat a moment longer, then got to his feet.

'I'm sorry,' he said.

Alina nodded. 'So am I,' she replied.

That night, she didn't sleep. It was a full moon, or close to one, and Alina sat looking out at the empty streets, watching as if she expected Jan to come wandering out of the dark in that slow, careless way he had, his attention fixed on some minor detail, a trick of the light, a shadow, a shimmer in the middle distance. He'd been so *not* of this world when he was alive, he would make a perfect ghost, Alina thought – and then she had been shocked by herself, at how venial the notion was, how lacking in due ceremony. She was grieving, she knew that; but she was thinking too, and she couldn't stop the thoughts that came, stupid memories, grudges from the past, absurd notions like this, of Jan as a ghost, or of his not being dead at all, as if this were some elaborate test he had contrived for them all. She couldn't stop the thoughts, and she couldn't stop herself thinking about other things – about Heather's wedding, about work, about whether she would have to stay, and for how long, when the summer ended. She couldn't help thinking about Heather, about the wedding, and the dress, and the moment when the happy couple arrived at their hotel and went upstairs to the bridal suite. Heather had joked about that. She had said she'd been trying to find out what a bridal suite looked like, because she had never seen one. Alina imagined a wide, white bed and champagne in ice buckets. It reminded her of that story about Fatty Arbuckle, about how the room where she would die might have looked to Virginia Rappe at first sight, before the slow horror began.

Sometime during the small hours she heard a noise. The doctor had given her mother something to help her sleep and Alina could hear her now, her breathing troubled, even as she lay unconscious in her own room, the door open, the large moonlight filling the dressing-table mirror, watchful and silent, like a presence in the room. The sound was coming from below, the quiet sound of someone moving, not carefully so much as slowly, the sound a sleepwalker might make – and for a moment Alina wondered if her mother had got up and gone downstairs in her sleep. She had forgotten her father almost completely. The noise had begun in the hallway; now it was at the back of the house, in the kitchen, as if someone was fumbling around at the back door. She slipped on the dressing-gown she had bought at college, the one with the huge scarlet peonies that had seemed so beautiful to her before, but now looked like raw, open wounds, and hurried downstairs. There was a light on in the kitchen, but no one was there. Whoever had been there was outside now – the back door was open, and she could see, or rather, she *felt* someone was there, a presence as faint and tentative as a spectre, nobody she recognised, nobody she knew. She went to the door and looked out. She wasn't sure what she was expecting, but she hadn't been afraid until now, when she saw who it was, not a ghost, not a spectre, not even an intruder, but an ordinary man, a man she barely recognised, though he had only been gone two days, a white, thickset man standing at the far end of the lawn, his back to the house, gazing up at the lit sky. It was her father, and he was naked.

Alina took two steps towards him, then stopped. She didn't want to be there. She didn't want to see him like this. In the clear moonlight, she could see his back was marked, somehow, and she wondered if he had been in a fight himself; as she looked, however, she saw that the marks were old, white seams in the flesh, old badly healed scars on his back and shoulders. 'Dad?' She knew he had heard her, but he didn't look round. He was gazing up at the sky, gazing at the moon, bathed in the white light of it, lost to her. 'You should come in,' she continued. 'Mum's been waiting –'

He turned then, just a little. For a moment she thought he was smiling; then she saw that he was gone, that he didn't even recognise her. His face looked like something that had been torn to pieces and carelessly put back together, the features out of place, the eyes drained of intelligence. He shook his head softly. 'What is this light?' he said. He lifted his face to the sky and looked at the moon uncomprehendingly.

'Come on, Dad,' Alina said. Her father didn't answer – but behind her, in the doorway, Alina heard her mother's voice. 'It's all right,' she said. She was dressed in the same clothes she had been wearing earlier that day. She seemed calm, steady, as if this was something she had prepared for. 'Go to bed. I'll take care of him.'

'I'll help you get him in –'

'No.' Her mother crossed the garden and stood looking at her husband, as if he were an animal in a zoo. She put her hand on his arm. 'It's all right. It'll be easier if it's just me.'

Alina nodded. There was something terrible about her father, something terrible about his scars. For a single, ugly moment, the thought crossed her mind that they were self-inflicted, then she shifted her gaze and, after a moment, she turned away. 'Can I do anything?' she said.

'No.'

'OK.' Alina felt there was something more she had to say, some question she was supposed to ask, but either she didn't know how to put this question into words, or she didn't want to ask it. 'I'll be in my room if you need me.'

Her mother nodded. 'He'll be better in the morning,' she said – and Alina couldn't tell if she really believed this, or whether she was just saying what she was supposed to say. It was something she had said before, on many more occasions than Alina had realised till now. She had said it in the middle of the night when everyone else was asleep, to herself, and maybe to him, and she had kept it as much of a secret as she could. 'Go to bed,' her mother said. 'Sleep.'

Alina looked at her father. He seemed not to hear what they were saying; he hadn't even noticed his wife was there beside him, holding his arm, watching his face. He was staring up at the moon, a confused look in his eyes, as if offended, or puzzled, by its very existence – and Alina realised that she had been expecting something like this for years, and that her mother had expected it too, that she wasn't in the least surprised or even very troubled by what was happening. She had been expecting it, and she had been preparing for it. Two hours later, when Alina put down the book she was trying to read and listened as her mother finally brought the naked man indoors and sat him down in the kitchen, talking quietly all the time, boiling the kettle, stopping to listen occasionally as her husband spoke, Alina understood for the first time that her mother felt nothing, that she was only doing what she had to do, that she had been doing what she had to do for years, waiting for nothing, expecting nothing. Yet, at the same time, there was something else, something that had struck her as she stood in the garden, looking at her parents, the one stricken by grief, the other beyond feeling. It had taken her a while to work it out but finally, as she sat there in the lamplight, the unread book lying open in front of her, it had come to her that they were the same, her mother and her father, one and the same, as if made from the same body, white, oddly luminescent, like those animals who live deep in the sea and are lit from within, light without a source, colour without an origin. They had lived so long in the dark, they had become so dense with the weight of their unspoken history, that they had begun to shimmer, just a little, to shimmer with a light that was well-nigh invisible to others, but by which they lived, as they had lived for years, not quite blind, not quite lost. And when she finally saw it, she realised she had known it for years, she had sensed around them all the strange light by which they lived, and she had learned to accommodate it. It was what she feared more than anything, that accommodation. No matter what else happened to her, she wanted to live in the plain light of day; failing that, she wanted nothing but darkness.

The next morning Alina went out before her parents woke and started a fire at the edge of the garden, beside the privet hedge. Some petals from her mother's rose bushes had fallen, and now they lay here and there in the grass, or under the hedge, still blush-pink, like the icing on a wedding cake. In Canada, the early fall would be starting soon. The first golds would seep through the green of maple trees, the sumac would have already turned a deep flame-red. Alina could smell it on the windows in the morning, when it was still dusk, even though it was thousands of miles away. She could taste it, she could taste the journey she had never made, feel it on the surface of her skin, on her face and hands, on her lips and eyelids. Deer tracks in the woods. The fuzz of drifted pine needles on lakeside roads. Fire roads in the hills dusted with frost and charcoal. This was what she missed more than anything else – and she did miss it; even though she had never been there, she missed that new chill in the air, the promise of snow, the way a curtain billows into an upstairs room while the people sleep, dreaming of elsewhere. She had no idea if any of this was real – the only Canada she knew was the one in the old school atlas, with its deer trails and lakes, but the map of her own world was unconvincing now: The Works, her mother's garden, the stop across the road where she used to catch the bus to the baths on Saturday mornings, the Festival Hall, the lamps in the little park by the tennis courts, lit too soon on these summer evenings, white slurs of light against the hanging darkness: everything was there, yet something was missing. As soon as the fire was properly lit, she took the Bible they had given her at school and started tearing out the pages. They were thin as rice paper, with browned edges; in the fire they curled and burned out quickly, like flakes of snow melting: Genesis, Exodus, Leviticus, Numbers, Deuteronomy. Job, Psalms, Proverbs, Ecclesiastes. Matthew, Mark, Luke, John. Acts. Jude. Revelation. It was a pointless exercise – she hadn't believed in God for years, and she had despised the religion of her fathers for even longer – but it meant more to her than the mere exorcism of old bogeymen. In the encounter with her parents the night before she knew she had been allowed a fleeting glimpse of a new order, a logic that was at once savage and compelling, an order that would not allow for scriptures of any kind, or for formulas, or for the conventions she had lived by for so long, in a state of dismay and disbelief, unable to see what else she could want, amidst all that she refused. Now, she saw that the refusal itself was a beginning, a first step on the path that led, if not towards something known, then at least away from here. Now, it wasn't a Bible she was burning, it was a whole set of lies and pretences.

In no time at all, the whole book was gone. Alina was surprised that it had disappeared so quickly, all that begetting and smiting, all those plagues and commandments. Now she stood with her back to the house, looking out at The Works in that space where the snow had always seemed to begin when she was a child waiting at the kitchen window for Christmas to come. She felt clean and empty standing there, listening to the silence of God in the sky above her, the silence and absence all around her in the first light of day, the rose petals and smuts drifting across the lawn, the pink and the black, oddly beautiful in their different ways, equally fleeting, equally fine, black and blush-pink, melting away in the summer air.

The Air of the Door

Dear Jan,

It's five in the morning and I'm sitting in a roadside cafe, writing to you on this day of the dead – writing to a dead man, how odd that seems, not for the obvious reasons, but because I still can't believe you really are dead. I know and I understand and I've seen them put your body into the ground but I don't believe it and I didn't believe it that afternoon two years ago when I walked to the edge of the cemetery and found that other gate, not the gate I'd come in at, the gate the cars and the mourners use, but the narrow gap in the hedge that the dead follow, slipping away quietly while the rain is still drying on their graves. I hadn't planned on going – or so I tell myself now, though there is evidence to the contrary, when I look back and examine every minor, inconsequential event that took place during those first days, when I was completely numb, shut down as if someone had thrown a switch in my mind, all the lights off, the rooms echoey and large, the sudden absence of something – not you, or not just you, but something else, something like the world itself – overwhelmed me. In spite of all that, in spite of how numb I felt, how unthinking I seemed to be through those first days, some force was operating at the back of my mind, making plans, however vague, preparing for a journey, drawing the curtains and locking the doors in the life I had occupied for all those years when I was still Francis Cameron.

Maybe that sounds melodramatic, but there's a grain of truth in it nevertheless. I know myself well enough to know that what

I was trying to leave behind that afternoon wasn't Corby, or Tommy, or the summer we hadn't really shared, the summer when I had been distracted for a moment – only a moment, true, but long enough to betray you. No: it was me I was trying to leave behind. Otherwise, why would I have bothered going? There was no good reason to go – certainly, there was no reason to go the way I did, to walk away, to become one of the missing, leaving everybody to wonder what had happened. A few months later, I heard that Andrew Niven had been killed on his way home from the Maple Leaf, and it came as a surprise to realise that revenge had never occurred to me. In a hypothetical situation, if someone had asked what I would do if my best friend was murdered in cold blood, I know exactly what my answer would have been. I would have said that, for someone like me, vengeance would have to be precise and exacting, Old Testament vengeance, an eye for an eye, a tooth for a tooth, a life for a life. When it really happened, though, I was far too numb even to consider acting. At the time, it hardly mattered who had killed you, the one significant fact was that you were dead. The fact of that – the fact of death itself – made everything else irrelevant.

I remember you asked me a question once. You said: if the world was ending and I had five minutes' warning, would I go out and hunt down my enemies, or would I wait and watch as everything I loved disappeared, coming to terms with that loss, telling myself that something would continue, because nature cannot tolerate a vacuum, convincing myself that, when a world collapses, that collapse is, in itself, the origin of another world, that even if everything were to be lost, it would eventually recur, in all this infinity, just as it had been when I knew it, an eternal return of Christian Science and cycle races and chocolate-covered raisins. Friends would return; enemies would return. I would have to love and lose and exact the same vengeance over and over again, time without end, unless I learned to stop, to step aside and leave the circle. On the morning of the funeral, to walk away, to just go missing, was like the first step out of the circle, the first step away from the world where I had been trapped for twenty years and into something else.

People go missing all the time. I've read about them in magazines and books, and I usually imagine them living on the coast, eating their meals alone in guest-houses or tatty bed-sits or taking walks to the end of the pier and back just to gaze out at the blank horizon which, presumably, represents the unattainable country for which they are searching. I imagine them sitting in the cinema on Sunday afternoons, trying to recapture the old black-and-white matinees of childhood. Sometimes they might show up dead, pulled from a tangle of seaweed and litter out by the groynes, or sitting in a clouded Renault 5 with a half-finished bottle of vodka and a photograph album set by on the passenger seat. Sometimes they disappear and nobody ever sees them again. Sometimes they turn up in the Arctic Circle, or Kansas. I reckon it would be a comfort to their families to think that they might be alive somewhere, eating gravadlax or listening to country music on the radio: better than imagining petrol trails in the grass, wet wreckage, traces of burning hair or blackened skin; better than remembering those moments on woodland walks when you found the edge of some alien, sad territory of discarded clothes and muddy twine, the air blue as cyanide and tainted with rot and blood.

There was no reason to leave that anybody else would understand; no reason, other than to break something, to snap the thread that tied me to what I had been, to what other people thought I was. To have no more history. If I had to be alone, let me be truly alone, and no half-measures. Remember how we always liked those shows on television – *The Fugitive, Man in a Suitcase* – where the central characters had that lost, provisional look in their eyes, that same grey quality, the lack of precise definition that made them so much more interesting than the accomplished heroes everyone was supposed to admire. The teachers at school, Tommy's friends, Lizzie's relatives, they would all ask what I wanted to be when I was older, then wait expectantly for the appropriate answer: lawyer, doctor, teacher, whatever it was they had in mind – and I would always answer that I didn't know, I hadn't decided yet; meaning that, out of all the richness of possibility, I hadn't yet chosen the destined path that a clever boy like me – the kind of boy they could be proud of – might take. What I wanted to say – what I needed, in some fundamental way, to call out from the rooftops – was that I didn't want to be *anything*. I don't recall when it first occurred to me, but I know I was very young when the idea formed in my mind that I did not wish, in any meaningful sense, to participate in their world at all. I just wanted to be counted out, to go quietly, to be left to myself. Still, I hadn't realised how ready I was to go until it actually happened. When you died, I became a stranger to the world I knew, a being so different from those I had known all my life it was as if every word they spoke, every gesture, every look, was poison to me – subtle, quiet, gradual, but poison, none the less. I couldn't have stayed another day; I couldn't have spoken another word. I did not belong with other people. I belonged with you – and you weren't there any more.

When we were fifteen or so we used to have that game where you would say something – some word or phrase, the name of a plant, or some scientific term – and I would have to guess what it meant. Remember? The added difficulty was that sometimes, not very often, but regularly enough to make it interesting, you would be making it up. I was only allowed one question, then I had to take a guess. As far as I recall, we never played this game the other way around. It was always you who asked the questions, always me who had to guess.

'Tyndall Effect,' you would say, pointing to a window at the far end of the school corridor.

'What?'

'Scientific term.'

I would look hard. I always felt I should know the answer. It was always something that, afterwards, seemed glaringly obvious.

'There's nothing there,' I'd say. 'You made it up.'

'Wrong.' An accusation of falsehood always counted as a guess. 'Try again.'

'I don't know –'

'Look!'

It didn't occur to me, then, that people watched us all the time. It surprises me, looking back, that I was never aware of that; but then, we were so wrapped up in our own world, so wrapped up in the idea – no, not the idea, the sure conviction – that we were different from those others, that we hardly noticed anything at all. It was like the animals I saw at the zoo when I was a kid: the zebras, or the red pandas, or the chimpanzees might take a passing interest in their visitors, but all that really mattered in the world was what other zebras, other pandas, other chimpanzees were doing. That was how we were, then: a different species, with our own interests, our own language, our own ways of seeing and hearing. People found that sinister, or arrogant. They would say, 'You think you're so special', or 'What makes you so different?' and what they meant by *different* was *better*. Yet I can honestly say that *better* never entered my head: a zebra doesn't think it's better than red panda – the comparison simply wouldn't arise.

Alina always felt uncomfortable about our friendship. 'You think too highly of him,' she used to say. 'Like he's one step away from perfect. I mean, he's just a boy. He's not some kind of – I don't know –'

'What? Some kind of genius?'

'Is that what you think?'

I'd thought about it more than once. I did think you were smarter than anybody else I had ever met – but we lived in a small world. Even I was smart in that little fishpond. 'He's pretty bright –' I'd say, out of loyalty, but also, I suppose, to tease her a little. I thought she was jealous, though I wasn't altogether sure what she was jealous *of*.

'Sure,' she would say. I knew she didn't want to seem grudging about her own brother, even if there was jealousy there. 'But that's all he is. Bright.'

I wasn't so certain. But then, that wasn't the point. The point was that she had it all wrong about us. I didn't think of you as one step away from perfect; I knew you had faults. But admiration wasn't what it was about. It was about belonging. You and I belonged to one another from the day we first met – and I really think I loved you the way a brother loves a brother. You were my brother, my soul's friend, and I loved you the way a shadow loves substance, the way water loves gravity. As long as you were there, I felt real. I think you felt it too – though you did better at hiding it – and it meant something, to me anyway, that there was someone else in the world who knew what I was talking about. So when you died, the whole thing began to seem unreal. Or no, not that. Not unreal; not false – or not exactly. No: it was *inauthentic*. That was it. Lacking in authenticity. An accurate but somehow unconvincing facsimile. Not quite right. There are whole philosophies to make that distinction.

'So what is it, then?' I'd ask, squinting in the shaft of bright sunlight pouring through the half-open window. And as soon as I asked, I saw it.

And as soon as I saw it, you knew I had seen. 'That's right,' you would say. 'Tyndall Effect: the scattering of light by particles of matter in its path, thus making a visible beam, such as is caused by a ray of sunlight illuminating particles of dust floating in the air of a room. Beautiful, isn't it?'

I was always mystified by how much you enjoyed things like that, and I always felt I was missing something. I knew the definition was a quote from the encyclopaedia, or from some dictionary of optics. But it didn't sound like a quote. How you knew about these things, and why this game, which would have been so annoying played with anyone else, could be such a pleasure, were questions that only ever occurred to me in passing. It all felt right, it all felt *just*. When I was with you, the world I could see and hear and feel all around me would suddenly become a world that could be talked about and shared. Until I met you I never realised how alone I was. I never saw how sealed-up I was inside my own head, locked inside a magical space full of signs and wonders, with no one to tell it to, or no one who could begin to understand.

All through the funeral, I thought about sky burials. I didn't blame your mother, but I knew it was wrong for them to put you in the ground, laid down in a casket under the wet earth, sealed in a crumbling shell of wood and lead. I remember once how we talked about it, going over this very thing in the serious way children talk about death, without a hint of morbidity or relish, making it hypothetical, and so, beautiful. I said I wanted to be cremated; if I knew anything at all, it was that my soul belonged to fire, though I couldn't have said it then in so many words. I always loved that expression I'd read somewhere, in some Scripture or history book, 'consigned to the flames' – and I knew that this was what I wanted, to be consumed, to leave nothing behind but a handful of charred bones and ashes.

You snorted. 'What a waste,' you said. 'The only thing you have of worth is your carcass. Somebody ought to get some use out of it after you die, even if you didn't do much with it while you were living.'

'Oh, I intend to get as much use out of it as possible,' I answered. I was pretty annoyed by the suggestion that I was nothing more than a carcass. 'But what are you going to do with *your* carcass – donate it to science?'

As usual, my annoyance amused you. 'Perish the thought,' you said, laughing. 'No, when I die, I want a sky burial. You know, like they have in Tibet.'

As it happened, I didn't know, but I had only to think about it for a moment, before I guessed. 'What? Like you see in Westerns? When an Indian dies, and they put him up on a big pile of sticks?'

'Something like that.'

I hadn't liked the idea, but I could see its appeal for you. Sky burial: your flesh devoured by crows and vultures, the marrow sucked from your bones by passing dogs, the hair plucked from your scalp by nesting birds. Which left what, exactly? Fire consumes everything, or almost everything: whatever is left is marked, charred and blackened. A sky burial would have lasted weeks, maybe even years, and even after all that time, there would still be traces, evidence of being, patches of skin and bone, bleached teeth, a hungry spirit wandering among the rocks and stones, trying to cease, trying to become nothing. Fire would be better; fire swallows you whole and leaves a clean, empty space for something new to happen. Still, if the choice had been mine I would have dragged your body out into a field and set it on a pile of logs, or a heap of stones, to feed the crows. If nothing else, the ceremony would have been a quiet one: no priest rambling on about God and forgiveness, no paid funeral attendants to stand around outside the church sneaking cigarettes, no school-friends in their new or borrowed mourning clothes, weeping for a boy they had never really liked. If I knew anything at all, I knew you would have wanted to be buried alone.

Later, after they had set the coffin in the warm earth, I found myself at the edge of the crowd that had gathered – some to take their leave, others just to be present at the ceremony of the murdered boy they remembered from school, or from along the street, a handful of faces emptied by grief surrounded by those others that were vacant with curiosity. I found myself, first at the edge of this group, and then detached: turning, then walking away towards the tight, thorny scrawl of a hawthorn tree that stood at the far end of the path. I hadn't intended to leave, or not in any deliberate way. I just started walking, and when I came to the last headstone, I stopped a moment and gazed out at the empty space beyond. There was a gap in the hedge at the far side of the path that skirted the edge of the cemetery. It was the kind of gap animals use, deer coming in from the fields to browse the graveyard roses, foxes following a path they had used for generations, ignoring the lines of human settlement, hunting rabbits among the cool gravestones on a summer's night. I'd never really thought about such things before we met; the world was a static affair: buildings, steelworks, trees, water, gaps, tracks – everything was given, nothing had history, nothing seemed to change. But you had another way of looking at it all. You subsisted on guesswork; you lived by hypothesis and inference. You were like those Indian scouts in old Westerns, stopping suddenly to examine some mark in the grass or the snow, pausing on a country road to study a patch of hair or wool in a barbed-wire fence, lifting stones, peering into boreholes. For you, everything was flux, everything was a changing text. What I read once, then forgot, like a map, or gospel, you reckoned and scried, interpreting, finding clues, recognising the possibilities for transformation. I was always surprised by the extent to which you gave the world its due, recovering it from stasis the way an alchemist recovers the potential for gold from the flat proposition of lead.

There was a gap in the hedge – a gap, a piece of history, a portal – and I found myself slipping through. On the far side – a foot away from the grass and gravel of the cemetery – I was already in a different world, the earth warm underfoot, the sky suddenly high and bright over my head. The cemetery was bounded by a narrow strip of ground, not so much verge as scrubland, a narrow path through the summer weeds running away from the gap in the fence and up to where the road ran by, another borderline between the town and its environs. Beyond the road, a small wood; beyond the wood – I remember it all, in precise detail – a series of steep fields; beyond the fields, Rockingham village, and on, into Rutland, into Leicestershire and on, further north, into nowhere.

It was a simple matter then, to walk away. I had always planned to leave Corby, the only difference was that now I was doing it in one easy, flowing movement, crossing a road, following the road as far as the fork that led down and away from the smell and taste and noise of the town I had lived in all my life, walking away in the clothes I stood up in, with twenty-five pounds and my building society passbook in my pocket, a wristwatch Lizzie had given me, a set of keys. At that moment, I had no notion of doing anything dramatic, of making a clean break – of actually *disappearing*. One thing just led to the next: a gap in the hedge, a track through the grass, a stretch of road. Over the next few nights, I slept in an abandoned greenhouse full of potsherds and broken cold-frames. I could have found better, but I discovered that I liked sleeping rough under the open sky, close to the earth. For as long as the summer lasted, I could sleep anywhere – in farm buildings by the side of the road, in bus shelters on country lanes, in country graveyards. I liked the graveyards best: it was easy to find them, and nobody ever disturbed me once I was bedded down for the night.

It wasn't that I had no money. The building society passbook, which contained all my savings from working over the summer, was snug in my inside pocket. I have no idea how it got there; looking back, I realise I must have picked it up before I left the house, on my way to the funeral. Which means – does it not? – that even without knowing it, I had a plan all along, and my drift to the edge of the cemetery, my disappearance through the gap in the hedge, the whole process of leaving had been worked out in advance somewhere deep in my mind, before I even thought of going. It made sense, of course: I was taking the journey we had planned to make, with the money we were saving over the summer. I guess I resented the way you decided, without really consulting me, that we were going somewhere in Eastern Europe. I don't think you knew exactly where, but you must have imagined you'd find some clue to where your family really came from, or what they had done, before they were almost English. As for me, I was pretty certain we wouldn't make it that far and I imagined being in Italy, warmed by the southern sun, walking among the treasures of Siena or Assisi. When we first decided to travel, I'd had a sudden notion of going there, to Assisi, where my patron saint had lived, talking to the birds, befriending wolves – but I'd deferred to you in the end, maybe because your unknown history was hidden away in those eastern lands, a tangle of folk-tales and rumour buried in a region I could only think of as unbearably dark and still.

After you died I had no desire to go anywhere. All I wanted was to be away, to be on the move. I knew that, sooner or later, the money would run out and I would have to stop a while, find a job, save more, decide what I was going to do with myself. That was Tommy's favourite expression, the question he had levelled at me for years: *What are you doing with your life? What are you going to do with yourself?* It didn't matter that I went to college while Derek stayed home, sitting in his room between shifts at the plug mill, practising his guitar and writing songs that nobody would ever hear. It didn't matter because Tommy knew that I was the one he had to worry about – and he was right to worry. During those first few days, as I hitchhiked from place to place, sleeping in graveyards and parks in the August warmth, I felt at home as I'd never felt in my life till that moment – at home, meaning: in a good place and, at the same time, exquis- itely, almost joyfully *lost*. I would never have guessed how right, how authentic this life would seem – with nowhere to go, nowhere to be, I felt free, blown in the wind, unburdened. Every few nights I would make my way to a town and book into a cheap hotel, to sleep in a bed and have a long bone-deep soak in a bath; the rest of the time, I stayed out, walking or hitch- hiking through the year's gathering harvests, my lungs and blood filling with that late-summer gold, buying bread and sardines and bottles of milk from village shops and finding a graveyard to eat them in. I liked to eat in country churchyards, sitting apart with the vast company of the dead to which you now belonged, a company I envisaged not as so many individuals with names and histories, but as a single, seamless wave of potential shifting quietly in the earth under my feet like a dark inland sea. I was surprised by how quickly I lost track of time, by how soon I forgot every- thing I had left in Corby. Because I did forget, for most of the time. I forgot Tommy, I forgot Katrina, I forgot Derek. I even forgot you. When the money started to run out, I was alone in the world, disconnected, a soul apart. I dropped Derek a postcard from Lincoln, to say I was all right and would be gone for a while, then I stopped thinking about the people I'd left behind. I didn't want to think about Alina now. I certainly didn't want to think about Tommy or Lizzie, or how you died. Most of all, I didn't want to think about what I'd done on the night of the party, when I should have been looking out for you. I'd guessed something was brewing: I could see the mood you were in, and I was afraid something might happen – though I didn't really know what. So it was my fault, you see. I know that.

And yet, in spite of what had happened, in spite of everything, I was almost happy. For as long as the summer and the money lasted I could go wherever I chose, drifting from place to place, sleeping in the open, eating when I was hungry, alone, or rather, set apart in a wider world of birdsong and windy verges and sweet hedgerows on the road to York or Gloucester; alone, even when I was walking through a market town or a city car park; alone, even on the two or three occasions when I met a girl in a bar and went home with her for an afternoon, or a night, almost drifting into the beginning of something before I woke in the small hours and let myself out into the first light, walking away along a street in the suburbs, one step up from ghost as the last summer of your lifetime decayed around me.

Meanwhile, I was waiting. I didn't think much about it – but if someone had made me stop, if I had been obliged to say what I was waiting for, I would have known immediately. I was waiting to meet someone: a woman, I supposed, though it could as easily have been a man or a child, or even an animal. It had nothing to do with romance or sex, or any other narrative I knew from elsewhere. It was only a meeting, a moment's recognition. I would be crossing a meadow on a warm afternoon, or I would be sitting in a bus shelter out of the rain, and this person would appear, this figure I had never met before, but knew as well as I knew myself. There were times when I was beset by an absurd anxiety, afraid that the last decision I had made, the last fork in the road, the last missed opportunity to go on travelling with a driver I'd hitched a ride from would be the wrong choice, the choice that led away from this meeting, and not towards it. Instead of walking along a country road in Surrey, the air softening into grey, an owl calling out among the trees, I should have been drinking tea in a roadside cafe near Peterborough, or crossing a beach some-where near Arisaig, because that was where the meeting was supposed to happen and the other – the still, salt-blue phantom of the other that hovered in my mind – was moving into place, guided by destiny and chance, expectant, alert, incapable of betrayal. There were times when I thought – times when I *knew* – that this being was the only solid presence in the world other than my own body.

Finally, when the money was almost gone, and the first signs of autumn were unmistakable, I drifted to Cambridge and found a job as a kitchen porter at the Arts Theatre. The work was badly paid but undemanding: clearing tables, emptying bins, fetching vegetables from the market or carrying up boxes of food and drink from the stores, three levels below the kitchen, I was almost as invisible as I would have been if I'd still been on the road. I was working a split-shift system, which meant there was no point going back after lunch to the cheap bed-sit I had found in Cherry Hinton, so I would sit in pubs or cafes reading and eavesdrop-ping on people's conversations. After work, I'd stay in town, drifting from bar to bar, getting myself invited to strangers' parties or picking up foreign language students, anything to avoid going back to that ugly little bed-sit. After the summer on the road, I hated being indoors: if I wasn't exhausted when I got off work, or after the pub, or if I couldn't find a party, I would walk the streets till I was tired enough to go back and drop straight into oblivion the moment my head hit the pillow. It wasn't much of a life, I knew that, but it wasn't going to last for ever and, for the time being, it was as much as I wanted.

It might have gone on for much longer than it did. But then, one night when things were slower than usual, I met this short, prematurely balding Scotsman called Jim in the bar of the Eagle, and we spent the rest of the evening getting drunk. I don't know why I didn't just go home after a couple of pints – Jim was pretty dull, all said and done, but I kept going, for no good reason. It was like drinking with a phantom: Jim was soft, maudlin, barely noticeable: a hungry soul, desperate to tell some story he had locked away in his brain, while I did all I could to avoid having to hear it. Finally, when the pub closed and there was nowhere else to go, we bought some cider and sat by the river on Coe

Fen. It was a clear, cool night. Jim had some grass on him, so we smoked a joint and sat watching the water flow, till I finally gave in and allowed just enough of a silence for Jim to tell his story.

'Where did you say you were from?' Jim asked, for openers. He was being polite, you had to give him that.

I shook my head. 'I didn't,' I said. I was wondering whether to just get up and go, but by then I didn't much fancy walking back to Cherry Hinton and, besides, I liked being there, the cool night air soaking in through my jacket, the sky above us full of stars.

Jim wasn't offended. 'I'm from Grangemouth,' he said. It was all he said – a cue, a last check to see if I was ready to listen.

'My old man's from Fife,' I offered. I didn't want to be unfriendly. It's embarrassing, now, to admit it, but I realised I was homesick the moment I heard Jim talk, back in the bar and I wanted to hear that voice go on, soft and musical, the voice my cousins and old school-pals had kept, after I went to Corby: the voice of home.

'Oh. Whereabouts?'

'Cowdenbeath.'

'I know it,' Jim said, and he gave a crumpled little smile, to show he also knew how ridiculous this sounded. How could he know Cowdenbeath? What was there to *know*? I half-smiled back and waited for the story to begin.

A silence followed. Then, slowly, but with some deliberation, as if he had rehearsed it many times, Jim told his story. He had been in England for ten years, drifting, just as I'm drifting now, from one place to the next, doing garden work, mostly. At the moment, he said, he was employed at King's College, doing the donkey work while the head gardener, Dennis, wandered about giving orders, or tending the fancy chrysanthemums he grew in the college glasshouses. The glasshouses were supposed to supply cut flowers for the public rooms and offices in college, but Dennis had a nice little number going selling bunches of freesias and quality chrysanths to a few regular customers on the side. Jim wouldn't have minded this, he said, if Dennis had been a decent bloke to work for, but the old bastard was continually meddling, finding fault with his work, making Jim do stuff over again when it wasn't right and giving him all the worst jobs. What rubbed salt in the wound was the fact that Dennis made the other men come in at weekends to water the glasshouses, but he never once shared the profits from his unofficial florist's business with any of them. One of these days, Jim said, he was going to do something about Dennis – all it needed was for him to be up a tree, sawing through a bough, and for Dennis to be down below, mouthing off at him –

He broke off. 'You got family?' he asked.

'A brother,' I answered. I didn't much want to pursue that line of conversation, which was fine by Jim.

'I have four brothers,' Jim said. 'Three sisters. My mother is dead but, as far as I know, my dad's still alive. I used to have a fiancée, too. Ellen Mitchell, her name was.'

It took Jim a while to get round to telling what was in his mind to tell, but it was a simple enough story. Ten years before, when he was twenty-two, he had left home to go to Canada, where he had the prospect of a job. Or at least, that was what he told his four brothers and three sisters, his father and his fiancée, Ellen. The truth was, he hadn't wanted to get married to Ellen Mitchell, or not right away, which was what she and everybody else wanted, and he had invented the job in Canada, promising to send for her when he was settled. They had all come to see him off at the station – his sisters and Ellen in tears, his brothers variously proud or resentful. Only his father seemed suspicious. 'I think he knew,' Jim said. 'He wasn't really convinced. At one point, I thought he was going to ask to see my ticket. I didn't have one, and I think he knew. He kept looking from me to Ellen and back again, with this sad look in his eyes.'

'Maybe he was just sorry you were going,' I said.

'No.' Jim shook his head and took a swig from his cider bottle. The dope was gone now, and it was getting too cold to stay there much longer. I was wishing we had something warm to drink, a little whisky maybe. 'He knew,' Jim said, mostly to himself. 'He just didn't know how to stop me.'

I started thinking about Tommy when he said that. What was he doing now? I have to admit, I felt bad, then, about what I'd done. I knew Derek would be at The Works, counting the minutes, converting them into wages payable minus tax and national insurance. Or he would be up in his room, picking away at his guitar and dreaming about Amy Mackay, or Alina, or some other girl he thought he was in love with. But what was Tommy doing? I wondered if he was still in touch with Katrina, and if he was, whether she had told him anything about the night you were killed. It seemed unlikely, but I couldn't be sure. 'So where were you going, anyway?' I asked Jim, to change the subject in my own train of thought.

Jim laughed. 'I didn't know,' he said. 'I just wanted to get away.' He pondered a moment, staring out over the water at the lights in the hotel gardens beyond. 'I thought about going to Canada, right enough,' he said. 'But I never really believed I would make it.'

'So you ended up here?'

Jim let out another soft, haunting laugh. 'Not to begin with,' he said. 'To begin with, I had a job in a pub in North Queensferry. It was weird, being there, and my family and Ellen just twenty miles away. I kept thinking someone would come in and see me.' He smiled ruefully. 'Then I worked in Glasgow for a bit. Then I came down here.' He turned and looked me in the eye. 'We're not that different, I reckon,' he said, quietly.

I shook my head. 'No,' I said. 'I don't suppose we are.' I thought we were chalk and cheese, to be honest, but I didn't feel like pointing it out. Jim looked out over the water, almost black now, glossed over here and there with light. 'Nobody's that different,' I said, though I wasn't sure what I meant. 'And everybody is.' I was stoned, drunk, more tired than I had realised.

Jim laughed softly. 'Ellen and me,' he said, 'we were different. As different as could be.'

'You never got in touch with her?'

Jim shook his head. He was staring at the water. I couldn't tell if he was sad, or happy. He looked contented enough. 'Nah,' he murmured. 'No point.' He gave me a quick glance, then turned back to the river. '*If I had wings, and I could fly, I know where I would go,*' he sang softly, to himself mostly. '*But right now . . . I'll just sit here and watch the river flow.*'

I was embarrassed, now. For him, not for me. He'd given something up, some degree of necessary distance, and I was sorry for him that he'd done it. Not for his story: that was a decent enough thing, an escape he'd made when he didn't know what else to do, and I didn't think he was any unhappier drifting than he would have been married to Ellen Mitchell. I was sorry for him because he didn't know who I was, and he'd given something away to me. It seemed – ignoble is the only word I can think of. I took a last swig of cider, and, after a moment's deciding, struggled to my feet. 'I'd better get off,' I said. 'You staying here?'

Jim nodded, but he didn't say anything. He'd told his story. He didn't have anything else to add, and I realised, suddenly, that the boy wanted to be alone. That was what he'd been saying with that bit of singing he'd done. He wasn't giving anything away, after all – he was trying to retrieve something. 'Be seeing you,' he said at last, in a fair imitation of Patrick McGoohan in *The Prisoner*.

I nodded. I knew I wouldn't see Jim again, and I knew Jim knew it. I also knew that this was all either of us wanted from life right now, to meet and pass on, and not remember anything other than the simple pleasure of being a stranger in the world. Jim turned back to the river – and I could see that, by the time I reached the Silver Street Bridge, my erstwhile drinking companion would have forgotten me, much as he'd forgotten everyone else he'd ever got drunk with and told his story to, rehearsing it, getting it right, making it into a truthful narrative by a lifelong process of easy repetition.

A week or so later, I quit my job at the Arts. It was winter. I decided I would go to Scotland, maybe try and get a job in a ski resort, but I changed my mind after a day's hitchhiking, getting nowhere, standing in the cold, watching the motorists as they passed me by, the looks on their faces betraying something – what was it? fear? – as they flowed by, one after the next, glancing at me and looking away quickly, as if they wanted to believe I wasn't real, and they had never seen me. The only two lifts I got were from truck-drivers, and neither of them was going that far. I suppose I started to feel the weariness of performance after a while, sitting up in the cabs, shouting over the noise of the engine, smoking roll-ups and watching the world flow by, the verges and cold estates half-finished and dull, like pictures from a child's colouring book that hadn't been filled in yet. When the second driver stopped, just outside York, I made my way into the city and found a place to stay. I was signing on for a while, but I eventually got a casual job in a restaurant, then I worked on the

Christmas post. That was my first Christmas away from home: sitting in the post-workers' room at the station between trains, then running out every time a train got in, locating the post-office wagon, and unloading bag after bag of other people's Christmas presents, big chunky boxes inside the sacks that seemed to hold amazing things. I have to admit, I got homesick then. I remembered Tommy and Lizzie sneaking about at night on Christmas Eve, setting out our sad little presents – they were miracles to us, back then – then going back to bed, tired after a long day, scared we wouldn't like what they'd bought, knowing we'd rather have had the bike, or the fancy new toy that they couldn't afford. I have to admit it, I did get homesick – and that was when I broke my promise to myself, that I wouldn't go back, not even in my mind. A few days before Christmas, I stopped off at a telephone box on my way home from the station. I figured Tommy hadn't got a telephone yet – I don't know why he hated telephones so much, though part of me enjoyed the fact – so I called Mr MacColl, the next-door neighbour.

He didn't know who I was at first. I had to explain. 'Francis,' I was almost shouting it down the line, 'Francis Cameron.' I was annoyed with myself already. 'I was just wondering if Tommy was home –'

'Francis!' Mr MacColl finally got it. 'Where are you, son?'

'I'm up in Scotland,' I said. I didn't want anybody to know where I was.

'Oh,' Mr MacColl seemed confused. 'So you didn't go away, then?'

'Sorry?'

'No.' The old boy was thinking. 'I see it now. Anyway, that was the right thing you did. Everybody says so.'

'How do you mean?' I was really regretting the call by then, and I was about to put the phone down, when he said something that held me there, a cold feeling spreading through my chest and belly.

'That boy had it coming, for what he did,' he said. 'Nobody thinks you did wrong. An eye for an eye, it's in the Bible.'

I hadn't figured Peter MacColl for a Bible reader. 'I'm sorry, Mr MacColl,' I said. 'I don't understand.' When he'd said that boy had it coming, I'd thought for a moment he was talking about you.

'No need to worry, son,' the old man said. 'You did the right thing.' He was worried he'd said something wrong. 'Look, your dad's not in right now. He's at the Hazel Tree. But I'll tell him you called, all right?'

I nodded. He didn't see me. I was thinking about what he'd said. 'It's OK,' I said, finally.

'He'll be glad to know you're OK,' MacColl said. 'You'll ring again, right?'

'Yes.'

'Be sure and do that, son. Your dad's worried.'

I didn't know what to say. I wanted to know what he meant, but I didn't know how to steer the conversation back.

'Anyway,' the old man said, his voice dimming, 'like I said, that Niven boy had it coming. Even Tommy sees that.'

It was colder now. One of the boys from the station walked by and caught my eye. Big snowflakes were falling out above the nearby gardens. 'I don't know what you mean,' I said. 'What happened?'

There was a moment's silence, then the old man spoke again, loud again, like someone talking to a deaf person. 'Andrew Niven,' he said. 'You killed him, you know.' He paused a moment, still thinking. 'Didn't you know he was dead?'

It was sinking in. Somebody had killed Andrew Niven in a fight, and everybody thought it was me. That was why I ran away. That was why I wasn't getting in touch or letting anybody know where I was and, suddenly, I realised that to say it wasn't true – to let this old man tell Tommy that it wasn't so – would take away the only explanation he had for my absence. To them – I realised it with a shock, because I'd never thought about killing anybody – I was a boy who had done the only right thing he could do, which was avenge a friend's death. Maybe it saddened them, that it had to be that way, but it was better than thinking I'd just gone off on a whim, for no good reason. The way things were, me killing Niven was a story, something they could tell each other over a drink at the Hazel Tree, whereas me just walking away was nothing, an act of madness, a slight to their sense of an ordered world.

I put the phone down. I wished I'd never called. All of a sudden, I was a wanted man, a killer. Maybe the police were after me. Surely they were. But if they were, surely they would have found me. I hadn't been in hiding, or anything like that. I remember, once, I ran away from home, hitching lifts all the way to Edinburgh almost, before I got picked up in the small hours and taken into the police station. They didn't know I was a runaway, but it would have been a fair guess, a fourteen-year-old boy out in the night in an old anorak and basketball shoes, and they'd wanted to know my name, where I'd come from, all that. I tried to brazen it out, told them who I was, that I was sixteen, on my way to visit family, but they made one phone call and found out Tommy and Lizzie had reported me missing, and they called my uncle Dave to come down from Rosyth and pick me up. I got to stay a week in his house before they put me on a coach and sent me back. I've no idea why I headed for Scotland – I didn't even remember the place that well, though we'd only been gone a few years – but I don't suppose it would have taken them long to find me, wherever I'd gone. Which was enough to convince me, this time, that if they'd wanted to find me, they would have done it. That was all it took, to put the worry out of my mind. I finished the Christmas post, and I didn't call home again. I found another job in a hotel, but I packed that in when springtime came.

And I've been wandering ever since. It's amazing how little you need to get by, in England, in the warmer weather. I've been down a few times. I've slept in some strange places and I've felt dirty and tired and low, sneaking around, stealing food, staying in bed-sits. I'd rather sleep under a hedge, if the weather's dry enough, than in a bed-sit – but I can't imagine living any other way. Now, I'm sitting in a transport cafe on the A1, in the wee small hours of the night of the dead, and I'm writing this to you because you're the only person I can talk to, alive or dead, that would know what it is I want to say, if I ever manage to find a way of saying it. Because there is something I want to say, there is some purpose to all of this, if I could just find the right words to express it. It has something to do with belonging, and it has something to do with my not having killed anybody – because, and I didn't realise it, till that old man told me, what I *should* have done was killed them all, every last one of them, for what they did. But you see, I couldn't have stopped there. If the idea

245

of revenge had ever occurred to me, I would have wanted to kill the whole town, I would have wanted to destroy the whole world. I would have wanted to obliterate everything, every moment that happened after you died in that gutter. And the odd thing was, I didn't even think of killing anyone. I didn't think of revenge at all. Because they were irrelevant: the Nivens, MicMac, whoever else was involved, all the others who hated you and laughed behind your back, the whole miserable crew, they were all irrelevant. It didn't matter what they did, it mattered what *we* did. To have acted, to have taken my revenge, would have meant including them in our story – and I'm glad, now, that I didn't let that happen, and I'm glad, most of all, because that's something I learned from you. It was you – or no, it's you as you are now, the burden I carry, heavy and secret and rich, like those sacks of Christmas parcels in the post-wagons at York station – it is you, my phantom, my brother, who taught me that. I didn't know it then, going around in a daze after you died, but you were already there, in my mind, in my spirit, becoming a piece of me, buried in my sleep, talking, listening, watching. I think I began this letter – what other reason could there be for writing a letter to a dead man – to exorcise that ghost, to unload that burden. Now, though, I can't help feeling glad of your presence, even though I know that you are gone, that all I have is me, and that the phantom which is you in me, is really me and nobody else, the way I always could have turned out, the way I always was. God is no respecter of persons. I remember that from Scripture class and I used to think I knew what it meant. But I only knew the half of it. Because we aren't born with souls, we become souls, and that becoming is a process of mixing, of one person becoming another, or becoming two, or disappearing into thin air. Now you are gone, and you are here, sitting in this cafe, drinking warm, sweet tea on a cold October's night. I carry you with me always.

There. That was what I wanted to say. I carry you with me. And I am disappearing, even as I sit here, disappearing, and becoming something new, just as you are, fading away into space, going into the dark or the light, and emerging on some far side, in the plain light of day, matter-of-fact, commonplace, amnesiac. And I will stand up, go out into the cold, and stand among the ghosts, on this Hallowe'en night, while I wait for the next driver to take me wherever it is I'm going. Goodnight, *mon semblable, mon frère*. Sleep well.

Dear Jan,

It's autumn again. I thought my first letter to you would
be my last, because I knew, even in the delicate state I was in
when I wrote it, that I was really writing to myself. Or not to
myself so much as to the part of me that was also you, the district
of my soul, if that's the right word, where your ghost had taken
up residence. That was a hard time, and it seems impossibly long
ago. Now, though only two years have passed, I feel so much
changed that, had I walked into this cafe that Halloween night
two years ago, the person I was then would have real trouble
recognising me. And yet — and yet, as Tommy used to say: *here's a
thing*. No matter how much I think, or even know, I have changed,
I'm still the same person. It's still Francis Cameron sitting here,
the same handwriting on the page, the same ghosts, the same train
of thought. How do you work that one out? You were always so
scientific in your approach, you thought everything could be
described, if not explained, in some satisfactory way — and you
were always looking for that description too, like some seeker after
the Holy Grail. I remember, whenever one of the teachers said
something you didn't like in school, how you always reminded
me that they were just giving an explanation, and explanations
were no good, because they left out the mystery, they were too
exclusive. What you wanted was a description, something inclu-
sive, something with its mystery intact. You loved it when Miss
Scallan told us about the way the body changes completely every
seven years, how a 35-year-old man has none of the cells he had

248

when he was twenty-one, or twenty-eight. You loved it when she gave that bright, silly smile of hers and asked us – asked us, as if she was really waiting for an answer: 'So how can we meaning-fully say he's the same person at all?' I loved it too, but only because I had a crush on Miss Scallan, and I think, at the time, I wanted a few explanations to be going along with.

I don't know how many cells I've shed since I walked out this door two years ago – skin and hair and gut cells discarded all over the place – but I know I'm altered. I just don't know how much. I was doing more or less the same thing as I'd been doing, those first several months after I left this cafe two years ago – jobs here and there, bed-sits, rented rooms – and then, all of a sudden, something changed. Or maybe everything changed. The world had soured, the future we'd been foolish enough to imagine was lost for ever. The only thing I was glad about was that I was alone. Then, last summer, I was working in a restaurant, washing up, and I just got tired of it, so I quit and went out on the road again. I wasn't sure where I was going – I think a little part of me was tempted to go back to Corby and see what was going on, because I'd heard snippets of news here and there about a strike, and The Works closing down and I'd started thinking about them all, and whether it was safe to go back. I might even have given in to the temptation, if I hadn't gone to Scotland instead.

How I got there is a long story, and I'm not very sure of the details. After I left the restaurant job, I drifted along for a while, not doing much, wandering around, stopping for a while, moving on, going where the wind took me. Not much different than I'd been doing, in fact, only it was a different wind that was blowing me along. I felt empty, indifferent, rudderless. Most of the time, I was drunk or half-drunk, stoned or high or coming down from something – and that was what drove me, that detachment from the everyday, that sense I'd begun to have that something magical, something occult, was steering my course. One night, at a party in Grantham of all places, I met a girl called Cindy who said she knew about a great squat in the Scottish Borders and two days later, I was on my way north. I didn't really fancy Scotland, to be honest, but when the idea came up, I couldn't think of any reason not to go – though that's not the whole story. After the first couple of days, I felt strangely attached to Cindy; the idea of not being around her really disturbed me. I'm not talking about the usual thing, about love, or romance, or whatever. I mean, I found her attractive, but she wasn't that much different from other girls I've known. She was serious and confident and had what Lizzie used to call a real sense of herself, but I wouldn't have said she was particularly good-looking or sexually exciting or anything like that. In fact, when she wasn't actually standing right in front of me, I found it hard to remember what she *did* look like. There was a darkness in her face that I couldn't see through, a darkness and a strange familiarity, as if I'd foreseen her in a dream or something. Or maybe she just reminded me of someone.

Anyhow, we stayed on in Grantham for a couple of days, then Cindy got hold of a car – I'm not sure how – and we drove north together. It's all a bit of a blur: I'd been stoned or tripping for a couple of weeks without a break and all I really remember now is a cool morning in early winter, me standing by the side of a country road, feeling the muscles uncramp along my back and legs, just breathing the fresh, green air and wondering where in the hell we were, because I didn't recognise the place at all. Not that it mattered. As I stood at the roadside, gazing out at the bluish hills, I decided I'd come on this journey because it was the only way I had of breaking the cycle of dope and acid and speed and drink that I'd been caught up in for too long. I turned to Cindy, who was sitting on the bonnet of the car, smoking a joint. She had taken off her boots and socks to let her feet air. For the first time we were together in the daylight, and I noticed how young she was – eighteen or nineteen, maybe even less. 'Where is this place?' I asked her. 'Are you sure you know where we're going?'

Cindy smiled happily. 'Sure I do,' she said. 'We're going home.'

'What do you mean, home?'

Cindy looked at her feet and shook her head. 'I mean home,' she said. 'Well, it's sort of home for me.' She looked at me and smiled sweetly. 'Maybe it will be home for you too,' she said.

'I don't understand,' I said. 'How can it be home for me?'

Cindy laughed. 'That's up to you,' she said. 'You decide.' She hopped down off the bonnet of the car, still barefoot. 'You'll know what I mean when we get there.' She picked up her shoes and socks and threw them into the car. I wondered if she was still stoned on something. 'All you have to do is pay attention,' she murmured.

'To what?' I wasn't sure I'd heard her right and, all of a sudden, I wasn't sure I trusted her. There was something so assured, something so glib about her manner. It was as if everything was a foregone conclusion.

Cindy grinned and shook her head. 'To yourself,' she said, getting back into the car and starting up the engine, to let me know that, if I had any doubts, she could go without me.

A few hours later we took a turn off the road at a village in the hills and followed a wide, gravelly track through trees for about half a mile, till we reached a big house.

'This is it,' Cindy said, as we dipped our heads to peer at it through the foliage. 'This is Westwater.'

What struck me first about the place, when we finally emerged from a stand of rhododendrons and saw it looming before us, was how grand it was. It didn't look like a squat, quite the opposite: Westwater was only a step down from baronial, the kind of place that a minor Scottish laird might have inhabited once upon a time, a country estate in less than perfect repair, perhaps, but imposing, nevertheless, standing on a slope above the road in splendid isolation, surrounded by its own woods and lawns. If the woods were ill-managed, if the lawns were mossy, it seemed more a matter of choice than ordinary decay, a calculated affair, a piece of ironic theatre. I wondered aloud if we'd come to the right place, but Cindy just smiled, parked the car on the gravel drive in front of the house, and led me into the big echoey hall. Inside, the house itself was less imposing than its stately, if somewhat unkempt, grounds had suggested. Once we were through the front door, it was like a large family house, comfortable and lived-in-looking. Three doors from the hall stood wide open: one revealed the half-view of a sitting-room with big old armchairs and an ornate fireplace, the second, what looked like a library, while the third gave on to a large, friendly farmhouse kitchen.

'Hello the house,' Cindy called, stopping in the hall, just outside this third door. She waited a moment, then looked at me. I was standing uncertainly in the hall, wondering if this was some mad prank that would get us both arrested. 'Nobody home,' she mused.

She stepped through into the kitchen. 'Well, we'll have some tea and wait.'

I wasn't so sure. 'Who lives here?' I asked.

Cindy laughed. 'Nobody,' she said, then added, 'we do.'

'Who says?'

She didn't reply, but led the way into the kitchen. It was a huge, high-ceilinged room with a large refectory table in the middle of the floor and a stove off to one side. 'Don't worry,' she said. 'I mean, it's not as if you've got any place else to go, is it?'

We waited in the kitchen a while, but nobody turned up, so Cindy led me upstairs and showed me to a neat, white room with a single bed and an old-fashioned wardrobe. I suppose, in my confused state, I'd thought something was going to happen between us, but she simply smiled and left me there saying I should get some rest. For a moment, I stood in the middle of the room staring at the bed, wondering what the hell I was doing there. I didn't know Cindy, I had no idea what she was up to. I'd started this journey because of her — and as soon as she left the room, I wasn't even sure why she seemed so important to me. She was just another pretty girl, someone I could have met any night of the week in any pub and gone off with for a while. That thing about her reminding me of someone had been a superstition, nothing more. I knew enough about getting high to realise how superstitious it made me. A look, a tone of voice, something found on the street, a chance remark overheard in passing — anything at all could become an omen. Now, because Cindy had seemed familiar, I was in the middle of nowhere, moving into a strange room in a strange house, and I had no idea what was going on. It was as if I'd been drawn into something — and really, I couldn't help thinking there was something deliberate about this, something planned. I just couldn't see what possible purpose it might serve.

When people did turn up, they were a bit of a surprise, considering the house, and pretty much what I might have expected, considering where I'd met Cindy. I don't need to describe them all: I'll just say that I have never seen so many crazy people gathered together in one place. There was a sick-looking biker in full leathers but no bike who called himself Pigpen and said he was on the way to Prague to find his old girlfriend; a pair of twin girls with odd bubble-shaped eyes like those Japanese fish you sometimes get in ornamental ponds; a sullen, fat black woman who looked like she was forty-five, but swore she was twenty-two. Then there was Tim: a tall, thin, blond and very white boy in a fake leopard skin coat who claimed he was the reincarnation of Little Richard. I explained to him one night, patiently and at some length, that Little Richard was still alive and probably touring even as we spoke; Tim greeted this information, which seemed not to surprise him, with an expression of mixed scorn and pity. Tim's best friend was a tiny and apparently mute girl called Agatha. Tim said she was French; he told everyone he met that she was French, insisting upon the fact as a matter of some principle, which was a sure sign to everyone that she was nothing of the sort. They were all of them out of their heads, for most of the time, on something or other, but they were harmless enough and Cindy seemed to know them all – the regulars and the ones who were just passing through – as if they were family. The one she was closest to, a rather beautiful wasted-looking girl with terrible, dark blue eyes – might have been a sister, for all I knew. The girl's name was Shirley and, though she was obviously not quite there, Cindy treated her as a best friend, her only real friend, I suspected, among that tribe of hungry ghosts.

Over the next few weeks, I slipped into a kind of limbo. The house was full of people, but I rarely saw any of them, and when I did, usually nothing was said, no exchanges were made. I spent my days wandering in the gardens, or going through the books in the library, taking them down from their places one by one, then replacing them when I was finished, treating them like museum pieces, though they were nothing special: a few were bound in ancient, blurred leather, but mostly they were '50s and '60s paperbacks, an apparently random mix of foxed or dog-eared volumes, with everything from Vance Packard and Nabokov to cheap thrillers and sensationalist literature on drugs and juvenile delinquency. Now and then I came across one of the other residents on a landing, or at the edge of a lawn, and we would linger a moment to make awkward conversation, all the time watching one another with shy, curious suspicion. I would ask where they were from, and why they had come to Westwater, but the answers, when there were answers, were vague and evasive. Nobody seemed to know who owned the house, or even exactly where it was in relation to the outside world. Nobody knew how the place kept running; the common impression was that it ran itself. Nobody I met had any money, and there was no gas or electricity, but there was a stove in the kitchen, a ready supply of logs from the grounds and, like some miracle from the New Testament, food seemed to just turn up when it was needed. Obviously, someone was behind it all, but in the short time I was there, I never found out who – though after a while I had my suspicions.

Most nights, there would be a party. Parties were held in the old ballroom, a glittering cavern lit by candles and fairy lights, where the residents gathered in a state of excited expectation – for reasons that soon became obvious to me. The first few were pretty ordinary affairs: lights, music, dope, a fairly thin supply of beer and vodka. I spent the time trying to get closer to Cindy, with no great success, and I was beginning to think it was time to move on. Then, one night, when I came into the ballroom, I couldn't help noticing a bright energy in the room, a wave of excitement that flowed from person to person, touching everyone, even the ones who were standing off to the side, self-absorbed, attending to the music. After a while, Cindy handed me a paper cup of what looked like orange juice – though I didn't have to wait long to find out what it really was. After ten minutes or so, somebody put on some music, and the room began to flicker slightly, the lights taking on a new brightness, an almost palpable energy, as if they had come to life as tiny animals, or birds, and were floating free in the wide darkness of the ballroom. I saw Cindy moving through the room – the ballroom seemed more crowded now, though it still felt huge – and I tried to follow, but she eluded me, like the White Rabbit in the Alice stories, there one moment, gone the next. *Acid*. For some reason, I hadn't expected acid, but on this particular night, there was acid and nothing else and, as the spiked orange drinks took effect, everything began to soften, the people moving about the room slowly and with such total grace that I began to think of them as fish, delicate, colourful beings flickering through the bright undergrowth of a coral reef, their bodies suddenly illumined, almost indistinguishable from the coloured fairy lights that seemed to drift across the ballroom. I looked around. Some of the others were beginning to drift away from their groups, finding corners and patches of open space to set up local zones of fairground or carnival, of Hieronymus Bosch or Richard Dadd; some were coming together, smiling, not touching, moving together and apart as if dancing, becoming the creatures of their own imaginations, seeing themselves in one another, discovering new faces, new bodies. Someone had opened the row of French windows at the back of the ballroom – it was odd how things kept happening, though I didn't see anybody acting to make them happen: the music changed, the windows were suddenly open, flooding the room with cold air from the garden outside, even the weight and texture of the air seemed to alter from moment to moment, yet nobody was doing anything that I could see. It was as if the house itself was changing, as if some spirit, subtle and deft and infinitely sensitive to my mood, was controlling the air and the light, controlling the music, choreographing the bodies in the room as they moved, or came to rest, or shifted from light into shadow around me.

I was looking for Cindy. I hadn't been aware of the fact, to begin with, but as I drifted towards the cool air from the garden, I realised I was searching for someone – someone, I wasn't altogether sure who – in that drift of faces and bodies. Then, after I had been looking for a while, I realised it was Cindy. A group of about ten or fifteen people had wandered out into the garden, and I had followed; once outside, however, I saw almost nobody, just one or two figures moving out across the lawn, silvered by the sudden moonlight or vanishing into the rhododendrons: lovers in pairs, holding hands, or solitary individuals drifting to the far edge of the wide lawn, and away, towards the lake. I stepped on to the patio and looked around. It was cold outside, but not too cold. The air smelled clean, with just a hint of late-autumn sweetness, that slightly fermented sweetness of leaves and apple windfalls, a dark sugary scent that seemed to belong to the earth itself. The people who had left the ballroom just moments before had vanished into thin air. It was as if they had become invisible in this white moonlight, invisible, but still gathered around me, watching, hidden among the shrubs and rose beds. I looked back along the narrow patio towards the sundial. Alone, in a white dress that made her look impermanent, a temporary manifestation of the moonlight, stood Shirley. She was looking at me, a half-smile on her face, though I doubt if she actually knew who I was. I crossed over to where she stood.

'Hi,' I said. I sounded absurd, but I knew it didn't matter what I said, because as I approached her, I could feel something else forming, something that grew stronger the closer I came, a physical sensation, like static electricity.

Shirley nodded. The half-smile played about her lips, and she looked like she wanted to say something, but wasn't altogether sure of the right words. I waited. 'It's beautiful,' she said at last. She seemed surprised to hear herself speak, but the surprise was pleasurable, almost beatific. 'Look at the moon.' I looked up. The moon stood silver-white and huge in a blue-black, starless sky. 'Listen!' Shirley put her hand to her face, covering her mouth with the tips of her fingers. I listened. I heard voices, laughter and – under it all – a soft rushing sound that might have been the wind, had the night not been so still. 'Do you hear?' she asked.

I listened again – and I heard the same sounds again: the same as before, and different. 'What?' I asked her.

'They're here,' Shirley said, only half in answer to my question. 'Well, they're always here. But you can hear them so clearly tonight.' She turned to me enquiringly, and I nodded. I had no idea what she was talking about, but it seemed rude not to agree. Shirley laughed softly, mostly to herself. 'I love it when you can hear them so clearly,' she said. 'They sound so happy. Don't you think? Most of the time, you can't hear them, you have to use machines, and when you hear them on the tapes they sound so far away, they seem almost sad.' She looked away across the lawn. 'But when you hear them like this, in the night, you know they're all right. They're happy, because they understand how it all works. They know they're coming back.' She turned to me and smiled wistfully. 'I thought you were one of them, for a minute.'

'One of who?'

'You know.' Shirley studied me as if she had suddenly found something missing in my face, some detail that had been there a moment ago, and was now absent. 'The spirits.'

'Ah.' I nodded. '*Them*,' I said, as helpfully as I could manage. Shirley laughed. 'Who did you think I meant?' she asked.

I smiled and shook my head. I had forgotten about Cindy for the moment. This girl standing beside me on the patio seemed all of a sudden beautiful and straightforward and – loveable – in a way that surprised me every time I looked away from her, or when she stopped speaking, but which seemed so obvious when I looked into her eyes, or listened, not to what she said, but to the sound of her voice when she spoke. She was nineteen, or maybe a little younger. Her eyes, in this light, were even darker than I remembered them, and I couldn't stop looking at her. I wanted to touch her, I wanted to be alone with her, touching her face, kissing the white of her throat, staring into the black of her eyes as I lay beside her, our bodies touching, our spirits intertwined – spirits, yes, because that was how she saw the world, and it made sense to me, even if I couldn't hear what she was hearing. I wanted her to know that I was a spirit too, just as she was, just as those others, out in the dark, were spirits. I turned my head a little, so she could see I was listening.

'I wonder if they can see us,' Shirley said, her voice soft, pensive, directed at me now in a way that it hadn't been before.

'Maybe,' I said. 'Maybe not. But they can hear us, I'm sure. They can hear us, just as we can hear them.'

Shirley smiled and nodded appreciatively. I moved a step closer and I felt the current between us quicken, and I knew, now, that Shirley felt that current too, that she was waiting for something to happen, a touch, a word. Raising my hand slowly, carefully, my fingers extended, I touched her arm and everything in her shifted: all her energy, all her equilibrium shifted from the separate space she had occupied a moment before into the space I was in, a space that was now shared, where everything was possible because, for this unrepeatable moment, everything was understood. At the same moment – exactly the same moment – I realised that I didn't want her the way I thought I did: I'd been mistaken about that current and I felt ashamed. That was how I'd felt with Katrina that night, when I left you at the party. Ashamed, because I had tried to turn something large and complicated into a narrow, simple thing. I can't explain it any better than that – but I think you of all people would understand.

Eventually, we walked out to the lake, Shirley attending to the spirits all the while, stopping to listen among a grove of rhododendrons, catching something far in the undergrowth, a whisper, a centuries-old cry. It turned out, as far as I could understand from her disjointed conversation, that Shirley had been brought up by a spiritualist mother who had made tapes of the dead, the spirits who were always present, their voices travelling over the years, or through the ether – Shirley didn't seem to care about explanations of the physical sort – calling out to the living, plaintive, spectral, waiting for an answer. Shirley's mother had believed that she knew how to hear the spirits, even how to record their messages on tape, but it had grieved her, all her short life, that she didn't know how to respond. Shirley had always said that the dead could hear the living, just as if they were in the same room listening in, but her mother had never been convinced. Still, when the older woman had died of cancer, two years before, she had left a note for her daughter to say that she would get in touch as soon as she reached the other side and it perplexed Shirley that, in all this time, she hadn't heard anything.

For as long as we were out of doors, that current flowed between us – but later, when we drifted back to the ballroom, Shirley left me suddenly and fluttered away across the floor, like a winged bird. I felt some regret that she hadn't wanted to stay with me, or take things any further, but it didn't last. The ballroom was cold now. Most of the candles had burned out, though some still flickered here and there in the darkness. I sat down on the floor and waited to see what would happen next. Shirley sat off in a corner by herself, at the centre of a cluster of candles and fairy lights. She looked far away, tuned into some other world of cries and whispers that I could only imagine hearing. I started to drift, to accept the weightedness of my body, the ebbing out of the warmth, the stillness of the descent. I felt time passing: it was always a surprise, this return to fixedness, to the moment-by-moment passing of time, to a space that no longer felt elastic and infinitely mutable. Every trip I've ever taken, it's as if I've found a different space-time continuum, a field of ripples and folds, all dance, all movement. Sometimes there was a stillness right at the end where I would allow myself to be lost, willing it to go on, trying to evade that eventual return to clocks and walls – but every time, through it all, something else would begin: the sound of a car engine, the ticking of someone's wristwatch, the tight presence of furniture and clutter all around that felt like an extension of my body, an extension of *me*. This time, it was a voice that brought me back, though when I first became aware that I was listening to it, I didn't know who was speaking, or where the voice was coming from. It was a man's voice, soft-spoken and reassuring, with just a hint of schoolteacher about it. I looked around. I couldn't see a man, but Cindy was standing at the far side of the room watching me. For a moment, I thought the voice was coming from her, then I realised it was a tape. But then, in one sense, the voice *was* coming from Cindy, because she had put the tape on, and she was watching me, to see if I was listening. When she saw that I was, she turned and walked out of the room. I wanted to get up and follow, but I couldn't. The voice seemed to fill the whole space, to block me in and hold me where I was. To begin with, I couldn't make out what it was saying, I was just aware of the tone, and this immense pressure that prevented me from getting up and following Cindy. After a moment, though, I started listening.

'We want to think there's a logic to our lives,' the voice said. 'By logic, what we usually mean is something surface-level and linear, cause-and-effect, A leads to B, B leads to C. I don't know why this is. Isn't it more interesting to think of it in terms of a story, something complex, with undercurrents and secret processes waiting to be revealed, any number of possible paths and endings leading to the single, inevitable path that – though we cannot know it – is the true path, the single way upon which we were intended to travel all along? For while the story is in progress, it seems that anything could happen. Afterwards, though, we see that the outcome was inevitable – it was *written*.'

I looked up. The voice seemed to be coming from overhead, and I half-expected, when I raised my eyes, that I would see the speaker floating in the high vaulted ceiling of the ballroom, like Jesus in some old Ascension painting. Then, when the voice came again, it was off to the side somewhere, up by the long row of windows, where the coloured lights were dimming into the first daylight. 'The sleep of reason produces monsters. But then, so does the sleep of fantasy.'

I was coming down quickly now. I had begun to remember the beginning of the evening, the paper cup of thick, sweet orange juice, the change in the music, the way everyone had started tripping at the same time, and I was calculating now, wondering how much we had been given, and whether there was any science to it, any measurement to make sure everyone got the same amount. Though they didn't make that much sense, I was half-listening to the messages that kept fading away then returning, ebbing then flooding back into my mind as I slid back into the usual frame of reference: fixed time, fixed place, the kind of everyday logic that, an hour before, had seemed laughable. I looked over at Shirley. She had slumped down on to the floor and lay still, her white dress around her. She appeared to be sleeping, but she might have been listening, as I was, unable to do anything else.

'We can't allow ourselves to be defined by others,' the disembodied voice announced. 'Think of the people who run things – politicians, salesmen, priests. *Officials*.' The voice spat out the word with a benign, sweet contempt. 'Their world is irrelevant to us: they have never experienced *this*. The real world – this world, here, now – is beyond their awareness, and they don't care about it. Whereas we – we strive to become aware of the real world, to pay attention to it and take care of it. We are here in all humility to forget what society made of us and discover who we *really* are. Who we are and who we can be. In this respect, we're like a different species. The others, the officials, go by – and they are just background noise. Static.' The voice smiled. 'We mustn't delude ourselves. We aren't better than anyone. We're just different. We are becoming a new race, an ungodly, unofficial version of the human idea. We do not belong with these people, these officials. We owe them no loyalty. Yet it is essential, nevertheless, to treat them with impeccable courtesy, if not for their sake, then for our own. We mean no harm. We replace nothing. We are simply . . . beginning again.'

It was foolishness, I know, this talk of a new beginning, but it was also strangely reassuring, almost comforting. I closed my eyes and lay back. The idea of beginning again seemed terribly, almost painfully appealing, though I had no idea what it actually meant. To begin again, to stop the world and spin it around in the opposite direction, to make the clockwise counter-clockwise, to reverse the old order, to become new — I wasn't sure if this was something I was thinking by myself, or something I had just heard on the tape, a tape that seemed to be running inside my own head now, in the chambers of my imagery, as I drifted from not quite waking into not quite sleep, the voice growing softer and, at the same time, clearer as it whispered, deep inside my brain, something that seemed at once familiar and strange — a poem, I thought, or something from a film. It seemed familiar, but I couldn't quite make it out. Odd words stayed in my head, then vanished, merging one into another like raindrops running down a windowpane. I had no idea what any of it meant, but I knew it was supposed to mean something.

I woke up sometime in the middle of the morning. Someone had covered me with a blanket, but I was still cold. The windows at the far end of the ballroom were closed now, the curtains drawn, the room almost dark. The fairy lights, the candles, the litter of plastic cups, even the tables and chairs had been cleared away. I stood up. The sprung floor of the ballroom felt like it might open up under my feet, like the trapdoor on a stage or a gallows. I walked quickly to the door and looked out. Nobody was there. I stepped out into the clear, pinkish daylight. Behind me, the ballroom was another world, a world I might never see again, but all I wanted now was to go to bed and sleep for days, to be alone in the darkness of my own unmanaged dreams. The night seemed far away now, a half-memory tinged with the notion that I had been deceived, and I felt oddly embarrassed, as if I had fallen for a very bad conjuring trick. Then I felt nothing at all and, by the time I fell into bed, the whole thing seemed an illusion. Later, when I woke again, it was as if I had imagined everything, like one of those feckless men in old folk-stories who follows an animal or a fairy into the other world and loses consciousness there. In his own mind, he has slept for an afternoon, or just an hour, but when he returns to the human dimension, fifty years have passed, and the place that had once been home is lost for ever, a stranger's domain, where he is unknown and unwelcome.

Over the next couple of weeks, hardly a night passed when Cindy didn't dole out paper cups full of orange juice and acid

– it was always great acid, subtle and warm and friendly, better than anything I had ever had in the outside world. The trouble was, at some time during the trip, somebody – I never saw who, but it was probably Cindy – would start a tape machine and that soft, alluring voice would fill the room, imploring us to change our way of living, suggesting, ever so politely, that we create a new world. As far as I could see, the voice's philosophy was a random mix of half-truths, vague slogans and snatches of oriental and pre-Socratic mysticism, combined with what it called a technique for 'self-invention'. According to the voice, self-invention was a necessary step on the path to knowing the world – and it was the world, the voice insisted, the world out there and not ourselves, that we wanted to know. To know yourself was only to relearn the stories somebody else had invented for you: from our earliest years, the voice told us, we are bounded and limited by the way others invent images for us based on *their* expectations and fears. We had to break that, if we wanted to be free. From time to time, the voice would recommend different forms of self-invention: in the most extreme cases, it would suggest the complete recreation of a subject's life: new parents, a different school, imaginary friends, enemies, lovers. Each of us had a life story that was forced upon us: it was up to us to decide whether we were going to accept it, or replace it with something else. The trick, it seemed, was to turn the tables on those who imposed their narrative upon us and make them characters in our own stories. By looking closely at them, we could see who they represented: first love, only love, best friend, lifetime foe. The key to breaking the spell of the imposed narrative was to see other people – all other people – as acting out roles or stories in our own narrative, and not as people like ourselves.

I knew this voice had something to do with Cindy, because the voice and the acid went together, two elements of the same experiment or game, but I decided that I didn't want to know what was going on. Every now and then I decided I would be gone before the next party, but for a long time, I didn't make my move. It was cold and, as Cindy had said, I had no place to go. But there was more to it than that. The fact was, I'd been caught, I'd been drawn in. I wanted to go but I couldn't. I had no will, no mind of my own. It would be some time before I worked up the energy to leave.

The winter progressed, the days passing in a beguiling, slow procession, all the same, all slightly different. I kept trying to get Cindy to talk to me – about what was going on, about what I was still thinking of as *us* – but I was wasting my time. Meanwhile, Shirley was avoiding me – which struck me as unfair, considering what had passed between us at that first acid party. I say unfair, because I was pretty sure the distance Shirley was creating between us had something to do with Cindy, as if Shirley thought anything that might happen between us was an infringement on whatever she thought Cindy and I had going. Or maybe what she and Cindy had going, who knows? What with all this, and the general sense that the acid that was being doled out was either part of some sinister experiment in brainwashing that Cindy was somehow in on, or simply the bad practical joke of whoever owned or was behind Westwater, I knew I had to get out. When I felt strong enough, I decided I'd try one last time to get to the bottom of things. Cindy knew something, I was sure of that. And, for better or worse, Cindy was the reason I was there.

I found her in the library one snowy afternoon, having tea by herself and leafing through a large-format book. I was ready to go now, and I didn't have anything to lose – so I decided to be very direct. I'm not sure if that was the best approach, but it was the best I could manage.

'What's going on, Cindy?' I asked. I felt oddly nervous, like a schoolboy talking back to a teacher. 'Can't you tell me anything about who's behind all this?'

'Behind all what?'

'Westwater. This.' I cast around for some question that might break her defences, some thin end of the wedge that would prise the mystery open. 'Who's in charge? Who's paying for it all? Whose voice is that, on the tapes?'

'The tapes?'

'The tapes you play,' I said. 'At the parties.'

'Oh, *those* tapes.' Cindy shook her head. 'His name's Victor.'

'Who is he?'

'He's just a friend,' Cindy said. 'He used to own this house.'

'Used to?'

'Yes.'

'Where is he now?'

'Why do you ask?'

'I want to know what's going on –' I said. I probably sounded angry. I had promised myself I wouldn't sound angry.

Cindy sighed and put away the book she'd been looking at, a book on Dutch art. 'You don't pay attention, do you, Francis?' she said, after a moment.

'What does that mean?'

'It means you have work to do.' Cindy permitted herself a faint, half-sympathetic, half-pitying smile. 'You came here for the wrong reasons,' she said. 'But I'd hoped you would get beyond that –'

'What do you mean, the wrong reasons?'

Cindy shook her head. 'You know what I mean,' she said. 'Though I'm not criticising you for that. The best journeys can begin in the strangest places –'

'I came here because of you,' I said.

Cindy smiled. 'It doesn't really matter why you came,' she said. 'What matters is what you do in this place.'

'This place?'

'Westwater. *This* place.'

I shook my head. I felt sad, all of a sudden. 'This place isn't real,' I said. 'It's an escape. A dream.'

'Is it?' Cindy wasn't offended. She was too sure of herself for that. 'What do you mean by *real*?' she asked.

'You know what I mean,' I said. 'I mean the world out there. The world people have to live in. War. Hypocrisy. Politics. Deceit. That world.'

'So that's the real world, in your opinion?'

'Yes,' I said, exasperated. 'It's what there is. It's what you have to deal with.'

'No it isn't,' she said. 'You see, that's your big mistake.'

'What is?'

'The most basic mistake of all. The simple mistake of confusing the real with the human.'

Now it was my turn to ask the question. I felt that it was expected of me, that the whole conversation had been scripted from the beginning. 'So what do *you* mean by "real"?' I asked.

Cindy laughed. 'I don't know,' she said. 'But I'll say this. Whatever it is, it is always punctual.' She smiled sadly. 'Go out into that real world of yours. Look around you. See how people are. They live in bubbles, isolated from the world, plugged into the TV, listening to all that junk –'

'I'm not bothered with any of that,' I said. I was annoyed again. 'That's not what I'm talking about.'

'So you say.'

I could feel something in my chest giving way, folding up, and I knew I had no hope of getting through to her. I suppose I could have hung around, done some investigations, maybe found out what was happening. But I didn't want that. I wanted Cindy to tell me, of her own accord. 'Come on,' I said. 'Tell me what's going on. I know you know more than you're saying. What is this place? Who is this Victor?'

Cindy pondered a moment; then, without warning, she changed the subject. 'I read a story once,' she said. She didn't look at me. 'It was about a village of more than two hundred people, somewhere in northern France, I think it was, sometime in the nineteenth century. It seems all the people in this village disappeared, all at once, every man, woman and child, in the space of a single summer's evening.' She looked up and I nodded. I remembered this story. I'd heard it somewhere before. 'It happened over a Lammas weekend,' Cindy continued. 'Though how it happened is another question. Did they steal away in the dusk, vanishing into the hills with their children? Did they go all at once, all together, or did they slip away one at a time, or in twos and threes, walking quietly through the birch woods at the far end of the lane and receding into the shadows?' She paused for a moment, as if to listen to her own voice talking. 'All we really know is what they left behind: a scatter of tools and nails in an empty yard, a woodcutter's cart abandoned in the lane, a white apron dusted with flour and dew outside the baker's shop.' She shook her head in wonder and turned to me. 'Maybe they had waited years for the moment when they could go, working patiently at tasks they knew did not matter, enduring the incidentals, the ceremonies of a church they didn't believe in, the years of pretence. The smell of cut grass or cordite on their hands.' Cindy looked at her own hands then. It was an absurd theatrical gesture that made me want to laugh out loud. 'We're waiting too,' she said. 'I don't know what for, but I know one thing, and it's that I don't care about the world out there, I don't care about what's *real*. I want my own world. I want *home*.' She gave me a soft, questioning look. She still seemed sad, as if she knew I was already a lost cause, but she was determined to stay with me, to give me every chance to change my mind. It seemed sincere, this sadness – which was exactly why I mistrusted it.

'I don't know what you're talking about,' I said. I felt sad too, all of a sudden. 'You're evading the question.'

'No,' she said. 'You're evading the question. That's all you've done since you got here. Evaded the question.'

I gave up. I hadn't known it before, but I didn't really care who owned Westwater, or what was happening there, or who 'Victor' was. Not any more. I'd just needed this conversation to get up the resolve to leave. Two nights later, I was letting myself out the front door, when a light came on. It was Cindy. She stood at the foot of the stairs in a silk dressing-gown, her face calm but alert. I had no idea why I was leaving in the dark, secretly, as if ashamed.

'You don't need to sneak away,' she said. 'You could have said goodbye to the others.'

I looked at her. I didn't want to speak, I wanted to be gone, silent and unseen, gone away and my presence there forgotten.

'What's wrong?' Cindy continued. She spoke quietly, without a hint of emotion. 'Do you really miss the real world that much?' There was only the tiniest hint of irony in the way she said it: *the real world*, but it was enough to show her disdain for it.

I smiled, but I managed to stop myself from responding. It was important, I felt, to be silent, to go away and have nothing to say for myself.

Cindy waited, watching from the foot of the stairs, mildly curious. 'Do you know what you're going to do?' she asked finally, when she understood I had nothing to say to her.

I shook my head.

'Tell me something.' She inclined her head slightly, her face impassive – though I thought I detected a trace, just a wisp, of disappointment in her voice at the end, and I wondered if it was genuine, or if she was putting it on, to make me change my mind. 'Before you go. Indulge my curiosity.' She looked at me and smiled like we were old friends. I waited to hear what she was going to say. 'What was the first band you ever went to see?' she asked, still smiling.

I thought about it. Then I remembered; Rory Gallagher, just after Taste split up, at the De Montfort Hall, Leicester, when I was — what? Seventeen? I remembered it clearly, in a rush of images and sensations, as if, with that innocent question, Cindy had just thrown a switch in my memory and filled it with light. Still, I didn't want to say anything.

Cindy smiled. She knew my game, and she was playing along, trying to get me to say something before I left — but she wasn't taking it *that* seriously. It was just a game, after all. 'What was it like?' she said.

It had been great. I was a little embarrassed by the memory: a whole theatre full of boys like me, excited and crazy with the music, jumping up and down on the seats, demanding encores, Rory Gallagher up there on the stage, with his long dark hair and pointed sideburns, tearing 'I Fall Apart' out of a Stratocaster. It seemed callow to me, all that noise and heat, all those adolescent boys going crazy while the security men looked on — but there had been an energy there, too, an honest wildness.

Cindy nodded. She seemed to be remembering something too, and for a moment, I was tempted to turn the question back on her. But I held my tongue. 'OK.' Cindy turned out the light. 'If you have to go, you have to go.' She stood where she was, in her silk dressing-gown, the memory of another time and place lighting her face in the near-darkness. 'Good luck.'

'Thanks.' I felt lonely for her all of a sudden. 'See you.' I opened the front door.

'No you won't,' I heard her say quietly, as I stepped out into the dark. It was cool, fresh, utterly clear, and the sky was full of stars. I hesitated a moment, wanting suddenly to explain, to say, yes, I believed in another world, I believed in another way of living, but I wanted to do it by myself, wanted, just as I had always wanted, back at St Brendan's, or in Scripture class, to keep that life my own. It wasn't a rejection on my part that I didn't want to join anything, I just felt more authentic when I walked off by myself, as I was walking away that night, hesitating a moment, but drawn out and away by the cool of the night air and the wide sky peppered with stars.

It was cold, still, and the roads were empty. I sat in a bus shelter for a while, then walked to the nearest town – a village, really, with a pub and a couple of churches, a sub-post-office and a play-park for children, the slide and the roundabout coated with a thin layer of ice. I wandered around the park for a while, then found the pub again and went in. There was nobody else there – or nobody but the barmaid, a woman of around thirty-five, pretty in a way that struck me as familiar, though I couldn't think why at first. It wasn't until much later, when we had struck up a conversation, that I realised that the woman, whose name was Carol, seemed pretty to me in exactly the way a friend of my mother's had been, when I was fourteen and passing through that brief, mystified phase of beguilement when every smile, every word, every ounce of attention from any woman older than twenty-five rendered me weak with desire, almost senseless, tongue-tied, rapt and utterly bereft of logic. At the same time, I was aware of an urgent, almost uncontrollable lust, a lust that had been growing all the time I'd been at Westwater House, a lust that Shirley's withdrawal, and Cindy's inaccessibility, had only heightened.

'What was the first band you ever saw?' I asked, as Carol poured me another pint. I was calculating how much money I had in my pocket. I figured I would stay there till closing-time, and decide what to do then.

'The first band?' Carol looked amused, but she was lonely in that bar, and she liked the fact that this young guy was paying her attention. I nodded. 'Let me think.' She *was* thinking too, pleased with the question, taking it seriously. Then she smiled. It was as if she had discovered something – as if my question had revealed to her – some moment she had been trying to remember for years. 'Oh yes,' she said. 'I remember now.'

I waited, but Carol didn't say anything more. 'Who was it?' I asked finally, when I realised that she was teasing me.

Carol smiled. 'I'll tell you later,' she said. 'If you're still here.'

I liked her – and I stayed till closing-time, just as I'd planned. To begin with, I only wanted her, but later, when we had made love for hours in her cold, dimly lit bedroom, and she had turned aside and drifted off to sleep, I realised that I liked her too. I suspect I would have liked anyone, after the months at Westwater, but that wasn't the point. While she slept, I lay beside her, listening to her breathing. She was less pretty now, in her own house: the light in her face, a light that she kept for the bar, had dimmed, just a little, and I wondered if it would dim a little more, once I was gone. She was lonely, and that light came on because everything – every conversation, every small flirtation, every smile – was reason for hope. One day someone would reach out and touch her. One day, she would be absolved. The first band she had seen had been Fairport Convention, she'd said, and her favourite song had been their version – not the Bob Dylan version, which she didn't even seem to know about – of 'I'll Keep It With Mine'. She said she had no idea what the words meant, which meant she could interpret them any way she liked.

Later, when I knew she was so deeply asleep that I wouldn't wake her, I got up. The house was small, but I knew there was something I hadn't seen, some secret Carol had kept from me that was the real truth of her story, the key to her loneliness. Somewhere along the landing – one door, two doors away – there was something I needed to see. I went from room to room until I found the one I wanted. It was the room where a little girl had lived, growing up and moving from one fad to the next – miniature animals and Russian dolls, a litter of soft toys, a poster of a blithe Snoopy lying atop his kennel, a clothes brush with a horse's head for a handle. The books went up to Famous Five and *The Observer's Book of Horses and Ponies*, then stopped. I could see that something was missing; the room had an unfinished, arrested quality. Whoever the girl was, she had left before she reached the stage when she stopped thinking about animals and started thinking about boys. I picked up a worn, amber-coloured teddy bear and gazed into its mournful eyes. No doubt the girl who had once inhabited this room had told this scrap of rags and stuffing all her joys and sorrows. She would have lain in bed on summer nights, listening to the last birds in the tree by the high window; from time to time, she would have glanced over at the picture of a little girl, a girl just like her, only touched with the light of the fairies, on the wall opposite. She had treasured herself, not as herself, but as that girl: the girl whose story she told herself every day, the girl who drew pictures in bright wax crayon at school and brought them home to show her mum and then pin on the wall in her bedroom to yellow and darken over the years of her absence. It seemed odd to me that a child should pin her own drawings to the wall in her own bedroom – I imagined a parent doing that in the kitchen or at work – but here they were: the sun, a pair of white clouds, a house with its own garden and fence set between two waxy green trees shaped like lollipops. I couldn't help wondering why kids always draw a certain kind of house – four windows, a roof, a tree outside, flowers in the garden, all that thick, rich colour – no matter what their real houses were like. Still, it was these drawings – these very conventional, ordinary drawings – that revealed Carol's secret.

I wandered downstairs, thinking about the little girl who had lived here once and was now lost – was she dead? Had someone come and taken her away? There was no sign of a child anywhere else in the house: the front room was tidy, too tidy, in fact, with nothing but the two wine glasses from earlier on the coffee table by the fire to show that anybody lived here at all, and the kitchen was even tidier: nobody cooked here, nobody sat at the table in the middle of the afternoon, reading a book or drinking tea. I came to rest at last in the little dining-room and sat by the patio door, half-naked in just my shirt, gazing out at the cold garden. It was well-tended, though a little too tidy, just as the house was a little too tidy. The girl had gone, someone had come and taken her away, and Carol was upstairs dreaming of her at that very moment. I thought about how warm she was, how smooth her skin felt, and I wanted to go back, to get back in beside her and stay a while. I wanted to give her something, to do her some kindness before we parted and saw ourselves for what we really were: phantoms brought together by need, longing for contact and desperate to be gone. I knew she would tell me her story if I stayed long enough – and then, all of a sudden, I had to leave. I didn't want to know. I didn't want her to tell me what had happened to that little girl – and I didn't want to be there long enough that she could tell anyone about me, even herself. I didn't want to be part of her story. I didn't want to be part of anybody's story. I just wanted this: a moment, the cool of the evening, a stranger's improbable skin. I just wanted to be a stranger, to stop a while and then be gone. No name, no history. Nothing to remember or forget.

And now I'm here. Much changed and still the same. I have no idea where I'm going, and I don't much care. It doesn't matter. All that matters is

Dear Jan,

I just found the letter I wrote you, a couple of years back, and I was trying to work out what it was I was going to say when I broke off, trying to remember, because it seemed – not important so much as interesting, a clue to something. Right now, I'm looking for clues, and I don't know how to find them, because I don't know what I'm looking for. Clues to *what*? To how I could have found something amazing, then lost it again. Or not lost it as much as thrown it away. For nothing? Or maybe not nothing. No, that wouldn't be fair. A hard lesson – because there is something to salvage from these last few months. There's always something to be salvaged from any situation, all it takes is a little thought and imagination. So let's just say I've learned a hard and necessary lesson. Which is why I'm writing this letter now, I suppose. I'm trying to work it out, trying to retell a sad and fairly humiliating little episode so it's more of a story than an episode, more of a lesson than a humiliation.

All right – let's go back and start again. Start at the beginning – which is where I broke off with that last letter, a moment I cannot remember, though I remember what I did next, that day, and the day after that, all the way down to now. So: to begin.

After I left Carol's house, it seemed logical to be going south, heading to where it might be warmer, but there were times over the next few months when I almost scared myself into going back to Corby. It was something I knew I really didn't want to do, but I kept worrying away at it, like a man with a broken tooth, going back to it, testing it out, making sure it was still there, that jagged edge, that flaw. I was starting to follow well-worn paths now, up and down the country: York again, Lincoln, Peterborough – coming dangerously close to Northamptonshire, to the road home. By the time I reached Cambridge again, months after I left Westwater, I needed to stop a while to take stock, to just be still. Of course, I didn't realise that to begin with. I'd intended to pass through and move on, maybe find somewhere out on the Fens, or the Suffolk coast and see about work and a place to stay: I liked the idea of myself out on the Fens, under a cool, wide sky, or walking on the beach at Aldeburgh, or Walberswick, but I met a girl called Karin in the Bath and decided to stick around for a bit. So, as usual, my fate was determined by an accidental meeting: Karin was a thin, nervy student from Bremen, doing some kind of summer course at one of the language schools; two days after I moved into a room in Grantchester, she helped me christen the place with a few beers and some oddly pungent grass. The woman who owned the house, a former journalist, was asleep downstairs in the front room, and she managed to stay asleep while Karin and I had very noisy sex for a couple of hours, then went out into the summer gloaming and walked over to the Blue Ball for a drink. It was a good time, for exactly two months. Then Karin went home, and I was alone. With the summer coming to an end, I needed a better job, with more money and less unsociable hours – which led me to the job centre and, in turn, to the ancient splendour of King's College Garden. Which I'd heard about before, but couldn't quite remember where.

Now you begin to see how small my world has become. Almost seven years after I leave home I end up, not only back in Cambridge, but working in the very same job Jim had been doing. You remember Jim, of course. Apparently, he disappeared again a few weeks before I was appointed so, in effect, it was his job I was taking over. It seems he came to work as usual, and nobody noticed anything odd about him, but sometime during the morning he just put down his rake and walked away. Nobody's seen hide nor hair of him since. It was a warm, sunny day, late in the summer, and maybe it just got to him, all that light and space he was missing, all that light and space somewhere else, a sunny street, a park, a bottle of cider, who knows? Or maybe he went to Canada after all. The most likely explanation is that he just got tired of Dennis Guilford. Which wouldn't be surprising: I got tired of him after about a minute, and that was just the interview. I got even more tired of him when we met at the stock-ground, at about nine o'clock one morning late last summer – or was it early last autumn? There he was in his tweed jacket and a dumb little fisherman's hat that was supposed to make him look like a real countryman type, with a tie thrown in to show he wasn't a countryman of the labouring variety. I'd had a bit of trouble finding him, so I was about five minutes late. He nodded at me, then he glanced at his watch. He raised an eyebrow.

'We start at eight thirty around here,' he said.

I nodded, but I didn't say anything. I didn't want to get petty about it. So Dennis starts walking away, without even waiting to see if I'm following. 'All right,' he sings out, over his shoulder. 'Let's see if you've got any hard work in you.'

This is how he talks all the time. The man sounds like bad television. He'd struck me at the interview as a plump, smug little fool, in spite of his pleasant manner: sitting in the bursar's office at King's College, his hat perched on his knee, he had assumed the manner of a good boss, the kind of boss the authorities flattered themselves they had done well to set in place above the men, a thoughtful, considerate head gardener of the old school, a little better with plants than he was with people, but kindly and firm, a senior figure who had earned the respect of his men. I know how that particular scenario works: even if the bursar can see through Guilford's act, it wouldn't do to acknowledge the fact; as long as the gardens are tidy and the college is well-stocked with cut flowers, nobody cares what petty injustices go on in the potting sheds or the greenhouses. When I applied for this job at King's – I'm as unqualified for gardening as anyone could be, but it's slightly better paid than washing dishes, and the hours are less unsociable – I had forgotten all about Jim, or his stories about King's. It was only when I heard the head gardener's name that everything came back from that slightly drunken night: Jim, the chrysanthemums, the glasshouses. It was an unfortunate memory: as Guilford sat down, he must have noticed something in my expression, some flicker of amusement or contempt, and he kept glancing at me throughout the interview, studying my face as if he thought he ought to know me from somewhere. It was the bursar who told me about Jim's disappearing act – or rather, talked about it to Dennis, so I could hear, to let me know they both hoped for something better from me.

But that first day on the job, I could see Dennis was testing me out – and there was no bursar to impress with his avuncular, kindly-but-firm management style. 'I want you to hoe this area here,' he said. He was standing in the middle of a plot of around quarter of an acre, a plot that, as far as I could see, contained nothing but weeds. I was 99 per cent sure that they had machines for this sort of thing – and Dennis was not trying very hard to keep the smirk off his face. 'All right?'

'You want me to hoe it?' I asked him, looking sceptical. Maybe this was just a joke, one of those initiation games they played on new men everywhere. 'What's wrong with the rotovator?'

Guilford shook his head. 'Nothing's wrong with it,' he said. 'But I want you to use the hoe.'

'Why's that then?' I knew now, from the man's manner, that this was no joke. Guilford was there to show me who was boss.

He shook his head wearily. 'Let's get one thing straight,' he said. 'Around here, I'm the one who asks the questions. And I'm the one who decides what needs to be done. I give the orders, and you do what you're told.' He gave me a tight little smile. 'Got that?'

I looked away across the nursery ground towards some willow trees in the distance. Rain was threatening. It was the end of the summer, the beginning of the autumn, with that sugary taste that comes when the apples are ripe and the leaves are starting to turn. It was a very quiet moment, and I felt an odd sadness, though I didn't know why. I waited till Guilford was just about to underline his point then, before the man had time to speak, I took the two steps that separated us and stood close to him, my face inches away from his. 'Look,' I said. I said it quietly; I wanted him to know that I wanted to be reasonable. 'I don't mind what I do. I'll dig. I'll sweep leaves. That's fine. But don't piss me about. All right?'

Guilford took one backward step, then another. 'Are you refusing to do the job I'm telling you to do?' He was trying to hold on to something, but I could see he was scared. 'Because if you are, the bursar —'

I shook my head. 'You tell anybody about this and I'll come back and break your fucking neck. Do you understand?' I waited a moment to see what he would do, but he didn't move. I could tell that he wanted to walk away, but he didn't dare turn his back on me. 'So,' I said, finally, when I'd given him a moment to take it all in. 'What do you *really* want me to do?'

Guilford thought. His face worked, then he decided. 'I'm going to forget this happened,' he said. 'Obviously, there's been a misunderstanding.' He still sounded like bad television. 'You'll find rakes, brushes and a barrow in the big shed. The bridge and the paths all along the back of college need sweeping.'

I nodded.

'That's your job, every day, from now on,' Guilford said. 'Sweeping up.'

I had to smile. I could hear the intended slight — to a man like Guilford, sweeping up was the lowest job he could hand out — but I didn't care. I looked the head gardener in the eye, and smiled, to let him know that this was just the job I wanted: sweeping leaves. Then I headed off to the big shed to pick out my tools.

In the old stories, when a man became a Zen monk, he would be required to sweep leaves or gravel for ten years before he was allowed to ask the master a single question. Then, when the ten years had passed, he would go to the master's room and sit there, waiting to be enlightened — but no matter what question he asked the master only sent him back to his work in the courtyard. I understood that story: over the next few months, as I stood on the narrow stone bridge at the back of King's, I found a rhythm that my body had been waiting years to discover, a rhythm arising from the steady performance of a task that, as time passed, was an answer in itself — or not an answer so much as a negation of the question that I might have been tempted to ask. Not that I felt particularly enlightened by the performance of this work: it was just that I was suddenly disposed to understand, as I raked and swept, that this was all there was: a body, a rake, an autumn day, the leaves falling slowly across the path I had just swept, blanking it out again, even as I worked. This understanding, this rhythm, wasn't profound, and it only lasted for as long as I was working, but being there, working *in* that steady rhythm, I felt everything slip into place around me: good, bad, ugly, beautiful, indifferent, painful, it was all one, all just as it was and not otherwise. It wasn't that I felt more at peace, or more accepting, I just saw what was there and, after a while, saw myself sweeping leaves, not thinking, empty. It would last for hours, this emptiness – and then it would break and I would become aware of myself thinking, separating out my thoughts from the rest of the world, and I would be annoyed when it happened, annoyed at myself for letting this break happen. It was like when I was sixteen, and first started on acid, I had always become annoyed with myself towards the end, when I started to come down, because I knew, at the back of my mind, that I was letting it happen – that, if I hadn't let it happen, I would never have come back to where everything was fixed in its allotted place, immovable, fixed, beyond transformation.

Anyhow, that's been my life for a year or so. I raked leaves while there were still leaves to rake, then I dug snow, or kept the potting shed tidy. In the spring, Dennis retired; he was given a cool send-off by the men, and replaced by a younger guy, Dave Greene, who had new ideas, which bothered the men for a while, till they saw he was going to be much fairer than Guilford had been. He also knew his stuff. I'd not gone for the job for any other reason than that it was fairly undemanding – I certainly didn't know anything about being a gardener – but after a few weeks working for Dave Greene, I started taking an interest. As the spring progressed, I did jobs around the glasshouses and the potting sheds, sowing seeds, taking cuttings, learning the names of things. That was enjoyable for a while, learning to identify plants by their flowers or by the way the buds were aligned on the stem, and I settled into a fairly routine existence. I moved into another, nicer place in Grantchester; I bought a push-bike; I joined the library. I even found a girlfriend of sorts, a girl called Stella who worked in the cafe at the Fitzwilliam. I didn't tell anybody that I'd been to college, or anything else about myself for that matter. It had started to be a matter of policy, to say as little as possible about myself. I was trying not to have a story, I think. It was the world I was interested in, not myself. So maybe Westwater had taught me a few lessons after all.

I don't know how my friendship with Tim and Adam started. They were at the university: Tim was studying German; Adam was doing archaeology, if I remember rightly. They were fairly well-off, middle-middle to upper-middle-class, I suppose, and they were decent enough guys, though some of their friends weren't. I think they struck up a conversation with Stella at the pub, then started talking to me when they saw I was with her. One of them – Adam, I think – was trying to pick her up, but when they saw me, they played innocent, and we got into a fairly stupid conversation, which led to another stupid conversation the next time we met, in the Eagle about a week later, when I was on my own. We took it from there, I guess. I liked observing them; it was amusing, how they managed themselves around someone like me, a real working-class person. I think it excited them a little, in spite of their feelings of natural superiority. They had spent their whole life seeing working-class people as either (a) comic relief, like the peasants in a Shakespeare comedy, or (b) salt-of-the-earth types in old black-and-white films, miners who *talked like that*, or dour Scots infantrymen who gave the officers a bit of lip for the first few reels but died bravely at the end. It seems I didn't conform to either of these models, though, because they couldn't quite figure me out. I was a cause for them, but I was also a game they were playing, a bit of a joke, when all's said and done, though not quite a joke to be laughed at. I hammed it up a bit, too, of course. They were always telling me that I could do better than garden work and I would string them along, letting them suggest various alternative careers. Tim's father operated some kind of countryside development business, and Tim was pretty sure, if I was at all interested, that he could put in a good word with the old man. Adam thought I should go into garden design on my own. I'd be much happier working for myself, he said: nobody ever made any money working for somebody else. They couldn't work out that I might not want to have all – or at least, some – of the things they thought were important; they couldn't see why I didn't want to belong to the big bright world that they were about to inherit.

And there it is: the story of their lives in a single word – theirs, and all their friends, all the people they knew and understood, the people they liked, the people they hated – they were the inheritors, boys who would be middle-aged in ten years' time, working in the city, or Whitehall, or running the family business, property owners, members of the club, men to be reckoned with. I could see Adam on his veranda on a Sunday afternoon with a G&T and an intelligent thriller or a well-crafted novel about the British Raj; I could imagine Tim with a gun and a dog, out shooting with his betters, grateful to have been noticed and eager for preferment. They were simple souls, clever, but not intelligent, perceptive and blind, thoughtful about all the wrong things, moral within the narrow bounds of a system that refused to consider the intrinsic immorality of their position. I saw through them – and I found them amusing. I also liked them, for no reason I could think of and, over a period of time, I started to hook up with them. We drank together now and again; they even introduced me to some of their friends. There was one group – three men and two women – who came into the Eagle or the Bath from time to time, a band of dramatic types with semi-famous parents in the theatre or television, stalwarts of the ADC and May balls, the boys cinema-tough, the girls fragile and self-aware, self-consciously slumming it with the likes of Tim and Adam – not to mention their dubious townie friend – but prepared to tolerate anybody for the sake of an audience. Mostly, this group was a fixed unit: all for one and one for all, but now and again they brought other people in, sometimes invading the narrow little lounge bar of the Eagle in gangs of twenty or more, on their way to a show or a party. One night they brought a girl called Ursula Black and, because Adam knew her, I got to meet her too.

Until that very moment, I'd been fairly happy with the life I had: the room in Grantchester, the garden work, drinking in the Eagle or the Bath, going out with Stella, sitting around with boys like Adam and Tim. I didn't see anything wrong with that. I'd managed to convince myself I was really fond of Stella, though in my quietest times, I knew she could have been anybody, and even when I considered that this Adam and Tim would soon be leaving, only to be replaced by other Adams, other Tims, it didn't much bother me. I wasn't like them. I had nowhere to go, nobody to impress. Somewhere at the back of my mind, I liked the idea of being fixed, a feature of this particular piece of terrain, like the weather, or one of the trees in the college garden, something that was there all the time, but hardly ever noticed, one of the elements of the place. It didn't matter if Adam and Tim thought I was wasting my time as a gardener. It didn't matter if they really meant it when they said I was better than that – it was something they were saying for their own gratification, something that revealed to them the depth of their own perceptions. I didn't care where I went or what I did, one place was as good as another, so why not stay where I was? For a while there, I started to enjoy the passing of time. I enjoyed the feeling that the world was flowing by, not quite touching me. I knew men who had been in Cambridge for years, teaching EFL, or working as postmen, just for that sensation of time passing them by. There was something earth-brown and quiet and warm about that life: earth-brown and warm and acquainted with dust, like the workings of an old radio, or the space inside a terraced house in the midwinter, warm with the glow of the hearth, a theatre of the banal and the miraculous, the quiet illusionist's trick of an ordinary life. I found the prospect of that ordinary life as appealing as anything else that was on offer.

'Isn't there something you'd like to do?' Tim asked me one night. We were sitting in the Bath, watching the foreign language students come and go. Tim enjoyed being concerned about me, this was his project: the recovery of another human soul. Adam was along for the ride, mostly.

'Like what?'

'I don't know.' Tim glanced at Adam for moral support, then back to me. 'Something more satisfying. Something more – engaging.'

I laughed. 'I'm fine where I am,' I said.

At that very moment, Ursula Black walked in. I didn't know who she was, of course, though I'm surprised I hadn't seen her before. She seemed to be a friend of Adam's – a real friend, not just another ADC poser – because she smiled when she saw him, and he got up quickly and went over to where she was standing, perched at the edge of the crowd waiting to get to the bar. At first I thought she was more than a friend, because he'd stood up so quickly – Adam rarely did anything quickly – and because of the way she smiled as he went over. He even kissed her on the cheek, which didn't seem like Adam at all.

'Who's that?' I asked when Adam returned, an odd, slightly embarrassed smile on his face.

'That's Ursula Black,' he said. 'I know her from back home.'

'Really?'

'Oh, no, it's not like that. She's going out with Freddie Lyndon.' He gave the word a suitably derisory note for my benefit. 'His father owns half of bloody Scotland. He's not that bright, from what I've heard.'

'Linton,' Tim chipped in. 'And he's a good bloke.'

'Lyndon, Linton.' Adam gave him a sour look. 'You would know.'

'What's that supposed to mean?'

I thought I'd better get in quick before they went off on one of their scraps. They were like Tweedledum and Tweedledee when they got going. 'So – what about her?' I asked.

Adam looked confused. 'What about her?' he asked.

'How do you know her?'

'I told you, from back home,' he said. He turned back to Tim. 'I've never understood what you see in those people. They swan around –'

Tim snorted. 'Adam's jealous,' he said, but I could see he'd finally noticed my interest. 'Anyway, why are you so interested?'

I shook my head. 'No reason,' I said.

'Good.'

'I just thought she looked interesting.'

Tim gave me one of his man-of-the-world, man-to-man, all-chaps-together looks. 'She's not for you,' he said. 'Don't waste your time.'

It was something Tim and Adam said every time I took any notice of one of their fellow-students. Language students were fair game, town girls were fine, but university girls were always a waste of time, as far as I was concerned. They were right, too. I'd talked to girls they knew at parties I'd crashed, and they'd been polite enough, in a lady of the manor kind of way, but it's obviously a step too far to take any real interest in the gardener, no matter what D.H. Lawrence says. What always struck me about those girls was how sensible they were, how very grown-up. It was pretty annoying, to tell you the truth. I know you wouldn't think much of all this; I don't think much of it myself, if I'm honest. Now that it's all over – though there was never anything there to be over in the first place – I realise what a fool I was. I knew – I had always known – that the worst mistake I could make was to want something. I could do without money, I didn't want any kind of success, I didn't need to belong. After Cindy, I'd sort of worked out that there was a certain type of woman that I should avoid – but there were plenty of others, women to like and have good times with and not get serious about, women like Stella, who was sexy and funny and not at all sensible or grown-up. But that was the problem. Women like that were easy to be with because they were interchangeable: some were pretty, others weren't, but that didn't really matter to me. They all had something. It's the best luck a man can have, liking women. Not just the pretty ones, or the ones who want to go to bed with you, but all women. It's the worst luck when he chooses one woman and sets her apart, then lets his imagination go to work on her – because that's all it is, in the final analysis: imagination. Of all the bars in all the world, Ursula Black had to walk into the Bath one Tuesday night when I was bored and my imagination was ready to work overtime.

I'm not going to go on about how beautiful she was – she *was* beautiful, but then how much of that was my imagination I couldn't say. I can't really describe her either: she was tall, she had long, dark hair, she had blue eyes – those are all facts, but they don't say anything about how she was, or how she looked to my mind. At the time, it was like when you see somebody in a photograph and then meet them in the flesh, it's that degree of difference: when she was in a room, everybody else looked like they were the people in photographs, and she was *real*, she was there. She was with a whole group of other people – I knew a couple of them from the Eagle – and they were like wallpaper, they were background noise. She talked to Adam for a while, then he came back over – without her, I was sorry to say. Or was I that sorry? Even then, before the farce even began to unfold, there was someone at the back of my mind calling out like some thirsty customer at the back of the queue at the bar, waving his hands and calling to the barman, trying to get his attention. Naturally, I ignored him.

I sat for the rest of that evening waiting for her to come over. She didn't. I asked Adam about her when Tim wasn't listening in – casual questions, nothing that might arouse his suspicions – but his answers were fairly vague. He knew Ursula because he'd gone out with her older sister when he was seventeen. To judge from what he said, the sister had given him a pretty hard time. It wasn't easy to imagine Adam mooning around with a broken heart, but everything he said suggested one of those painful summer romances that everybody should have once and no more than once. This is the voice of experience speaking, I'll add. The voice of a man salvaging something from recent humiliation. I couldn't get much more out of Adam that night – it would have been indelicate to have pursued the matter, and I'm sure he didn't really want to go baring his heart to the college gardener – but I picked things up again later, the next time we met. It was a Saturday lunch-time in the Eagle: for once, Tim wasn't there, but it so happened that Ursula Black was – only now she was with someone, not touching him, not even really looking at him but with him in that unmistakable way that lovers have of being connected, even in a crowd of people, moving apart but always ready to come together again, tethered to one another by some invisible energy.

'The famous Linton, I presume,' I said, nodding at the happy couple.

Adam nodded. 'The very same,' he muttered. It was obvious he didn't like Linton, for some reason – which was striking enough in itself, since Adam didn't usually go to so much trouble in his personal relations. People were OK, or they weren't. Few people merited such extremes as love or loathing. It would probably have struck him as bad form, in some curious English way. He studied the landowner's son a moment longer; then he turned to me. 'So,' he said. 'Is your future decided?'

I nodded. 'I think so,' I said. I wasn't interested. The future didn't exist, but Ursula Black did. Standing at the far end of the bar, cocooned in a little band of like-minded souls, she existed the way Antarctica exists, visible on all the maps, but utterly inaccessible.

But here's a thing, as Tommy used to say. I still remember him now, standing at one of the slot machines in the pub, watching the wheels go round, studying the machinery, trying to pretend there was some kind of science to it all, as his hard-earned pay slipped through his fingers. That's a specific trait of our race, I suppose: we take the most random processes and make-believe we could understand them if we only had all the facts, or if we were only skilled enough, perhaps because it makes it that much easier to pretend that the inexorable, the entirely predictable processes that decide our fate from the cradle to the grave – money, work, somebody else's interests – are actually haphazard and so potentially avoidable. It's a great tradition – I admire every fool who's gone before me, pulling the wool over his own eyes as he walked gladly into the fire – and I'm quite prepared to carry it on. I'm not sure what Tommy wanted from those one-armed bandits in the Hazel Tree – it wasn't the money, I think, more a sense that, for a moment, just that once, he really could be lucky, that, for once, the script allowed for a change – and now, looking back, I don't know what I wanted from Ursula Black. Nothing I couldn't have had from Stella, if I'd allowed my imagination to go to work on her – or from someone else. As it happened, I only really noticed Stella after we split up. I met her outside the Fitzwilliam, just after New Year, and I could see that she was already happy to be on her own. She stopped to talk a moment, and I asked her how she was, what she'd been up to over the holidays, the usual stuff. I wanted to ask if she'd met someone else – she looked so easy, so over me, that I assumed there had to be somebody – but I managed to stop myself just in time. I found out later that she was on her own; I also discovered she was happy with that arrangement. I don't know why I should have imagined otherwise.

So here's a thing and the thing is, there's no story here, because nothing ever happened, or nothing anybody could tell. It's like Victor used to say on the Westwater tapes: we think it's the big dramatic happenings that make a difference, but it isn't. It's the long-drawn-out, drip-by-drip processes of loss or betrayal or grief that break us down; it's the weeks and months of growth after some revelation, and not the revelation itself, that make us wise. I saw Ursula Black on Trumpington Street a couple of days later:

she was on her own, it was quite early, she'd been out for a walk, I suppose, or maybe she was just getting home from somewhere, going back to her rooms to face another day with the glow of the night on her. I hoped not. I suppose she noticed me looking at her, but she didn't remember me from the pub – why should she? – and I was in my work-clothes, cycling in from Grantchester, enjoying the cold of the morning, the clear, crisp air, the sunlight glittering on the frosted grass. It would soon be Christmas; all the students would be going away, but first there was the annual round of parties, all bakery warmth and nostalgia and mulled wine, the beautiful young people going out in the dark and over the snow, warmed with spirits, wrapped in their winter clothes. I knew, from the previous Christmas, that it was my place, in all this privileged confusion, to carry a big fir tree into the bar and set it up for someone to decorate. I even got to help Mike, the handyman, hang the decorations, standing atop a wobbly stepladder, my mouth full of tacks, while the lads from the bar stocked up the wine, all of us caught up in the colour and noise and business of a party we wouldn't be allowed to attend. It hadn't bothered me the year before, but it did now. Meanwhile, I saw Ursula everywhere – from a distance – sometimes alone, some-times with friends, occasionally, though oddly enough, not that often, with Freddie Linton. I never spoke to her, nor she to me. I never touched her. I never looked her in the eyes. Can you imagine that?

And that's all the story there is, that desire to go to a party where I didn't belong so I could meet a woman I could never have. I knew, if I asked, Tim or Adam would get me in as a guest, but I had always been too scrupulous to ask – not because they were great friends of mine, but because they weren't. We all knew that, in our honest moments. Now Ursula had turned up and I was desperate to go. I know, I know, it's beginning to sound like some *Blue Angel* story: man falls in love with totally inappropriate woman, man turns into abject, shameless wreck, woman toys with man for a while, cat-and-mouse style, then lets him go. But it wasn't like that at all. Believe me, I'd have been grateful even for that little game. I'd have been glad of anything that added up to some kind of story, anything that would have made a connec-tion between us, however tentative.

You're wondering why I didn't just go up to her in a bar and introduce myself. I was always good at that kind of thing, I know you noticed it, even if you didn't have any time for such business yourself. Or so you said. At times, I thought, you did protest too much, but we'll let that go: even if it was all a bit of an act, all that contempt for romantic love, you would never have allowed yourself to get into difficulty in the first place, would you? The world was too big for that. That's what I liked about you: it wasn't that you were grown-up and sensible, you were just too interested in other things. It's like the time when they were announcing the prize-winners for the year at the end of fifth form, and you asked me afterwards if I'd won the house prize. It was you, of course, but you hadn't been listening. Something had caught your eye out on the playing field, and you'd not heard your name being called. All those kids sitting around staring at you, and you were just gazing out of the window, watching a rabbit cross the football pitch or something. I imagine they thought you were being modest. If only they'd known. The fact is, their prizes didn't mean anything to you at all. On the big day, when you went up on to the stage and received your book token from the chairman of the governors, you were so obviously thinking about something else, even old Collings noticed. And, just as you had been given credit for modesty before, now you were faulted for being proud. And all the time, you were just you. You weren't proud – if anything, I was always the proud one. That time the Nivens attacked you and tried to cut your hair, you didn't care – or you didn't seem to. That was what bothered me, as much as anything that bunch of idiots did. You didn't care, you wouldn't fight back, you let stuff like that go by. I never understood that.

Of course, it was pride that kept me from saying anything to Ursula. I knew – oh, I knew all along – that she was exactly where she wanted to be: even if he was no great intellect, Linton was a bit of a catch, and she was obviously happy with him. You only had to watch them together to see that. For his part, he played it a bit cool – there was all that money to think about, I suppose – but that was just guy stuff. It's interesting how this kind of thing works: women are always lamenting the fact that men are attracted to looks and nothing else, but they should see themselves when it comes to men with money. I don't mean the big spenders, I don't mean flash, I'm talking about that quiet confidence that comes of having a trust fund behind you, the confidence that comes of wearing the right clothes, driving the right car, going to the right ski resorts for Christmas vacation. When Ursula got out of bed to find a delivery man at the door with three dozen red roses, when she sat late into the night drinking champagne with the right crowd, when Linton telephoned her from wherever it is these people go for the holidays, she didn't wonder about how smart he was, she just thought it was romantic. Who was she, anyhow? A solicitor's daughter from Worcestershire. She'd spent her whole life being taught to find money attractive: not money in the abstract, but what it can buy. I'm not saying she didn't like Linton. Whether she did or not, that's pretty irrelevant now. Or it is to me. In spite of spending all that time mooning about, thinking I was in love with her, Ursula Black was really just an object lesson for me, a lesson in pride, and in the power of glamour.

Glamour. That was it. Beauty isn't enough, intelligence isn't enough, not for the world. They need the frame that sets it off, and the frame is glamour. You have to see how angry I was, knowing that Ursula was falling for that and nothing else, for the glamour of money, for the way it rubbed off on her, being with the rich landowner's son. If she didn't love him to begin with, she came to love him for the way his money made her feel about herself, the way it made her feel about the world.

All right. It's time to talk about the day of the party. Not the party itself, which I didn't attend – though I'd asked Adam if he'd get me in, and he'd reluctantly agreed. I don't know what I was thinking, I know there was some half-baked plan in my head to finally talk to Ursula Black, to catch her when she was alone, or to infiltrate her little group and say something that stopped her in her tracks, or made her laugh or – you get the picture. The claw marks on the bottom of the barrel were getting pretty obvious, even to me. I don't think I ever really believed I stood a chance and this isn't chip-on-the-shoulder stuff – I love that expression, chip on the shoulder: I bet nobody ever said it who was ever hungry and it was somebody else's world. I knew what I was dealing with, but I just decided to ignore the odds.

As I said, it was my place to bring in the Christmas tree and plant it up in the corner of the bar, next to the window. I enjoyed that: I enjoyed the smell and the weight of it, enjoyed dragging this big dark body into the lit room, enjoyed the feeling I had of carrying something from the woods into the polite world of indoors. For an hour or so, while I was setting it up, and before it was dressed, that tree was a pagan presence, a dense, shaggy mass of darkness that seemed to fill the room with phantoms from an earlier, less confined domain. I suppose I thought I was the only one who'd ever noticed the effect that tree had when I raised it up, a wild beacon in the angle of the wall, so it came as a surprise when someone behind me – a voice I didn't recognise at first – broke in on my labours.

'What an amazing tree,' the voice said. 'It's so – elemental.'

I looked round. It was Ursula Black. I had just finished setting up and I was about to step back and see how it looked; as I let it go, it shuddered a little, as if it really did have a life of its own, and I thought for a moment it was going to topple over and bury us both in its cold, dark-green branches. It held, though.

'Where did it come from?'

I stepped away from the tree and looked up. 'I don't know,' I said, feeling the letdown as soon as I said it. I felt I should have known. 'From the woods,' I added lamely. I looked at her.

'It's beautiful,' she said.

'Yes.' I really didn't know what to say. Lizzie always used to say I would meet my match some day. I was just beginning to realise that I'd met my match. 'It is.'

Ursula Black laughed softly and gave me an odd look. 'I know you, don't I?' she said. 'You're a friend of Adam Hodgkin's.'

I nodded, but I couldn't manage any words.

'So what are you doing?'

'I'm sorry?'

'What are you doing with the tree?' She was smiling oddly, as if she thought I was slightly mad. 'I mean, isn't there someone to do this kind of thing.'

I shook my head. 'I'm not sure I understand,' I said, quite certain I did.

'Well,' she said. 'Couldn't you get someone else to do this? Slip him a fiver? A gardener or somebody?'

I looked at her. She seemed slightly offended on my behalf. 'I am the gardener,' I said, finally.

'Oh.' She looked puzzled a moment, then stepped back. 'Oh. I see. I thought you were a friend of Adam's?'

'I am a friend of Adam's,' I said. 'I'm also the gardener.'

'Oh.' She gave an odd, nervous laugh. 'I see. Sorry. I see it now. Because I thought −' She looked up at the tree as if it had played a significant part in the confidence trick that she was beginning to realise had been perpetrated upon her. 'Well,' she said. 'I'd better go and let you get on with your work. Sorry.'

'There's nothing to be sorry about,' I said.

'No.' She laughed again. 'Sorry.'

'I quite like being the gardener.'

'Of course you do,' she said. She was backing away now, shaking her head, half-amused, half-annoyed with herself. It was bad form to have made such an obvious mistake, and she didn't want to compound it by letting the conversation continue. Though, oddly enough, even now, that was all I wanted.

That would have been an end of it, I suppose, if I hadn't been drafted in to help restock the house plants in the various public rooms and stairways the next morning, pretty much first thing. I was looking a bit rough when I arrived, I guess, and Dave probably gave me the job so I'd be able to coast through the day: it was one of the better jobs, checking the house plants, cutting out dead stuff, replacing any that were looking the worse for wear. In winter, it was mostly cyclamen and Christmas cacti, which are pretty resilient. So I was doing the rounds, taking it easy, nursing my head. It's a slow time anyway, but there's a pleasure that comes of making things run even slower. It was chance, of course − not bad luck, not even good luck, but chance pure and simple − that placed me in a narrow alcove above the staircase in the hall, at the exact time when Ursula Black met her old chum from back home and thought it would be funny, or at least some kind of conversation, to tell him all about what had happened the day before. I hadn't seen anyone since the party, of course, though I must confess I'd thought about their revels once or twice as I sat alone in the Eagle, drinking a little more than usual. I'd split up with Stella by now − or rather, I'd drifted so far that she'd felt she had no choice but to split up with me, and if I'm honest, I have to say I enjoyed it a little, feeling sorry for myself and drinking too much. Now I was hung over and taking it slow, thinking, putting it all in place, making absurd leaps, plunging into deep depression one minute, then laughing at myself wryly the next. Then Ursula Black met Adam Hodgkin and I overheard what, for them, was nothing more than casual conversation.

'Christ, Adam,' Ursula was saying. 'Why didn't you tell me your friend was the bloody gardener?' She didn't sound like herself; she seemed strained, awkward, trying too hard to make it seem funny.

'You didn't ask,' Adam responded gruffly and, I'm sorry to say, rather defensively. I realised I was about to hear the sound of cocks crowing. 'Why? What have you done?'

'Nothing. It's just that I met him in the bar yesterday and I think offended him.'

Adam was puzzled. 'What was he doing in the bar?' he asked. He probably thought I hadn't noticed that, while he and Tim were happy enough to have a pint with me in the Eagle or the Bath, they never invited me to King's.

'He was putting up a Christmas tree.'

'Oh.' Adam softened. 'So how did you offend him?'

'Well. I mistook him for – I don't know.' Ursula was beginning to see that it wasn't very funny, however she told it. 'I just didn't know he was the gardener. How do you come to be so friendly with the gardener, anyway?'

'I'm not.' Adam sounded slightly nasal, and I wondered if he was hung over. 'Tim's taken him on. You know Tim and his lost causes. So.' The cock had crowed and he was keen to change the subject. 'You going home today?'

Ursula said something but I didn't hear what it was and a moment after, they were gone, receding into the cold outside, off to their own Christmas trees and walks in the snowy woods in Hants or Worcs, drifting away to new flirtations, new loves, new mistakes.

And that was that. A boy I had always considered inconsequential had betrayed me in the most casual and inconsequential fashion, and a woman I didn't know had called me 'the bloody gardener'. It's not much of a story. Though maybe it's a lesson.

I did see Ursula Black, once, when the students came back

from vacation. She saw me too, but she pretended she hadn't. Which was all for the best. The odd thing was, watching her as she cycled by on King's Parade, I couldn't remember what all the fuss had been about. The only thing I knew was, it had much less to do with her than I had imagined. Something in me had needed to descend, and I'd chosen the most trivial, the most farcical descent that I could come up with. I'm not sure what else to make of it. A farce, nothing more. So why do I feel so ashamed? And why, as I stand here, packing my few belongings into a bag and making ready to move on, do I feel so *right*? Not happy, you understand, nothing like that, but right, just, authentic. It's like I've just received the confirmation of something I'd known all along. More than that, I've learned the hard and necessary lesson I was talking about. For a while there, I almost stopped moving. I almost gave up. I would have thrown everything I've ever learned away for – what? Something I didn't want, my own idea of glamour. An illusion, nothing more. A flattering and very commonplace illusion.

Four in the morning, mid-October, Stinson Beach, California. At least, I think this motel is in Stinson Beach, I'm just not 100 per cent sure. I got here in heavy rain – *heavy* heavy rain, heavy enough to wash the soil from the hills and send it sprawling in thick dark waves across the road, and even heavy enough, in places, to create landslides of rock and mud, so I wasn't sure I was going to get here before it got too bad to drive altogether. I certainly couldn't have made it back to San Francisco, much less back to the Bay Area, and I guess I wasn't the only one who underestimated the weather: outside, when I arrived, a whole row of motorcycles, maybe ten or more, stood gleaming in the rainlight, red and silver and electric blue glimmers of neon streaked across the clean machinery like something from a '60s road film. Turned out these guys had taken all but one of the rooms in the motel, and I'm in the one. I'd half-expected some mad bikers' party to be going on all around me, with guys lumbering out of the rain in leathers and those peaked caps they all wear, like Lee Marvin and Marlon Brando in *The Wild One*, but I've not seen or heard a thing. I suppose they're tired after a long day of whatever it is they do on a Sunday, north of the Bay, riding around in the rain. I'm a little disappointed, to tell you the truth.

I've never seen rain like this. Certainly not here. I've seen fog, and one night I drove through an amazing lightning storm over the open country to the south and east, the sky filling with electricity, the thunder rolling across the open land between the Pacific coast and the mountains, down near Mariposa, on the way home from Yosemite, but that was picturesque, that was the kind of theatre that runs for a while then ends in a sudden cascade of black and silver rain. Nothing like this. The smell is amazing: this vivid, dark green scent of water and ozone, charged and bright and almost tangible, like a live presence in the air all around me. When I got here, I was reluctant to go inside: I thought it would stop at the door of my cabin – but I needn't have worried. It's everywhere. It's in the room, it's plastered across the TV screen and the windows, it's in my clothes, it's a film on my skin, a second skin of sky and water and static.

Four hours ago, I was wondering what the hell I was doing here. Or not here, exactly – out on the weekend, driving around the north of the state, having what my occasional boss, Stefan, who claims to have been a helicopter pilot in Vietnam, calls R&R – but where I am in life, doing all the things I never meant to do, working in an office, taking orders from Stefan – who has to be the crudest person I have ever met anywhere, Corby included, though he's pretty decent next to some of the other people I have to work with. Sales guys. Guys who used to be hippies who now have SHAMELESS CAPITALIST stamped on their foreheads, which makes me a shameless capitalist too, even if I am just a visitor from the despised English office of Synergism Inc. That's who I work for. Synergism Inc. Expert solutions for tomorrow's problems. Or something. Of course, I'm not here for *that* – or not really. It's the *reason* I'm here, but I'm actually *here* because this is California, the spiritual home of acid, and I'm on a pilgrimage, connecting back to something, finding my roots in a dream that was only ever cinema and pop songs for me, as I dropped what passed for California Sunshine in my psychedelic bedroom in rainy Corby under the glower of The Works, all the while listening to *Electric Music for Mind and Body*, or *Happy Trails* and imagining I belonged to the first wave of the new world culture. *That* is why I'm here – the job is just an explanation. I'm a pilgrim, which is to say, a sentimentalist. I thought I'd drive north, up to Calistoga or Point Reyes and drop some acid, for old times' sake. As a gesture of acknowledgement, a gesture of allegiance. Instead, I settled for a drive up the coast in heavy rain and *Maiden of the Cancer Moon* on the tape deck of my company hired car. It was enough. I remembered one thing and I forgot something else, which was all I wanted from this particular trip.

So there I was, driving on an empty road in northern California, wondering what the hell I was doing. And for the first time I thought: I'm lost. All those months and years on the road, or living in cheap little bed-sits, I never thought I was lost; now, in a rental car that somebody else was paying for, with money in the bank and a well-paid, ridiculously easy job, I was a lost soul, a hireling, a traitor. It all started three years ago, when I met a guy called John in a pub in Croydon (I'm not even going to begin to explain how I ended up in *Croydon*) and he told me that, with my background, I could get a job in computing, no problem. That was how he talked. 'You want money. No problem. We're hiring people right now. I'll talk to Ray. He's a good guy.'

'Don't I need some kind of experience?' I asked. I was broke, which was probably obvious to John, and I was attracted by the idea of some quick money.

'Nah,' said John. 'Just tell them something. They won't check. You sound plausible, they'll hire you. Just be smart. You got a degree, right?' I told him I had a degree in experimental psychology. If he was counselling dishonesty, I figured I might as well start right then and there. 'Great,' he said. 'No problem. You'll walk in.'

I didn't really know what being smart consisted of, but I went along a few days later and got the job. It was less money than I'd been led to expect, but more than I had hoped for, and it rose quickly once I'd been working a while. And what John said was right: it was easy work. Common sense, really, with some basic mathematics thrown in. Which brings me to here, now, three years later. I worked in that company a while, then got this job – no problem, as John might have said, common sense really, or common sense and some imagination typing up the CV – at Synergism Inc. When I went for the interview, they didn't even ask me what I studied at college. Some nervy ex-pat New Yorker in a crumpled suit – I've never seen anybody look less comfortable in his clothes – took me to lunch, and we talked about baseball and old movies for a couple of hours. Three days later he rang me up to say I'd got the job. Which, in turn, is how I came to be here, unpacking, in my wet clothes – wet through from

walking the ten yards from the car park to the reception desk –
with the rain hammering on the roof and the bikers sleeping all
around me in the American night. And as I was unpacking, I
came across this bundle of papers, which turned out to be my
letters to you, over these last – how many years? I have no idea
how they got there, but when I found them I was glad, as if I'd
planned to bring them all along. When I got the job, they gave
me some on-the-job training at the Croydon office, then packed
me off to head office in Mountain View, about a hundred miles
south of here, in what people who work there don't like to call
Silicon Valley, to see what I was made of.

Of course, the guys in Mountain View saw through me right
away. They were the real thing, the nerdy math geniuses and ex-
hippies who had given up being Deadheads to build a new
machine world, guys like Rubin, an arrogant, hyperactive thirty-
year-old who looks like a balding eighth-grader and monitors his
blood sugar on an hour-by-hour basis, for the sheer bloody-
minded hell of it, or Sam, the gentle, quiet-spoken back-room-
boy type who used to think technology would change the world,
but now spends the few hours of any week he's not at his desk
driving up to Candlestick Park for Giants games. Most of the
people in Mountain View have come here from somewhere else
– Chicago, New York, Texas – and they probably thought they
were here for a reason other than money once, but only a few
still cling to that notion. Still, even the ones who are disillusioned
think they are the élite: the smartest, the quickest, whatever, they
think what they are doing is the whole world. Sure, they talk
about other stuff – politics, baseball, music, their families – but
you know what really matters is the new feature they just added
to the system, or the contract the company is about to land with
Third Cotton and Hosepipe of Carolina or whatever. There's
something comical about this, I recognised that right away but,
at the same time, I found myself treating these people with an
exaggerated respect, even an odd, fairly awkward, but well-
meaning deference. I couldn't figure this out for a while, but
then, one night, as I was having dinner with one of the VPs, I
saw it: this skewed respect was inspired by the recognition that
these were the ones who had sold out the '60s, these were the
ones who betrayed the revolution and I realised they probably

lay awake in the small hours – not all, but some, some for sure – and they went back over the trail step by step, trying to work out exactly when and where that betrayal started. They are the collaborators, and they don't even know when they started to collaborate. Not all of them, but some. They lie awake and tell themselves they did what they did for their families, or because they believed in the promises the technology made, but they can't convince themselves. They fucked up, and they know it. This is America: spell that $$$$$$. They serve $$$$$$. Their kids go to school every morning and pledge allegiance to $$$$$$. They love $$$$$$ because it betrayed them and if they didn't love it they would have to admit they had allowed themselves to be betrayed. They feel contaminated by $$$$$$ but they have worked day and night for years to love their contamination. And you know what's really ironic? What's really crazy, what makes me want to weep, it's so tragic, is the fact that America – not $$$$$$ but *America* – is unbelievably beautiful. I don't just mean the landscape, I mean the cities, the air, the light, the houses, the games people play. If these people could only give a damn about something other than their own beautiful lives, they would be extraordinary.

The odd thing about all this is that I quite enjoyed trying to pull the wool over their eyes for a while. It had been too easy back in Croydon. The day after I'd been hired I met the sales director, a smiling damned villain named Peter Weekes, who told me straight out he could sell anything to anybody, he didn't really need to know what the system did, it was his job to read what the customer wanted and make sure they believed they would get it. He said they were hiring on the basis of plausibility: we had to put people into customer sites who seemed credible, and it didn't really matter how technically sound they were. What mattered was presentation. I assumed from this little speech that I scored high on presentation, but I wasn't sure I knew what that meant. Or what that made me. Anyhow, I somehow scraped through. I passed that first audition at the Mountain View office – mainly because of Stefan – and they let me come back. They don't give me anything important or interesting to do, but I suspect that, even if I was some kind of genius, they wouldn't give me anything important or interesting to do because I'm not

American. They don't trust me. They have to get along with the European side of the operation, so they take in waifs and strays like me for appearances' sake. Nobody thinks I'm clinically stupid or anything like that. They just know I'm not American, and that's enough.

The one exception in all this is Stefan. He's from somewhere else like everybody else, but he's also *not* Californian, which is different. He's in charge of sales, or customer relations, or some such thing, but he's technically aware, aggressively smart and, in his off-hours, makes crude, inelegant jokes, mainly at the expense of minorities, women and the US government. In spite of all that, he reminds me of someone. I think he reminds me of Victor, that mysterious voice on the Westwater tapes. Or he reminds me of him in one respect: he believes in stories.

Which brings me to my point, finally. I think I might have said this before, but I'll say it again so you don't think I'm compli- cated, as Stefan would say. Conclusion: it seems to me that the world is divided into two camps: (a) people who believe in stories and (b) people who trust the isolated, fleeting moments that stories seek to string together, like the little black points in one of those old join-the-dots puzzles you used to get in comic books. It never works. The picture turns out awkward and ugly, the story is, at best, a half-truth. Unless you let them go, the moments get lost. Stefan pointed all this out to me one evening when we were having a drink in a Sundowner in Sunnyvale where one of the waitresses, according to Stefan, was an old acquaintance of Lou Gehrig's.

'What matters is to have a good story,' he was saying, as the waitress, a thin, nervy woman of around sixty-five with bright red lipstick and a pronounced New York accent, brought our margaritas to the table. One of the reasons I liked Stefan was that, apart from anything else, he defied California and all its works. He liked strong liquor, quality cigars and cuss-words. In the Bay Area, that made him loveable. 'This world is run by people with good stories,' he said.

I nodded. 'True stories,' I said, pretending I'd got it wrong.

'No.' Stefan slapped the table with his palm. It was his substi- tute for good old-fashioned fist-banging. Like alcohol and tobacco, like sex and drugs and rock and roll, fist-banging was out in the new California. '*Good* stories. It doesn't matter if they're true or not. Better if they're not, in fact: true stories are far too fucking complicated. You see those movies where they say: THIS FILM IS BASED ON A TRUE STORY. Well, when they say "based", you better believe it. Nobody in America wants to fuck up a good story with the truth. That's why we don't got history. It's too fucking complicated.'

He turned to the waitress. 'Tell me about Gehrig,' he said.

The woman beamed. 'I knew Ruth, too,' she said.

'The hell you did,' Stefan roared, without a trace of doubt in his voice.

'Knew them all, honey,' the woman said, smirking. 'But Gehrig was the best of 'em. A real gentleman.'

Stefan kept it up for a while, then let her go. 'See what I mean,' he said. 'That woman's got a good story. Well –' he looked around. 'Good enough for this place.'

I nodded. 'You think she's lying about Gehrig, though, right?'

Stefan roared like a bear in pain and raised his fist. It was all an act, and he knew I knew it, but he also knew I loved him for it. 'It doesn't matter a goddamn whether she's lying or not,' he said, making a good show of being exasperated. 'That's what you people don't seem to understand. It's about quality. It's not about truth.'

And that's my point. I've been writing this letter to you for over a decade now. It's the only thing that's stayed with me in all that time, my touchstone, my one true possession. To begin with, I didn't know what I was doing, writing to a dead person, then I thought I would go back some time and lay this sheaf of papers on your grave – an offering, I suppose, a tribute to the man you could have been. Because you have been there, all this time, growing up and growing older, changing, becoming, learning new things, forgetting others, exposed to all the ordinary disappointments and betrayals that any man gets to experience in a life. I used to think this was all for you in some odd way – a way of keeping you here. If I was writing to you, you had to be somewhere, reading what I wrote, even if it was only somewhere in my head. Which is exactly where you are. You haven't gone away. You're here, you're me. Some kind of exchange has been taking place all these years, some kind of reconstitution. You get to continue in me, if I give something up to make room for you. I've been carrying you around in my head for so long, there's been this gradual exchange, a transfer of the spirit. It's as if I'm living out the story you couldn't have, the story that was stolen from you, and it's too much, it's too crowded. I'm not sure if we'd even still be friends if you were alive today: to be honest, I think we were drifting apart in those last weeks before you died and maybe that was partly why I left the party with Katrina. Yet you're still there, all the time, at the back of my mind, like a ghost, or a tumour. And maybe it was for you that I gave up the good story I should have made up, in order to belong.

But that's not it. That's not what I wanted to say. That sounds petty and bitter and resentful and I'm none of those things. Not here, not now. I'm sitting in this motel room in Stinson Beach as the light starts to break through. The rain has stopped, more or less, there's an eerie silence, though I know if I went out and pressed my ear to the door of the next cabin I'd hear the gentle, sweet sound of some biker snoring away in his narrow bed, lost to the world, dreaming who knows what. It's a fine notion, suddenly, in this motel at the edge of the world, with nothing between us all and the Pacific but a row of bikes and a sodden escallonia hedge, and for a moment I feel like Alice, when Tweedledum and Tweedledee tell her she's only some figment of the Red King's dream, only for me it's a sleeping biker splayed on his bed in the next room, wreathed in the smell of stale beer and smoke and gasoline. A sleeping biker. A pale woman with dark roots to her dyed blonde hair dreaming away the hours over a movie magazine in reception. An elderly waitress who used to know Lou Gehrig. Any of them could be dreaming this. Stefan could be dreaming this. Stefan, who works far too hard at being unpopular, a man who thinks America is the new Rome because, like Rome, America has no history, has only myths – he could be dreaming it all, moment by moment, making us all up as he goes along.

It was Stefan who sent me here. When I first came, he told me to go out and see America – or California at least – and I was happy to oblige. I drove up and down 1 and 101, south to Los Angeles, east to Yosemite, north as far as British Columbia, west to the Pacific, which was as far as I could go. And I fell in love with it all. I could see the land as it was, the old fruit farms, the old forests, the land before whites, the land before people and I fell in love with it, because that was the first time I'd ever seen anything without centuries of human history laid over it all. And I think this was what Stefan wanted me to see. He works so hard at being crude and disliked because he wants to live in that America, the America before people, the America whose only history is natural. He sent me out here and then he waited to see what I would say when I got back – but I didn't say anything, I just told him where I'd been each long weekend he allowed me, I even sent him a couple of postcards from Vancouver and Yosemite, but I didn't tell him what he wanted to hear.

But now – now after all this rain, I have something to say. Not words, or not exactly. I have something to say to Stefan, and I have something to say to you. It's taken a long time, it's taken many miles and just as many random and given moments. I've stood in a redwood forest at dawn and listened to the quiet. I've watched pelicans drift along the rim of the Pacific in the dimming light. I've sat on the edge of a rock face at Glacier Point in a lightning storm and I've stood silent and stock-still at dusk as a family of deer passed a few feet away at Big Basin. I've parked the car at midnight and gone walking in East Cupertino to see if it was really as frightening as they said it was. I've watched whales pass close to the lighthouse at Point Reyes – and all this time, or every time I stopped at the edge of a road and stood leaning on the roof of the car studying the map, the wind blowing softly through the orange-gold poppies and grasses on the verge and through me, through the illusion of the self I pretend I am, I've been in love with it all, in love with this one story that includes all the others, includes you and me and Stefan and the woman who knew Lou Gehrig. So I guess what I want to say to you is exactly the same thing that I want to say to Stefan, and it is this.

The rain has stopped. I'm going out. I'll pay my bill and get in the car and drive south, but I'll not be going back to Mountain View. I'll go to the airport and leave the car and I'll catch the next flight out. I don't know where I'll go, but I'm going to do something else now. It doesn't matter where I go and I have a little money set by from the obscene wages they've paid me all this time for doing nothing – what matters is that I go alone, and do what I was intended to do, instead of trying to carry, or dodge, or reinvent the stories other people write for me. By other people, I also mean you, my old friend. It's time for you to let go now. It's time for me to let you go. From here on in, I'm on my own.

Dear Jan,

It's one in the morning and the rain is falling, as it has fallen all day, heavy and loud at the window and on the roof: dark, salty rain, making that slow drumming sound the Japanese supposedly have a special word for, but which makes me think of you all of a sudden, for the first time in weeks. It's been so long now, and I suddenly wondered how far away you were – because I realised, after a long time, that the only way I could think about death was as a journey, and the only way I could think of you, dead, was as a long process of moving out and away, a long recession into the stars and the dust, not decay in the earth, after a while, but a slow receding into the fiery dust that drifts for ever in space. That image, that idea, sits at the back of my mind all the time – when I said I hadn't thought of you in weeks, it was true, but this image is different, the difference, you might say, between talking about a living person and a ghost, or a word and a phrase of music. It's part of a change in me, I suppose, this transformation of you as a thought – a name, a face, a regret – into you as image, you as idea: a transformation that allows me to think of you, not as you were, but as you are now, not as a historical fact, but as a potential, like one of those torch-beams we used to shine into the night sky years ago, knowing the ray of light would go on travelling for ever or, at least, till it found the edge of the universe. I remember how odd that idea seemed to me, at the time: the edge of the universe. I used to wonder what there could be, when what there was stopped.

The last time I thought about you was also the first time I talked about you by name to anyone since you died. I was sitting in the gallery after hours with Sally and somehow your name came up. I suppose I should explain who Sally is – explaining her to you might make it clearer to me why we were together for so long – but right now I don't really want to get into some long account of *I said this, she said that*. Besides, I have to go back so far to make any sense of where I am now: here in this house, a house by the sea, working – I mean working, finally, doing something I want to do, taking pictures, like you always said I should, but also painting, which is as much a surprise to me as I'm sure it would be to you – half-living, in between-times with this woman who is, beyond any doubt, smart, beautiful, decent, warm and, though I know this is just one big cop-out, far too good for me. But then, she *is* too good for me. She understands me too well, and so not at all; she talks to me about what I'm feeling and I think what she says makes perfect sense, in some abstract way, but not for me; she sees me as she thinks I could be – happy, at peace, whatever – and she doesn't understand why I wouldn't want what she wants for me. Which is, oddly enough, where you come in.

I don't remember how we got on to talking about you, but we did. Maybe it had something to do with the Westwater affair, I don't know. I guess I was giving her something, making a gesture, allowing her a glimpse of the inner life she so obviously wanted to be a part of. Whatever the reason, we talked about you, and about what I'd been doing since you died, and she suddenly saw, she suddenly understood the reasons for why I am the way I am.

'You've been grieving,' she said. That's how she talks: she listens for a while, takes it all in, then she says something abrupt and to the point, with this amazing confidence that makes her seem, if not exactly right, then at least sincere. 'Sometimes a person who's grieving doesn't know that's what it is. Grief. They don't see that it's a temporary thing, a stage they're passing through. They think it's something else, something permanent. You don't want to stop moving, you don't want to belong anywhere, because you think that's just how you are. But it isn't. It's because you're grieving, it's because you're angry. Maybe you're guilty too.'

I perked up at that, I have to admit. 'How do you mean: *guilty?*' I asked her.

'Guilty because it was him, not you,' she said. She made it sound very logical and matter-of-fact. An everyday thing: grief, guilt, anger. For a moment, though, I thought she'd stumbled on to something – because I know I'm guilty, don't I? Guilty – and not in some psychological sense, but really, truly guilty, as in *at fault*. Which is something these amateur psychologists can't see, of course. They're so devoted to *normalcy* and in normal situations, guilt is nothing but a burden. But I am guilty because I did wrong and I'm guilty for ever even if I forgive myself for the sin: it's part of who I am to be guilty. And it's part of who I am not to want to belong, not to want to stop moving. Grief – of course I know I've been grieving, though I wouldn't have used the word as such before Sally used it – grief just allowed me to focus that desire not to belong, to clarify it and make it whole. Grief just allowed me to see it for what it was: an attribute, a characteristic of my psyche – though wouldn't it be better just to say soul and have done with it?

No. This is going to get all complicated if I don't go back and start again. Not from the beginning, I hope, but from somewhere. I'll start with where I am and what I'm doing right here and now. Then the history, or as much of it as I need to spell out. A few days ago, just before we broke up, probably for the last time, Sally wanted to know how long I would be staying in Fasthaven. She wanted to know if we had a future together, if I was prepared to stay here with her and call it home. That's what she said, in so many words: if you don't have a home, you find some place, and you call it home. It's that easy. After you've made the decision, you just have to work at it.

'Maybe home is overrated,' I said. 'From what you're saying, one place is much like another.'

She shook her head – there was that mixture of mock-pity and patience in her face. 'That's not what I'm saying at all,' she said. 'It's a question of choosing. You don't just settle down in any old place, you *choose*. You come to a place and you say: *this* is where I want to be.'

'What?' I asked, mock-innocent. I felt vaguely ashamed, but I couldn't help it. The more serious things get in these conversations, the more I want to undermine them. 'For ever?'

'You know what I mean,' she said, a trace of sadness in her voice, though I couldn't have said if it was altogether genuine. A little maybe, but a little put-on too.

'I'm happy here for the time being,' I said.

She shook her head. 'Not good enough,' she told me.

'Best I can do,' I murmured.

She smiled grimly. 'No it isn't,' she said. She thought a moment, then she let her face show she was giving up, letting something go. It had to do with us, I knew, but I didn't know how much. '*Your* trouble', she said, 'is that you don't want to live anywhere.'

'No,' I said. 'My trouble is that I want to live nowhere.' I didn't smile. I didn't want her to think I was being flippant, or trying to make some kind of smart-aleck joke. 'There's a difference,' I added. I don't know if she understood what I meant; probably not. I don't think I understood it myself when I said it, but I've been thinking about it ever since: about what we mean when we talk about home, and belonging, and how this is a world where nobody should feel altogether at home, this is a world where no honest person can feel he belongs – or not altogether. In a world like this – not the real, wide world of grass and earthquakes and bullfinches, but this world, this human state – grief, and anger, and guilt for that matter, are only natural. Home, wherever and for however long we find it, is, by its very nature, provisional and tainted.

Today, provisionally, I am as at home as I have ever been. I live in a tall, narrow house facing the sea and it feels right to be here. For a while, when Sally was coming over every other night, I used the whole house; now that I am alone, I keep to the upper rooms, where the good light is, and I leave the downstairs empty. If I had the money, I would put land and distance between me and my neighbours; as it is, I keep to the third floor attic, gazing out over the firth, high above the street. The lower house is all I have of space, my substitute for fences and woodlands, or a moat. Not that I'm unhappy with these arrangements for the time being. It's how I always imagined myself, years ago: a man alone, living a simple life, doing what he finally knew he wanted, or needed to do. The attic is sparsely furnished: a bed in the corner, a large church wardrobe I bought at an auction, a moth-eaten armchair by one of the dormer windows and space around the other for an easel, and a table littered with brushes and paints. All I want now is quiet and a place to work. I have music, and on good days I have the near-perfect light that comes off the sea. I've started painting you see and, though I'm still taking photographs, I think this is what I was meant to do. It's like alchemy, it's like I was transforming something – not an idea, not an image, certainly not a thought, so much as a charge, an energy – into something material, something people can look at.

My daily routine is simple. I work in the mornings, absorbed in whatever it is I am doing, trying and never quite succeeding and trying again for a fabric of colour and light that I cannot put into words, cannot paraphrase. I need this marine light; but my work has nothing to do with painting from life, it is not something outside, in the world, that I am trying to capture. On the other hand, what I am after has nothing to do with me – with my own soul, or heart, or mind. The best way I can explain it is to say that I am trying to paint what is imagined. But not what is imagined by me.

In the afternoons, I take to my bed, though I don't always sleep. There are days when I lie awake, staring up at the light as it moves across the walls – but there are also days when I lie dreaming for hours, and there is a deep pleasure in rising in the dark and sitting up through the night while the rest of the world vanishes into blackness. If I had to give an example of happiness, it would be this: rising at the start of a long night, fixing tea, settling down by the window in the full light of the moon and feeling myself alone with the universe. Sally used to wonder if I was happy, and I couldn't explain it, but if I have to think in those terms, I would say that this state I am in when I am working is a perfect example of happiness because, in spite of all we are raised to believe, happiness is not personal, not at all. Not ever. I used to think I would be happy once I had got away – *clean* away, as Tommy would have said, leaving the taint of the old life behind and waiting for as long as it took till the old, tarnished skin began dying and flaking away, the new tender flesh adjusting slowly to a different air, a new body.

And surely this is the idea – isn't it? To be rid of the self, to be transformed. Once *I* have gone – once *I* have disappeared – the task will be done, the work complete. Every day I wait for the noise and the unnecessary movement of cars and people and business to subside, and it is I who remain, finally alone and free, clean, not from having left something behind, but by staying put and paying attention to the light and the tides and the sky. That voice on the Westwater tapes used to say that, to gain one thing, you have to give up another – and, as usual, it was almost right. Yet at the time I didn't understand what it all meant: I thought Victor, or whoever was talking, was telling me about the choices I had to make, about the ordinary calculation of wishes and fears. It's taken me till now to see what he was really saying. When I emptied out the lower rooms of this house, when I chose to be still, in a defined space that I could gradually vacate, when I turned my back on all that noise and business down below, I was giving something up, but it wasn't the world, it was my presence in the world. My presence as a person, you might say, my social being. I did it willingly, thinking that I would receive nothing in return. But when you give up one thing, you have to gain another: it's a law of nature, a fact of life. The process isn't one-way. In exchange for my absence as a person, I have to be given a presence in a wider world, a presence alongside the weather and sky and light, alongside birds and seals and the horizon, alongside water and the stars and you, receding one moment at a time into infinity.

Anyhow. To go back to the beginning. It seems odd to consider how long it's been; even more odd to think that I've been writing these letters, off and on, for fifteen years – but then, I've finally begun to realise that I have only the most rudimentary understanding of time. I'm so much a creature of the moment that I can't put the past into anything like an orderly, continuous narrative. I can't plan for the future either: it just doesn't seem real to me. I could never have constructed one of Victor's life stories for myself, even if it was mostly a matter of invention. True, I'm aware of the days and weeks ticking by, and I know there are people elsewhere who wonder where I am and what I'm doing, but every now and again, when I stop for a moment and realise it's been three, or five, or eleven, or fifteen years since I last saw Derek or Tommy, I'm surprised. I'm sure, if I suddenly turned up in Corby, I would expect everything to be much the same as when I left: The Works, the house, the people, all preserved in glass like the fairytale world to which stolen children return years after they were first lost.

In the meantime, I was drifting. After Synergism Inc., I needed to be alone again, to be invisible – but it was getting more difficult just to wander, doing odd jobs, or house-sitting. I was getting too old for that. I wanted to be alone, but I also needed something worthwhile to do, something to keep me occupied. That was the quaint expression that came to mind, one afternoon two summers ago, as I sat dreaming on a northbound train, just outside Newcastle. I'd been back in London for a couple of months, but when it turned warm, I decided to go to Scotland, to see Fife and maybe, if my path took me that way, to look in at Westwater and find out what Cindy and her little gang were getting up to. I didn't know if I'd be welcome; I didn't even know if they would still be there, but I felt a nagging curiosity to see the place again.

It was an odd expression – *to keep me occupied* – something Lizzie might have said, as she sat knitting by the fire, or rather, when she sat unravelling the sweater or ski-hat she had just finished, so she could start again, keeping her hands busy, keeping herself occupied. I'd always thought it was the indication of an unhappy mind, this need to be busy. Now that I felt the same need, however, I began to see that it wasn't so much a matter of unhappiness as a mere lack of will, an absence of direction that afflicts people like Lizzie and Tommy and Derek, people like me, people who grew up without a plan. The poor in spirit, who are not at all blessed as far as I can see. The unprivileged. The work fodder. It doesn't matter that I've been to college: my will had been drained away long before then. That doesn't mean I could never *do anything* with myself, as Tommy always said. It's just that, if I do anything at all, it can't be for the usual rewards, because I've already assumed – because I have been carefully trained to assume – that the usual rewards are reserved for others. If I do anything at all, it's to occupy myself.

Once off the train in Edinburgh, I changed my mind about Westwater and continued north instead, washing up some days later in this little Fife coastal town where I rented a house with some of the remaining computer money and proceeded to settle in. I had a hunch about the place as soon as I saw it – or rather, as soon as I encountered its people. I remembered the dour Fifers of my childhood: the miners were bad enough, with their hard, set faces, but I'd always known that was a front, that underneath there was blood and sinew and sentiment they were afraid of showing. On the coast, however, the people weren't so much hard as indifferent: their regard was fixed wholly upon themselves; if you weren't from there, born and bred, you didn't really exist, you were an incomer, a non-person. Which suited me right down to the ground in so many ways. That was why I took this tall, narrow fisherman's house I saw advertised in a shop window, paid the rent for six months in advance and settled in. Around me, the locals played bingo and squabbled among themselves, and I was invisible, a stranger with no name and no history. It was a matter of satisfaction, four months after I first moved here, when the assistant in the little grocery store I'd been using ever since I arrived, a woman who had never spoken to me till that very moment, lifted her head slightly and asked, with no obvious irony, if I was on holiday.

I nodded. 'That's right,' I said. 'I'm on holiday.'

The woman nodded back, and rang up my purchases. She didn't say anything else, or even look at me again as I left. She had probably never looked at me in all the months I had been shopping there. She had probably never seen me. That was the pleasure of the place: nobody saw me. This strange, inward-looking, oddly fascinating race, the children and grandchildren of fishermen and sea-traders, coastal people whose history encompassed the whole of the North Sea, trade with Holland and Scandinavia, or long voyages to the Orient for the East India Company, were now reduced to this narrow world of gossip and intrigue, a community of souls caught up in lifelong self-regard and half-hearted Christianity. I sat in my former fisherman's house and watched them come and go: the unco' guid and the wily chancers, the local beauty from the florist's shop and the dignified, good-humoured carpenter, the men who still ran boats for crab- and lobster-creeling and the old fishermen who gathered each day by the little marina, obviously a new development with its pleasure boats and holiday sailors in denim caps and Arran sweaters. It was still a place where people came and went all the time: German or American holidaymakers would pass through on the marked coastal path that ran the length of the county, wandering alongside the endless golf courses for miles, then dipping down to typical little harbour towns like this one, with its gift shops and its pocket lighthouse at the end of the pier. Yet there was only minimal contact between tourists and locals: the people from the town kept to themselves, like the elect from some old presbyter community, the only ones who mattered in a world they didn't much like.

I'm being unfair: I know that. I know every person out there – alone in the dark when the television has shut down for the night and there's only the silence or the sound of the tide – every person, asleep and dreaming or lying awake in the dark, lives in that other world of grass and wolves and bullfinches. You see it best at night because, at night, all our houses are holy. They cannot help being so: asleep or awake, we are transformed by the night, transformed, not just altered, we come to life like people who unexpectedly find themselves in a theatre, the stage lit, the scene set. Not that anything will happen, as such: there is no action here, no melodrama. What I mean by *holy* is the sense a theatre-goer has of the magic of things, in that moment when the lights go up, soft and golden, or blue-green and rich with the impli-cation of rain, singling out and illuminating everything they touch, making everything visible for the first time. Anyhow, I was telling this from the beginning, like a story. I'm not doing very well, am I? What I wanted to talk about was Sally, not these others. I was going to tell you about the day I met her, and how we got to be lovers, and why we decided to part. Well, one thing at a time. One thing at a time.

There was a thick mist in from the firth that first day. I'd noticed it was a feature of the summer weather – I had no idea why, but on some days, after a bright, warm morning, this cold mist, the haar, would creep in off the water, stealing up through the harbour, rolling slowly up the narrow wynds, whiting out the town street by street, house by house, till everything stood isolate in a cold white stasis. A couple of times, I had been down at the waterfront taking photographs, or watching the men at work on their boats, when that fog came in: warm in a T-shirt and jeans, in the bright, clear sunshine, I was always surprised when it touched me, a contact two degrees colder than the air of moments before, cold and total, like being wrapped suddenly in a caul of ice. I could walk down the slope from the top of the town and meet it halfway, stepping into it, crossing a borderline between light and fog, between warm and cold. I kept going out to try and catch it with my new camera – after all these years, I bought a good camera and started taking pictures again. I felt self-conscious at first, trying not to imagine your ghost peering over my shoulder, telling me I was making too much of something, that I needed to avoid tricks, to let the thing I was picturing speak for itself. After a while, though, I relaxed, just taking the world as it came, trying to empty myself, to find that unbiased, attentive mind's eye that everybody talks about but very few ever attempt to become. It was, I realised, a way of keeping myself occupied, but it was also an absorbing, sometimes even satisfying occupation. I couldn't get what I wanted from the haar, though. The image I had in mind – something I would only know when I saw it – kept eluding me.

I liked walking in the haar best of all, but I went out every day, no matter what the weather, and took a stroll to the end of the quay, or up along the shore past the pig farm in one direction, or the golf course in the other. I rarely stopped off in a pub or a shop: what I wanted was to avoid contact, to be invisible. Just stopping to talk about the weather with a waiter or a barman forced me back into being a person, someone with a past and a present, someone with a history – which was exactly what I most wanted to avoid. I have no idea, then, why I walked into the Salt Box Gallery that afternoon and started talking to the owner, a slim, dark-haired woman about my age or slightly younger, a soft-spoken, rather attractive woman with an obvious English accent, whose name, I discovered that very day, was Sally Clarke. I had been seized, all of a sudden, with a desire to look at pictures, and I had seen a drawing in the window, a free-flowing, energetic image of one of the local wynds, that struck me. Inside, I was pleased to discover that I was the only customer: the gallery, which was long and narrow and full of daylight, was empty, but for the woman who sat with a book at the far end of the room, her head bowed, totally absorbed in what she was reading – though not too absorbed to glance up, as the door opened, and bestow upon me a welcoming smile. I smiled back. It still wasn't too late to take a quick look around then escape before words were exchanged. I'd done it before. In a town like this, it isn't a difficult task to go unnoticed.

The woman had other ideas though. It was probably nothing more than politeness on her part, but when she saw me taking an interest in the show — all work by the same artist whose drawing I had seen in the window — she put down her book and came out from behind the table. 'If I can help you with anything,' she said, 'don't hesitate to ask.'

I looked at her. She was more attractive than I had realised, with bright, dark eyes, but it was her soft, almost unbearably musical voice that drew me to her. 'I'm just looking,' I said. 'I'm renting a house just along the street for a while, and it was looking a little bare.' This was true, but what it implied, that I had been thinking of buying pictures when I came in, was a lie. What I liked best about my new dwelling place was its spartan decor: I had no more desire to buy pictures for it than I had of going to the moon. It was just that I wanted to keep the conversation going — an impulse I felt sure I would regret, but couldn't resist.

The woman nodded. 'You're in Maggie Tennant's house,' she said, a statement of fact, not a question. She moved closer and stood a few feet away. 'The house on the front.'

'I don't know Maggie Tennant. I rented it through an estate agent,' I said. 'But it's on the front.'

'Maggie's a friend of mine,' the woman said. 'I'm Sally. Sally Clarke. The work you are looking at, as it happens, is by Maggie's nephew, John.'

I turned to the painting nearest to where we were standing, a dark, powerful landscape. I wanted to tell Sally Clarke how good I thought it was, but I couldn't think of the right words to say so without sounding fatuous. I shook my head. 'You're not from around here, though,' I said, apropos of nothing.

Sally laughed. 'How could you tell?' she said.

'You smiled when I came in. That was the first giveaway.'

'Ah.' She made a mock-serious face. 'You're not much taken with The Car People, then.'

'The Car People?'

'That's what Maggie calls them,' Sally said. 'Like some primitive tribe, with their fetishes. This lot just love their cars. They give them names. They make sacrifices to them when the moon is full. If they are forced to leave their vehicles, even for a moment, they become confused and distressed. They leave the engine running, to keep it warm. They leave the radio playing so it won't feel lonely.' She laughed. 'One day, an archaeologist will excavate the local burial ground and find whole families buried in long mounds with their Ford Fiestas.'

I smiled. 'Is it that bad?' Now that she mentioned it, I'd been aware, in the evenings, of a certain level of noise from the streets below, but as my own house faced the water, I hadn't been too bothered by it. 'I'd not really noticed,' I said.

A strange interruption. I was sitting here writing this letter – it's two in the afternoon, two days after I began, and I'm aware of how disjointed this is, but then surely you of all people under-stand, not what I am saying, but what I am trying to say. Or do you? Who are you anyhow, that you have stayed alive in my head for almost twenty years? Did I ever confess that, towards the end, during that last summer when you started in with the mood swings, I was beginning to wonder about you? No – I don't need to mention it; you knew, even then, that things were changing. We were drifting apart – college had contributed to that, but that wasn't all it was – and I didn't feel I knew you any more. You had become – absolute. I think that's how I'd want to put it: you had become absolute, the way an absolute monarch is absolute, the way absolute zero is. You were so isolated, so far into your own world, it had become hard to see you. It was like looking at some figure on the horizon, a man far in the distance striding along a ridge or the brow of a hill, like those figures in *The Seventh Seal*, faraway, abstract, metaphysical. You were a recognisable shape, it was obviously you, but you were so far-off I couldn't be sure.

Anyhow, I heard the knocking, down below, and for some reason I went to answer. Did I think it would be Sally? Well, if I did, I don't know what I expected or wanted from her. I miss some things, I miss the way we were together before she made a story out of our life, but not enough to go back to her. Though it turned out it wasn't her anyway. It was someone she had sent, some guy who'd bought one of the pictures at the gallery, and asked how he could get in touch with me. So she's still thinking about me. She's still looking after my interests. I sent him away, of course. Too serious. I'm sure she knew I would, but you never know. She thinks I've 'got something' and, like most people who grew up hoping they had something themselves, she thinks it would be a crime for me to squander my talents. It was one hell of a burden, living with somebody who believed in me so much more than I believe in myself. It was even more of a burden, living with somebody who believed in me so much more than she believed in *herself*.

And we did end up living together, in a manner of speaking. I kept my place, she had hers. I could go into all the romantic details, but it was a fairly quiet thing, really. In a place like this, with so few other people to take any interest in, it was almost inevitable that we'd end up together. I'd only been here a few months, but I could see that – so how much clearer would it have been for Sally, who'd been here for years? Maybe she had been waiting for someone like me to come along for as long as she could remember. Someone like me, but I suppose, in the end, not *me*, as such. Anyway, we slid quietly into something: friendship, sex, a kind of logic. We had laughs, we knew we were different from the rest of the people here, so we allowed ourselves to imagine we were much more similar to one another than we actually were. It was a fairly ordinary affair, but it had its passions and eccentricities. For example: we both loved art, but we were scandalised by some of the work that was getting shown in the big galleries and even more so by the stuff that was winning all the awards and subsidies. We thought we could do better, or if not better, then no worse, so we would sit around and make things up for fun. I would describe a project off the top of my head and Sally would have to think of a title. She was good at titles, they were sufficiently odd, or sufficiently ordinary, to give us both pause.

'A hundred coal miners' lamps in a black room,' I'd say. 'But there has to be something else, some kind of counterpoint. Scarlatti playing on an invisible sound system, say.'

Sally would think for a moment. '*Preparations for the Golden Mean*,' she pronounced, like an oracle. It was a good role, oracle; one she enjoyed. Her titles didn't have to be very meaningful or profound, they just had to sound right, they just had to be plausible. We devised a whole range of installations involving light: a country lane, with trees on each side, lined with miners' lamps or ships' lanterns. *Founders' Day*. A cupboard full of burning candles. *Domestic Science*. Specially constructed bowers full of Christmas tree lights and flickering liquid quartz displays. *Natural*

History. We never took it very seriously, yet we kept going back to it. Meanwhile, Sally ran the gallery, was friends with some of the local artists, and a polite enemy to others. As for me, I went on taking pictures – but I started painting too, not knowing if it was any good, and not really caring.

The computer money was about to run out, though. I hadn't done anything I was very sure about, not from the selling point of view. Still, I was happy enough in myself. I've always held on to that expression: *happy in myself.* Tommy used to say it from time to time: it was a way of saying: don't look for anything outward, don't fall for all the usual claptrap about what success means; a way of saying to the world: don't expect me to want what you want. Happy in myself; meaning: I have my own way of doing things, my own rules, my own eyes and ears and heart. Still, happy in myself or not, I needed to pay the bills. I wasn't going to live off Sally. I did some photographic work – that was fairly easy and brought a bit of money in, but what I really wanted to do was paint.

I'd got interested in the idea of the pentimento. I would see a painting in a book, and it would be a picture of three girls standing on a pier, or a dog's head, or a strange face laughing, or shrieking. Then, when I went to see the thing in real life, there were flaws, runs, smudges, scribbles – and sometimes there were places where the artist had changed his mind, where the third girl on the pier had been painted out, or a second dog's head was just visible in the neutral, slightly sinister mauve background, or maybe there was another face, ghostly and barely visible, under the one I already knew, the head the artist had thought of first time around, the face of a friend or a lover who had fallen out of favour, or a model who had just looked insufficiently anguished or ecstatic. That was a pentimento: that visible evidence of an artist changing his mind. In the history of art, there are thousands of these; some well-known, others unnoticed. But what if the pentimento was the very point of the painting? What if you did just enough *almost* to conceal the thing you wanted the viewer to see, *almost* to hide the image that, because it wasn't too obvious, would be all the more haunting? Such a thing, done well, had the potential to insinuate itself into the soul, to follow the viewer home, to turn up in dreams, conversations, secret fears.

I didn't say anything to Sally. I just started sketching things – copies of well-known pictures initially, recognisable images with just the barest hint of a pentimento thrown in. A vase of roses with the vaguest rumour of a martyrdom almost, but not quite, concealed by the opulent, slightly blown flowers. The ghost of a slaughtered hare hanging in the background of a well-known portrait. It took a long time to get it right – it struck me, of course, that there were ways of doing this using photographic images – but I kept to the painting. Finally, I thought I had something. To get it right, I realised, I had to abandon the literal: the meaningful juxtaposition, the telling contrast, no matter how well camouflaged, didn't quite work, it just felt smug, or didactic, or clever. I didn't want to be smug, or didactic; most of all, I didn't want to be clever. I remember hearing somebody say it once at an exhibition: the world is full of clever art, by clever people. There's just too much cleverness.

Gradually I began to see what I was doing, to understand that it was better when nothing was depicted and the pentimento was a matter of pure colour or texture. It was like those walls on the Underground, or at the seaside, when they strip off the old posters in readiness for a new image. Sometimes one layer of the old shows through, or several show through, here and there, just ghosts of colour or form, nothing specific. It would be like that, I thought, only more haunting. Now, all of a sudden, I was starting to take the whole thing seriously. I wanted to make real art. I wanted to haunt people. Finally, I showed Sally what I'd done. She loved it, of course. It moved her. It almost put me off continuing, how much she liked what I was doing. And of course, I didn't know how objective her response was. There's an arrogance in that, and I recognise it; but I still know that Sally was the wrong person to discuss it with, because, with Sally, everything is personal.

It was about that time that I found Dog. I remember you and I wondering why people called their pets Rex, or Fred, or Tabitha, as if they were other people. Of course, I have no idea, really, why people keep animals at all, unless they are there as toys, or ornaments. I would never have dreamed of keeping a dog, much less of calling it Rover or Flash, or some other dumb name. When I found Dog, though, I had no choice but to take him in. I wasn't looking for a companion, I was just letting him shelter from the rain for a while. Later, Sally said it meant something, that I was giving myself away when I couldn't even bother to give Dog a proper name, and though I didn't bother to argue the toss, I thought it was the other way round. For me, Dog was a better name than most. Dog wasn't a person, and that was the point. If he'd been a person – a kid, say – the woman who left him out on the pier, tied to a railing, would have been in deep trouble.

I found Dog one late September morning, when I was out on one of my shore walks. I was just starting to get things right with the painting, and I was making a bit of money with photography, so I was fairly happy, living in that little seaside town, seeing Sally every other day or so, but not in too deep, or not so I felt crowded. The sex was good and she made me laugh. I was happy to be able go out walking on a weekday morning, when there weren't too many people around, to feel the rain on my face, or the wind at my back. Weekends, I stayed in, or took a bus further along the coast to one of the little inlets where the crowds didn't normally venture, but during the week, when the main holiday season was over, it was good to walk on the pier, with no other company than the gulls, and the odd fisherman. It was something of a ritual, that walk; it cleared my head before I went back to the house and started work. As I say, I had already started doing some good stuff and, though I wasn't as taken with it as Sally was, I felt it was worth going on with, that there was something waiting to be found, somewhere along the line. I didn't know then that it would always feel like that, that it would always be a tentative, slow-moving, uncertain business, stopping and starting, taking false trails that ran for weeks then came to nothing, finishing something only to realise that, even when it was honourable, even when it had some merit, it bore no resemblance to what I'd had in mind when I started. I didn't know this then, and I certainly didn't know that I'd end up being glad it worked that way.

I never worked first thing in the morning. After a night's painting, I would have a pot of tea, then go for a walk. There was a process going on that I didn't think too much about, a process of erasure, where everything that had happened the day before – the work I'd been doing, the conversations I'd had with Sally if she had been over to stay, whatever I'd seen or heard on the news, or talking to Sally's friends in the pub – everything extraneous was erased and forgotten. It was a necessary ritual, this process of erasure: I had to become myself again, a non-person, someone with no defined identity, without family or friends, or fixed abode. There were times when I thought I'd already stayed in that little town for far too long, that I was sinking into it, becoming settled, but the work I was doing had become interesting there, and I couldn't bring myself to move away, while that promise of something still hovered, undefined, in the air. I had found a routine that worked, a life that had been stripped down to its essentials: a clean, well-lighted house by the sea, a basic, almost invariable pattern to the days, the space and the quiet to work. I could have gone on there for much longer, I suppose. Maybe I'll go back some day.

It was windy that morning, with fine rain blowing in off the sea – a perfect day for walking. If it was out of season, I always took the same route: down the narrow wynd to the shore road, right along the front to the harbour, across the car park, past the new marina, where a few pleasure boats bobbed up and down on their moorings, and out to the old pier, where the handful of fishing boats that still worked that stretch of the coast were moored on long thick ropes dripping with green weed in the morning light. When the tide was out, the boats would settle at odd angles on the harbour floor, the keels oxblood red or navy blue, the decks littered with rope and fishboxes or great, heavy-looking lobster creels bound in orange netting. The near end of the harbour was a strip of dark, sweet-looking red sand, studded with blood-coloured pebbles and fragments of pottery and glass; a few yards out, though, it was all silt and mud, a thick, clotted bed of sludge criss-crossed with spidery wet tracks where the gulls had gone, or where they still stood, heads tilted to watch as I passed. Every now and then a stranded jellyfish would be visible, half-buried in the mud, its clouded, dying flesh turning from silver to a dull bluish mass. Stars of weed would appear in the silt, glittering on the surface, jade-green, or purple, or black, elaborate, still vividly alive, waiting for the tide to resume possession of their true, expanded form. I would take time, on these walks, to study the harbour floor: if I knew anything about what I was starting to think of as art, it was that the truth was in the details; that we live, in spite of ourselves, at this forensic, homeopathic level of glints and shimmers, of grace notes sifted out of the wind, of everything that happens between the obvious events of life that we usually notice and talk about.

I saw the woman when I reached the end of the pier. She was dragging the dog along on a leash, trying to act casual, so nobody would notice that the dog was resisting her every inch of the way. I didn't pay her any mind, though, not at first. She walked off along the pier, pulling the dog behind her, and I stood watching the gulls pacing up and down on the grey, patchy mud, their wings folded behind them, their heads bowed, like hopeful suitors, or old-time diviners, waiting for a sign. I was always fascinated by this mud: usually it looked thick and creamy, with a wet, ash-grey crust, all pocks and blisters, punctuated by spidery gull-trails, though occasionally it would seem dangerously wet, like quick-sand, almost, and there were stories of men falling in at night, on the way home from the pub, back in the old fishing days. The locals guarded these stories like best china: they would bring them out from time to time, handling them carefully, taking more than enough time in the telling to allow not only for the neces-sary suspense but also for elaboration, creating legends whose magical power was more than the sum of their content. I remember the first time I heard the story of a fisherman who'd spent too long in the Salvation Bar and had wandered off into the night, drunk and alone, towards the pier, where he'd tripped off the edge and sunk, slowly, the mud sucking him down, while his cries went unheard by the sleeping town. I had accepted this narrative as a matter of principle – it seemed a dishonourable act not to believe the stories the old men told in the bars, from the tales of eerie lights out on the open sea, to accounts of the myste-rious sea-creatures that occasionally turned up in the nets, two-headed, many-eyed, hermaphroditic, dying or melting away as soon as the catch hit the deck.

I was still at the head of the pier when the woman appeared again, walking briskly towards the town. It struck me as odd that the dog wasn't with her: odd, but not sinister, certainly not enough to be distracted from the process with which I was engaged. The rain was heavier now; one by one the gulls spread their wings and drifted lazily across the harbour, towards the wooden docks by the marina. I pressed on along the pier, my face to the wind, the smell of the rain and the sea-water filling my lungs, and suddenly I felt at home there, the way I had felt at home in other places, in anonymous hotel rooms on the road, in the suburb where I'd spent a summer house-sitting for a friend, in all the temporary shelters and halfway houses I'd ever known. I had been at home; but I had never wanted to stay – or rather, I only felt capable of being at home in those places because there was no option of staying, they were fleeting havens, harbours for a night, or a week, or a couple of months, but no more than that. This was their special charm, their particular beauty. When I lived in that suburban house, with a near-stranger's furniture and clothes, tending his garden and doing routine maintenance on a home that he would soon repossess, I was happiest in the middle of the day, when I knew the other houses were empty, the parents at work, the children in school, house after house standing silent and still in the warm summer sun. I would go out and walk to the end of the street, out to where the woods began, and I would stand enthralled, gazing into the live borderline of trees and Queen Anne's Lace. Then I would turn and walk back, drinking in the stillness, passing the house fronts and gardens I already knew by heart down to every last detail: the door-knockers shaped like dolphins' or foxes' heads, the rose beds, the grey and white cat perched on the larchlap fence by the edge of a disused railway siding, the child's tricycle abandoned on an empty lawn two doors from the house that, for a summer's lease, was mine.

Yet none of this felt so much like home as being out in the wind, in the late summer rain, the day I found Dog. Nothing felt so much like home as being out-of-doors did. That day, I was happy for reasons that nobody else would understand. By the time I reached the end of the pier, I was wet through, which only added to my happiness, so that it was several minutes before I noticed the dog standing at the end of the pier, tethered to a railing. It was a medium-sized animal with long, black-and-white hair, and a narrow, despondent face, part-collie, I supposed, though I knew nothing about dogs. Its eyes seemed too large for its head, and oddly protruding, giving it a dissatisfied, froggy air – which wasn't surprising, considering it was as wet as I was, its coat dripping already in the quick, hard rain, turning first one way then the other in a hopeless attempt to slip its leash, whimpering and crying out. I didn't register, at first, what had happened: I assumed the woman had left it there for a reason, that she, or someone, would return for the creature and take it home, feed it, give it a warm bath, whatever people did with a wet dog. It was only when the animal saw me and lurched to the end of the line, a desperate look on its face, its mouth hanging open, that I realised it had been abandoned.

As I say, I wouldn't have chosen to have a pet. At that moment, however, as the dog became more and more agitated, waiting, hoping, desperate to be freed, I didn't know what to do. I could call somebody, I supposed, but that would probably lead to the dog's being returned to the woman who had left it here in the first place, or kept in a home for a week, then destroyed. Dog wasn't what I imagined the average pet-owner would consider attractive; it was unlikely to be selected for a good home, out of a crowd of cuter, glossier, smugger-looking beasts. So I untied it and took it home. I didn't really know what to do with it – give it a bath? dry it off with a towel? – and I regretted my decision a hundred times a day for the next week or so, but gradually we got used to one another, me and this unwanted animal, in my house by the sea.

About a month later, I was sitting in the studio with Dog, watching the news. There was an item I didn't register at first, I was busy with something I suppose, and I didn't start paying attention till Dog did. I can't really explain this, but there's a quality of attention this animal has, maybe all animals have it, I don't know, a quality of attention that registers as a change of atmosphere, or a frequency, or *something* that makes me stop what I'm doing and pay attention. Which is what I did – and at the very same moment, or just a split second later, the announcer said *Westwater*, and I hurried over to where I could see the screen. I'd missed something – I didn't know how much – but there was a film playing, a badly made, fuzzy film that showed some people lying in rows in a room – I recognised the ruined ballroom at Westwater immediately – and, after a moment's disbelief, I saw that all the people in this film were dead. I knew this, not just because the announcer was saying so, but because I had always known, without knowing it consciously, that something terrible was going to happen to those people, sooner or later. I'd known it when I was there, and I'd known it, in some recess of my mind, ever since. Yet I had almost gone there, on the way to here, not that long ago. I couldn't help wondering what would have happened if I had made it, if I hadn't decided, on a whim, to come to Fife.

There were almost fifty people in the film, and apparently they had all been poisoned. The voice-over was wondering if they had taken the poison voluntarily. Then another film began to run, a film of the same people, alive, talking to the camera. They seemed calm and happy, or the few who had been filmed, Cindy, Pigpen, a few others I remembered from the acid parties, seemed happy and calm. But what of the others? What about Shirley? What about Victor, or whoever was behind it all? As I watched, I found myself wondering what had happened, not believing that what I was seeing was the whole truth, partly because it was on television, but mainly because of the omissions – the ones, like Shirley, that I couldn't see on the screen, the ones I knew were there, whose names weren't mentioned, whose faces were not pictured. At the same time, I couldn't make the connection between the people on the screen, and the people I had known, identical in every respect, and at the same time different. There was Cindy, talking about leaving her body, then lying very still, peaceful, the look on her face not that dissimilar from the one I had observed so often – calm, sure of herself. Had she been the one who'd set all this in motion? It occurred to me then that I had not seen the actual discovery of the bodies, I had only seen them taken away in those dark zipper bags the authorities use for the improper dead, men and women we do not know, people for whom we feel a mixture of pity and contempt, for the absurdity of their gesture and for the questions it raises in our own minds about the life to which we have allowed ourselves to become accustomed. The camera is still running when the police burst in and find them, laid out in rows, mutilated, dead, at peace. Later the other tape – the tape they made when they were still alive – is shown on the news and the world sees them for the first time: doused in a washed-out, primrose-coloured light that suggests early porn, or the Zapruder footage, they smile for the camera and repeat the stories they have memorised, though God knows for whom. Family? Old friends? Strangers? They are wearing odd, brightly coloured robes — though nobody ever wore robes, or any other special clothes, all the time I was at Westwater — sitting together, with their odd, fixed smiles, they reminded me of the ardent church-goers of my childhood, the would-be genteel Corby women who served the priests, cleaning the church, bringing flowers from their gardens for the presbytery, neat women with a taste for milky tea and the banality of spiritual truth. As they sat on the patio in their silly robes, smiling mechanically and preserved on the film for ever, like a new kind of flora, I felt sorry for these people, but I wasn't convinced they were who they said they were. Or who the authorities said they were.

I stopped working for a while after that. I bought the papers the next day and cut out all the photographs, studied them for some clue, some sign of foul play. The newspaper reports said that Westwater had been in financial trouble, that it had been rife with dissent and power struggles, that there had been fric-tion between what they called the 'cult' and the local commu-nity. A range of theories were proposed to explain what had happened: the Westwater residents had become deranged from a life of isolation and drug abuse, their suicides had been the result of mass hysteria, a kind of group madness. Nobody once consid-ered the possibility that they had just decided to do what they had already said they were going to do, that they had taken the appropriate action to leave their bodies behind. The phrase was repeated on film again and again by any number of smiling, contented people, yet even in death their words counted for nothing. Oddly enough, though, I believed them. The initial suspicion I'd had — the suspicion of foul play, or some kind of conspiracy — still held, but it wasn't the deaths that troubled me now so much as the way the words of these smiling dead were being so carefully set aside. The conspiracy I had imagined against their bodies was actually being perpetrated against their ideas, against their words. As I began working, studying the pictures I'd cut from the paper, rereading the reports, I found myself on their side. I'd started to wonder why nobody was saying that, in a world like this, there was a logic in wanting to leave, espe-cially if you believed another, better life was possible elsewhere?

Surely it was no worse to die *en masse* in silly coloured robes than to give your life on some foreign field, blown to smithereens because a prime minister or a president was running low in the polls. Might it not be better to die for your own, home-grown crazy idea than for some abstraction? That was the idea that took shape in my head – or not an idea so much as a notion, a set of images – as I began to work on a series of pictures, large stark paintings of the faces of the dead that Sally found morbid, but which gave me an oddly spiritual satisfaction. I was paying tribute, I think, to their madness. Meanwhile, Sally kept asking why Westwater was so important to me; she wanted me to go back to the stuff I was doing before, the stuff she was certain she could help me sell. I couldn't tell her about my time there, of course. No – that's not true. I could have done; I just didn't want to. Westwater was my secret.

It was about then, I suppose, that she and I began to drift. The shock of Westwater opened me up a little and, to compensate for keeping that secret, I probably talked too much about other stuff – you, for instance – which, of course, was exactly what Sally was waiting for. I don't blame her for that, either. She's learned all her life that what she wants is relationship, and that healthy relationships thrive on shared stories, shared emotions, shared everything. But I didn't want that. I wanted to be able to be with her when I was with her, and forget her when I wasn't. I wanted to keep my secrets. Most of all, I wanted to be alone when I chose. I'm surprised, looking back, that it went on for as long as it did, but after Westwater and more or less overnight, it had stopped working, like a machine that runs down one afternoon and ticks to a halt in an empty kitchen.

Which brings me to now, and the absurd notion that entered my mind a couple of days ago. And it *was* an absurd notion: going home. I don't really know where it came from, or why it expressed itself in that particular phrase: for as long as I had lived in Corby, I heard people talking about going home, and I remember the wistfulness, the longing in their voices, as they sat around in the Hazel Tree, or in Lizzie's front room, conjuring up images of else-where, a place they had never really known, a home that did not exist. Even then I had wanted to tell them – wanted to grab them and shout in their faces – that there was no such place as home, that, at best, home was where you happened to find your-self. It certainly wasn't this *elsewhere*. Depending on who was talking, home could be anywhere – the only thing any of them knew was that home never meant Corby, never meant the place where they were, at that moment, there and then. Home was a fraud. Or so I thought at the time – but now, all these years later, I found myself thinking about Corby while I worked, remembering small details I thought had been erased from my mind, as I painted in the studio, or when I went walking on the front. I even dropped Derek a note, just to ask what was going on, and he wrote back right away, first a short letter, then a much longer account of everything that had happened while I had been gone. He'd been laid off at The Works and he'd been involved in the strike, which didn't surprise me; he'd also got married and now had a baby son, which did. All of a sudden – and it may have been no more than an easy means of escape from Sally – I decided I wanted to go back. Sally would stay here and look after Dog. Or so I thought.

So there it is. Sally took Dog in, but she said she wasn't going to wait for me. Which is fair enough. She's no fool. I know there's a less than fifty-fifty chance I'll return here – and even if I do come back, I'm not sure who I'll be by then. I only know that I need to go. Meanwhile, you go on drifting into space, along with Pigpen and Cindy and Lizzie, and, for some reason that I can't quite fathom, I miss you all. Maybe that's why I'm going back, maybe that's why I'm ready to talk about home. And maybe that's what home is, anyway: the place where you bury your dead. For the dead are real, are they not, real and fixed and true? It's the dead who give us, the living, our place in the world: the dead are our roots, the one sure anchor in an otherwise provisional existence. When they say that home is the place that, when you go there, they have to take you in, they're only recognising the point that whoever *they* are, they have no choice, being dead and buried, stories to be picked up and retold, names and faces to be remembered and changed in the recollection, till some semblance of home is there to be claimed, in the subtle balancing act between healing and decay, in the miracle of imagination and the calculated lie that we, the living, do so well, for as long as we are able.

Earth Light

HE ARRIVED IN the middle of the summer, at about the same time of year that Jan was killed. In fact, the weather was unnervingly familiar as the train pulled into the station at Kettering: the same dense heat hung on the air, the same lowering threat of rainstorms hovered in the distance. Without really thinking it through, he had been planning to visit for a couple of days, more or less, before moving on; but when he stepped off the train and Derek came forward to meet him, he knew he would have to stay longer. There was something he had to do – some kind of unfinished business that he had never thought about but had left simmering at the back of his mind. All of a sudden, he had the impression that he'd come home on false pretences and he was annoyed at himself for not realising sooner that this visit was going to mean much more to everyone than he had expected. And how could he not have expected it? He hadn't been here in seventeen years, he hadn't seen Derek and Tommy in all that time. They would be expecting more from him than a flying visit. Which was fine, when he thought about it; what he hadn't expected was the feeling he had that there was something he needed to do, some conflict he needed to reconcile in his own mind. It was as if he had deliberately tricked himself by treating this trip so lightly, as if one part of his mind was working against another. As if, in other words, what Sally had said was right, that he didn't really know himself at all. And she *was* right, he thought, only she was wrong, too. It wasn't as simple as she made it out to be, like a problem out of a self-help book.

Emotional maturity. Self-awareness. He didn't want nice formulas for living; he couldn't trust that business of treating each day as an exercise in self-management or assertiveness. He would rather live unprepared and accept the surprises than spend his whole life getting in touch with his inner self. He didn't want to work at it so bloody self-consciously.

As soon as Derek saw him, he stepped forward and took the large overnight bag from Francis's hand. 'You're here,' he said. He seemed genuinely surprised, as if he'd imagined until the last minute that Francis wouldn't come.

Francis nodded. He could see that Derek was already being careful, that he had probably rehearsed being careful while he waited on the platform for the last half-hour, determined to stop himself asking all the obvious questions, trying to act as if nothing out of the ordinary had ever happened. Derek had aged, which should have come as no surprise, but did; his hair was thinning, his eyes and mouth were lined with wrinkles, he looked almost preternaturally thin. In most respects, though, he was no different from the gauche boy Francis had always been slightly embarrassed to have as an older brother: dressed in a pair of tattered jeans and a sweatshirt he had obviously bought in a charity shop, he still didn't care, much, how he looked; and though he wanted to seem as unsurprised by Francis's sudden return as he had probably tried to seem about his disappearing act, all those years ago, the expression on his face was already betraying him. Derek had always been an open book – and Francis had always thought how ironic that was, because his brother had so much on his mind that he wanted to hide, so much that should have remained private. Now, in spite of himself, Derek was wearing the look, the awed *gaze* that people who stay reserve for those who have been away and then returned, still dusted with the scent and glamour of elsewhere. Francis was to encounter that gaze more than once over the next week or so: Derek, Tommy, the handful of old friends he encountered, even Alina – they all had that slightly wondering, awed look, in one form or another. At least, in Derek's case, it was awe, pure and simple. He seemed incapable of resentment.

Still, as they walked to the car, Francis felt watched, felt how Derek was studying his face, waiting for something to happen, for some word or gesture that would finally reveal what it meant to have been *away*. It was almost irritating, the way Derek had stayed put, not only in the one place, but also in his habits, in his manner of being in the world: he had always waited for the other person to make the first move; he had walked around shrouded in this pained half-smiling diffidence for close to forty years and he hadn't even noticed how badly it served him. At the same time, Francis was a little irritated that Derek had no idea, that he wouldn't have guessed in a thousand years, that he himself didn't think of his arrival at Kettering station as anything like a homecoming – that, as far as Francis was concerned, there was no such place as home. He wanted to stop and explain, right there on the station forecourt, that in all the time he had been gone, in all his travels, there was no place that had ever felt more real, or more like home, than the home he had left without a word, so long ago that he scarcely remembered being there. All that mattered, in all that time, was that those places *weren't* home, that they *were* somewhere – anywhere – else. Finally, he stopped in his tracks, turned and looked his brother in the eye.

'What is it?' he asked. He was smiling, and he had been careful to put the question gently, half-mockingly, but without malice; he didn't want Derek to think he was annoyed.

'What?' Derek knew what he meant, but he still managed to sound innocent.

Francis shook his head. 'What's so fascinating?' he said. 'Am I so different?'

Derek laughed out loud, then put down the bag. He seemed pleased with this turn of events. 'Of course you're different,' he said. 'It's been a long time.'

Francis nodded. It was odd, then, to think how little they'd known and how much they had misunderstood one another over the years – and at the same time, how Derek had always been in awe of him, even when they were kids. It was as if Francis were some strange animal that Derek couldn't quite imagine as his own flesh and blood. But then, all of a sudden, Francis saw that this wasn't the whole story. There was something else, some-thing his brother was holding back that he couldn't quite put his finger on.

'Have I changed much?' Derek asked.

Francis shook his head. 'No,' he said – and he really was being honest. In spite of his thinning hair, and the obvious signs of age in his face, Derek hadn't changed in all the ways that mattered. 'I don't think you've changed much at all.'

Derek stood a moment, gazing at him incredulously, then he picked up the overnight bag and started towards the car. It was an old Ford Escort with a cracked wing mirror and bad upholstery. The inside was a riot of sheet music, chocolate wrappers, a couple of battered guitars, splayed heaps of library books and – for some reason that Francis could only guess at – half of an egg box, with three eggs, all cracked, perched precariously on the edge of the back seat. Derek cleared a space in the passenger seat, tossing a plastic bag full of bread and milk and a couple of dog-eared books into the back, dumped Francis's overnight bag in the boot, and got in behind the wheel. He didn't speak again until he was driving out of the car park.

'I've changed out of all recognition,' he said. It was odd, the way he said it; not the kind of thing he would usually say, and Francis had the impression, once again, of something rehearsed, the words carefully chosen, the tone of voice measured. There was no obvious sadness, no self-pity, certainly no bitterness in Derek's voice. What he was saying was nothing more than a statement of fact – the result, no doubt, of a long process of accommodation and, finally, acceptance, in the small hours of the morning, and on the way home from auditions and pitches for gigs that he hadn't got. 'We all have, for better or worse,' he added meaningfully. He glanced at Francis significantly. 'Tommy's not well,' he said. For a moment, Francis thought this was the secret Derek had been keeping from him, the simple fact that he had been waiting to tell. 'He's been pretty bad. Linda thinks he's been better lately, but I don't know. I think it's serious.' Francis could feel his brother watching him. 'Still, you know what he's like,' Derek continued. 'He tries to pretend it's nothing.' He paused, waited, watched. 'I'm glad you've come home, though. I know he's been missing you.'

'I'm glad to be here,' Francis said, lamely.

Derek nodded. 'I thought you'd be here sooner,' he said, with an obvious effort not to sound resentful. 'After your letter, I thought, you know.'

Francis didn't say anything. He knew Derek hadn't intended to be cruel, that he didn't want Francis to feel guilty. He never had, even though he had always been overshadowed by his younger brother. Francis had been the clever one. Francis was the one they all said was good-looking, when they were boys. Francis had been Lizzie's favourite – and, in spite of their constant warring, he had been Tommy's favourite too, no matter how hard Tommy might have tried to hide the fact, no matter that Francis had broken his heart, before he'd disappeared for good. But Derek had never held any of that against him. It was both irritating and humbling, this goodwill. As they drove away, talking quietly about their father and the plans Derek had made for the next few days, Francis began to understand what his brother had been holding back all this time – not just since he had stepped off the train half an hour before, but for as long as they had known each other. It came as a surprise, because he knew he had never deserved anything from Derek but mistrust, or maybe a dignified indifference, but it was unmistakable, in spite of everything, that, from boyhood, through all the time he had been away, till now, when he was returning like some caricature of the Prodigal Son, Derek loved him more than he could have said. He was probably as mystified by that love as Francis was, but that didn't change anything. Derek loved him, as one brother loves – or is supposed to love – another. It was like something from a fairytale, or a textbook.

The drive was shorter than he remembered. Corby loomed up on them much sooner than Francis had expected: it had grown, or rather, it had sprawled, since he'd last seen it, but it was also smaller, less vivid, because the dark spectre of The Works had been erased from the background, leaving nothing where there once had been fire and darkness, or nothing but a sickly, luke-warm sky. New estates reached out into the countryside where he and Jan had gone on picnics and bike rides with their cameras; they had sprawled out as far as Great Oakley, swallowing up the woods, the reaches of waste land, the open fields where Francis had hidden out for hours, looking for birds' nests or smoking dope when he should have been in school. The map of the place that he had in his mind, that indelible map everybody carries of their childhood places, had always been clearest here, the ink fresh, the details exact, everything to scale and perfectly accurate. It wouldn't have mattered to him if some of the other places – the town centre, the school playground, the area around their old house – had faded, but he had never forgotten the woods and fields between Corby and Oakley. They were faithfully reproduced, down to the last tree, down even to the last ditch, in his imagination – but now they were lost. Now they only existed on that private map, and nowhere else. He turned to Derek, looking for some reaction, some shared sense of loss.

'What happened to everything?'

Derek shot him a swift, questioning look, then turned back to the road. 'What?'

'What happened to the woods? Remember?'

Derek considered the question for a moment, then shook his head. 'God,' he said. 'I'd forgotten how long you've been away.'

Francis waited, but Derek didn't say anything else. For him, the change was historical: he had probably even forgotten what it was that had been lost. After a moment, Derek turned and smiled sadly. 'You know who I saw the other day?' he asked.

Francis wasn't really paying attention. He was gazing out at the dead land around them: the anonymous estates, the colourless tracts of ground cover. 'I don't know,' he said, after a moment. 'Somebody from the old days, I imagine.'

He hadn't meant to be sarcastic, but that was how it came out. Derek shot him a hurt look. 'It *was* somebody from the old days,' he said. 'She's back in town for a while. Not for long. She went away not long after you disappeared.' The use of the word was pointed: disappeared. It was made to sound active, deliberate: Francis hadn't gone away, he hadn't left – he had *disappeared*. The diffidence had broken for a moment, just enough to let Francis see how much hurt he had caused.

'Who's *she*?' he asked. He'd already guessed, of course, just from Derek's manner. His old reverence for Alina, the reverence that had preserved her impossibility just as surely as it had kept her perfectly beautiful and beloved in his mind's eye, that old trick he had played on himself was still at work.

Derek laughed softly and shook his head. They were turning

into Gainsborough Road now, just a couple of streets from home. 'You know who,' he said.

Francis was touched, then. Touched, or perhaps moved. He didn't know exactly *what* he felt but, for a moment, he was moved to look into his own heart in an attempt to find the mirror image of that commonplace, secretive love Derek had harboured all these years, in spite of everything Francis had done. And he did find something – if not a mirror image, then an echo at least, a fondness, a slightly remote, almost fictional affection. It wasn't love, perhaps, in the usual sense. He had to admit that he hadn't thought about his brother much while he'd been away. It hadn't even crossed his mind to wonder how Derek was, or what he was doing before the letters started to come, describing a world that had seemed so remote, so irrelevant, that Francis had been tempted, sometimes, to throw the envelopes away unopened, the moment they arrived. He hadn't even given Derek much consideration on the journey home, other than to wonder if he would recognise him at the station. For that one moment, though, seeing how childishly pleased Derek was to have read his mind, Francis felt a surge of affection for this brother he'd almost forgotten, an affection tinged with pity, perhaps, but still no less real for that, a surge of affection that, no matter how temporary, was not only stronger, but also more satisfying, more just, than he had expected it to be.

'So what are you doing now?' Francis asked, as they drove the last few streets before home. 'You didn't say in your letter.'

'No.' Derek looked puzzled. 'I'm not sure. A bit of this, a bit of that. I'm still playing. It was pretty hard for a while, after The Works closed down. Especially for Tommy. I've done OK.' He smiled and put on a fake brain-dead voice. 'I didn't go to college, but,' he said.

Francis could see that the remark wasn't quite as innocent as it seemed. 'So what?' he said. 'What difference would that have made?'

Derek was already looking repentant. 'Well. I didn't have the openings –'

'You know what, Derek?' Francis made an effort to be very level, very calm. 'When I was finishing up college, they had a recruitment fair in the Union. I went along, just to see what they'd say. They told me I had a promising future in retail management. Is that what you mean by openings? Retail management.'

'Well –'

'You did fine staying right here –'

'How would you know? You left.'

'That's right. I left. But that had nothing to do with college.'

'So – where did you go?'

It was out at last, the first of the many questions. Francis smiled sadly. 'Nowhere much,' he said. 'Here and there. You know –'

'Oh come on –'

'No. I just . . .' Francis cast around for something to say. He could hardly tell his brother that he'd been an accidental member of a cult, a cult whose every other member Derek had probably seen dead on television, and he didn't want to talk about California, or driving to British Columbia, when Derek had never been out of Corby. 'I travelled around a bit, here and there. I was one place, then I was someplace else. Time passed. More than I thought.'

'Almost twenty years.'

'Don't exaggerate. Anyway.' Francis looked at him. 'Tell me about Linda. Tell me about your little boy.'

Derek suddenly brightened. 'He's a bright kid,' he said. He was like a kid himself, delighted and proud. He fished a tattered snapshot from his jacket pocket. Francis could see that it was tattered, not because Derek showed it to that many people – he probably didn't have that many people to show it to – but because he was always taking it out and looking at it, like some precious and unexpected gift that someone had given him for no good reason. He grinned, remembering something. 'The other day I found him sitting by the washing-machine, watching the clothes going around and laughing his head off. He kept saying *funny*, *funny*.'

'I think that falls firmly into the category of making your own entertainment,' Francis said.

Derek pulled up outside the house. Nothing had changed. It was the same house, the same square of grass, maybe a little untidier than before, maybe a little cleaner. This was where he had been so unhappy for so long, fighting with the neighbours' children, watching his mother die. He recognised every detail, but it was as if he was solving a puzzle, or looking at a picture that he'd seen hundreds of times, a picture of some place he had never been, but knew at one remove, familiar and strange at once, like the indelible images of New York, or Monument Valley, that years of cinema had printed on his mind.

Tommy was dying. He had the quiet, slightly darkened aura and that faint baby-shit smell to him that Francis remembered from Lizzie's last few months with the cancer and, though he seemed able to get around, he was slow, careful, held in check to conceal the fundamental awkwardness, the potential for clumsiness of a body that no longer functioned as it ought. Francis didn't know if Derek knew, if he'd been hinting at it in the car, but he could see that Tommy did. From the moment he walked into the room, and found his father playing with the baby on the floor, Francis sensed, not just Tommy's resignation to his impending death, but a reinvestment, a transfer of all that the old man had ever loved or wanted from life to this smiling, beatific child, who looked so like Derek that Francis was obliged to look at his brother again, as if for the first time, to look, and to see in him a beauty he had never noticed before, an odd, almost angelic quality that had probably been present all the time, had Francis taken the trouble to notice. The baby – who looked big for eighteen months – was dressed in faded blue jeans and a blue and white striped Breton-style jersey; he had straight blond hair, huge attentive blue eyes and a very red mouth. When Francis and Derek came in, he looked up, considered Francis a moment, then scrambled into his grandfather's arms and buried his face in the old man's chest. Tommy looked up.

'You found your way all right, then?' he said, with no apparent irony.

Francis nodded. He had expected awkwardness, perhaps even some difficulty – emotion barely concealed, the kind of incandescent bitterness he remembered from the old days shining through the surface civility – but Tommy seemed easy and relaxed, in spite of the darkness in his eyes and the obvious diminishment in his face, the old fullness gone, the flesh around his mouth slack and grizzled, his eyes a faded grey.

'This is Gabriel,' Tommy said, cradling the boy carefully to his chest as he got up. Standing, he looked even more diminished and, at the same time, even more self-contained. Francis remembered the days when his father seemed to fill every space he entered, all presence, carrying a force-field of energy that was only partly rage wherever he went; now, he seemed terribly still, though Francis couldn't have said if this was the outward sign of a kind of peace, or evidence of some final resignation.

'He's not good with men, for some reason,' Derek said, as Tommy passed the boy over. 'He'll get used to you after a while.'

Tommy lingered a moment at Derek's side, then turned to Francis and held out his hand. 'Welcome home,' he said, without a trace of sentiment, his grey eyes clear and watchful, taking Francis in, sizing him up.

For the first time, Francis realised how much he had changed over the years he had been away. He could see it reflected in his father's eyes, but he couldn't tell what the old man thought. 'It's good to be home,' he answered, hoping he didn't sound too glib. He took his father's hand and he was stunned by how cold it was, how reduced to the basic elements of skin and vein and bone. 'It's been a long time.'

Tommy nodded, letting the moment last just long enough, before he turned to Derek. 'So,' he said.

Derek smiled softly. 'So.' It was a deliberate echo, not so much a question as the bringing of something long-considered to a conclusion. The baby, meanwhile, had plucked up the courage to venture a shy, cautious peek at Francis. Tommy crooked his head and smiled at him.

'You're not shy, are you?' he said. 'Say hello to your Uncle Francis.'

The baby studied Francis thoughtfully for a moment, then looked at his feet. 'Shoes!' he cried happily.

Francis looked down. He was wearing his brown desert boots. 'That's right,' he said.

Derek grinned. 'He's got a thing about shoes,' he said. 'He's just started wearing them.'

Gabriel was still looking at Francis's feet. 'Shoes!' he said. 'Shoes!'

Francis smiled and held out a hand. 'That's right,' he said. 'Shoes.'

The baby jerked away and buried his face in his father's shoulder. They all laughed awkwardly.

'He's shy of strangers, still,' Derek said. 'He'll be fine, when he gets to know you.'

Francis nodded.

'You were aye shy with strangers, too,' Tommy said. Francis wasn't sure which of them he meant. It was difficult to look Tommy in the face: he was so old and still.

'I still am,' Derek said, and they laughed again, remembering, or thinking they remembered, some moment, long ago.

Francis's room had been redecorated as a nursery for Gabriel, so the only familiar feature was the awkward shape. He felt guilty to be ousting his nephew, but Derek had explained that the boy loved sleeping with his parents, and would be glad of the move. The only difficulty would be persuading him back into the nursery after his uncle was gone. Francis nodded and accepted defeat graciously, but he would have been happier on the fold-out sofa in the living-room. Now, while he stood in the nursery, unpacking his few things, Derek lingered at the door, not wanting to intrude, but somehow unable to leave.

'So,' he said, with obvious pride. 'What do you think of Gabriel?'

'He's beautiful,' Francis said – and it wasn't just the expected response, the child really had struck him as remarkable, not cute, not winsome, like the babies in television adverts, but possessed, in some way, of genuine beauty.

'He sure is,' Derek said. 'Takes after his mother, I suppose.'

Francis stopped unpacking and looked him in the eyes. 'He looks just like you,' he said.

Derek looked pleased and embarrassed for a few seconds, till Francis went back to unfolding his shirts. 'Wait till you meet Linda,' he said.

He didn't have long to wait. Linda arrived from work about an hour afterwards, and Francis saw right away that Derek was right: Gabriel did look like his mother. There was something in the two of them – a vitality, a warmth – that was unmistakable. But where Gabriel was all noise and energy and self, Linda was calm attentiveness, a watchful presence, someone who came into a room and sized everything up at a glance, a conductor of energies, a catalyst, she seemed to do nothing much, but changed everything.

'You must be Francis,' she said, as she set down her bag of shopping. She held out her hand and, surprised, Francis shook it. Somewhere at the back of his mind, he wondered what she had been expecting, and he experienced a sudden, pungent desire to be able to say no, he wasn't Francis at all, he was somebody else altogether. Linda was taller and slimmer than he had expected, and a good deal younger. She had thick dark hair and very clear blue eyes, but what struck Francis most was the way she moved. It was as if she were holding something in reserve all the time; or rather, not holding so much as enjoying that reserve of life and power. Francis was reminded of nature programmes he had seen on television, where a hunter – a fox, say, or some big cat – is out stalking its prey, relaxed, unhurried, ready to strike, but just as ready to wait, to see what happened, to let the world unfold around it. Linda had the kind of confidence – a supreme confidence – that Francis had never seen before in anyone from Corby, much less a woman, and it was with some shame that he wondered, more than once in the course of the evening, how this astonishing woman had come to be married to his brother.

Still, there was no doubting that Linda was happy with things just the way they were. She enjoyed Derek's open admiration, and she enjoyed the fact that Tommy was obviously a little in love with her, too. It wasn't until after she arrived that Francis realised they had been waiting for her to come, the two men, the child – waiting because, even with the prodigal returned, actually *present* in the flesh, the moment wasn't real until Linda was there to share it. Everything – the household, their lives, the thoughts they thought and the dreams they dreamed – revolved around Linda, and she just sat at the centre of it all, watching, listening, not saying or doing very much at all. Later, after they had eaten, and sat making small-talk, Linda stood up. The men had been drinking – beers at dinner, whisky afterwards – but she hadn't touched a drop.

'Time for bed,' she said, stretching. 'I've got work in the morning.' She looked at Derek. 'Come on you.'

Derek looked disappointed. 'I thought I'd sit a while,' he said.

340

'No you don't,' Linda said. 'I don't want you coming up half-cut and waking me up.'

Derek looked at Tommy. 'All right,' he said. Tommy gave him a wry, man-to-man grin, but he didn't say anything.

Francis stood up. 'See you in the morning,' he said.

'You will,' Linda said. She came and gave him a quick, tight hug, then hurried out. 'Goodnight, all,' she said.

Derek followed. 'Sleep well,' he said. 'I'll see you tomorrow.'

Francis watched them out, then sat down on the sofa. There was a long silence that he didn't want to break. He didn't think Tommy wanted him to break it either. They would have to take things slow, as Lizzie used to say. Francis knew that. 'So,' he said at last. 'How are you doing?'

Tommy shook his head. 'Oh, no sae bad,' he said, but he didn't make much of an effort to hide the lie.

'Really?' Francis permitted himself a sceptical look; he didn't want to be bothered with that strong silent routine, and he didn't mind if Tommy saw it – and Tommy did see it, was probably looking for it, looking for an excuse to talk to somebody who – the thought occurred to Francis for the first time – was enough of a stranger to listen, and not show too much emotion. This thought – the thought that he had been away so long that Tommy could think of him as both son and stranger – shocked Francis a little, even as it seemed entirely to be expected.

Tommy poured the whisky. 'Well,' he said. 'I suppose I can tell you. But I don't want you saying anything to Derek or Linda –'

Francis grimaced. Did the old man really think Derek couldn't see what was happening right in front of his eyes? 'I'll not say a word,' he said.

Tommy nodded gravely. 'It's the usual,' he said. 'I've read about it in the magazines, how a man won't go to the doctor till it's too late. Though I don't know if it makes that much difference. I mean look at your mother. She was going to the doctor with one thing and another for years, and they still didn't know what was wrong.' He took a sip of his whisky. 'Anyway, I don't want to be bothered with hospitals and such. They'd only tell me to give up this –' he set his glass down carefully on the coffee table, 'and this –' He produced a packet of cigarettes from his cardigan pocket, flipped it open and offered it to Francis. Francis shook his head. 'Anyway, I've been one of the lucky ones,' Tommy continued, lighting up. 'I've had a good innings, considering.' He looked at Francis's brimming glass on the table top. 'Are you no going to drink that?'

Francis leaned forward and lifted his glass; his father did the same. 'Here's to you,' Tommy said and knocked it back in one. Francis followed. He hadn't drunk whisky in years, but after the first, slightly sickening moment, it felt warm and good in his throat, a memory of something he had let his body forget, the warmth of it a settlement of some kind, an old belonging renewed in his blood, some kinship with the earth at once as real as it was treacherous, touched with sentiment, suspect and compelling. Tommy refilled the glasses. 'Aye,' he said. 'I've been one of the lucky ones.' He looked up at the mantelpiece, at the row of gilt-framed photographs: an old one of Lizzie in her twenties, before Derek and Francis were born, another of Derek and Linda, in their wedding clothes, a row of snapshots of Gabriel at various stages from birth to the toddler Francis had seen earlier in his designer jersey. Tommy shook his head. 'I've not done bad, all things considered,' he said. 'And probably better than I deserved.'

Later, when the rest of the house was asleep, Francis rose quietly and went downstairs. He was surprised, now, by how small the house felt, and he was surprised by his surprise; he had never thought of it, consciously, as larger than this, never thought of it as anything but the box where he had grown up, lonely and angry, among strangers who lived in identical boxes around the little patch of dirt and grass they laughingly referred to as the square. Now, as he passed through the front room, on his way to the kitchen, he remembered the house as it had figured in the dreams he'd had, while he still lived there, and long after he was gone, and he realised that it was the dream house that he remembered, just as the town he remembered wasn't the cramped, noisy estates with their stray dogs and litter, or the line of shops on Corporation Street, but the hushed, empty theatre of lights and small rain from his early-morning paper round. He had missed that house from time to time during his long absence, and he was less disappointed than relieved by the realisation that he missed it still, now that he had come home. This house – the place itself, the bricks and mortar, the cluttered front room with its over-sized furniture – this house wasn't real, it was just the physical marker of something larger and more precise, a marker to represent the home he'd imagined for all those years, making what he could out of what he had been given, living for years in a half-made world and finishing it in his mind's eye, making it whole like a blind man walking around in the smooth darkness, learning to match the outward and the inwardly seen on the tips of his fingers, in the echoes and resonances unique to the place, making a home of the world by a long process of discovery and invention.

He walked through to the kitchen and, by the surprisingly bright moonlight that streamed in through the window, he put the kettle on. It was only the half-moon, but the earth light was so strong he could see the dark side clearly, a kingdom of broken rings and tumuli bathed in a cool, grey luminescence, like the light he had imagined for limbo, back in school, when people still spoke of such things. He had never thought much about heaven and hell, in those near-daily catechism lessons the teachers had inflicted on him, but he had imagined limbo often enough and he had always seen it like this, a place half-lit, a space to wander in, a visible nowhere. Now, in his father's kitchen, he gazed out at the same cool light, the perfect light of the moon, untainted by the glow of The Works, making a limbo of the only house he had ever considered his own. He was glad he had sat up a while with Tommy; glad, too, that he'd taken a drink with him, but he needed something, now, to balance out the whisky, something to bring him back to earth. There was no tea in the cupboard – Lizzie had been the only other tea-drinker in the old days – so he made himself a cup of instant coffee from a jar of the cheap, freeze-dried stuff Derek had always maintained was as good as anything else and stood at the window, staring out at the garden. He couldn't see much, but even in this light it looked different – though it was a moment before Francis worked out what the difference was. He had forgotten Tommy's spring ritual, the hours of digging, the bags of stolen fertiliser base from by-products, the raking, and the leaving things to settle. He had forgotten how the garden lay fallow for the rest of the summer, as the weeds gradually re-colonised the bare earth where Tommy had planned but never got round to growing vegetables and pota-toes. Most of all, he had forgotten how he'd sneered at Tommy's inability to make anything out of all that work. He had forgotten it all, because he had wanted, more than anything, to forget that sneer – so it was a moment before he saw how green it was, green, not with weeds, but with what looked like a real garden. He leaned closer to the glass and peered out: there was definite order out there, a simple, linear order, perhaps, but a garden never-theless, with shrubs, flower-beds, what looked like a vegetable plot, with onions and potatoes, by the fence at the back, and spectacularly, a climbing rose trained along the side wall, thick clusters of pearl-white flowers gleaming softly in the moonlight.

He wasn't sure how he felt about it. He'd always been a little suspicious of the garden at Jan's parents' house. He found the neatness of it unsettling: it made everything smaller to have things tidy and ordered like that; the flower-beds and clipped lawn made all the gardens and patches of open land look too contained, so The Works and the grey housing estates only seemed that much bigger. He preferred it when the garden was overgrown after Tommy had dug it over in the spring and it had reverted, all through the summer, to wild: a patch of irises here, a straggling lupin there among the tall grasses and weeds. Francis had grown up on pieces of waste ground, on the land claimed from the woods for the new estates, on the patches of wild out near the sludge beds. He remembered how people were always saying that kids needed playgrounds, and neat little parks, but that wasn't right at all. Everything he could remember had happened on patches of waste ground – games of hide-and-seek amongst the willow-herb and nettles, encounters on the paths through the woods and the guesswork of sex after school, pressed to the damp stone walls under the railway bridge, acid trips out on the empty roads at evening, his lost loves mingled with the smell of water and moss, the taste of fallen leaves in a kiss, the taste of himself on that first trip, the pure surprise of it, to have a body that was suddenly real and mysterious, not the wet machinery he had read about in school textbooks, or the theatre of shame they had taught him to loathe in church.

Now, as he stood at the window looking out at the trans-formed garden, he began to understand how similar he and his father were. They had both become gardeners, they had both chosen to live apart, to do work that could only be achieved in isolation. Tommy had finally made the garden he'd planned because he had nothing else to do: The Works had closed down, and he was too old to get another job, so he had taken all his energy and put it into the earth, trying to create something that would feel like home in this foreign place – because it *was* a foreign place, even for Tommy, it wasn't home, it was a temporary encampment, a settlement he had been obliged to reach with his circumstances. He remembered Tommy talking, years ago, about some uncle of his, a man who worked on the land up north, and how happy he had been – as the boy Francis had never known, and couldn't even begin to imagine – when he had been allowed to visit this uncle – Francis couldn't remember the man's name, though he had known it once – in a place that, for Tommy, had felt like home. That was what had set Tommy apart from the others, Francis realised, all the years he and Derek had been growing up, listening to Lizzie talk about going home to Fife, going back to Cowdenbeath, or hearing their neighbours reminisce about Glasgow, or Ireland. That was what made Tommy different, that connection to some place that he knew didn't exist any more, so he could never talk about going home, could only look around in this foreign place and see it for what it was, a settlement, a compromise. Tommy had wanted to go home just as much as anybody else, but he'd had the nous to realise that home wasn't there; that, even if there were names on the map that corresponded to the names inside his head, that didn't mean you could still go to those places. For the others, the words were repeated, over and over, like incantations, like a kind of magic, but they didn't make anything happen in the world. Tommy knew that. He wanted to go home, but he knew home didn't exist any more. Maybe it never had. Maybe it could only exist as an idea, a word, or a picture, or a remembered song buried in the mind, as much imagined as remembered, as much invention as given fact. It was like the past. Somebody said once that the past was another country, but Francis thought that wasn't quite right: for him, the past was a series of names and landmarks and roads from an old map that he couldn't quite put together, a country that, in spite of the given facts you thought were there and unchanging, would always be no more than an invention, would never be a country in itself, with its own laws, its own vegetation, its own fauna. When he thought about the past, he kept coming up with events and landmarks that didn't match, though officially they all belonged to the same 'other country': Tommy and Katrina, himself and Katrina, Lizzie, this house, The Works, the town, the Nivens, the taste of anger like blood or rust in his mouth, the taste of his body on summer days when he sat out in the woods tripping on acid, watching, listening, catching glimpses of another world that he would never be able to inhabit. Jan alive. Jan gone. Alina. He wasn't sure he wanted to see Alina again: it would remind him of something and he wouldn't know if the memory was true or false, something that had really been, or something that he wanted to remember. All these years, he had been careful not to think about it too much, careful not to betray the unknowable truth of the past for that other country where they did things differently, but were still recognisable, still capable of being betrayed. Those who remember, forget. He had read that once – it was an old Chinese proverb, he thought, though he wasn't sure where he had heard it – and he believed it was so. He didn't want to remember, because he didn't want to forget. He wanted the past sealed up in a box, he wanted to feel its power without knowing what it was, the way, some mornings, he would wake with the knowledge of having dreamed, but unable to remember the details of what had happened. Those dreams were more powerful than any he had remembered, they had made him ready, they had made life strange again, made him, and the world, capable of anything.

He wasn't sure if he wanted to see Alina: part of him did, but another part wanted to avoid any further complications. He had as much as he could deal with, he thought, with Derek and Tommy making this short visit into a homecoming, without having to mull over old times – whether that meant talking about Jan or studiously avoiding the subject – with a woman he hadn't seen since they were fresh out of college. Derek had left her number on the sideboard where he could easily find it, but he hadn't called. There was a telephone in the house now – Tommy had probably relented for Linda's sake – but it was obvious that nobody used it much, and he didn't want to do anything out of the ordinary, to emphasise his status as Prodigal Son. He could feel them all watching him when they sat down to eat, or when they gathered around Gabriel and made a fuss of him in the front room, playing with his brightly painted wooden toys, chasing his toy mice around the floor, making odd little Lego houses that always came out looking like something from a spaghetti western, for some reason.

Derek had other ideas. He kept nagging Francis to call, or go round. 'She'd love to see you,' he said.

'How do you know?'

Derek grinned.

'You told her I was coming?'

Derek nodded.

'Well, she's bound to say that,' Francis said. 'What else can she say?'

Derek shook his head. 'She's curious to see you,' he said. 'It's been a long time.'

'I don't want to dredge up old memories –'

'It's good to talk.'

Francis thought. There was no way of getting out of this. Not with Derek around. 'I'll think about it,' he said.

He didn't call her, though he'd decided he would – he met her on the street before he had a chance. She looked so different, he almost walked right past her. If he'd been asked to pick this woman out from a line-up, he still wouldn't have recognised her.

'Francis!'

The woman who stopped him opposite the Festival Hall looked too faint to be Alina, too washed-out and insubstantial, even though close examination revealed the same eyes, the same mouth, the same curve of the chin.

'Alina?' He felt like a character in a film. 'Well –'

'I heard you were back –'

'I was going to call you.'

She nodded, but she didn't believe him. 'Well,' she said. 'Here I am.'

'Here you are.' Francis was embarrassed. He'd not been sure what to expect, but he hadn't expected to feel so disappointed. 'Are you on your way somewhere?'

'Not really. Just shopping.'

'Have you got time for a coffee?'

'Sure.'

'Great.' He nodded. He felt guilty; he hoped his disappointment hadn't shown in his face. 'Where do people go these days?'

'I don't know.' Alina smiled. 'I'm a visitor too.'

It took a while, but over coffee, the awkwardness melted away. They were careful, but it wasn't too obvious; they didn't talk about Jan, they didn't really talk about the old times at all. Alina told him about her life: she was a history lecturer; she lived in Birmingham; she shared a flat with a woman called Tania. She came home every couple of months, she said, more often if she could, to see her mother. Her father had died not long after she finished college. Francis knew what she really meant; Derek had told him the old man had pretty much had a mental breakdown after Jan was murdered, and he hadn't really recovered.

'Mum's still soldiering on, though,' Alina said, smiling in that stoical way that always looks practised, no matter how genuine it might be. It was an odd expression, too, coming from her: *soldiering on*. It made her sound old.

Francis nodded. 'Derek said she's still got her garden,' he said.

'That's right.' Alina looked proud. 'Just like your dad.'

Now it was Francis's turn to feel proud. 'Who'd have thought that?' he said.

Alina shook her head. 'I think it's great,' she said. 'It's been the saving of Mum.' She smiled awkwardly at that, or maybe something in Francis's eyes had betrayed his surprise: *the saving of*. 'But you know what's odd,' she continued. 'You know what really surprises me?'

Francis shook his head, though he knew what she was going to say. It was what he had always thought about her mother, from the day he'd first met her.

'What surprises me is how happy she is,' Alina said, seeing that he had guessed what she was going to say, and saying it anyway, to make it that bit more true. 'She's finally happy, after all these years.'

'She deserves it,' Francis said, not knowing what else to say.

Alina nodded. 'She paid up front,' she said. 'It's a pity it took so long in coming.'

Francis nodded. He didn't really know what more to say in this vein.

'So,' Alina said, to break the silence. 'How have *you* been?'

Francis felt awkward. He didn't want to do small-talk. 'I thought it was going to be different,' he said, then regretted his words almost immediately.

'I know you did,' Alina said, not looking at him. 'You always did.'

'No.' Francis suddenly felt it was important that she should understand him, that she shouldn't think he was just talking about himself. 'I thought all that old stuff would be swept away,' he said. 'All that old Christian myth, all that joylessness. That fear of pleasure. The daily injustices. The complete denial of the imagination.'

'*Imagination au pouvoir.*'

'Yes.'

'That was a little before our time though, don't you think?'

'Maybe,' he said. 'But I thought something had started. I'm not sure what I ever hoped, but I thought something was going to change. No; I didn't think it, I felt it in the air. It felt *real*. I don't understand why it all stayed the same.'

'It's not the same,' she said. 'You didn't really think it was a straight line, did you? Revolution? Turn on, tune in, drop out? That's the kind of linear thinking that got us into so much trouble in the first place. That was how they thought in the Fifties.'

Francis looked at her. Her face had come alive: for the first time, he could see the Alina he remembered, a girl on her first acid trip, walking in the snow, in love with the world, taking it all in. Her eyes looked bright. 'Don't listen to me,' he said. 'I've been lost for seventeen years.' He smiled apologetically. He didn't want her to take any of this too seriously, but he had finally realised it was something he wanted – needed – to say, and it occurred to him suddenly that she wanted to talk about it all as much as he did. 'I've been lost ever since Jan died. And you know what? I'm glad I was lost. I'm glad I couldn't have just gone on with things.'

Alina shook her head. 'So what do you think? We all just got on with things?' She seemed annoyed, and Francis realised how insensitive he had sounded.

'I'm sorry,' he said. 'I don't mean –'

She interrupted him with a small, almost imperceptible wave of the hand. 'I know you didn't,' she said. 'I know.' She composed herself. 'Anyway,' she continued after a moment, her voice warm and even again, as if nothing had happened. 'What have you been doing all these years?'

'Various things.' Francis had to think for a moment. It was as if, all of a sudden, he really was the man he had wanted to be, someone with no history, the final erasure of a self. 'Working. Travelling around.'

Alina smiled. 'Wooden Ships,' she said quietly, to herself almost.

'What?'

'That was your favourite song. Back then. Don't you remember?'

Francis shook his head. He remembered the song, of course: 'Wooden Ships', from Jefferson Airplane's 1969 album, *Volunteers*. He'd had it among his records, along with The Grateful Dead, Quicksilver Messenger Service, Country Joe and the Fish, most of the other Airplane stuff. He didn't remember it being his favourite song, though.

'You couldn't get enough of it,' Alina insisted. 'You kept playing it, over and over –'

'Really?' Francis thought back: it was so long ago – or rather, it wasn't so much to do with time as distance; not long ago, so much as far away. 'I don't remember.'

'Oh yes.' Alina smiled at the memory – and there was more than a hint of mockery in her face. 'You would sing along.'

'No.'

'Yes.' She shook her head and chanted the words softly. '*We are leaving, you don't need us –*'

'Ah.'

'So you left.'

'Yes. There wasn't that much of a choice, was there?'

'Oh, I don't know.'

'I did. I couldn't wait to get out.'

'So you did.'

'What was the alternative? Staying put?' He could hear the note of disdain in his voice, and he felt ashamed immediately. He didn't want to justify himself, any more than he wanted to hurt her.

'It depends who you are. I didn't stay put. But I do come back. I need to stay in touch, for some reason.'

Francis was tired now. It had been a mistake, he thought – and he was annoyed with himself for coming back, or for staying long enough that this conversation had become inevitable. If he had just gone through the motions, if he had pretended they were nothing more than old school-friends – which, in fact, was all they were now, no matter what had happened in the past – he would already be on his way back to Tommy's house, to see out the rest of the visit and be on his way. Perhaps it was this – the fatigue, the annoyance – that made him bring up Jan, though he'd intended not to talk about it. He had come so far, he thought, he might as well go all the way. Yet as soon as he spoke, as soon as he heard himself say the words, he regretted it. But by then, it was too late. 'Do you miss him?' he heard himself say and, before he could take it back, before he could leap in and change the subject, he realised he wasn't really just asking a question, he was surrendering to something he had kept locked away for half his life.

Alina didn't appear to be surprised by the question. Annoyed, perhaps, but not surprised. 'Of course I do,' she said – and, at the same time, Francis detected a note in her voice, a deliberation, a practised quality, that made him doubt what she was saying.

'Really?' he said. He was ashamed now, and he tried to lessen the blow. 'I mean – still? After all this time?'

Alina shook her head. 'I don't know,' she said. There was an admission, or an acknowledgment of something in her eyes and, with it, Francis thought, something close to relief. 'He wasn't like a real person to me. More of a rumour.'

'What do you mean?'

'I don't mean it badly,' Alina said. 'It's just – I didn't find him altogether convincing. Not as a person. If he'd been a character in a book, say. Or a saint, maybe.'

'He wasn't a saint.'

'No. But he had that same – inhuman quality.' She looked penitent immediately, but she was evidently glad to have said it, finally. They were silent a moment, mulling it over, then she looked at Francis, too obviously all seriousness. 'You know,' she said. 'I used to wonder why you two were friends. Then I figured it out: you were swapped at birth.'

Francis laughed.

'No, I'm serious,' she continued. 'You were swapped at birth. He was living a little part of your life, and you were living a little part of his.'

Francis nodded. What she had said made sense, in an odd way. She hadn't said it right, but then, there was no way to say it right. 'I know what you mean,' he said. 'I always felt there was something – I don't know, interchangeable about us. I mean – we were different –'

'You were that,' Alina said, a little too enthusiastically.

'That last summer, though, I didn't feel that way any more. It was like I was alone in the world for the first time in years.' Francis glanced away. 'I didn't want to turn around and see him there somewhere, watching –'

'You were growing apart.'

'Maybe,' Francis agreed reluctantly. Just to be saying what he was saying felt like a betrayal. 'But it seems a little too straightforward when you say it like that.'

'I know.' Alina shook her head. 'You know, back when you went away, I was angry with you. I thought you should have stayed and faced it, stayed and helped.' She looked at him sadly. 'I even blamed you. I thought: he admired you. You don't know that, but it's true. And I thought what he did, he did it because *he* imagined it was what *you* would do –'

Francis shook his head. 'You're wrong,' he said. 'We were growing apart, you just said so yourself. That's a two-way street. And even before, I don't think we were so – I mean, I admired him, but I never wanted to *be* him. And I'm sure he didn't want to *be* me.'

Alina nodded. 'I know that now,' she said. 'I know it was stupid, the whole thing. But I was grieving. I think we should allow ourselves a little irrationality in grief.'

Francis nodded, but he wasn't really listening. He was thinking about what she had said. It was true, or partly true, of course: there had been something between Jan and himself, a kind of exchange, a potential for transformation. 'I don't know that you're right,' he said, finally. 'The odd thing is, though, the thing that I've only just started to notice, is that I've become more like him over the years. Or the part of me that most resembled him has come out more. I don't know.'

Alina was watching him. She seemed interested, ready to hear more – which made Francis want to change the subject again. What he had just said to her – that admission, that affirmation – had come unexpectedly, like a gift, and he wanted to consider it at length, in his own good time, before speaking again. He smiled and shook his head. 'It was a long time ago,' he said, apropos of nothing. 'We were all a bit crazy.'

'Were we?'

'Sure.'

'I don't think I was crazy enough,' Alina said.

Francis couldn't tell if she was joking or not. Then he remembered her father, and her own bad spell, just before she went to college, when she'd been in hospital for a while, with depression. Feeling awkward, he changed the subject. He had been changing the subject, it seemed, all afternoon. 'Did you know my brother had a big thing for you?' he asked.

Alina laughed. 'Did he?'

'Are you telling me you didn't notice?'

'I didn't –' She shook her head. 'Poor Derek,' she said quietly.

'He came to see you,' Francis continued, knowing he was on shaky ground. 'When you were in the hospital.'

She looked up, startled. 'No, he didn't,' she said, with surprising vehemence.

'He did.' Francis pretended not to notice her reaction. 'He told me. He came to see you, but you wouldn't see him –'

'I'm sorry.' Her face betrayed real regret. 'I thought it was someone else.'

They were quiet for a long moment after that.

'Actually, I used to think you had a big thing for me,' Francis said, to break the ice. The remark was meant ironically, of course, but she seemed to give the matter serious consideration before she shook her head and smiled sadly.

'Not really,' she said. 'I liked you. I don't know why.'

'Thanks.'

'You know what I mean.' She was unshakable in her seriousness. Perhaps she had an idea of what was to come. 'I liked you more than most of the boys I knew,' she said.

'That's not saying much,' he said.

She laughed softly. Her laughter had an eerie, unsettling quality.

'No,' she said. 'It isn't saying anything at all, really.' She studied Francis's face, as if she hoped to find some trace of the boy she had known, all those years ago. 'They all had so many problems, I didn't have the patience to wait while they sorted themselves out.'

'And you preferred girls,' Francis ventured.

Alina looked surprised. 'Not really,' she said. 'I thought about it for a while.' She sounded very lonely all of a sudden, like one of those spinster schoolteachers from Our Lady's. One of 'The Misses'. 'I suppose I'm happiest in my own company,' she added. 'Like you.'

Francis nodded. 'Best way,' he said, lamely. He sounded like Tommy.

'So.' She shifted in her seat, changing the subject. 'What will you do next? You won't stay here long, I imagine.'

Francis grinned. 'Maybe I will,' he said. 'Maybe I'll get married and settle down. Give Tommy some more grandchildren.'

'Huh.'

'Or maybe I'll just disappear —'

She gave him an odd, beseeching look. 'Don't do that again,' she said. 'It's not — fair.'

'On whom?'

'On your father. On Derek.'

'You want me to stay here for their sake?'

'No. But talk to them before you go. Tell them where you're going. Stay in touch. It would mean a lot.'

Francis felt sad, suddenly. The idea of staying in touch, of writing letters home wasn't so bad but the thought of receiving their sad, cheerful replies was unbearable. He thought again how awful pity is. How it rots the soul. 'Listen,' he said. 'There's something I need to tell you —'

She interrupted him immediately, her face suddenly hard, her resolution final. 'No,' she said. 'Don't.'

'You don't know what I'm going to say —'

'Don't!' She reached out, almost touching his hand, before she drew away. 'Leave all that alone. It doesn't matter now. Do what you like, but don't come back and try to salve your conscience, after all this time.' She gathered up her bag. She wouldn't look at Francis. 'While you've been away, the rest of us have been living with it. With the space you both left behind. Maybe you should think about that.' Finally, she looked him in the eye. 'I know what happened, that night. I have my version, and you have yours. The trouble is, you think yours is the truth –'

'Well,' Francis said. 'Maybe it is –'

She looked at him coldly, then, but there was a trace of pity in her eyes. 'It would be,' she said, 'if everything was as simple as you imagine. But it isn't.' She shook her head in not quite mock-disbelief. 'You're like one of my students,' she said. 'You think, while you're doing something, while you're *acting*, nothing else is going on. It's like a film. The camera is here, pointing at you, so it can't be anywhere else, can it? It's all about you, and what you do.'

Francis felt angry now. She had got hold of the wrong end of the stick entirely. 'I don't understand,' he said. 'I just –'

'That's just it,' she interrupted. 'You *don't* understand. You never did.' She stood up. 'I'm sorry,' she said. 'I have to go. It was nice seeing you. Give my best to your father. And to Derek.' She looked serious, formal, casting around for some gesture that would make her going seem like an ordinary departure and, for a moment, Francis thought she was going to shake his hand. Instead, she bent her head and smiled sadly. 'Look after yourself,' she said.

Francis nodded. 'You too,' he said.

She lingered a moment. Francis thought there was something else she wanted – or needed – to say but, whatever it was, she didn't say it. Maybe she didn't have the words; or else she did, but had thought better of it. Either way, it didn't really matter.

When she was gone, Francis stayed where he was. He was thinking about what he had said, about how he felt that he had become more like Jan over the years – which was part of the truth, though it wasn't really what he had wanted to say. What he had realised – in that moment, saying one thing to Alina, and meaning another – was that, all that time, all those years ago, he had felt complete, he had felt that he and Jan had lived apart, in their own world, far away from other people. Together, they had been different; together, they had been special. They had always been told they weren't, but they were, and they knew it. Together, they belonged to another world: in fact, together, they weren't people in the usual sense at all. Or they were persons, rather than people. That was how Jan described it, without rancour or any hint of superiority, just making an observation in his usual abstract way. For him, people were the ones who kept things in order, they were the ones who took what was going and didn't hold out for more. Nothing they liked – nothing they watched on TV, none of the records they listened to, none of the books they read, nothing they consumed – had anything to do with the world he and Francis inhabited. Every year, the best films or books were announced, and the films that Jan and Francis loved, the books they read again and again, stunned by the clarity and beauty of the writing, were scarcely ever mentioned. Every week the charts came out, and their favourite songs were never there. What *was* there seemed to Jan nothing more than a compromise, a middle ground of the commercially acceptable, the harmless, the undemanding. Jan used to say that was exactly what mediocrity meant: a middle ground, a defined territory from which both squalor and excellence had been banished. That was the world of people, that mediocrity. You didn't have to be stupid, or crass, or undiscerning, to inhabit that world; you just had to accept it. Persons, on the other hand, were the ones who moved through this territory, on whatever journey they were making, leaving almost no trace. They didn't make the adjustments and they weren't trying to sell anything – especially not themselves. They had nothing to prove, they stood by what they did, their only concern was with the excellent. Most of all, they accepted their place in the world as transients, as mortals. All the boys Francis had known in school had wanted to be the opposite of that, to be permanent, to be immortal – which was exactly what made them pitiable. They would end up in the cemetery, just as Jan had; the only difference was that *they* were afraid of the grave.

The next morning, Francis walked the mile and a half out to the cemetery, clutching a bouquet of flowers Tommy had cut from the garden. Japanese anemones, asters, chrysanthemums, a painter's bouquet. He had planned to buy a wreath, but Tommy wouldn't hear of it.

'Don't waste your money, son,' he'd said. 'You'll get better here than any florist can do.' And he had gone out and cut two large bunches of pink and dark blue and purple blooms, one for Lizzie, the other for Jan.

Francis wanted to be alone that morning. He'd been pleas- antly surprised, coming home, at how much everyone had done to make him welcome – and by how welcome he wanted to feel – but now he was tired, worn out from all the smiles and from pretending not to notice the sidelong looks. He went out early, in the freshness of the late-summer morning, a film of dew over everything, the world new and sweet, the grass, the trees, the gravel paths that ran between the headstones shimmering in the first sunlight, the air cool and still and clean-tasting. He found Lizzie's grave right away – he remembered where it was, near a thorn tree at the end of a long gravel path, out by the edge of the cemetery – and he stood a while, his head bent, waiting to feel something. He felt he owed her *something* – a lingering sadness for the life she had been obliged to endure, a moment's thought, something that might resemble, or substitute for, prayer, a long- awaited reconciliation with the ghost that, somewhere towards the end of her painful life, had looked into his eyes and seen less fondness than she had hoped for. But he felt nothing at all – or nothing save the warmth of the sun, and a slight heaviness in his arms. He stared at the headstone: there was something wrong, he knew, but he couldn't decide what it was. Maybe it was that the stone was too big, too ornate. Francis knew she wouldn't have liked it. Maybe it was the mistake – after a moment he noticed it – that the stonemason had made with her age, making her dead at forty, shearing seven years from an already brief life. Maybe it was his own guilt, but the fact was, he could find no ritual, no ceremony to mark this visit. He stood a while longer, trying to discover some form of words, some gesture that might suit the occasion, but he had no sense of his mother being there, either in the lettering of the stone, or in the earth, or in the air around him. He had no sense of anything other than the cool of the morning and the graveyard reaching away, stone upon stone standing mute in the pale light – and he realised that he didn't believe in the dead: not Lizzie, not Jan, not in himself dead, some day, or Tommy, or Derek or Linda. He laid his bunch of flowers on the wet grass in front of his mother's grave and walked away with no sense of urgency, with nothing in his head but the sudden beauty of the day. He looked for Jan's grave for a while, but he couldn't find it, and he didn't much care if he found it or not. That wasn't why he was there. He didn't believe in the dead, or not in the dead these stones remembered. He believed in the living, in life itself, in what the dead had been when they were still alive, and in what they became when they passed from one life to another. More than anything, he believed in the dead that the living carried with them everywhere. It didn't matter now, that these people had gone away or had fallen asleep in Jesus on such and such a day, at such and such an hour. Lizzie hadn't fallen asleep, she had fought and been overcome, and she had gasped out her last breath in a bed sticky with sweat and the smell of cancer; Jan hadn't passed on, he'd been beaten to death on the street by a gang of idiots – but even this bleak description of events was better than the lie, even these cold facts were more acceptable than life with the angels, or eternal slumber in Christ.

It was odd, though, how little grief he felt now; odd how calm he felt, as he walked among the headstones, looking for Jan's resting place. He remembered reading about the old alchemists and how they weren't really that interested in gold, for its own sake – for them gold was an emblem, a symbol of the last stage in a process that had to be considered entire. It was like the gold medal you got for winning a race at the Olympics: what mattered wasn't standing on the podium, receiving the medal, what mattered was how you got off the blocks, how you ran the race, how you crossed the finishing-line. After that, the race was over, and the medal was only there to mark what had happened. Gold was chosen for medals because it lasted for ever and never tarnished: the alchemists chose gold as their symbol for the same reasons. But what they cared about was the process in all its stages, and you couldn't help thinking it was the intermediate elements they loved, the ones that arose between lead and gold – mercury, anti-mony, the ambiguous elements that belonged on the borderline between one state and another, between liquid and solid, between metal and non-metal. That was what the Westwater tapes had missed with their life-stories – those moments on the way that could never have been invented, the gifts that chance offered, the obligation to make what you could from whatever you had been given. Francis remembered the quote Jan had repeated so often, when he was first at college: 'Freedom is the recognition of necessity.' He couldn't remember who had said it, Marx maybe, and he hadn't really understood it at the time, it had just sounded like one of those clever but not very meaningful paradoxes that people were fond of quoting back then. Now he saw that it meant, or at least suggested, much more than he could have imagined – maybe too much. It was like those tags from Buddhist stories and the Pre-Socratics, there was too much in them, they could be read so many ways – the way up and the way down are the same; what is the sound of one hand clapping; to the wakeful mind, the cosmos is always one. What was necessity, anyway? Wasn't there such a thing as chance? If you wanted to be free, you had to recognise the bounds of the given world, but what about Victor's idea that you could make things up as you went along? Where were the borderlines between necessity and invention? The real trick wasn't in being free, or in how interesting your made-up life-story might be; what mattered was that process of recognition, of not drawing the lines too tight, not making artificial limits out of what was, in the end, ordinary fear. Francis remembered that story, the old story, the essential father-and-son story, where a man put his child on a table and said: *Jump. I'll catch you. That* story. When the boy jumps, the father steps back and lets him fall. Francis had heard that story so often, not as a fact, but as an exemplum: trust nobody, trust nothing. Which was nothing but cowardice. It was cowardice to turn away and pretend that the ills of the world didn't exist, Francis knew that, but it was just as cowardly to dwell on the dangers, to dedicate your whole life to not being a victim, to avoiding risk. Better to live from one moment to the next, using your imagination, but accepting what came. Maybe making it up wasn't really an option, or not in the way the Westwater tapes had seemed to suggest, but even if it wasn't, there was something noble in working with *everything* you had been given.

The sun was high, almost at the zenith. It didn't matter now, but Francis kept walking, for the walking's sake, because he had chanced upon something, standing on a path a few yards from Lizzie's headstone, chanced quietly upon a sense of the moment, of the now. Not this moment, or the last, or the next; not time passing not time standing still, but the way it is *always* now, *always* here. Always *now here* and always nowhere. Looking up at a sycamore tree at the edge of the graveyard, turning to see a bird, catching the faint damp smell of grass and water, or the glitter of dew on the cellophane at the corner of his vision, he kept thinking it would end, this now, this here, but it kept going, kept continuing, *was* continuous, and Francis felt calm, calmer than he had ever been, as if he really had come home, if not to a place or to people who remembered him, then at least to a way of being in the world, open, empty, unseen. He walked on and he heard his own footsteps on the gravel path, but there was nothing uncanny in the sound, nothing was out of place. When he found Jan's stone, he stopped and stood a long time, but it was a while before he realised that he was waiting for something, that he was listening – and when he did, when he came back to himself, he realised that it had nothing to do with Jan, or with Lizzie, nothing to with them, and everything to do with himself.

He remembered the girl at Westwater, Shirley, the girl who believed that the dead are always with us, their wavering, plaintive voices bleeding through the background noise of radio and atmospherics, desperate to be heard. Now as he sat listening, he realised that, if Shirley had been there, she would have heard whispers on the air, the massed dead speaking in tongues, their stories murmured softly through the summer grass, beautiful in the way that anything finished and complete is beautiful, beyond sadness, beyond bathos. If Shirley had been there, she would have wanted him to listen through all that noise for the one voice, the one recognisable pattern that only he could pick out. But Francis heard nothing, or at least, nothing that stood out. A blackbird called, away across the graveyard; there was a faraway hum of traffic from the industrial estate; somewhere close by a tap was dripping, a thin sound, almost negligible in the overall scheme of things, but just as essential, just as important to the fabric of the whole as a Mozart aria or the explosion at Hiroshima – and all of a sudden, Francis realised that he wasn't that much different from all those others with whom he'd prided himself in thinking he had nothing in common. Like them, he had allowed himself to become too concerned with the self, with histories, real or invented, with strands torn from the fabric of the whole and given undue weight. He had to learn to begin forgetting, not just the dead, or the past, but the person he had been, the person he was, the person he wanted to be. It was time to forget himself altogether and *be* in the world, time to begin learning how to be free. He didn't want a personal history any more, he wanted to live in the world. If he could hear nothing, in this quiet graveyard, or nothing other than the distant hiss of traffic and the odd flourish of birdsong, he was glad. He wanted his dead to have moved on, to have already become what they were fated to become: loam, new souls, fire. He didn't want to belong to them any more. He didn't want them to belong to him.

Later, as he was walking back from the grave, he remembered something that had happened years ago, something that had seemed inconsequential at the time, one of Jan's sillier pieces of eccentricity. In the memory, they were twelve years old, or maybe a little older, but not much, because they were still at Our Lady's. It was late in the winter, or early in the spring. Jan had boiled a kettle in his mother's kitchen, and left it boiling, the steam filling the room, clouding the windows, condensing on the little group of knick-knacks and rubbish – bits of broken glass and crockery, feathers, all kinds of junk that she must have found in the garden and brought in – the kettle whistling away until Jan turned off the gas, carried the kettle to the table and filled a cup with water. Francis could see the cup in his mind's eye: old-fashioned, with one of those elaborate curved handles, it was painted with flowers, a single piece that was probably left over from a service lost or broken years ago. Or maybe Jan's mother had found it in a junk shop and brought it home, a private treasure, cheap because it had no matching saucer, or because it had a tiny, almost invisible hairline crack at the rim. Jan filled the cup almost to brimming, then he set the kettle down on the cooker and stood at the table, silent and motionless, as if he were waiting for something to happen.

'What are you doing?' Francis had asked, finally.

'Nothing,' Jan answered, not taking his eyes off the cup. A haver of steam continued to rise from the surface of the water, thin and almost invisible now, the heat from the water bleeding away into the cold air of his mother's kitchen. Nobody else was at home: Alina was in school, which was where they should have been; Jan's dad was at work; Mrs Ruckert must have been out somewhere, shopping probably.

'So what's the water for then?'

Jan looked up at him. 'Put your finger in,' he said.

'Don't be daft.'

'It's cooled down now,' Jan said.

'So?'

'So where does the heat go?'

'I don't know,' Francis said. 'Into the air, I suppose.'

'Put your finger in.'

Francis stuck his finger into the water. A minute ago, it had been boiling; now it was hot, but not so hot that it burned. He left his finger in the water a moment, as if to prove a point, then pulled it out. His skin was red.

'Now it's part of you,' Jan said.

'What?'

'The heat.'

'I suppose so.'

'That's what happens when an animal dies,' Jan said. 'The heat goes out into the surrounding air. It goes into the soil. It goes into water.'

'I suppose it does.'

'The principle of the conservation of energy says that energy cannot be created or destroyed,' Jan said. 'Which means that any heat, when it seeps out into the air, or the earth, or water, or into someone's hand' – he glanced at Francis – 'continues to exist, it's never lost, it carries on –'

'You're talking about heat –'

'Yes.'

At the time, Francis had laughed. He didn't see what heat had to do with anything. Now, he wasn't so sure. It really was as if Jan had been trying to tell him something, all those years ago, something about loss, and about the impossibility of really losing anything and, even if it was all too easy, even if it was a child's fantasy of how everything was connected to everything else, at this most basic level of primary physics, it made sense, suddenly, to think, not of spirits, but of heat, not of the afterlife, but of some kind of transfer, a continuum of warmth and light in a world where the dead left themselves behind as trace elements, waves, local areas of brilliance or noise or heat, to be used or inhabited by others, to be made use of, one way or another, to be, quite simply, continued. It was a good thought: not a comforting one, necessarily, just a starting-point, a way of seeing. As he reached the cemetery gates, Francis paused a moment, not looking back, aware of something behind him, but deliberately not turning to see what it was.

When he got back to his father's house, he found Derek and Gabriel playing in the dinette, the boy sleepy-eyed and irritable, wanting something, and frustrated because he couldn't say what it was.

'I hate it when he gets like this,' Derek said. 'I wish he could tell me what's bothering him.'

'Maybe he doesn't know,' Francis ventured.

Derek grinned and shook his head. 'It's easier when they're small,' he said. 'Their needs are so simple. Eat, sleep, drink, play. I remember when he was just a baby, and he had a bit of colic, he would get so *angry*.' He broke off and smiled at Gabriel, who glowered back, as if he knew they were talking about him. Maybe he did, Francis thought. 'I used to go in and give him my thumb to hold,' Derek continued, 'and I'd sing him songs. Not baby songs. I never thought he liked songs like that. You know, twinkle, twinkle, that stuff.' He picked Gabriel up and sat him on his knee. The boy clambered off immediately, an indignant look on his face, and wandered out to the kitchen. Derek laughed. 'I used to sing Etta James, Baby Washington, old Sam Cooke numbers. Bessie Banks, all that old soul stuff. And he would just latch on to my thumb, and he wouldn't let go. And he'd be listening, you know?' He shifted in his chair slightly so he could see what Gabriel was doing.

Francis nodded. He understood all this, at one remove. He could see his brother singing 'I'd Rather Go Blind', or 'A Change is Gonna Come', not quite in tune, his voice too breathy, leaning over the cot, slightly self-conscious, even with nobody there to see him. He managed a smile.

'Then when he went off,' Derek continued, 'I'd stay around just to watch him sleep. I'd not want to leave him alone. Linda used to get annoyed about it, the way I was always in there with him, watching him sleep, singing him old R&B songs.' He gave Francis a long, appraising look, and asked the question he'd obviously been dying to ask since his brother had arrived. 'You never wanted kids, I suppose?'

Francis shook his head, but he didn't say anything. It hadn't taken long to see that the whole house was besotted with Gabriel: Derek was a changed man, in spite of his outward appearance, and changed for the better, mostly; Linda was quietly happy, just getting on with her life, going to work, bringing up her son, keeping an eye on her odd husband. But Francis didn't want to talk about it. The last thing in the world he wanted was a child. He needed to be alone, he needed to keep moving; even if he decided to settle in one place, he knew the decision could never be final, he would have to be free to go if the need arose, it was who he was, and there was no changing that. Still, it had surprised him, seeing Tommy's quiet but all-consuming delight in his only grandchild, and Francis felt oddly ashamed of his childlessness, as if he had deliberately deprived his father of yet one more of life's pleasures.

'Well.' Derek poured himself some more tea and rolled a cigarette. 'There's still time. I mean, look at me.'

Francis managed a smile. 'You're lucky,' he said. 'It's nice to see you so happy.' He almost winced at how awful he sounded, but Derek nodded sagely.

'I *am* lucky,' he said. 'I had no idea it would be like this.' Francis put on a good listening face. 'It wasn't my idea, I can tell you,' his brother continued, flicking ash carefully into one of Lizzie's old souvenir ashtrays, A PRESENT FROM OBAN stencilled on the rim. 'It was all Linda's doing. She kept on at me —' He broke off and grinned. 'Anyway, I'll not bore you with a load of baby stories.'

Francis shook his head. 'Go ahead,' he said. 'I've got nothing better to do.'

Derek was watching him, now, with that old look of his, the look that said he was trying to figure him out, trying, from compassion, and kinship, to make some impossible connection. 'I suppose you'll be leaving soon,' he said.

Francis nodded. 'Fairly soon,' he said.

'Well.' Derek looked at the floor. 'Can I ask you a favour before you go?'

'Of course.'

'Don't feel obliged. If you can do it, fine. If not, don't worry.'

'What is it –'

'Tommy needs somebody to help him dig the garden over at the back. He can't manage it any more, and I don't really have the time.' Derek smiled apologetically. 'Well, I suppose I could. But I think he would like it if you –' He broke off as Gabriel reappeared, clutching an apple. 'Hey, Bobo,' he said. 'Do you want me to cut that up for you?'

The boy nodded solemnly. Derek reached into his pocket for a pen-knife. 'It just needs a bit of work,' he said, as he cut a piece from the apple and handed it to Gabriel. The boy stood between them a moment, looking from one to the other, before Derek picked him up and perched him on his knee. He looked at Francis and shook his head. 'He'll pretend you're interfering, but it would make him happy.'

Francis nodded. He knew he had fallen into a trap, but he didn't really mind. His brother had taken advantage of him, and he didn't care. Between them, there was a contract. There always had been.

'Stay a while,' Derek said softly, the shift of his eyes showing that he was already half-aware he'd gone too far. 'Get to know your nephew. He's a bright kid.'

'He is,' Francis said. 'Bright as a button.' Meaning: he'd stay for as long as the garden took. That was part of the contract too.

'He reminds me of your friend,' Derek said suddenly. 'The boy who died.'

'Who? Jan?'

Derek nodded – and Francis noticed something in his face then, a shadow, a buried secret. It only lasted a moment, but it was a glimpse, through some wavering curtain, of the one thing Derek had managed all this time to keep hidden. 'My God,' Francis said. 'It was *you*.'

Derek didn't speak. His face was set, motionless, but even then he was giving himself away. 'I didn't know what you would do,' he said.

Francis waited, but his brother didn't elaborate and he knew, if he didn't say another word, if he let it go, nothing more would be said. But he couldn't let it go. 'I phoned up, that first Christmas, and old man MacColl told me what had happened,' he said, remembering the call he had made from York, standing in that cold telephone box in the snow, so numb with pain and guilt he hadn't even been able to admit how homesick he was. 'He thought I had done it –'

'He told me,' Derek said. 'I told him not to tell Tommy. It would only have upset him.'

'Tell him what? That I'd killed Andrew Niven?'

'That you'd called.' Derek shook his head. 'I didn't want Tommy waiting around to see if you'd call again. If you had, that would have been fine. But you didn't.' Derek gave him a long, pitying look – and, suddenly, Francis saw it. Derek had killed Niven, and he hadn't felt a thing. Not a moment's self-doubt, not a moment's guilt – because that was what he had to do, or thought he had to, to protect his family. To protect his brother. Francis was ashamed.

'You told me to look after him,' Derek said, out of the blue. He meant Jan. 'And I didn't.'

'So you killed Niven?'

'I told you. I didn't know what you would do.'

Francis nodded. He couldn't tell Derek that he'd never wanted revenge, that he'd never once thought about killing anybody. 'It wasn't your fault,' he said. 'It was mine. I should have been looking out for him that night.'

'He should have looked out for himself,' Derek said. It was obviously a thought he'd lived with for a long time, accommodating it, draining it of venom till, finally, now, it was a simple statement of fact.

Francis shook his head. 'I let him down,' he said. 'Something was up. And I went off with –' He stopped talking. He couldn't bring himself to say it. Tommy was somewhere in the house, shaving, or lying on his bed waiting till the pain had passed.

'I remember,' Derek smiled sadly. 'I always meant to ask you what all that was about –'

'Nothing.' Francis sat back and shook his head. It all seemed so long ago. 'Nothing at all.'

Derek nodded. 'I'm glad,' he said. 'I'm glad of that, at least.'

That night, Derek and Linda went out. Tommy had agreed to

baby-sit and it was obvious, from the way he settled in, waiting for the boy's parents to go, that he enjoyed the chore. Francis decided to sit with him and Tommy made tea, but after a while his resolve wavered, and soon a bottle of whisky appeared on the table. They sat drinking a while, but it wasn't like the old days, or even like the first night: Tommy was more relaxed now, he took his time, sipping at the whisky, enjoying it. Francis guessed it had something to do with the baby: Tommy had always been able to hold his drink, but he would still be taking it easy, being careful, in case the boy needed him. The baby monitor sat on the mantelpiece. At first, it had been quiet, or maybe Francis hadn't noticed the sound, but after a while he became aware of a sequence of three descending tones, oddly musical and haunting, filtered from the air, like the voices in one of those machines Shirley had told him about. This was the world now, Francis thought: a web of sounds and movements that nobody had ever known about before, signals on the air, distant storms, event horizons, phenomena that only showed up because of the increased sophistication of the instruments. Now the best knowledge they had of the real universe, the universe of waves and unseen rhythms, came by accident, because of a flaw in a system, or a random scatter of white noise that nobody could have anticipated.

'Is he OK?' Francis tipped his head to the monitor.

'He's fine.' Tommy nodded. 'It always makes that noise. You can't hear it in his room.' He lit a cigarette and sat back. 'This is the only smoke I get now,' he said. 'When wee Gabriel is in bed.'

'You're very fond of him,' Francis said. 'I can see that.'

Tommy gave him an odd look. 'I love him,' he said. 'Same as I loved you and Derek when you were little.' He shook his head. Something still mystified him, some old misunderstanding between men. It hadn't gone away, it had just been laid to rest. 'You never thought you'd want a bairn, then?' he added, to get beyond that reminder.

Francis smiled a little too broadly. 'I thought about it,' he said. 'I just never met the right woman.'

Tommy shook his head and glanced up at the photograph of Lizzie on the mantelpiece. It was an old snapshot, taken when she was around twenty, on the very day she met Tommy. She had been invited to a fancy-dress party, and was on her way to meet a friend on Stenhouse Street in her cowgirl outfit, when Tommy had come walking by in the opposite direction with a box camera. That was when the photograph was taken, at the moment they first met, before they knew one another. Francis waited: he hoped Tommy wouldn't say anything: he was afraid it wouldn't be true, and he didn't want to hear his father lie, not now that there was something like peace between them. At the same time, he realised he had to wait, he had to give the man a chance to speak, if that was what he needed – but Tommy didn't say a word, and his face betrayed nothing, no regret, no resentment, only the weariness he was managing, moment by moment, for Gabriel's sake, determined to be alive for as long as he was still living, so the boy would have a grandfather for a few more weeks. Managing that weariness, balancing that pain, was all he could think of now.

'Anyway,' Francis said, when the moment had passed. He cast around for something more to say, then gave up. It had been a long day.

Tommy pursed his lips. 'Anyway,' he said. He leaned forward stiffly and poured them both another drink. 'Old times,' he said, raising his glass. Francis thought for a moment that he was being ironic, that he knew more than he was letting on about Katrina – but as Tommy downed his whisky and set the glass on the table, he saw that the old man was thinking about something else, some moment from the life he had known before Francis was born, a moment from a world that was lost for ever now, a moment – and Francis could see the doubt in his father's eyes – that might never have happened.

Early the next morning, as Francis struggled awake, a little muggy from too much whisky and another late night, Gabriel ran into the room clutching a big soft roll, the kind they use for burgers in fast-food restaurants. He was obviously feeling pleased with himself, his face smeared with what looked like piccalilli.

'Bread!' he shouted, waving the roll in Francis's general direction.

Francis sat up. He had the mildest of headaches, nothing too bad. Gabriel came closer and waved the bread under his eyes. It smelled sweet and sickly after the night's drinking.

'Bread!' the boy repeated, his face a rictus of delight with the world, with himself and, most of all, with the crumpled roll he held in his fist.

Francis nodded. 'Yes,' he said quietly, a little too adult-to-child. 'Bread.'

Gabriel laughed as if Francis had said the funniest thing he'd ever heard. 'Bread!' he cried, and then again, almost shrieking, 'Bread! Bread!'

Francis laughed. 'That's right,' he said, louder this time. 'Bread.'

'Bread!' The child was grinning like a thief now. 'Bread!' He waved the roll close to Francis's hand, so he could take some. Francis pulled off a piece and ate it, chewing slowly, making a pantomime of it. 'Very nice,' he said, smiling.

'Bread!' The child was beside himself. 'Bread!'

'Bread,' Francis replied, swallowing quickly.

'Bread!'

'Bread.'

The boy was still grinning, but Francis knew there was something else he wanted to say, something he meant Francis to understand, something that was serious for him. Francis nodded, then he scooped the child up and swung him on to his lap. Gabriel shrieked with delight.

'Bread!' he cried. 'Bread!'

It was a form of welcome, Francis saw, after the days of indecision. And still there was something else he wanted to say, something he didn't have words for. 'What is it?' he asked, peering into the child's face. Gabriel's eyes were astonishingly blue: astonishing, and astonished, delighted with the world and, at the same moment, puzzled, not by what he could see and hear, but by this new feeling, whatever it was, that he couldn't find words, or even noises, to express. 'Bread?' Francis enquired gently, gazing into the big, watchful eyes.

The boy laughed and slid free. He dropped to the floor and stood there, next to the bed, looking at this stranger in his room.

'Dammit!'

Francis was almost shocked. 'What?'

The boy laughed, pleased with the effect he'd created. 'Dammit!' he cried. 'Dammit. Dammit. Dammit.' Then he ran away, shrieking with laughter, the whole house ringing with his words.

Francis got up, dressed quickly and sat down to breakfast with Derek and Linda. Tommy was still in bed.

'He sleeps late, sometimes,' Linda explained. 'He's always annoyed to miss some of the day, but we don't have the heart to wake him.'

Francis nodded, but he didn't say anything. He was looking forward to getting to work, suddenly. Gabriel sat at the end of the table, in a high-chair, taking everything in. Every time Francis looked his way, he broke into a big grin.

'We've finally got him to take it easy,' Derek added. 'You know what he's like.' He took a sheet of paper towel from his pocket and wiped egg from Gabriel's mouth. 'Do you want anything else?' he asked.

The boy shook his head. 'I'm finished,' he said.

'OK.' Derek helped Gabriel down from the chair; then, as the boy clattered off, he turned to Francis.

'So.' He looked worried. 'What's your plan for today.'

Francis stood up. 'I thought I'd get started,' he said. 'See what I can do out there.'

Derek relaxed. Francis realised he'd been hoping for something like this, hoping Francis would get started while Tommy was still in bed so the old man couldn't do or say something to put him off. 'The tools are in the shed,' he said.

'Thanks.'

The morning was warm and bright. Francis was surprised, again, at how good the garden looked and he realised, as he unlocked the shed and carried a hoe out to Tommy's garden, that he was going to enjoy the coming day's work. It was odd, how his path had mirrored Tommy's: they had both taken refuge in a garden, they had both found a provisional and hard-earned peace with themselves in working the soil. In the beginning was the land – Tommy's uncle used to say that, years ago, on their country walks – what? sixty years ago? Francis wondered what his father had been like as a boy: how he had looked, what he had wanted, what had frightened him, what he had lost. Then, as the morning wore on, he thought about himself: about who he had been, all those years ago, when he was Gabriel's age, about how he had looked, and what he had wanted, about what had frightened him and what he had lost. He had lost something, he knew that, but he had found something too and, if he had learned anything at all, it was that you have to lose something to find something, you have to give something up every time you make a choice, or even when you refuse to choose, when you turn back, when you say enough is enough. He had lost something, and he had found something, but neither had been what he had expected to lose or to find, and it struck him, thinking back, that the Westwater tapes were right: every life really was a story – though not exactly in the way Victor had meant. It had something to do with the details you remembered but couldn't string together, something to do with the texture of things, with warmth and light and weather and those moments, late at night, when you wake from some labyrinth of a dream in a state of inexplicable joy, aware, just for a moment, of everything you had forgotten, trying to grasp the truth you have just glimpsed, to find a word or an image to fix it before it disappears.

The sun rose in the sky, and Francis worked on, sure of what he was doing, confident that he was making the changes that Tommy would have wanted. He had been afraid, at first, of doing something wrong, of offending the old man, even by being there, in his private domain, but he already knew, even before he looked up and caught Tommy at the back-bedroom window, watching him, that he was doing the right thing. He didn't know how long the old man had been standing there: he looked thin and frail and maybe a little afraid, but when Francis stopped and rested on his spade, Tommy raised his hand and gave a tiny, almost imperceptible wave, only the smallest gesture, but enough to let Francis know that his father was happy with what he was doing. A moment later, Linda appeared with a glass of barley water.

'How's it going?' she asked, as she handed him the cold, wet glass.

Francis looked around and nodded. 'It's a beautiful garden,' he said. He looked up at the bedroom window, but Tommy was gone. 'I'm just tidying up,' he added.

'It soon gets out of hand, if you don't keep an eye on it,' Linda said. She smiled. They were talking for talking's sake, and she knew that they both knew it. They had been talking for talking's sake ever since he'd arrived, because there were no actual words to say, there was no information to convey, only a warmth, and a preparedness to be kith and kin, acknowledged in small-talk and smiles and gestures. 'I'm glad you could find the time.'

'So am I,' Francis said.

'Take it easy,' Linda said. 'If you need anything, give me a shout.'

Francis nodded. The glass was already empty, so he handed it back to her.

'Would you like some more?' Linda asked.

'Not just now. Thanks.'

Linda took the glass and started back towards the house; then, halfway across the lawn, she turned and looked him in the eye. 'I'm glad you came,' she said. It sounded like something she'd been planning to say, when the right moment came.

Francis smiled. 'I'm glad to be home,' he said. And he was glad. In a day or two, maybe a week at most, he would be going, he knew that. But now, for the moment, he was here, and it was good. He would come back again, he thought; he would come and see Tommy before he died, he wouldn't be a stranger to his nephew, or to this woman, who had inexplicably chosen to make his awkward, kindly brother her kin. No matter what happened, they were connected, all of them. They were all connected, and they were all alone with their phantoms, but the phantoms were warmer and less unknowable than Francis had thought. They would slip away from one another, and they would come again in new guises but, no matter what happened, they would always be connected. There were millions of little stories, but all the stories were connected and, when you stopped for a moment, you saw that there was only one story, and the one story wasn't nature, or time, or human existence, or space, or God, or anything that could be named. As Linda turned and walked away, Francis looked up at the sky and he saw the high blue of it, empty and clear and still, and he could feel something moving, receding into the distance, returning to its origin. It was gone now, it was else-where. Everything changed so that this – the sky, the earth, the summer light, a man working in a garden – could continue. For the moment, he was that man and this was the garden. It was his light, it was his sky, it was his body that worked, tuned to gravity, assured and careful and skilled. Then the thought passed, and he went back to work, forgetting himself: a man working in a garden, then a garden and nothing else. A bird was singing; there was a smell of sap. Somewhere along the street, a radio came on, and music drifted across the hedges and lawns, a song from another time, an old music that Francis was sure he recognised, recurring on the summer air.

ACKNOWLEDGEMENTS

The epigraph is from the final pages of Gustav Mahler's *Das Lied von der Erde*, in which the composer adapts Hans Bethge's German translation of poems by Mong-Kao-Yen and Wang-Wei. The rather free English version quoted here is my own.

The research for this book was carried out during my term as TLS Research Fellow at the British Library; my thanks to both those institutions, and to the Library staff who gave so generously of their time and energy.

Special thanks to Emily Gilbert, Rob Perks, Richard Price, Graham Smith and Janet Zmroczek. Also to Dag and Tove Andersson, Andy Brown and Amy Shelton, Melanie Giles and my sisters, Margaret and Elaine, who helped talk it through.

As always, I cannot adequately express my gratitude to Robin Robertson, not only for his good advice, but also for his confidence. And thanks to Sarah, for everything.